For anyone who's been told they're too loud.
Too emotional. Too much.
You are the perfect amount of enough.

AUTHOR'S NOTE

Dear Reader,

While this romance is primarily kooky, chaotic, and fluffy, please note that it contains some sensitive topics, including pregnancy and discussions about abortion. There are also moments of potentially triggering content with ableist language regarding ADHD. This last is condemned by the narrative, characters, and myself.

 As always, I've tried to handle these topics with the utmost respect and care.

All my love,
Mazey

Chapter 1

THERE was no place in the world Lizzie Blake loved more than Philadelphia. From the food, to the people, to the kaleidoscope of neighborhoods, energy pulsed in every crack and crevice of her city, coursing through her with a bubbly type of joy.

But, as Lizzie stared down at the massive pile of shit she'd just stepped in, she *hated* that she had to question whether it was dog or human.

Lizzie dragged her hands over her face then shoved her knuckles in her mouth, biting down to suppress a frustrated howl. After sucking in three deep breaths, she scraped the sides of her shoe along the edge of the sidewalk, removing what she could before walking the last block to her apartment and stopping outside the door.

She stared at her pale pink sneakers, now ruined by the brown stain embedded in the fabric. With a sigh, she took off the shoes, pinched them between her fingers, and took a few sock-clad steps to the dumpster on the side of her building, hurling them in.

What a fucking day.

She tiptoed across the sidewalk, into her apartment, and up the stairs to her unit.

"Honey, I'm home," Lizzie crooned as she walked in the door.

Indira, her roommate, shot her a grin that quickly turned into a confused frown as she took in Lizzie's mismatched neon socks and lack of shoes. She lifted her eyebrows in question.

"Stepped in shit," Lizzie explained, peeling off her socks and chucking them through the open bedroom door as she made her way to the couch, plopping down beside her best friend.

"Animal?" Indira asked, dropping her head to Lizzie's shoulder as she scrolled through Netflix.

"Indeterminate source."

"Mm, life's fun little mysteries," Indira replied. "How was the rest of your day?"

Lizzie let out a long-suffering sigh. "Not the best. I got written up again," she said, digging the heels of her hands into her eye sockets.

Indira shot up. "Lizzie, *again*? That's like the third time this month."

"Second," Lizzie corrected, although she'd gotten both in just as many weeks.

"What did you do?"

Lizzie groaned and sat forward, planting her elbows on her knees and burying her head in her hands. "I forgot to prep a catering order for one of George's bigger repeat clients—some company party or whatever. The woman came in to pick up the cupcakes, and I found the order info scribbled on a gum wrapper that I'd taped inside my locker and completely forgot about. It was a shit show."

Indira gave her a look of horror. Although she worked in psychiatry, Indira was familiar with the wrath of an angry boss. "What did George say?"

Lizzie let out a humorless laugh. "What do you think? His face turned a new shade of purple as he yelled. Said I'm on thin ice." Her boss, George, was a millennial-hipster nightmare of a person, constantly having his bakers chase Instagram trends to the point that the shop was a hodgepodge of deconstructed quiches, ombre cakes, and overdecorated cookies shaped like sloths. All the while, he sipped nitro cold brew and scrolled through his phone, regularly barking out orders for everyone to "stay on brand," like any of them had a damn clue what that meant.

There was an awkward silence as Indira examined her perfectly manicured nails, avoiding eye contact. Lizzie wished she could have pretty hands like that. Instead, her nails were jagged and bitten down, the cuticles picked raw and butchered from Lizzie's constant, pulsing energy.

"You can't really blame him, though, Lizzie. For being mad, I mean."

Lizzie's shoulders slumped as shame gripped her around the throat. Lizzie didn't want to be like this. It wasn't like she enjoyed her mind rioting and rejecting normal executive functioning. But the past year had been a loop of one step forward, five steps back. She'd made the jump from working as a baker/barista at a coffee shop next to Callowhill's Medical School, to being hired on in a pastry kitchen of a bougie hotel chain.

But within two months, she'd been fired, having accumulated a mountain of citations ranging from chronic lateness to setting small kitchen fires, the last straw being her boss walking in on her hooking up with a server in the employee bathroom during a break.

Lizzie had flitted from job to job after that, unable to turn on the responsible-adult switch everyone else seemed to have.

Instead, she floundered with the basics—struggling to organize and execute tasks in an order that actually made sense, failing to remember important things that needed to get done, even keeping track of the damn time felt like an impossible feat—while the need for stimulation and impulsivity prickled across her skin.

Lizzie let out a deep breath. "Nope, I can't blame him. Can only blame myself," she said with fake cheeriness, patting Indira's knee and pushing up from the couch. She headed toward her room, making a mental note to schedule an appointment with her psychiatrist. It'd been a while since they'd evaluated her medication. She was on a nonstimulant drug that wasn't always as effective at bolstering her focus as she wished, but other options like Adderall gave her nasty side effects she had a hard time dealing with.

Lizzie made a second mental note to actually *take* her medication instead of continuing on ADHD's most ironic loop of forgetting to take the thing that will help her remember.

"Well, do you want to order a pizza or something?" Indira asked, getting up and following Lizzie. "Or we could splurge on a twelve-dollar bottle of wine, maybe? I bet that would cheer you up."

Lizzie laughed as she pulled her T-shirt over her head and flung it in the general vicinity of her buried hamper. "Twelve dollars? In this economy?" she said. "I'll take a rain check, sweets. I have a date tonight," she added, digging through a pile of wrinkled tops by her closet door.

Indira made a crooning *oohh* sound. "With who? That last guy that called himself 'the milkman' during sex?"

Lizzie shuddered at the memory. "*Fuck* no. I told him to get off me and blocked his number as soon as he asked me if I was ready for his 'whole milk.'" Lizzie made a gagging face that was more real than pretend. "No, this is just some guy on Bumble. Strictly looking to break the dry spell."

Lizzie had a strong sex drive and had used her early twenties perfecting a mutually beneficial dynamic of no-strings-attached hookups with carefully vetted people found on apps. But an unusual monthlong stretch of celibacy had her crawling out of her skin with want for the contact of another body. Another pair of hands making her feel good. The pressure and reassurance of another person's weight over her rioting nerves.

"Don't you get sick of having to figure out a new person?"

Indira asked, bending to pick up a crumpled skirt by her feet and holding it to her hips. "Wouldn't a consistent fuck-buddy be more ideal?"

Lizzie snorted. Going back for seconds was a recipe for disaster, leaving the door open for people to decide she's a little too emotional. A little too crass. A little too much.

For her to get attached and hurt.

"No way. You know I'm a one and done. Slam and scram. Hit it and quit it. Wham, bam, thank you, man. Screw 'em and—"

"Yes. I know all of that to a graphic degree," Indira said, holding up her hands to stop the onslaught. "I'm begging you, if you bring him back here, make it to your bedroom. I can't walk in on another naked person on our couch at two a.m. and expect my heart to last me."

"You got it, boss," Lizzie said with a salute, slipping a pale blue sundress over her shoulders.

"But leave your phone-tracker thing on so I know where you are. Or where to find you if you get murdered or whatever," Indira said, tucking the skirt behind her back like a dirty thief and moving toward the door.

"Duh," Lizzie said, twisting her long red hair into a knot on the top of her head, giving her armpits a quick whiff in the process. "You can borrow that skirt by the way!"

Chapter 2

LIZZIE was four minutes and a half a drink away from giving up on dating. Or hooking up. Or whatever the hell phrase best described her desperate need for an emotionless, physical connection to a willing body.

Hooking up would probably suffice.

But she was being stood up.

Nate, five foot ten, brown hair, ironic mustache, who liked hiking (barf) and dogs (aw), was standing her up.

Lizzie finished off the last of her drink and gnawed on the ice cubes, knee bouncing and eyes fixed on the door. Being stood up wasn't something she was used to, but it was happening with greater frequency, which was simultaneously disruptive to her regularly scheduled sex life and a kick to the tit confidence-wise.

She checked her phone for the seventy-third time, then tossed it back in her purse, resigning herself to the fact that he was ghosting her.

Whatever. She'd have one more drink, head home, and find comfort in her vibrator. It wouldn't exactly calm the dead sprint of her thoughts the way the press of another body did, but an orgasm was an orgasm.

The bartender darted up and down the length of the bar,

pouring shots and sliding beers across the glossy wood. She watched him work, quick and efficient. Focused.

If she were working behind the bar on a busy Friday night like this, she'd be forgetting drinks and neglecting patrons. Her sticky brain would latch on to a pretty face or the beat of a song, never following through the way the current bartender's quick hands reached and grabbed, seeming to do one hundred things at once in a fluid sync.

He walked past her, and she tried to catch his eye, but he was looking ahead. She'd get him on the next pass. The place was packed, Center City's young professionals grasping at all the joys (discounts) happy hour offered.

A warm body pressed a bit into her side to get closer to the bar, and the crisp brush of a cotton shirt against her bare arm made her want to purr at the contact. Lizzie needed touch like plants needed sun. It was fundamental.

The bartender rounded back, and Lizzie leaned forward to get his attention, but before she could get any words out, the body next to her spoke.

"Oi, mate, can I get another?"

The body spoke. *In an accent.*

An *Australian* accent.

Her brain pirouetted to attention. This was not a drill. There were few things Lizzie loved more than a man with an accent.

Please, merciful Lord, let that beautiful voice belong to an equally beautiful face so I may have sex with a hot Australian. Amen.

She turned and was confronted by a man who looked like the sun shone through him. He was tall and broad, his wide shoulders decorated with the slopes and valleys of lean muscles obvious beneath the clean lines of his button-down. His sleeves were rolled to his elbows, and a loosened tie hung from his neck, practically begging Lizzie to stroke the shiny silk.

Her eyes scoured over him, the pleasure centers in her brain going off like winning Vegas slot machines with each new discovery: sharp jawline. Tempting textures of stubble. Firm slant to his mouth. Dusting of hair on his forearms. Peek of an Adam's apple.

He was sensory overload.

He must have sensed Lizzie's ogling, because his eyes flicked to her, then back to the bartender, before doing a double take. He blinked at her with something close to surprise. Her brain hyperfocused on his eyes, a fascinating blue-green that reminded her of when she would hold pieces of sea glass up to the sun as a child.

Lizzie smiled, and his eyes flashed to her lips before his own mouth ticked up at the sides. As she continued to study him with an almost anthropological type of fascination, his smile grew, wide but bashful, the tiniest hint of pink kissing his cheeks.

"See something you like, Birdy?" The words were gravelly and deep, purring across her skin and tickling down her spine.

"God, yes," she said and laughed. He laughed back, a quiet shaking of his shoulders that contrasted sharply to the sonic boom of her own.

He crossed his arms over his chest, leaning lazily against the bar. Settling in.

This was going to be fun.

"I'm Lizzie." She stuck out her hand in the few inches that separated them. She needed to touch his skin, even just his hand. She wanted to know if his body felt as sun-kissed as it looked, like each cell collected the rays.

"Rake," he said, closing his long fingers around hers.

Lizzie couldn't help the cackle of amusement that burst from her lips, making him flinch in surprise. He quickly recovered with a look of bemused curiosity.

"Something funny about my name?" he asked, raising his eyebrows.

"*Rake?* Of course there's something funny. That's not a name, that's a type of hero from a Julia Quinn novel."

"A historical romance fan, I see?" he said, leaning an inch closer. Damn, he smelled good. Something heady and fresh, like a summer night filled with bad decisions and good memories.

"You too?" she asked dryly, arching an eyebrow.

"I've dabbled to keep up with the references," he said.

"Tell me, *Rake,* are you an infamous one? Do you have a string of scorned lovers littered across London's *ton*? Or—er—Australia's? I'm guessing?"

He grinned at her. "Oh, sure, I'm Sydney's finest libertine." He laughed, sending a ripple of enjoyment through Lizzie's chest. She loved making people laugh. "But if I'm the rake here, what does that make you? The virginal wallflower? Bookish spinster, perhaps?"

"Spinster? I'm not old, you ass. And I'm the opposite of virginal."

Heat and humor flashed in his eyes as he did a quick perusal of her body, a playful smile firmly in place. "That so? What archetype are you, then?"

Lizzie chewed on the inside of her cheek, thinking.

"A rogue," she said at last, nodding. "I'm definitely a rogue."

Rake shook his head. "A rogue and a rake? We won't have any fun at all, will we?"

"Doubtful," she replied, giving him a wink.

"Can I get you something?" the bartender interrupted, pulling them out of their little bubble. Rake straightened a bit, turning to the man.

"Oh, uh, yes. A pilsner and that cider you have on tap."

Lizzie's heart sank a degree as she registered he ordered two drinks. Both men turned to Lizzie for her order.

"Macallan. Neat," she said, giving the bartender a bright smile.

"Put it on my tab," Rake said, and the bartender nodded.

"Don't bother, I'm waiting on someone," Lizzie said to Rake. "And clearly you're . . ." She waved at the two beers plunked in front of him.

His eyebrows pinched together for a moment in confusion, until he got her meaning. "I'm here with some coworkers, on an overseas work trip. And it just so happens to be Jan from Sales's birthday," he said, opening and closing his hands in little bursts of mock excitement.

Hope perked back up in her chest like a wolf catching the scent of prey. She decided to go through the checklist, no point in wasting time.

"Married?" she asked, glancing at his ring-free left hand.

He laughed. "No."

"Girlfriend?"

"No."

"Boyfriend?" she asked, taking a prim sip of her scotch.

"Single," he said, pointing a finger at his chest, humor dancing in his eyes. Lizzie nodded.

"Emotionally unavailable?"

His smile dropped a notch, something almost like sadness flitting in his eyes, gone before she could get a good read. "Probably," he said, shrugging and running a hand through his dirty-blond hair. He was all too charming and all too tempting.

"Good," Lizzie said, her smile growing. "Me too."

Rake's eyebrows shot up, amusement glinting in his eyes. "Do you do this a lot?" he asked.

"Do what? Pick up guys?" She looked him up and down. "Need me to go easy on you, tiger?"

"No," he said, still chuckling. "I mean, talk to strangers so easily. Like you've known them for years."

Lizzie shrugged. "You'd have to ask the other strangers that."

Rake considered this as he took a sip of beer. "So, Lizzie." He focused his attention on his bottle, scratching at the corner of the label with his thumb while a tang of sheepishness crept into his voice. "How set are you on this someone you've been waiting on?"

"Less and less by the second," she said, taking a sip of her drink and licking her lips. His eyes flicked to her mouth, watching the movement.

"My coworkers are about to leave," he said, nodding toward the darker recesses of the bar, swarms of people packing into the large space. "If I go say goodbye, will you still be here when I get back?"

"Why wouldn't you go with them?" she asked with her best attempt at tantalizing indifference.

He gave her a pointed look. "Because you're much more interesting, and marginally more beautiful."

Lizzie hid her smile behind the rim of her glass as she took another sip.

"Will you be here?" he asked again.

Lizzie shrugged, trying to play coy. "Depends on how bored I get in the meantime."

"If you can have patience for just a few minutes, I have some ideas that I think can keep you entertained for the rest of the evening."

"Care to share?"

"I think we'll be sharing a lot of things tonight."

Lizzie's eyes roamed his face, taking in the heated meaning behind the contrived words, and she couldn't help the burst of laughter that broke from her lips, the sound ricocheting in the space between them. Rake's eyes went wide, taken aback by her less-than-swooning reaction.

"I'm sorry," she said, trying to hide her grin. "But do lines like that actually work?"

"Clearly not on you," he said when her giggles subsided, his expression somewhere between amused and indignant.

"I'll be here," Lizzie said, biting her lip, allowing herself to picture the feel of his body beneath her hands, how the thick ropes of his muscle would feel pressing her down into a mattress. He was exactly what she needed.

"Then I'll be right back," he said, rapping his knuckles on the bar.

"Try to think of some better lines while you're gone," Lizzie called to his retreating back, smiling at the wave he gave her.

She sipped her drink, warming at the thoughts of what came next.

Sex calmed her restless mind in a way nothing else did, and she threw herself into it like an enthusiastic hobbyist. Some people had yoga, some had meditation, others kickboxing or knitting. Lizzie had sex.

She loved the rush of someone new, the puzzle of how to get what she wanted, and the freedom of doing it all without emotional attachments. Lizzie was sensitive by nature, but she'd long ago figured out a way to detach from the pesky feelings that people often attached to sex. You couldn't get hurt if you went in knowing it was only a one-off, a means to an orgasmic end. Feelings couldn't be stepped on if you were in control of the duration of the encounter and the rules surrounding it. She'd structured the entirety of her "dating" life around that philosophical pillar. She was basically a modern, horny Descartes.

Her mind was flicking through images of the night ahead like pages of a magazine, when a hot puff of sour breath hit her cheek.

"There you are." The words were slurred and dripping with alcohol. The closeness of the voice made her jump, and she reared her head back, turning to the source.

It took her a second to place the vaguely familiar face, matching it with the pixelated version she'd squinted at through her phone screen.

"Oh," she said, frowning. "You showed." Nate, her original date for the night, swayed in front of her. "You're an hour late," Lizzie added, glancing at her phone.

"*Issss* me," he drawled.

"And me!" Another drunken idiot draped his arm around Nate's shoulders and gave him a bro-pat.

"And who the fuck are you?" Lizzie asked.

"Dis' is my best friend," Nate said, slapping a hand to the man's chest. "We both wanted to know if you're a natural redhead." He leaned in conspiratorially. "I've never hooked up with a fire crotch before."

Oh, Jesus Christ.

"Continue to talk to me and I'll light both of your crotches on fire," Lizzie said, riffling quickly through her purse and throwing some money on the bar for her drinks.

"Easy, babe," Nate said, leaning closer still, his breath rank, making every hair on Lizzie's body stand alert. "What're you doing?" His mouth was slack and eyes glassy as he watched her slide from her barstool.

"Leaving. Bye, asshole."

And goodbye hot Australian Rake. No amount of tempting accent and good looks were worth waiting around with aggressively drunk guys.

She shouldered her purse and took a step toward the door, hating that she had to walk past Nate and his friend.

"No you don't." Nate's voice suddenly rose, startling Lizzie. "We have a date." He stumbled a step from the bar, blocking her path.

"We really don't," Lizzie said, trying to sidestep him.

"Bitch, yes we do. I've been talking to you for days. I've put in the work."

Lizzie was about to let him know that two days of light flirting on the internet was no one's definition of work, when Nate made the biggest mistake of his life.

He grabbed her.

Chapter 3

TIME stopped with Nate's attempt at possession, making Lizzie feel like she was moving underwater.

She turned her head, staring at the spot where his thick fingers pressed into the bare flesh at her shoulder, the skin puckered and blanched around his unclean nails. She registered from somewhere far away that he shook her a bit.

The vibrations of his voice near her cheek forced her head to turn back to his face. His mouth was moving, but she couldn't hear the words. A sickly tongue peeked out to wet his fumbling lips as a lecherous smile broke across his face.

Lizzie smiled back as rage flooded her body, her lips curling to bare her teeth.

Casually, she reached for her drink from the bar, bringing it toward her mouth.

Nate's bloodshot eyes followed the motion, hungry and predatory.

Right before her lips touched the rim of the glass, she willed her fingers to release, letting it fall to the floor. Nate followed its path, head moving with its descent. Lizzie could tell the moment it shattered by his flinch, but she couldn't hear anything over the blood rushing through her ears.

Things sped up then.

She cocked her right fist back, swinging it up in a gorgeous arc to his down-turned face, making square contact with his nose. She found a perverse joy in feeling it crunch beneath her knuckles.

Nate's head whipped back from the impact, blood pouring from his nostrils. Before he could stagger away, she grabbed his shoulders and thrust her knee into his groin. He crumpled over, and Lizzie stepped back, letting him fall to the floor.

A moment of silence spread through the bar like a crack traveling through glass, as the last ten seconds registered with everyone.

Then all hell broke loose.

Shouts erupted, a woman shrieked, and the pure commotion in the bar vibrated against Lizzie's shattered nerves. She tried to suck in a deep breath, needing to escape, but before she could get her bearings, Nate's friend advanced on her.

"Fucking bitch! I'll—"

Lizzie didn't get to hear what he intended to do. In a blinding flash, the asshole was pinned to the bar, his face smashed against the wood and arms twisted behind his back, while Rake hovered over him, rage in his eyes.

"You'll do nothing." Rake's accent was much less sensual and far more terrifying now. He pressed his large palm against the friend's face, digging it into the bar and making him yelp. "You and your mate won't even look twice at a woman again, or I'll find you. Understood?" The man whimpered out a yes, and Rake pushed off him.

"Are you okay?" he asked, turning to Lizzie, worry marring his face. She nodded, a numb feeling ebbing across her skin and lips as a weird haze blanketed her senses. Rake continued to stare at her, before nodding in return. He stooped down and picked up her purse, which she'd dropped in the commotion, then stood, creating room for her to move forward. He seemed to know how badly she didn't want to be touched, and he managed to usher her out of the bar, creating a protective bubble without invading her space further.

Out on the street, Lizzie started walking—quick, sharp steps—not caring where she was going. She wanted as many inches, feet, miles between herself and that stupid fucking bar with its stupid fucking boys. Rake kept pace with her, and while there was something oddly comforting about his presence, a protective energy humming from him, the tears that pricked at her eyes made her want to tell him to fuck off too. She picked up speed. He matched it.

One block passed. Then another. And another.

She was running now. If she ran, she could concentrate on the muscles in her legs, and not how Nate's touch still pressed into her skin. If she ran, she could suck in more breath, get his stench out of her nose, get the feel of his words off her cheek.

She felt stupid. Dirty. Why was her life always like this? Why was everything such an ordeal? Why did a cloud of chaos seem to permeate from her pores and stick to her skin?

She wanted to run and run until she finally outpaced the feelings. She always felt too much. Too sharp.

"Lizzie."

The sound of her name on Rake's lips pulled her from her thoughts. She stopped short, placing her hands on her knees as she gulped down lungfuls of the humid May night.

"Are you okay?" Rake's question came in heavy pants, his hands resting on his hips as he caught his breath, Lizzie's giant purse still clutched in one of his fists.

Lizzie nodded and grabbed her bag, not wanting to look at him, not wanting to see the wary pity people always wore in the wake of her messes.

"Was that . . . 'someone'?" Rake asked quietly.

Lizzie's head shot up, meeting his eyes. "That," she said, her nostrils flaring, jabbing a finger in the direction she'd run from, "was absolutely fucking no one."

It was Rake's turn to nod. He continued to stare at her, his chest still rising and falling as he worked to catch his breath. His eyes bored into her, like he could see the wild circuits going off beneath her skin.

Thoughts and noise continued to build in her head, humming into her bones. She needed an off button. She needed him to stop looking at her like that. She needed . . . something.

She pushed forward, pressing herself against the hard wall of Rake's body. Her lips, hungry and desperate, found his, and she wrapped her arms around his neck, pulling him closer.

He pulled his head back, surprise and want lighting up his features. "Wait. Are you—"

Lizzie cut him off, straining on her tiptoes to press her mouth back against his. Words were pointless and trite. She didn't need to describe her feelings or analyze why she attracted chaos. She needed lips and teeth and hands and heat.

His initial shock melted into subtle exploration, kissing her back, molding their bodies more tightly together, opening her mouth with a swipe of his tongue and tasting her with hesitant desire.

Lizzie let out a sigh, tension evaporating from her skin, as he pushed even closer, pressing her between the rough stone of the building behind her and the hard planes of his body.

Calm spread through her limbs, her muscles focused on Rake's reassuring weight, her mind centered on the feel of his mouth against hers, the gentle scratch of his stubble. Lizzie twined her hands through his hair, pulling him closer, feasting on the soft groan he made.

But then, he pulled back.

Why was he pulling back?

Rake's hands dropped from her body, and he flattened his

palms on the wall behind her, one on either side of her shoulders. He arched his head back and blinked up at the sky, sucking in a breath. Lizzie watched the movements of his throat as he swallowed.

"Why'd you stop?" she asked, snaking her hands around his trim waist. Touching another person was a decadent luxury, and Lizzie was the embodiment of greed.

He looked down at her, his eyebrows pinching together as he searched her face. "Because a guy just laid his hands on you in a bar, and it seems shitty to feel you up right after." His voice was gruff. Lizzie wanted to feel the way it would vibrate against her thighs.

"I'm fine," she said, trying to tug his mouth back to hers. He didn't budge, just continued to study her. Lizzie blinked away. He was looking too closely, searching for something that wasn't there.

"Take me home with you," she said, dragging her fingers down the front of his shirt, enjoying the small vibration of the fabric scratching against her nails, the subtle shiver of his body under her hands. She looped her fingers in the waistband of his pants, pulling his hips closer to hers. "Use another one of your cheesy pickup lines, and take me home with you."

She knew she had him when he laughed.

"Are you sure that's a good idea?"

Lizzie leaned in and pressed a kiss to his jawline before lightly biting the spot. "Sex is always a good idea."

He stared at her for another long second before he shook his head and grabbed her hand.

"You should write holiday cards," he said, pulling her away from the wall and guiding her down the street.

Chapter 4

RAKE took a deep breath, trying to rationalize what was happening as he shoved his keycard into the lock and opened the door to his hotel room. He must have lost his mind somewhere between Lizzie's barstool and the corner block where she'd kissed him. It was the only explanation for the bizarre, light-headed feeling he'd had since they first started talking. He'd sworn off women—he'd stuck with it too—but something about this one's wide smile and booming laugh muddled his brain.

He pushed open the door and Lizzie waltzed in, flipping off her sandals and walking farther into the place like she'd been there a million times. He stared at the discarded shoes and was simultaneously unnerved and warmed at the foreign sight of someone else's things flung next to the precise line of his lonely shoes.

Lizzie let out a low whistle, spinning around as she took in the suite. "Hot damn, do you always stay in such nice places?" she asked, pulling her hair from the bun on the top of her head. Rake watched the red waves tumble free and cascade down her shoulders, the ends skimming just below the swells of her breasts.

"Work tends to set us up in nice places, I guess," he said,

watching as she pushed her fingers through it, making the strands dance like flames licking at her body, glints of orange and gold sparking in the mass of her hair.

He was transfixed. And in desperate need of a good fuck if he was this turned on by her hair alone. It'd been almost two years, he reasoned. He deserved to bend his rules a bit.

He'd done so well at avoiding women and sex—avoiding any demonstrations of human intimacy, really—that he hadn't seen Lizzie coming. But the second he'd caught her looking at him, his mind had focused in on her, the single thought of *want, want, want* throbbing through him.

He might have been able to push away the urge, come up with an excuse for his coworkers, and head for his hotel alone, but seeing those assholes harassing her filled him with such a primal, protective instinct, he knew he couldn't leave without her.

It didn't help that he actually seemed to like the odd little stranger. Lizzie made him laugh easily, and laughing wasn't something he'd done in a long time.

But now that he had her here, he wasn't really sure what to do with her. And he was mildly flipping out.

Lizzie, on the other hand, couldn't seem more at ease.

"Are you going to offer me a drink?" she asked, moving toward the small kitchenette in the corner of the suite and peeking into the fridge.

"Water's, uh, the best I can do," Rake said, rubbing a hand over the back of his neck. She smiled at him over her shoulder.

"Aw, really? I was hoping we could split the lo mein," she said, stepping to the side, revealing the stark fridge and the one sad carton of Chinese takeout that Rake had picked at last night while he sat alone in his hotel room, the city noises and his own self-loathing keeping him company.

Rake forced out a laugh, but awkwardness settled heavily on his shoulders. This was a bad idea. He shouldn't have brought her here. He definitely shouldn't sleep with her. He'd worked hard to cut out destructive pleasures like this.

Lizzie poked through the cupboards, grabbing a glass and filling it at the tap, humming as she did it. She padded toward him, holding it out.

"Want some?"

Rake shook his head, wondering if he looked as uneasy as he felt. Lizzie eyed him as she finished off the water, then set it down and stuck her hands on her hips.

"What's wrong with you?" she asked.

Rake blinked at the question. "Huh?"

"What happened to the cocky guy I picked up at the bar?"

That shook Rake out of his spiral. He had a role here, and it wasn't being some overanalyzing, blushing prude. He wanted sex. She wanted sex. Now was not the time to overthink things.

"I think I was the one picking you up," Rake said with a smile, trying to fall back into their easy flow from earlier.

"Sure, kid." She winked at him, then started undoing the line of buttons down her sundress, plucking at them efficiently and without ceremony. Rake was out of practice, but he was fairly certain undressing her was supposed to be his job.

But an embarrassing wave of shyness kept his hands shoved in his pockets while he gently rocked back and forth on his heels, watching her while his cock swelled almost painfully with a rush of blood.

"Do you have condoms?" Lizzie asked, slipping the straps of the dress off her shoulders and letting it fall to the floor.

"I actually don't," Rake said regretfully, scrubbing a hand down his mouth and chin as he took in the full curves of her body. The lace edges of her lilac underwear and bra. The splattering of freckles covering every inch of skin. He had the ridiculous urge to memorize them all.

"No biggie, I'm sure I have some in here somewhere," she said, dumping out her giant purse on the couch. She dug through the mountain of random crap—Rake could have sworn he saw socks and a Tupperware of snacks—before she finally pulled out a glorious handful of wrinkled silver packages.

"Aha! Always gotta come prepared," she said, shooting him another wink as she let the strip of foils unfurl from her hand.

"Holy God, I hope those aren't all for me. You'll kill me," Rake said, his eyes bouncing from the rubbers to her triumphant smile.

"Aw, sweet dove. I'll be gentle," Lizzie said, laughing as she ripped off the packet at the end and threw the rest of them back into her purse. She fixed her gaze on him, slinking forward with a hungry glint in her eyes. Rake swallowed.

"Damn, you're slow," Lizzie said, closing the space between them. She pressed the condom into his hand then went to work on the buttons of his shirt with quick, clinical efficiency. "It's like this is your first time hooking up." Lizzie's fingers stalled halfway down his torso, her eyes bouncing up to his as she took a step back.

"Wait. Are you a virgin?"

"What? No!"

The corner of her lips twitched, but she took another step back. A step toward the bed. "It's fine if you are." Another step. Rake found himself inadvertently following her, undoing the remainder of his buttons and shucking off his shirt. "It's just that I'm not in the business of corrupting innocents," she said, shrugging as she continued her backward retreat. "A lady must have boundaries. Guidelines, at least, for her sexual conquests. I'm not"—she paused for dramatic effect, her eyes sparkling with teasing—"a *rake*," she finished.

There was a second of silence while Rake stared at her, slack-jawed, before she burst out laughing.

The sound pulled him in like a magnet—making him smile, making him close the distance between them. Making him laugh.

He laughed as he kissed her and as he picked her up, her legs wrapping around his waist. They laughed together, their bodies shaking as Lizzie reached between them to fumble with the button of his pants. Laughed as she greedily pushed the pants off his hips, and laughed harder when he nearly tripped stepping out of them. Her laugh turned into a delicious sigh when he pressed her into the mattress.

She reached between them again, snaking her hand into his boxer briefs to grip his erection, causing him to hiss out a breath.

"Oh, shit," Lizzie said, looking up at him in wide-eyed alarm. She pushed at his chest and he rolled off her immediately.

"What's wrong?" he asked as she stared at him.

She sat up onto her knees, sliding off his underwear without delicacy and staring with something close to horror at his cock.

"That's your dick?" she said, her eyes flying between him and his crotch. Rake instinctively covered himself.

"Um, yes?"

She pushed his hand away, continuing to stare, before giving her head a resigned shake.

He moved to pull up his underwear. "I'll just . . . put it away, then?"

She sighed and stopped his progress with her hand. "No, no. It's fine."

"'Fine' isn't exactly something a man loves to hear when his pants are around his knees, Birdy."

"I was just hoping to be able to walk tomorrow. But really, it's fine," she said, giving him an experimental poke that made him slap her hand away. She looked up at him and grinned.

"I can promise if you keep talking about it with such disappointment, it'll shrink. Give it another five seconds."

Lizzie laughed again and swung her leg over his hips, straddling him. "No, no. I'll resign myself to sex with a hot stranger sporting a giant hammer-dick. Poor me."

Rake blinked at Lizzie. "You're a strange one," he said at last, giving in and laughing with her. He'd never laughed this much during sex. He actually couldn't think of a time he'd *ever* laughed during sex. But she was just so damn . . . fun.

All laughing officially stopped when she started grinding along his length, the silk of her underwear a maddening texture against his throbbing cock. She pressed her chest against his, giving him a deep, rough kiss as he unhooked her bra and ran his hands down her back until he reached her ass, squeezing it in handfuls as he pushed her hips harder against his. She moaned, breaking off the kiss and moving down his body, dragging open-mouth kisses along his chest and stomach.

"What are you doing?" he said on a hoarse breath. There was no way he was about to get as lucky as he was thinking.

Lizzie stopped her descent and shot him a playful look. "I'll give you three guesses," she said, dragging her teeth over his hip bone and shooting bolts of pleasure down his spine.

"You s-sure?" he stuttered out, right as she took him into her mouth. She gave one long suck before pulling away, sitting up to stare at him with a lusty smile.

"Want me to stop, big guy?"

"God, no."

Lizzie let out a husky laugh and went back to her task, positioning herself so her butt gave him an enticing view while she moved, using her sweet mouth and hands, gripping the base of him and following her lips with each deep stroke in a way that had him blinking away stars from his vision.

Rake needed to touch her. Feel her. Reaching out, he traced up the back of her thick thighs. He brushed his fingers along the edge of her panties until he reached the small bloom of wetness marking the silk. He dipped his fingers beneath the fabric, tracing the luscious slickness of her slit, his eyes devouring the outline of her through the thin fabric. The feel of her moan against his cock made his hips buck in response. Rake tried to focus on his fingers, needing to regain some self-control before he lost himself in under two minutes. He circled her clit, moving with smooth strokes that soon had her grinding against his hand. She was so wet, so hot, he couldn't decide what he enjoyed looking at more, her lips stretched around his length, her long hair spilled out around his hips, or the sight of her cunt as she slid over his hand.

It was too much. He needed a moment to regain his wits.

Pulling his fingers from her underwear, he grabbed her hip, nudging gently. "You better stop. I'm not ready for this to be over."

Lizzie cocked her head slightly, looking at him as she went down once more, and Rake squeezed his eyes shut, nearly ripping the sheets in an iron grip as he held off coming right then and there. With a soft *pop*, Lizzie released him from her mouth and climbed back over his body, grinding against him again.

"Come here," Rake said, grabbing her by the hips and pulling her farther up his body. He really did need a minute without stimulation if he was supposed to continue without embarrassing himself.

Lizzie looked down at him with something close to disbelief from where she straddled high up on his chest. "What are you doing?"

Rake shot her an arrogant grin before dragging his open mouth along the silk of her panties, pressing his tongue right above her clit.

"I'll give you three guesses," he said against her, imitating her voice from earlier. Lizzie let out a breathy giggle that turned into a moan when he laughed into her skin.

"Come closer," Rake said, tugging her hips a bit more, encouraging her to fully cover his mouth. She abandoned any of her previous hesitation, gripping the headboard as she circled her hips over him. He sucked on her through the silk, alternating between tight circles and thick drags with his tongue. He encouraged her rocking with one of his hands at her hip, the other snaking around to dive beneath her underwear and pushing into her center. Lizzie let out a hoarse gasp, dropping her forehead to rest by her hands, her fiery hair creating a brilliant curtain of red around them. Rake continued to press his fingers into her, curling them to hit a spot she seemed to like. He pulled his mouth back from her thrusting hips.

"Do you want to take these off?" he asked, snapping the elastic band with the hand that was resting on her hip.

"Holy shit, don't *stop*, you idiot."

Rake took that as a no, pressing his mouth back to her and sucking through the drenched fabric. He was ridiculously turned on, every one of her moans and sighs sending a bolt of electricity down his spine and to his cock. After a few more thrusts of her hips, Lizzie's eyes snapped shut and she let out a gorgeous cry, her muscles clenching around his fingers and her body shaking as she came. After the final trembles stopped, she went limp over him, breathing hard. Rake pulled out his fingers, running a soothing hand over her thighs and hips before gently pulling her down his torso and rolling them so he hovered over her.

Lizzie blinked up at him, a contented smile curving the corners of her mouth, lovely strands of her hair curling and sticking to her forehead. He licked his lips, tasting the whisper of her on them. He was hungry for more.

"Hi," she said after a moment, dragging her hand down his body.

"Hi," he said back, pressing a kiss to her neck. "You okay, or are you ready to stop?" *Please dear God, don't be ready to stop.*

Lizzie guffawed at that, pressing up to rest on her elbows and forcing Rake to move back a bit. "I'm no quitter. Let's see what you've got," she said, shooting a goofy, cross-eyed look straight at his penis.

Rake patted around the bed for a moment before finding the discarded condom. He tore it open and rolled it on, anticipation thrumming through his veins. Lizzie shifted her hips, finally pulling off her panties and tossing them across the room.

It felt ridiculous that they'd done all of that with her underwear still on.

She opened her legs for him, and he knew he didn't have the restraint to drag it out any longer. He positioned himself between her thighs, planting his forearms on either side of her face before surging into her wet heat with one long thrust, making them both groan. He moved in and out of her, ducking his head to take one of her nipples in his mouth, cataloguing the feel of her fingers pressing through his hair then down his neck.

"Harder," she gasped out, digging her nails into his back. He obliged, their skin slapping in a wet, crude way that made him wild. He reared up onto his palms, then used one hand to grip her thigh, getting a handful of luscious freckled skin, as he pushed her leg higher, moved into her deeper.

"*Yes*," Lizzie groaned, arching her neck and pressing her head into the mattress. Rake dragged his teeth along her throat and collarbone, needing to taste her and feel her with as many parts of himself as he could.

"It's so good," he ground out, pistoning into her with even more force, earning him a moan of satisfaction from her lips. It shouldn't be this good. It shouldn't be allowed for a random hookup to be this raw. Reach this overwhelming type of pleasure.

Their eyes locked, and Rake knew she was close. *He* was close. Pleasure rippled between them, and her body felt poised to snap as she looked into his eyes. But at the last minute, she slammed her lids closed, blocking him out. Riding that wave on her own with a raspy cry.

The loss of her eyes punched sharply at him, but he brushed it aside, his own release barreling through him, ripping the air from his lungs and the strength from his arms as he collapsed down, rolling off her.

They lay there for a moment, the heavy sounds of their

breathing mixing with the hum of traffic floating in through the open window. Rake waited for awkwardness to settle between them in the bed, but it didn't. Just a foreign feeling of contentment as his pulse calmed.

"I feel like I need a cigarette after that," Rake said to the ceiling. More accurately, he felt like he might need to pass out.

"Do you smoke?" she asked, turning her head to him with an amused smile.

"Not a day in my life. But after what you just did to me? It only seems appropriate."

"What *I* did to *you*?" Lizzie said with an incredulous laugh, slapping her palm against his sweaty chest with a loud smack. "You were a very active participant." Her eyes sparkled with mischief and humor as she looked at him, and Rake couldn't help but pick up her hand from his chest and lay a kiss on her palm.

Lizzie watched the movement, blinking at him, the humor draining from her features. She pulled her hand away gently, hovering it between them like she couldn't decide where it belonged. A decision seemed to click in her mind, and she gave him an almost familial pat on the cheek and turned away, sitting up and swinging her legs off the side of the bed.

"Where are you going?" he asked, dragging his fingers along the splattering of freckles across her back. She looked over her shoulder at him, smiling, while she pulled her mane of fiery hair into a ponytail.

"A lady always pees after sex. It's one of the ten commandments of womanhood." She laughed and stood, giving him an excellent view of her full ass as she padded across the room, scooping up her clothes on her way to the bathroom.

Rake flopped back onto the pillows, blinking up at the ceiling.

That had been . . . incredible. Better than incredible. Sure, it had been a long, *long* dry spell, but that was up there with some of the best sex of his life. Dirty. Uninhibited. *Fun.* He dragged his hands over his face, trying to get a grip. Trying to find the stamina to do it again if he was being honest with himself.

After another minute, Lizzie walked out of the bathroom and back toward the bed. Rake sat up, the sheets falling around his waist and his heart sinking as he saw she'd put her dress back on.

"Are you . . . You aren't leaving, are you?" Rake was embarrassed at how needy his own voice sounded.

Lizzie tilted her head, giving him a funny smile. "Did you expect me to . . . stay?" The words weren't mean, just filled with a genuine curiosity that made Rake feel like a fool.

"No, sorry. Of course not." Her leaving was the best thing that could happen. This was a one-off. Something he needed to get out of his system.

Her eyes lingered on him for a moment longer, catlike and focused, studying him with a soft smile at the corners. The power of those beautiful eyes was the only explanation for what he said next. "Can I get your number?"

Her eyes shot wide. As they should. She'd made this clear it was a one-night stand, and Rake similarly wasn't interested in anything more. And he was heading back home to Australia in a few days. He couldn't use her number. *Wouldn't* use it, even if she gave it.

Definitely wouldn't call.

Probably.

"Uh, sure. Um." Her eyebrows pinched together as she riffled through her large bag. She pulled out a green marker and stared at it then looked around, bewildered. Her eyes landing on Rake, she closed the distance and grabbed his wrist, scribbling her number on the back of his hand.

"I could have just given you my phone," Rake said, unable to hide the smile in his voice.

"Huh? Oh." She blushed, illuminating the dusting of freckles on her cheeks. "Yeah, that would have made more sense. Sorry."

She capped the marker and tossed it back in her bag, taking a step away from him.

"Do you always carry markers?"

She dropped her chin to her chest and let out a quiet, almost sad laugh, one that sounded like defeat. "Yeah, keep them right next to the condoms," she said, looking back up at him and winking. "This bag's a mess. I probably have half my life in here. Pulled out some old cheese sticks just this morning."

Rake scrunched his nose. "Delicious."

An awkward silence fell between them, and Lizzie fidgeted, looking toward the door.

"I'll get dressed."

"I'll see myself out."

They spoke at the same time, both cringing.

"I can walk you out," Rake said, scanning the floor for his underwear, feeling ridiculously modest all of a sudden.

"Don't worry about it. I know the way," Lizzie said, backing toward the door.

"Just give me a minute. I don't mind." He stretched out his arm, trying to reach the crumpled trunks.

"Seriously, it's cool," Lizzie said, shooting him little finger guns before she backed up into the wall with an *oof*.

"Oh my God, would you just wait a second." Rake's finger hooked the fabric, and he pulled it toward him, trying to hurry.

"Thanks for the, er . . . sex," she rushed out, turning and getting to the door just as he pulled on his boxers and leaped out of bed.

"I really enjoyed—" The door clicked shut behind her before he could get the words out. "Meeting you," he whispered to his empty hotel room.

Chapter 5

LIZZIE woke up the next morning and stumbled out of her room and straight to the kitchen for the coffeepot.

Indira was lying across the couch, a book in one hand and coffee in the other. "Morning, sun—"

Lizzie made a noise somewhere between a shush and a grunt, waving away her friend's perky voice as she reached the pot. She grabbed her favorite mug from the shelf, the words WORLD'S SEXIEST GRANDPA printed on it in large block letters, and filled it to the brim. After taking three long sips, she plastered a smile on her face and turned to Indira.

"Good morning, you sweet gorgeous angel with a face like a delicate orchid. How did you sleep?"

Indira snorted and moved her legs off the end of their couch, making room for Lizzie to sit. "You're ridiculous," she said. "And an addict," she added, pointing at the mug.

"We all have our fatal flaws. What do you have planned today?"

"Errands," Indira said with a wave. "Gonna try to get lunch with my brother too, but I'm on call tonight so I'll be bumming around here after that. Fabulous life of a resident."

Indira was wading her way through her psychiatric residency, focusing on pediatrics and regularly wowing Lizzie with her compassion and hard work. Lizzie was so proud of her friend, it felt like her heart would burst from her chest every time Indira talked about it.

"Can I be you when I grow up?" Lizzie asked, taking another sip of her coffee. "Like, seriously. You're gorgeous *and* a certified boss ass bitch? Incredible."

Indira giggled, pressing a kiss to the top of Lizzie's head. "You're a boss bitch too, ya know."

Lizzie almost choked on her sip of coffee. She'd lost countless jobs, was on thin ice with her current one, and still ate instant ramen over the sink like a raccoon foraging from a trash can on a regular basis. There wasn't really a comparison.

Indira's phone trilled from the coffee table, and she grabbed it. "Harper's FaceTiming us," she said, swiping open the call.

Lizzie and Indira smushed their faces together to fit in the screen, both screaming in excitement as their best friend, Harper, popped up. Harper's gorgeous, gangly boyfriend, Dan, hovered in the background, smiling as he rested his chin on Harper's shoulder.

"We miss youuuuuu," Lizzie squawked. "Move back to Philly immediately, please."

Harper had moved to New York a year ago after graduation for an oral surgery residency. She was so brilliant, Lizzie sometimes wondered how Harper's tiny body could support such a giant brain.

"We miss you too!" Harper said, shooting a sweet glance at Dan. They were so in love, it was almost disgusting. "But hold on, let me get Thu-Thu in here," Harper added. Thu was the final piece of their best friend quartet. Whip-smart and sarcastic as hell, she was living in Los Angeles as she finished up her orthodontics residency. After a few seconds of fiddling, Thu's face filled the bottom half of the screen.

"Harper, did you tell them yet?" Thu asked by way of greeting.

"No, I thought I'd let you do the honors."

Thu looked into the screen, her gorgeous smile brighter than normal. "We're visiting!"

"What!" Indira and Lizzie screeched in unison. "Both of you?"

"Yup," Thu said, popping the *p* sound at the end. "Harpy and I have been coordinating, and we've found a weekend we can both get home to Philadelphia. Dan's coming too," she added.

"When?" Lizzie asked, happy tears poking at her eyeballs. She loved her friends more than anything and was too excited to function.

"A few weeks. We'll forward you our travel itineraries and stuff," Harper said. "It won't be a long trip, but at least we'll get some time together."

Indira made a squeal of excitement. While this wouldn't be the first time they'd all gotten together since Harper, Thu, and Indira had graduated, visits occurred less often than any of them would like.

"Do you need to stay with us?" Indira asked.

"I'll be staying with Alex," Thu said, referring to her boyfriend who was still in dental school in Philadelphia.

"Dan and I will get a hotel," Harper said, reaching up to press her hand to Dan's cheek, his head still resting on her shoulder.

"Need some privacy for all that wild fuckin'?" Lizzie said. Harper turned beet red and slapped her palm over her face, but Dan laughed, his mouth breaking open into a crooked grin.

"God, I've missed you, Lizzie," he said, once he'd gotten his laughter under control.

They chatted for a few more minutes before a low-battery warning popped up on Indira's phone.

"Shit, my phone's about to die," Indira said. "I better run. But I can't wait to see you guys."

"Same," Lizzie said, giving Thu, Harper, and Dan a big smile and wave before Indira ended the call.

"The battery life on my phone *sucks*. Can I have my portable charger back?" Indira asked, turning to Lizzie.

Lizzie's eyes widened and her mouth pinched as she tried to remember where she'd put the battery pack that Indira had loaned her.

Indira's shoulders slumped. "Don't tell me you lost it. That thing was like forty bucks."

"I didn't lose it," Lizzie rushed out, even though she'd probably lost it. "Hold on, let me check my purse."

Lizzie moved to the floor by the front door where she'd dropped her bag when she got home the night before. After riffling through it and enjoying a soft tickle of pleasure as she saw the remaining condoms in her bag, memories of the fun with Rake purring through her, she realized the charger wasn't in there.

She bear-crawled to her room next, digging under piles of clothes and random papers. Indira let out a long sigh, leaning in the doorway.

"You lost it."

"No, no, no," Lizzie said, rising to stand but tripping over a discarded bra on the floor. "I think I left it at work." Shame tickled its nails down her back at the disbelieving look Indira shot her.

"You think?"

"I *know*," Lizzie lied. But she couldn't handle being looked at like that. Not a look of anger. Not even annoyance. Just resigned pity at Messy Lizzie. Always Losing Things Lizzie. Unreliable Lizzie. "I'll go get it right now."

Indira plastered on a half-hearted smile. "It's okay, dude. I gotta run anyway. Just . . . I don't know. Try to find it if you can."

"Okay wait, hold on." Lizzie sprinted to the kitchen, pulling out a tin of her luscious raspberry almond biscotti she kept stocked for moments like this. She grabbed a handful, then slid across the floor in front of Indira, pushing one of the biscotti into her mouth and pressing the rest into Indira's hand.

"Please don't be mad at me," Lizzie said as Indira chewed with a look of shock.

Indira swallowed then narrowed her eyes. "Damn you, Lizzie. You know I can't even be *annoyed* at you when you make something that tastes that good." She popped a second bite of biscotti into her mouth and groaned.

"I know what I'm about, toots," Lizzie said, spanking Indira on the butt and pushing her out the door.

As soon as Indira was gone, Lizzie's smile dropped and she hung her head, indescribably frustrated at herself. She was always like this. Forgetting the tiny details that ended up making life so much harder on everyone else. Her mother had never made a secret how much of a burden her scatterbrained nature was to everyone else, and it seemed to be a debilitating trait she was carrying well into adulthood.

She spent another few minutes ransacking her messy room, before realizing her last hope of finding the charger really would be at work. Which sucked, because the last thing she wanted to do on her Saturday off was go into the bakery and weave through the rabid line of people desperate for a donut.

Changing out of her pajamas and throwing on the first things she grabbed from the floor, she then scooped up her purse and began digging through it for her key ring. While she needed a key to get into Baking Me Crazy, her apartment had lock pads, so she rarely had her keys at the ready.

As she was searching, her phone buzzed. She looked at the screen, seeing a text from a number she didn't have saved. After she opened the message, her eyes went wide.

Missing something? it read, with a picture of a large hand holding her key ring. A naughty buzz of pleasure shot low through her belly as she recognized the hand. The same one that had gripped her thighs the night before.

The same hand attached to the body of a man she never planned on hearing from again.

Another text buzzed through that made Lizzie let out a bark of laughter.

This is a nice touch, the message said under a second picture of her key chain shaped like a small, pink penis—veins, balls, and all. The head detached to reveal a tube of ChapStick.

I should have guessed you'd rob me, Lizzie typed back, biting the inside of her cheek as she smiled.

A new message popped up immediately: We both know this is a desperate ploy to see me again. You could have just asked ;)

He followed it up just as quickly with: Is there somewhere you want me to meet you to hand them over?

Lizzie thought about this. The smart, responsible thing would be to give him a corner street to meet on, offer him a brief smile, take her keys, and not look back.

But her impulsive, hornier side knew exactly how much more fun it would be to meet back at his hotel room and enjoy a second round of the night before.

Which was odd. She wasn't one to want more after a hookup. She was exceptionally good at separating emotions from sex at a first encounter, but going back for seconds was a recipe for disaster; a chance for those pesky feelings to gain purchase.

But Rake seemed to be an exception to her rule, and with a dick that good and an accent that pretty, it wasn't hard to reason *why* she would want to see him again.

Without giving it any more thought, she typed out her reply: I'll swing by your hotel if that's cool with you.

An odd thrill of anticipation had her heart thumping in her chest when she saw the typing bubble pop up and disappear a few times. She felt a giddiness about this guy that she hadn't experienced since high school.

She wanted to know what he was thinking, what he was feeling, as he continued to type and stop, type and stop, that traitorous little text bubble giving away just enough of his struggle to tempt Lizzie to the highest degree.

Finally, three delicious words popped up on her screen.

See you soon.

Chapter 6

RAKE wasn't doing this right. His night with Lizzie was supposed to be a one-off. Something to get it out of his system. A mistake he could beat himself up for, a slip in self-control that would feed nicely into his self-loathing.

What it wasn't supposed to be was something that kept him up all damn night; every time he would finally close his eyes and think he was surrendering to sleep, he'd hear an echo of her laugh or sigh. It was *not* supposed to be something that he welcomed again into his life.

He wasn't meant to have attachments or feelings, and his odd craving for Lizzie needed to be stopped.

Which was why he decided that although he'd invited her over—or, more accurately, she'd invited herself—he would turn her away. He would open the door, hand her the keys, make an excuse, and firmly close the door. Bolt it for good measure.

But the thing he didn't take into account was all reason flying out the bloody window the second he heard her knock.

He took a deep breath, walking himself through a mental cold shower before he opened the door.

Like an unstoppable, lovely wave, Lizzie breezed into the hotel room, dragging one palm across his chest and fixing him with an effervescent grin as she went. She kicked off her sandals like she had the previous night, the shoes flinging off to different corners of the room like she planned on staying awhile. Rake's blood heated almost to discomfort with the hope of her staying awhile.

"Hi," she said brightly, turning to him and wrapping her arms around his waist in a familiar hug.

Rake wasn't used to physical affection—it very well might have been two years since he last received a hug—and the feeling of it sent his whole body off-kilter, like his knees would crumple beneath him if he didn't have her to lean into. To hug back.

Which was absolutely absurd because he didn't even like hugs or affection or anything of the sort. And he certainly wasn't one to swoon.

"How's your morning been?" she asked as she pulled away, moving farther into the hotel room with a soft smile.

He wasn't sure of the polite way to say he'd been kept up all night with thoughts of her, and when he'd finally gotten a few hours of sleep, he'd woken up achingly hard from memories of the night before. Then he'd spent the morning agonizing over what to text her, until he didn't even recognize himself any-more, overanalyzing every word of her response. His morning had been shit.

But instead of explaining this, he settled on: "Your keys are just there," pointing brusquely at the metal pile sitting on the coffee table.

"Thank you," she said, grabbing them.

And then she did something that nearly killed him. She pulled the head off the penis key chain from the ring, twisted the balls around and around to reveal the pink tip of ChapStick, brought it to her lips, and made a sensual circuit around her mouth, before reversing the process, clicking it back onto the key ring, dropping the whole damn thing in her giant purse, and popping her lips with a satisfied smack.

They stared at each other for a long moment, Lizzie fixing

him with a small smile that was a mix of amusement and flirtation.

Rake had to get her out of there.

He had to get every trace of her out of that hotel room because he wanted her with such a raw physical force that the intensity of it screamed danger like a blaring alarm through his skull, his pulse pounding through every joint and muscle of his body. Wanting something this much could only be a bad thing.

"So you probably—" He lifted his hand toward the door, but at the same moment, she talked over him.

"You're odd, do you know that?" she said, her smile growing.

Rake's head jerked back at this as he spluttered, trying to understand her words. "*I'm* odd?" he finally managed, jabbing a finger at his chest.

"Yes, *you*," she said with a little laugh, taking a step toward him.

"Coming from the woman with a penis ChapStick on her key ring and a pack of questionable cheese in her purse?"

Lizzie let out a booming laugh. And, as off-kilter as she made him, Rake couldn't help but smile at the noise. He'd heard her laugh more in the past twelve hours than he'd heard anyone laugh his whole life. *If yellow was a sound*, he thought, *it would be her laugh*. Bright and booming, warming and joyful. Different varieties ranging from sunbeams and lemon zest to the soft puffs of golden wattle.

"You're odd," she repeated, amusement still dripping like honey on every word, "because you're a big gorgeous mass of contradictions."

Rake tilted his head to the side, not understanding. He wasn't complicated. He wasn't *complex*. He was a normal guy who got up every day and went to work, stayed as long as he could without seeming weird, then went home to his empty apartment and watched boring TV until it was reasonable for him to go to bed, only to repeat the cycle the next day.

"What parts of me are a contradiction?"

"All of this," she said, gesturing between them, before closing the space and curling her fingers in his belt loops. "You're quick to flirt with me at a bar or over text. It's obvious you're attracted to me"—Rake still had the wherewithal and pride to send her a sardonic glance at that, which she accepted with a waggle of her eyebrows—"and it's even more obvious I'm attracted to *you*," she added, expertly stroking his ego. "But when it comes down to it"—she pressed their hips closer together, his erection a glaringly obvious third party in the conversation—"you clam up. Why?"

Rake didn't know what to say. If he was being honest with himself, his brain was having trouble working with his aching cock pressed so firmly against her. He couldn't seem to form a coherent thought, not with the fresh scent of her skin—a mix of sweet vanilla and tart fruit—tangling with the sound of her laugh and clogging up his brain.

"I don't do this a lot," he admitted. "Hookups don't come naturally to me." Embarrassment flooded him. He was a man. He was supposed to be good at hookups. He was supposed to be able to fuck and hook up and do it all without overthinking or having any damn feelings about it. . . . Right?

Lizzie stared at him for a moment, her eyes traveling over his face like she was looking into him, pulling him apart layer by layer, trying to translate some code. Then she smiled.

And stepped away. Rake's body jolted with the sudden loss of her heat.

"I'll stop bothering you, then," she said, giving him a goofy little salute. "It was nice to meet you, Dreamy Rake from Down Under."

She moved to pass him, heading toward the door.

And then an odd thing happened.

Rake lost complete control of his body, his arm darting out to grab her waist, pulling her back against him, his mouth pressing to hers in a hungry, searing kiss, before he could form a rational thought.

Rake couldn't make sense of what she did to him, why she disrupted his balance so badly, but he knew he couldn't let her leave.

Chapter 7

LIZZIE responded instantly to him, gripping his jaw between both her hands and deepening the kiss, lifting up onto her tip-toes to mold her body more firmly against his.

Rake pressed even closer, moving them until she was pinned against the wall, one of his hands gripping the swell of her ass, the other braced by her head.

"Why couldn't I stop thinking about you last night?" he said through gritted teeth, his hands searching her body in hungry circles, bunching up her shirt, until he was finally able to press his palm to her warm skin, making her suck in a breath at his touch.

Lizzie didn't answer, she was far beyond talking. Instead, she went to work ripping off his clothes, pulling and tugging at every layer until he was stripped to his boxer briefs.

He grabbed her roughly, hoisting her in his arms, her legs cinching around his waist as she ground against him. He walked them toward the bed, his lips and teeth and tongue dragging across her skin as he went.

He tossed her onto the mattress, pulling off her shirt in hurried handfuls. She fished out the condom she'd stuffed in the pocket of her shorts just before he tore them down her hips, dragging her underwear with them.

His eyes scoured over her with a hunger that scorched across her skin. Her body felt hot and restless, a naughty, delicious tension she wanted to drown in.

"Why do I feel like I can't get enough of you?" Rake said, more to himself than to Lizzie as he lowered over her, something close to frustration underscoring his tone. He tore open the condom, rolling it on with one hand as his other went between her thighs.

"God, you're so wet," he murmured, grazing his fingers over her in luscious circles before plunging them inside, causing Lizzie to cry out at the pleasure.

He pulled his fingers out, bringing them to his mouth and tasting her. His eyes fluttered closed, his lashes sweeping across his cheekbones. Lizzie groaned at the sight, grabbing his hand and taking his fingers into her own mouth, tasting herself and him all at once. It was so overwhelming, her body tensing almost to discomfort at the waiting.

"Now," she said impatiently, tugging at his neck, pulling him closer.

"I should make you wait," he growled, pushing her thighs apart and staring down at her. "Make you beg me." He fisted himself, dragging the head of his shaft through Lizzie's wet heat, making them both groan as she squirmed against him. Lizzie's fingers twisted in the sheets until she worried she would rip the fabric as he dragged himself over her again and again. Circling. Pressing. Almost entering. Never fully giving her what she needed.

"Fuck me," she panted out. "Please. Please."

With a satisfied smile, Rake pulled back, gripping her leg and draping it over his shoulder.

They both watched where he pushed into her, their breath coming in ragged pants.

Rake pulled out slightly before plunging deeper. And deeper still. He held there as their eyes locked for a moment. And then

he started a near-punishing rhythm that sparked electric pleasure through her body.

"How is it this good?" His words were almost inaudible
over the sound of his flesh crashing against hers. Lizzie couldn't
think. Couldn't speak. She closed her eyes, her breath catching
and back arching as he hit a perfect spot inside of her.

When she opened her eyes again, her gaze locked with Rake's
hot and searching stare. A foreign and unnerving crash of intimacy prickled across her skin and snaked through her chest. It
scared the shit out of her.

The sex *was* good.

Too good.

Sex with Rake felt the tiniest bit different from people she'd
been with before, and Lizzie didn't know why. But she didn't
want to think about it.

Sex wasn't for words or thoughts or answers to questions. Sex
was for physical sensations. And that's what she focused on—the
feel of his hands roughly gripping her hips, the circling of his
clever fingers against her clit, the delicious sting of his bite against
her neck, and the feeling of her nails scoring down his back.

"Harder," she demanded, moving to wrap her thighs high
around his waist, tugging him deeper.

He did as she asked, pounding into her in a delicious, re-
lentless rhythm, his deep grunts like music against her ear. He
shifted a bit, pulling her hips higher off the bed, moving her
body as a counterpoint to his. Emphasizing his movements with
soft words like *good* and *wet* and *sweet*.

Her body sprinted toward that explosive finish line, every
muscle pulling taut and tense, aching for release. But she couldn't
quite get there, couldn't quite reach that point, and she whimpered in agony.

Rake's mouth was on her ear, his stubble scratching the delicate skin of her cheek. "Come for me," he growled, his accent
pulsing through her. "Come for me, sweet girl."

And she did. She bit into the muscle at his shoulder and let out a raspy groan as her body deliciously convulsed under him. She lost all sense of time and place as she drowned in the pleasure.

With one final thrust forward, Rake followed her with a deep groan, his body shaking over hers for a few seconds before he collapsed and rolled to the side, their bodies tangled in a sweaty, satiated heap against the pillows.

They both stared up at the ceiling for a few minutes, their breathing a loud mix of pants and gasps as they tried to come back to earth.

*　*　*

RAKE WASN'T SURE how long they lay there in post-sex bliss, but he was acutely aware of the moment Lizzie shifted, some part of him understanding that she meant to leave. And that part turned frantic, wanting her to stay.

Lizzie sat up, shooting him a smile before swinging her legs off the side of the bed. She was about to push up to standing when Rake reached out, circling his hand around her wrist and giving it a gentle tug. "If you keep ditching me like this after sex, my feelings will be hurt."

She pressed her lips together to try to hide a smile as she quirked an eyebrow. "Is that so?"

"Yes, I'm quite sensitive," he said dryly, tugging a bit more until she fell back onto the bed, pressing a giggle to his chest.

"You do seem rather sentimental," Lizzie said, a smile in her voice as she spoke against his skin. "I think you got a bit misty-eyed there after you climaxed."

"I was practically weeping," he said with feigned melodrama. "I'm just really proud of myself for being so good at sex. I'm basically an artist," he added, squeezing her sides and making her body jolt with a piercing shriek.

"For someone so damn awkward before a hookup, you

certainly are good at the follow-through," she said through her gasping laughs.

She was a ball of energy and fire and noise, so different from the calm and controlled way Rake measured his days. Some deep hidden part of him was trying to scramble out of its cage and bask in her energy. He knew he should resist it, but a little indulgence couldn't hurt, right? He was leaving for home, back to his empty apartment and well-managed life. He could be this other person for a few hours in Lizzie's delicious company.

"Have lunch with me," he said, pressing his nose into the soft silk of her hair. "I'm leaving tomorrow and I've barely seen any of Philadelphia. Be a Good Samaritan and show me your filthy city."

Lizzie reared up and scrambled away from him, retreating with a look of horror and outrage that sent genuine fear into Rake's gut. She was silent for a moment, appraising him from the opposite corner of the mattress, like a bizarre naked predator deciding how to kill him.

"What?" he asked, genuinely at a loss for the seething look she gave him.

"What did you say about my city?"

Rake ran through his previous comments. "What? That it's filthy? That can't be news to you. I saw someone throw up on the side of a building and then just walk away the other day."

The corner of Lizzie's mouth twitched in a snarl. Like a hunting lion—her red mane of hair tumbled and wild, her honey-colored eyes blazing—she stalked toward him across the bed on hands and knees until the tip of her nose touched his. Rake swallowed.

"Don't you ever"—she reached up, clasping his cheeks between her palms in a strong grip—"*ever* insult Philadelphia. It's the best city in the world."

Rake let out a disbelieving huff. "My shoes stick to the pavement here. I've seen more random mannequin heads on the sidewalk than in entire department stores, and yesterday a tum-bleweed of condoms and human hair rolled past me. Even the rats are offended," Rake said, words distorted from her grip. "You can't tell me this city isn't dirty."

Lizzie seemed to think about this, staring intimidatingly into his eyes before giving a curt nod. "It's filthy but amazing," she said with definitiveness. "And if you refer to it with anything but utter respect and admiration, I will give you the worst pur-ple nurple of your life."

"What's a purple nurple?"

She reached down and pinched his nipple then twisted a bit, making him yelp in surprise. Having enough of that, he eas-ily set her off-balance and flipped her to her back, pinning her hands to the mattress.

"If Philadelphia is so great," he said, pausing to place a sharp bite on the top of her breast that made her suck in a breath, "then prove it to me. Show me around."

She studied him, a surly insolence across her sweet face that made him want to laugh, before she finally nodded. "Fine," she said. "But we should probably have sex one more time before we go."

Rake couldn't argue with that.

Chapter 8

AS Lizzie dragged Rake block after block around Philadelphia, it was hard to say who was the tourist. She took him to the Schuylkill River and the Liberty Bell. Walked him past the sky rises of Center City and the historical colonials of Old City. Guided him through Chinatown and the overcrowded Reading Terminal Market. And she talked all the while, asking him about his favorite foods, his favorite season, his favorite things about Australia. He didn't offer much detail in his responses, but always returned the questions, seeming genuinely interested in the off-track direction she ended up taking her answers, going from talking about a local brewery she liked to the belief that, if she were a sea creature, she was fairly certain she'd be a Dumbo octopus.

At the Rodin sculpture garden, she forced Rake to mimic the pose of *The Thinker* as she set up her camera timer, sprinting over to join him next to the statue. She snorted at the picture as Rake looked at it over her shoulder.

"You're very stoic," she said, turning to look up at him. Despite his initial reluctance, he'd played along and held the pose perfectly.

"You're very . . . not," he said, using his thumb and forefinger to zoom in on her. She was a red blur, a laugh and huge grin evident on her fuzzy features as she'd darted over to stand beside him.

Lizzie laughed. She had more pictures of herself like that than not. It had always driven her mother up the wall, Lizzie's brother, Ryan, a perfect little model in all family photos while Lizzie had blurred in and out of the frame like a wild spirit. *Why can't you hold still?* her mother would bark out at the less-than-perfect results. *Why can't you control yourself for just a minute?*

Lizzie had never found an answer for that.

"Will you send that to me?" Rake said after a moment, drawing Lizzie out of the painful memory that tickled across her skin.

"For the spank bank?" Lizzie asked, biting her bottom lip to suppress a laugh.

"Yeah," Rake said, not missing a beat. "Nothing spurs on my masturbation quite like blurry pictures of vibrant redheads."

She snorted and sent him the picture, secretly enjoying that he wanted it, a little reminder of the day.

"Wanna get some ice cream?" Lizzie asked after they'd left the gardens and headed toward the historic Rittenhouse neighborhood. Rake nodded, and she led him to a nearby spot.

The shop was small and crowded, and despite the copious minutes Lizzie had in line to decide on a flavor, indecisiveness gripped her so tightly by the time she stepped up to the counter, it felt like a physical punch to the gut, the buzz of bodies around her adding to the indecision.

Rake ordered immediately, getting a single scoop of vanilla ice cream on a sugar cone. Lizzie envied the calm confidence with which he ordered. She knew she'd never order something in such a seamless process. Sometimes, deciding on what to eat felt like the biggest decision of her life, the endless options overwhelming her, swarming her brain in a dysfunctional tangle of choices, until she knew she'd make the wrong decision regardless and just blurted out the next thing her eyes landed on.

"Can I try the . . ." Lizzie's eyes scanned over the colorful flavor tubs at warp speed. "A sample of the lemon," she said to the waiting server. "Wait, no, the birthday cake," she said, right before they dipped the tiny plastic spoon into the lemon. "Sorry, actually pistachio. No, the sorbet."

The server jerked up to standing, staring at Lizzie for a long moment. "You can try more than one," they said at last, and the annoyance in their voice made embarrassment trickle across her nape.

"I'm sorry. I'm so sorry. I'd like a sample of the brownie batter and the mint chocolate chip, please."

But, as the server reached toward the tub, indecision spiked again. "Wait. Sorry, I'll try . . ." Someone in line behind Lizzie groaned, and the server closed their eyes for a moment.

"You okay?" Rake said in her ear, the kindness in his voice making her jump out of her skin. She was mortified by her inability to do something as simple as order a flavor of ice cream.

"I'll have a scoop of the peanut butter chocolate and . . . uh . . . the mango. In a waffle cone," Lizzie said, naming the first two flavors she read. The server stared at her for a solid ten seconds, waiting for Lizzie to change her mind on that objectively gross combination. Lizzie didn't even like mangoes. But when Lizzie didn't say anything, they bent to scoop it.

"With sprinkles," Lizzie added weakly, reasoning that a little festive decoration would help the palatability of her choice.

After paying for the treats and excessively apologizing for the fiasco, Lizzie and Rake left the shop. At the corner, Lizzie stopped next to a trash can and pushed off the scoop of mango sitting on top of her cone with her finger.

"There," she said, licking her finger clean and pasting on a goofy grin. She couldn't look at Rake. She knew what would be written all over his face—incredulous scrutiny at what an obvious lunatic she was. She received that look every time she went out with her family growing up.

But she also didn't need to prove anything to this (hot) almost stranger, she reminded herself. Steeling her nerve, she shot him a quick glance. What she saw made her do a double take. He wasn't looking at her with harsh judgment or appalled concern like she'd come to expect. His eyes traced over her softly like he found her . . . intriguing. Like he wanted to learn more.

Warmth flooded through her body.

They continued walking through the historical streets. Rake didn't say much, but that was okay—Lizzie kept up a consistent enough commentary for the both of them.

Neon signs are so fucking cool. Have you ever watched a video on how they're made? No? You should.

I love the color of that door!

Oh la la floofer-fluffer puppy! So squishy.

Wow, how nice would it be to have that rooftop garden? I'd blow someone for a view like that.

I bet that place has good food. It smells heavenly.

I really like the flowers in that coffee shop window. I think pansies are such an underrated flower.

On and on, the city a kaleidoscope of wonders as they walked.

"Look. At. This," Lizzie said, halting in her tracks, Rake bumping into her. They'd made their way back to City Hall, the epicenter of Philadelphia's energy. The building jutted into the sky, its marble and granite facade sparkling in the sun, while the statue of William Penn rose at its peak, looking down at the splendor of the city.

Delicious details were carved into every inch of the structure, intricate swoops lining each window and ledge as delicately as white frosting on a gingerbread house.

Lizzie stared up at it, her eyes devouring every detail and nuance while her forgotten ice cream dripped down her hands.

"Have you never been here before?" Rake asked, pulling her out of her reverie.

Her eyebrows furrowed. "Of course I've been here. I come here all the time. I actually work, like, three blocks away. Why?"

Rake blinked a few times, looking between her and the building before answering. "You just . . . You look at everything like it's . . . new." His eyes roamed across her face, like there was some hidden answer just below her skin that he was trying to decipher.

Lizzie grinned. "There's *always* something new to find," she said, turning back to the building. It was what Lizzie loved about her city. No matter how many times she revisited a spot, there was something new to spark joy in her brain. Something beautiful and delicious to devour.

She walked closer, Rake following. She moved to a shaded area under one of the building's awnings, pressing her back into the cool stone as she licked her ice cream cone.

"God, I'm sweating my tits off," Lizzie said after a minute, plucking at her sticky T-shirt. While she loved her city, its humid summers did not love her back. She wasn't made for the heat. Her thighs chafed almost raw within the first week of the season, her pits sweat until at least September, and she lost a layer of skin every time she got up from the sticky plastic subway seats. Lizzie was made for fall, and she spent nine months out of the year wishing for it.

Rake paused with his cone halfway to his mouth, a drop of vanilla ice cream trailing across his knuckles as he looked at her. Like she had two heads.

"What do you do for a living?" he asked at last.

"I'm a baker. Why?"

"Because if that doesn't work out, you should consider writing children's books. You have quite the colorful vernacular, Birdy," Rake said, making her laugh.

"Why do you call me that?" she asked, taking a long lick of her quickly melting treat.

"Call you what?"

"*Birdy*," she drawled, mimicking his accent.

A flash of uncertainty crossed his features like the question caught him off guard, but it was replaced with his cool mask of cocky handsomeness. "It was your hair," he said, ducking down to catch a melted droplet of vanilla.

"My hair?"

"It looked like a bird's nest the first time I saw you."

Lizzie rolled her eyes and flipped him off, making him laugh.

"I'm just kidding," he said, and Lizzie looked at him expectantly. "It's because your voice sounds like a squawking bird."

Lizzie's jaw dropped in indignation as Rake tried to hide his teasing smile behind another lick of his ice cream cone. Without thinking, Lizzie reached out, pushing the cone into his face, smearing ice cream from his nose down to his chin.

He blinked at her for a few beats as her face broke into an evil grin. "Oh, you'll pay for that one," he said, dropping his cone and lunging for her.

Lizzie tried to sidestep him, but he caught her easily, cinching his arms around her waist and making her squeal. He pushed his sticky face against her cheek and down her throat while tickling her sides, causing her to squirm and make the mess even worse.

"You're such an ass," she screeched between her giggles as he nuzzled deeper into her neck. She tried to push free, her arms weak from her laughter, but he pivoted them, pinning her back against the stone of the building.

He dragged his mouth up from her neck to her chin, the movement straying from playful to intimate. The pleasure centers in Lizzie's brain lit up like fireworks, causing her to drop her own ice cream and plunge her hungry fingers into his hair, tilt his head so she could seek out his mouth, and press into a deep kiss. Rake returned it, tasting her as if she were the sweetest thing he'd had all day.

"You made quite the mess," he said, pulling away just long enough to nibble at her bottom lip.

"I like to stay on brand," she replied, letting one of her hands lazily travel down his body, fingers scraping against his abdomen before lightly resting at his belt buckle. Rake groaned into her mouth and deepened the kiss.

"Take me back to your room," she said after a few more kisses as her body buzzed with the want for contact and pressure and more.

Without a word, Rake laced his fingers with hers and led them back toward his hotel with quick steps. It wasn't long until they broke into a run, laughing as they weaved and bobbed through the crowded streets of Philadelphia. Lizzie felt like a teenager, like this young, wild thing that was in desperate search of the next rush of pleasure. In the hotel elevator, they laughed and kissed, Rake pressing her against the shiny golden wall, rubbing against her as she wrapped her legs around his waist.

They stumbled through the hallway, Rake bracing her against the door as he fumbled for the keycard, Lizzie's hands making desperate circuits across his body—back, arms, neck, hair—any part she could reach, until he finally got the door open and they collapsed inside.

Clothes were ripped off in a blur, and they fell to the bed in a tangle of limbs and lust, soft groans of pleasure.

In the aftermath, they looked at each other, sharing goofy, sheepish grins, before deciding, in some unspoken understanding, to close their eyes.

Lizzie woke some time later, the last rays of early summer casting a glow around the hotel room, bathing Rake in beautiful golden light as he slept with one of his muscled arms draped carelessly over her. Her heart beat with a spastic rhythm as a pesky feeling tried to creep into its chambers.

Her instincts told her to run, told her to get out before a feeling could gain purchase. But she was so comfortable and weighted down. Her mind wasn't far away in a different world, and she wasn't meandering off in the twists and turns of some distracted thought.

This has an end date, she reasoned. *It's okay to enjoy it for now. Nothing more can happen after tonight.*

She told herself it didn't matter that this would be the first time she'd ever *literally* slept with a guy, spent the night with someone she kind of . . . liked. It didn't mean anything that she cautiously cuddled closer to him, that she pressed her nose into the spot where his shoulder met his neck and breathed in like she could snort his sea salt and citrus scent straight into her veins. She told herself it was inconsequential that he made her come but also made her laugh. That he talked to her instead of just fucking her.

She told herself the little pangs in her chest had nothing to do with saying goodbye tomorrow to this gorgeous stranger she didn't have any feelings for. No feelings at all.

She lied to herself and let her mind drift back to sleep to the sound of Rake's breathing, deciding to enjoy the fling and not worry about it ever being something more.

Chapter 9

RAKE woke with a start as his alarm blared. He fumbled until he could turn off the screeching, letting out a low groan as he scrubbed his hands over his face before stretching his arms over his head and dropping them down to the mattress with dead weight.

Expecting them to land with a soft thump against the sheets, he nearly jumped out of his skin when the palm of one hand landed firmly on another person's flesh with a smack.

Heart thumping up to his throat, he turned his head slowly to see his large palm resting on a plump, freckled butt cheek. Moving his gaze farther up, he locked eyes with Lizzie's similarly wide-eyed stare.

"Well, good morning to you too," she said after a moment. "I've always said there's no better way to start the day than with a good ole-fashion spanking."

Rake quickly whipped his hand off her butt, and Lizzie giggled, pressing her face into the sheets. Something about the noise produced a warm feeling in his chest, but he rubbed it away, blaming the foreign sensation on his sleep-addled brain.

"I'm sorry," Rake said gruffly, sitting up and pulling the sheets around his waist. "Are you—" but the rest of the words lodged in his throat as Lizzie turned onto her back, stretching her fingers and toes as far as they would reach as she yawned. Naked. She did all of this completely naked and almost made Rake's head explode.

"No biggie," Lizzie said casually, throwing her long hair into a ponytail as she sat up. Acting as if it was completely normal for them to wake up together in the same bed totally naked and thoroughly tumbled. Maybe Rake was the only one who felt the hum of intimacy about the moment.

He was overreacting, he reasoned, as he turned away from her and snatched up a pair of boxers. He hadn't shared a bed with another person since Shannon, and he wasn't used to the odd feelings that swirled in the air the morning after sex. He needed to get a grip and get back to his normal, isolated life.

"What time is it?" Lizzie asked, surveying the room from her spot on the bed.

"Five thirty," Rake answered, scooping up her clothes from their various locations around the hotel room and gingerly laying them on the bed. "Sorry to have to wake you. I—uh—I mean I guess you could probably keep sleeping, right? I can just . . ."

Lizzie let out a loud laugh, and Rake's eyes snapped up to her face, taking in her massive grin.

"What's so funny?" he asked.

"Nothing," Lizzie said, trying to hide another giggle behind her hand. Rake stared at her. "You're just really cute the morning after," she said. "All awkward and shit. It's endearing."

Rake felt himself blush. *Oh for fuck's sake.*

"I'm not—I wasn't—"

"You better take a breath before you kill yourself there, sport," Lizzie said with a wink, hooking her bra and slipping her arms through the straps. "I hate seeing you so flustered."

Something about her shit-eating grin made it obvious that she hated nothing about his discomfort. But he couldn't help but smile back.

"I haven't done . . ." He waved his hand vaguely.

"The awkward morning after?" she cut him off, smiling. "Me neither. But I won't make you eat awkward morning sex pancakes. I'll spare you the misery."

"Sex pancakes?" Rake asked, his brow furrowing.

Lizzie waved the question off. "Never mind. Have you seen my purse?" she asked, sliding out of bed and hopping up and down as she pulled her tight shorts over her hips. Rake was momentarily distracted by the movement before he shook himself and started looking for her giant bag. He found it spilled by the door, a ridiculous amount of odds and ends littering the floor around it.

"Ah, there she is," Lizzie said, bending down to sweep everything into the gaping mouth of the purse with practiced efficiency. She stood, slinging the bag over her shoulder and turning to face him. They stared at each other, looking for the right way to say goodbye.

An odd sensation speared from the bottom of Rake's stomach up to the top of his throat. He couldn't name it, but something about it made him want to grip Lizzie to his chest and not let her go. Which was absolutely ridiculous. So instead, he stuck out his hand. "I really enjoyed meeting you," he said.

Lizzie looked at his proffered hand for a long moment before her eyes flicked up to his, her face creasing into a giant laugh. In a flash of movement, she wrapped her arms around his waist, pressing her face to his chest while she giggled, the vibrations of it amplifying that odd sensation puncturing his body.

"You're so *awkward*," she said through her laughter. "But I really enjoyed meeting you too."

Rake couldn't stop the smile that spread across his face as he squeezed her back, holding on for a second longer. But he absolutely needed to let her go before any more of these strange sensations took over him and he did anything else out of character.

"So, I guess this is goodbye, Gorgeous Rake from Australia," she said wistfully, tapping her foot. She seemed as reluctant to step out that door as Rake was to watch her do it.

"It's goodbye, Lovely Lizzie from Dirty Philadelphia."

Lizzie rolled her eyes but smiled at him, the look softening as her gaze caressed his face.

"God, this is super weird," she said with a half-hearted laugh, "because I actually kind of like you."

"This *is* super weird." Rake nodded in agreement. "Particularly because *you're* super weird."

Lizzie punched his shoulder with a laugh, and Rake surprised himself by grabbing her arm and pulling her in for one last hug, pressing his smile to the top of her head.

"Okay, okay, okay, longest goodbye ever," Lizzie said, pulling away and opening the door and stepping out. She paused. "But, uh . . ." Her leg started bouncing again as she looked at him. "Don't be afraid to, um, look me up if you're ever back in Philly. I mean, you totally don't have to. No pressure or whatever. I just meant—"

"Now who's being awkward," Rake said, rocking on his heels and giving her a huge smile. "Of course I'd look you up. It'd be the first thing I do."

With a poorly controlled grin and a few quick nods, Lizzie turned, heading down the hall. Rake watched her leave, letting out a soft laugh every time she peeped over her shoulder, sending him about six more waves before she finally turned the corner to the elevator banks.

A foreign impulse in Rake almost jolted his body forward to go after her. It was such a bizarre, over-the-top reaction, he firmly shut the door and bumped his forehead against it a few times.

He was being absolutely ridiculous. She was all but a stranger. A fun, out-of-character memory that would get him through another few years of celibacy.

It was nothing, it was nothing, it was nothing, he repeated over and over again as he jumped in a cold shower, not letting his thoughts touch the memory of her body. *Nothing at all*, he reasoned as he collected any stray items around the hotel room and tucked them neatly into his suitcase.

Absolutely nothing, he yelled in his head as the company shuttle took the team to the airport, as he pulled out his phone and opened his texts, losing control of his fingers as he typed and hit send.

> Thanks for a great time. Let me know if you ever
> find yourself in Sydney

Of course, that didn't mean anything either.

Chapter 10

TWO weeks later, Lizzie was startled awake, not by the screech of her alarm—that she'd already snoozed about eight times—but to the foreign trill of a phone call coming through. *Who the fuck* called *people anymore?* she thought as she wrestled out of her blankets to find her blaring phone. *Psychopaths, that's who.*

And her older brother, apparently.

The words GOLDEN CHILD flashed across her screen above an ugly picture of Ryan. Lizzie really, *really* didn't want to answer, but she also knew his ungodly level of persistence for their tense and obligatory once-a-month phone calls. With a sigh, she slid her thumb across the screen to answer.

"Lizzie's Sperm Bank, you spank it, we bank it. How may I help you?" she said by way of greeting.

There was a long silence on the other end before Ryan let out the world's heaviest breath. "Good morning to you too, Elizabeth."

The corners of Lizzie's mouth kicked up as she traced a pattern on her comforter. She and Ryan didn't have a . . . stellar relationship, but she got a shot of joy through her system by tormenting him, and she harbored the secret familial fantasy that he enjoyed her teasing too.

"What's up, Ry?" she asked. "How's Mary?"

This was all part of their monthly phone call script. Lizzie and Ryan spent their three-to-five-minute call volleying questions back and forth about everything but each other. It was a good way to say words without actually talking.

Mary was Ryan's wife—petite, gorgeous, put together, and sporting a ridiculously good personality.

"Mary's good," Ryan said then cleared his throat. A long pause followed. "She's actually part of the reason I'm calling."

Lizzie's head jolted back and hit the wall behind her. Ryan wasn't supposed to have a *reason* to call her. Their talks were supposed to be about checking off a little task box to assuage both of their guilts for not actually being great siblings to each other. These talks weren't supposed to have substance, let alone an actual purpose.

"Uh-oh," Lizzie said, sliding down the wall to land on her pillows. "Did she finally perish from your incessant discussions of golf?"

"Do you have to make everything a joke?"

"Yes. It's called deflection and poor coping skills."

Ryan sighed. "I'm calling because Mary wants to hire you to bake something. A cake."

Lizzie perked up at that. "Really? That'd be awesome. What for?"

"Mary thought it would be a good chance for you to build your . . . portfolio or whatever. Do bakers even have portfolios?"

Bakers did, but Lizzie did not. She had some random pictures scattered through her phone that she'd always meant to organize and never got around to. "No, I mean, for what occasion."

"Oh, uh . . ." Ryan hesitated, taking a few loud swallows Lizzie could hear through the phone. Gross. "Well, as you know, Mom and Dad's anniversary is—"

"No," Lizzie cut him off. "Absolutely not."

Ryan let out an exasperated groan. "Don't be so dramatic,

Lizzie. Mary is planning their thirtieth-anniversary party for the end of summer. You'll be there anyway, why not bake the cake?"

"Who says I'll be there? I'd rather burn the hair off my head than go to that."

"You have to."

"Oh yeah? Says who?" Lizzie's voice was rising.

"It's just . . . I don't know. It's what you're supposed to do. You're supposed to go to stuff like that."

"Yeah, well, I've never been great at doing what I'm supposed to do, have I?" Lizzie said, hopping out of bed and pacing her room like a captive cheetah. She hated being told what to do, especially when it came to family bullshit. She'd been so caged in by the dos and don'ts of unspoken family rules that the thought of being back behind those bars made her blood pound through her body like it wanted to burst through the veins.

"I know you have issues with Mom and Dad"—Lizzie snorted at this massive understatement—"so think of it as helping Mary out. She's always loved your baking."

Ryan had gone for Lizzie's Achilles' heel. Nothing motivated Lizzie more than being needed.

"Mary shouldn't even *want* me doing this," Lizzie said, her shoulders deflating, the fire snuffing out of her as quickly as it started. "We both know something will go wrong, and Mom will lose her shit and then that will look bad on Mary. She should save herself."

Ryan was quiet for a moment. "I told her that."

The truth shouldn't have stung, but it did. Lizzie hadn't ever done anything to earn Ryan's faith in her—leaning fully into the wild child role she'd always been cast in—but the confirmation of Lizzie's shortcomings still felt like a slap.

"She said she knows you *won't* mess it up," Ryan continued, unaware of the tiny little knife he'd twisted between her third and fourth ribs. "She begged me to convince you to do it. So here I am, asking for this favor."

Hearing that split Lizzie in two. Part of her rejected Ryan's words immediately, yelling at her that he was lying, that no one had faith in her like that. But the other part of her practically purred at the praise. The idea that Mary found Lizzie's talent for baking useful was a type of validation she was starving for.

"Ry, I highly doubt Mom even wants me there," Lizzie said weakly.

"Of course she wants you there."

"Noooooo," Lizzie said in a goofy voice, trying to mask her hurt with humor. "She wants *you* there. You and perfect Mary. She does *not* want me there. I'm sure she's afraid I'll burn the place down. Again."

"Come on, Elizabeth. Literally no one could believe you would burn a place down twice. And you were ten when it happened anyway."

Lizzie's lips quirked at the memory.

While the only casualties from her attempted bonfire on the restaurant's back patio had been a few table umbrellas and a wooden bench, neither of her parents looked back on the incident with anything close to humor.

Lizzie thought it was funny as hell.

"Please just do it," Ryan said, his patience running thin.

Lizzie chewed on the inside of her cheek, her thoughts swirling around her head, down her neck, and across her chest, tickling her heart. Maybe she could do this. Maybe she could actually pull this off with no screwups and start to defy every low expectation her family held of her.

"Okay," she finally said, her voice a tiny squeak. "I'll do it. Have Mary text me about her ideas for it and stuff."

Ryan blew out a breath. "Thanks, Elizabeth. Got to run. We'll talk soon."

And with that, he hung up.

Lizzie stared at the phone in her hand, her heart and stomach tumbling around her insides, each landing in the wrong place.

Ingrained inadequacy pulsed beneath her skin, every instinct telling her that she was going to screw this up and sink even lower in her status as family clown.

She sucked in deep breaths, trying to knock down the rock that seemed to have lodged itself in her throat, repeating the words her therapist had taught her when she was twenty-two: *Your brain was built different and that's beautiful, never a burden.*

Lizzie collapsed back onto her bed, exhaustion overwhelming her before her day had even really begun.

She'd been sleepy all week, but a sudden touch of queasiness made her squeeze her eyes shut.

She lay there for a few minutes, halfway asleep when some underused entity of executive function decided to do its job and suddenly jolt her internal alarm.

Her eyes snapped open as she grabbed her phone and looked at the time.

S.H.I.T.

Lizzie was running late. Like, *really fucking late.*

She tumbled off the side of her bed, speed-crawling across her floor as she searched for her work shirt and a clean pair of underwear. Ripping on the former and not able to find the latter, she slipped out of her pajama bottoms and hoisted her thighs into the closest pair of jeans.

Lizzie sprinted out of her room, her sock-clad feet nearly slipping out from beneath her as she dived for her shoes and hopped into them, grabbing her purse and continuing her breakneck speed out of the apartment.

Stupid stupid stupid, she cursed as she sprinted down the block.

George, her boss, was about to ream her a new clock-shaped asshole for being late again. And, to top it off, she still needed to put finishing touches on a blueberry-kale cake monstrosity that was being picked up in twenty minutes. If George's recipe wasn't gross enough, the customer wanted #BLESSED written on top. The thought of having to subject her beautiful buttercream to such depravity made Lizzie's hands recoil.

Lizzie skidded to a stop in front of her work, Baking Me Crazy, and yanked open the door, her ridiculously sweaty body instantly chilled by the over-cranked air conditioner and the heinously contrived minimalistic vibe of the bakery.

She dashed to the back, pushing through the swinging door and into the kitchen toward the lockers. She wondered if she herself was #blessed and could have her ridiculous lateness go unnoticed when George stepped in front of her path and she almost slammed into his plaid-decked body. While they didn't exactly belly-slap, she did cause him to lose his balance, and he dropped his mason jar of cold brew, droplets smattering both of their legs.

Lizzie and George stared down at the mess before their gazes slowly lifted and merged, George looking furious, Lizzie looking guilty.

"Do you have any idea what time it is?" George asked, ripping an AirPod from his ear.

"I know I'm late and I'm sorry. I'm so so so so so sorry. Very sorry. I swear it won't happen again. Deadass."

"You literally said that exact same thing last week," George grumbled, scratching at his patchy chin-strap beard. Lizzie stared at the bald spots that ebbed and flowed around the random tufts of hair. She was constantly distracted by the damn thing, wondering why he didn't just shave it off since he scratched at it so much.

George waved a hand in front of her face, breaking her train of thoughts. "Are you even listening to me?"

Her eyes snapped up to his as she realized he'd kept talking. *No.* "Yes."

"Really?" George said, raising an eyebrow. "What did I say?"

The question caught Lizzie off guard, and she sucked in a

giant breath, trying to think on her feet. (Un)fortunately, she also sucked down a bunch of spittle, causing her to double over as she coughed and choked on air.

"Sorry, George,"—*cough*—"I don't"—*hack, cough, grunt*—"hold on—"

By the time she regained her breath and stood up, eyes watering, George looked more weary and resigned than furious, and Lizzie jumped on that. "Sorry, don't know where that came from. What were you saying?"

George pinched the bridge of his nose, sighing. He looked at her. "You're an excellent baker, Lizzie. Truly. And I'd be willing to let you incorporate your own recipes here more and take on bigger projects if you could only figure out how to get your head out of your ass and your feet in the door on time."

Lizzie swallowed against the pinpricks of shame that needled at her throat. "I'm sorry," she said in a small voice, meaning it.

She hated the all-too-familiar look of exasperation that George was giving her. It was so damn frustrating that her mind was a constant tangled scribble that she could never seem to unravel.

"Am I fired?"

George stared at her for a hard moment before his features softened and he scratched again at his patchy beard. "This is your last warning. I mean it. Late again like this and you're done. I'll be watching you closely. Every shift, every break, you better get here on time."

"Oh fuck, thank you, George. I won't let you down," she said, bouncing on her toes as though the relief of still having a job could lift her from the ground.

George dismissed her with a weak flap of his wrist. "Don't leave this either," he said, waving at the shards of glass and spilled cold brew. "Grab a mop or something," he said, walking into his office.

Lizzie wiped up the mess quickly, then got to work on the

day's orders, losing herself in the calming rhythm of measurements and precision. While other tasks seemed to cost Lizzie's brain twice the fuel to go half the distance, baking was the one thing she could do on autopilot. It was like every delicate swoop of frosting, each powerful knead of dough, every carefully crafted confection, allowed her nervous system to sigh in relief. The constant flood and buzz of energy zipping randomly from neuron to neuron could finally be allowed to still, to focus. It made her feel whole.

She worked on a large order for a gallery, making simple and sturdy sugar cookies, but decorating each with an intricately piped frame, and hand-painting landscapes on the smooth, frosted surface.

While she lost herself in her art—gently piping and painting, absorbing the scent of sweetness and work—she decided she could do this. Be more responsible.

Turn a new leaf.

The problem was, Lizzie had turned so many new leaves, she could be a decaying forest floor for how many of them had failed.

But this time would be different. She would wrestle her brain into submission. She would force it to accurately keep track of time and to-do lists. She'd remember to take her meds and stay on top of chores. She'd yank on its leash every time it started to wander.

She didn't exactly have a *plan* for how she was magically going to do this when it was, you know, something that she and her therapist had been trying to develop coping skills for almost a decade. But she'd figure it out.

And she wouldn't fuck this up.

Chapter 11

THE day was barely halfway over, and Lizzie was fucking this up.

She'd had a good brain morning. She'd powered through a to-do list, which she'd written out with *details* and *color coordination*, thank you very much, and was pretty confident that operation New Brain Leaf would be a smashing success.

And then she'd gone to lunch.

She'd wandered a few blocks from the shop toward her favorite food truck in Rittenhouse Square and, gyro in hand, headed for a bench in the park. She'd gone into hyper-focus while eating, her brain completely absorbed by a Beverly Jenkins audiobook. It wasn't until a giant flock of pigeons took off in flight right in front of her, scaring the shit out of her and snapping her out of her brain trap that she realized she only had five minutes before her break was over.

Shitgoddamnitfuck

Lizzie jumped to her feet, a wave of queasiness almost knocking her back down to the bench, but she pushed it away. She fisted her trash and took off in a dead sprint, for the second time that day, toward work.

She could not be late.

She could not be this dumb.

Lizzie weaved and ducked around masses of people, only giving the quickest of glances before darting across intersections.

She was three blocks from Baking Me Crazy, with only two minutes to get through the doors, when she hit a massive traffic block.

A garbage truck was broken down in the middle of an intersection, bags of trash spilling out and open onto the street, blocking both cars and pedestrians from getting across. Lizzie came to a screeching halt right before crashing into a mass of sweaty people.

And then everything seemed to happen at once.

A wall of sharp, rotting scent slammed into her nostrils, singeing her nose hairs with its intensity, while nausea caused her stomach to plummet down to her kneecaps. The heat of the day and the crush of bodies around her heightened these terrible sensations, pushing and pressing on her skin. Her belly. Her throat.

And then she puked.

It wasn't a cute, *oops-mini-throw-up-haha-shake-it-off* type of puke. It was a massive, chunky, body-wracking hurl of waste. Just in time, she opened her plastic lunch bag, emptying the entirety of her internal organs into it. It seemed to go on forever.

People gasped.

She was pretty sure children started crying.

Hell, *Lizzie* was crying, as her body seemed to try to turn itself inside out. After multiple prayers for the devil to take her if he could just make it stop, she eventually regained control of her body. She lifted her head, sweat dripping down her temples and her back, a cold chill racing through her bones despite the heat of the day.

The smash of people had given her a wide berth, and she tied up the bag as tightly as she could, dry-heaving a bit at the slosh of its contents when she took it to the corner trash can and dropped it in.

She looked down at her phone and felt more tears slam against the back of her eyeballs.

She was officially late.

Dragging her body in a defeated trot the final distance to Baking Me Crazy, she prepared for George's worst.

And when she pushed through the swinging doors to the kitchen, he looked ready to give it to her.

They stared at each other for a moment, and Lizzie watched as the vein on George's forehead swelled with each passing second until it looked like it would burst through his skin.

She swallowed. "George, I'm so sorry. I can explain. I—"

George held up both hands, silently begging her to spare him. He then pressed his fingers to his temples like he wanted to push through to his brain and swirl it around, his nostrils flaring, and fake wire-rimmed glass fogging as his face turned six shades of purple.

After what felt like a lifetime, he spoke. "We literally had this talk five hours ago. *Five.* You can't even keep your act together for a single day?"

"I—"

"I don't want any more excuses!" he yelled, cutting her off. "How are you this irresponsible? How are you this—this—"

Lizzie knew what word was coming next, and her shoulders coiled around her neck as she braced for the slap of it.

"—*lazy?*"

Whoop, there it was.

If Lizzie had a dollar for every time she'd been accused of being lazy, she wouldn't need a job she'd show up late for.

She wasn't lazy. She *wasn't.*

Lizzie wanted to do well. She wanted to impress the people in her life so damn badly, her bones ached with it. But she couldn't get her brain to cooperate. Her brain felt like this separate entity tossed haphazardly into her skull, like a toddler she would never have much discipline over.

It twirled and raced and jumped rope up there, never ceasing in its activity, but also never doing what she needed it to do. And then she was constantly running around trying to pick up the pieces of the messes it made, collecting phrases like *you're just lazy* and *try harder* and *grow up* that created a poem of failure branded across her skin.

"You're fired," George said, emphasizing the world's most obvious point. "Empty out your locker and go home."

He turned on his artfully distressed ankle boot heel and left Lizzie standing there like a hollowed shell of a person.

Chapter 12

LIZZIE went home, stopping in her kitchen to make a batch of pity-party hot fudge sauce before carrying it to her room, throwing on her pj's, and curling herself into a cocoon of blankets on her bed.

While being fired wasn't a new experience for her, shame and frustration held her down like a leaden weight. She only left her bed to puke a few more times, her hot fudge long neglected when the usually comforting smell of the rich chocolate turned her stomach.

She heard Indira come in but couldn't find the energy to get up and greet her. She was so damn exhausted and felt poised between the sharp pang of uncontrollable sobs and projectile vomiting, so she stayed put, hoping Indira would come check on her.

A few minutes later, Indira knocked on the door and pushed it open.

"Hey, sweets," Indira said, leaning her shoulder on the doorjamb.

Lizzie lifted her head an inch and gave a weak wave before collapsing back down into her mattress.

"You okay?" Indira asked, shuffling forward across Lizzie's messy floor.

"I feel like shit," Lizzie admitted, as Indira ran a cool hand over her forehead.

"Oh gross, you're so sweaty," Indira said, wiping her hand on her pants.

"Throwing up all afternoon has given me that dewy look."

Indira took a giant step back. "Ew. You think you'll be better in time for the Family Reunion on Saturday?"

"I'll strap on a vomit bag if I need to. I wouldn't miss it." The Family Reunion was what Lizzie, Indira, Thu, and Harper had started calling their infrequent but always wonderful meetups.

"Atta babe," Indira said, taking a few more steps back for safety. "Anyway, I'm running to the store to get tampons. I just ran out. Do you need any?"

"You started your period?" Lizzie asked, her brows knitting together. Her and Indira's bodies were so hormonally in sync that Aunt Flow usually visited them both within a few hours.

"Uh, yeah," Indira said with a snort. "I'm on day four of asking my body what I did to offend it. You haven't?"

"No," Lizzie said slowly, a trickle of uneasiness moving down her spine. This was . . . odd. To say the least. Her body always worked with an easy consistency month after month, never spurring her to get on birth control to get it regular, her few experiments with it as a teenager leaving her feeling awful, nauseous, and weepy . . . when she'd remembered to actually take it, that is.

"Lizzie?"

Lizzie's gaze snapped to Indira's. "Sorry, what?"

"Do you need anything while I'm out?"

"No," Lizzie said, balling her hands into fists as a fresh wave of nausea crested through her. A different kind of nausea. A cold, dread-filled kind that had her fingers itching to get ahold of a calendar.

"All right," Indira said, eyeing Lizzie closely. "Text me if you think of anything."

Lizzie tried to nod, but her body had gone numb. As soon as she heard the door click shut, she bolted from her bed, scrambling around her room in a directionless tornado as countless, dizzying thoughts scratched and clambered to get out. She lunged for her phone, fingers shaking as she opened the calendar app, then switched over to her texts, thumbing through until she found his name, found the exact date of their nefarious weekend together. She flipped back to the calendar. Counting back days. Looking at weeks.

Two.

Two weeks.

The last time she'd had sex was two weeks and five days ago.

Her brain scrambled to draw up a mental ovulation chart, to remember anything and everything from sex ed. It was all blank. Her brain turned smooth and empty in her sheer panic.

She turned to Google. Her palms sweaty, her vision blurry, as the results she didn't want to see came up in image after image of a monthly cycle.

She couldn't be pregnant.

She couldn't be this stupid.

She bolted for the door, not even bothering to change out of her pajamas as she rushed out of the apartment, racing down the stairs and pushing into the cool May night. She looked left and then right, feeling both frozen and like her body would soon explode if she didn't move. Indira had likely gone to their usual pharmacy a block away, and Lizzie wanted to avoid her at all costs when she was in a panic like this. She went left, her rapid steps quickly converting into a run as she moved a few blocks to a nearby bodega. She burst into it, small chimes on the door sounding like sirens in her ears. She moved through the store, spinning around and around as she searched frantically for what she needed.

"Can I help you?" the burly owner of the shop asked, his

thick brows and mustache almost obscuring his face completely in a way that made Lizzie want to burst into unhinged
laughter.

"Do you have—" The words caught in her throat. She tried
to swallow past it, her foot stomping down repeatedly as she
willed the words out. She started to choke and splutter, as if
asking for it would literally kill her. The man's bushy eyebrows
rose, exposing a glint of dark, alarmed eyes. Something about
his concerned expression released her, allowed every tense muscle in her body to relax, and threatened to lay her out in the
middle of the store.

"Do you have any pregnancy tests?" she asked on a whisper.

His eyebrows dropped, but a soft, comforting smile kept her
grounded as he nodded and led her down the aisle.

There were a few options to choose from. The man left
her to contemplate, and she stared blankly at the boxes. Pinks
and blues and purples seemed to flood her vision, the word
pregnancy pulsating on every piece of cardboard. She reached
up, then dropped her hand to her side, repeating the movement
half a dozen times before finally squaring her shoulders and
grabbing one of each option.

With tears pricking at her eyes, she approached the register.

"Bathroom?" she asked weakly as she watched her receipt
spit out from the machine.

With another gentle smile, she was handed a key and
pointed toward the back-left corner of the shop. The bathroom
was small and gross, dirt smears and footprints marking the old
tiled floor, a single fluorescent tube flickering from the ceiling.

Lizzie didn't care.

She plopped down on the toilet seat, ripping open the first
box she grabbed from the bag. She tore open the plastic encas-
ing within, pulling out the ominous white stick. She squinted at
the directions for a minute, but the idea seemed simple enough.
Hovering over the toilet seat, she pushed her sleep shorts down

to her knees, trying to find enough inner serenity to release a stream of pee. After moments of hesitation, she was finally successful, and all that was left was for her to wait the three minutes.

180 seconds.

She made it maybe five before peeking.

She couldn't be pregnant. This was nothing but a major overexaggeration on her part. There was a highly logical reason her period was four days late for the first time in her life.

After the three longest minutes in history, Lizzie suddenly couldn't bear to look at the test. She gritted her teeth, clenched her fists, squeezed her eyes shut, until she finally found some willpower to pick up the stick and look at it.

Two pink lines stared back at her.

She checked, then double-checked, then triple-checked what those two pink lines meant.

And slowly, it started to sink in.

Two *positive* pink lines.

Chapter 13

THE next day, Lizzie stayed in bed. Her mind hummed and swarmed with a hornet's nest of thoughts, turning into a tangle she didn't have the energy to unravel. She rotated from crying, to puking, to sleeping, to staring down at her stomach in disbelief. She'd always felt at the mercy of her hyperactive mind, but now she felt a disconnect from her body too, like she was a passive bystander to what it was doing. What it was creating.

Maybe.

Maybe creating.

Because could you really trust five positive pregnancy tests? Trust those blue plus signs and double pink lines growing darker and stronger each time?

She managed to finally find the presence of mind to call a free clinic and schedule an appointment for the next morning, wanting to make the call before Indira got home.

When Indira walked in the door an hour later, Lizzie told her she still felt like shit and would probably go to bed early. Instead, she stared up at her ceiling for the rest of the night, blue plus signs, Rake's voice in her ear, and the howl of a crying baby chasing one another around her skull.

* * *

AT THE CLINIC the next morning, she sat in the waiting room, her leg jiggling up an earthquake as she filled out the paperwork. After what felt like an eternity, she was ushered into the back by a friendly but efficient nurse named Linda.

The nurse slid behind a computer, typing furiously as she looked between Lizzie's paperwork and the monitor, the pounding *click click click*s filling the room.

"And what brings you in today?" she asked without looking at Lizzie.

"I . . . uh . . . I think I need a blood test."

"A blood test for what?" *Click click click.*

"For, um." Lizzie coughed, the words wrapping themselves around her vocal cords and making her choke.

"Let me take your blood pressure," Nurse Linda continued, seeming to need to use every second to its maximum efficiency. "You were saying?"

"I think I'm, uh, maybe kind of pregnant . . ." Saying the word out loud was like being punched through the chest and having the fist squeeze her heart.

"Would you like to be tested for STIs too?" Linda asked, oblivious to the avalanche of emotions currently crushing Lizzie.

"Oh fuck, might as well," Lizzie said, throwing her hands in the air and giving in to the tears.

Nurse Linda finally seemed to pick up on Lizzie's distress, giving her fingers a moment of rest from their endless clacking. After a brief pause, she handed Lizzie a tissue. Lizzie took it and blew her nose, but all she really wanted from the woman—from anyone—was a hug.

"I just . . . I just don't know how this could have happened," Lizzie said, wiping at another bubble of snot from her nose. "I mean, I know how this happened. Despite the pretty picture I'm painting, I'm not a total fucking idiot. But we did use a condom."

The nurse gave her a sympathetic shrug. "Condoms break. Or expire. You're not an idiot."

"*Expire?*" The thought had never occurred to Lizzie that she might be toting around expired condoms in the bottomless depths of her purse. She knew it was technically possible, sure, but it seemed like such an *improbable* outcome that she hadn't ever given the idea much room in her already-crowded brain.

She dug to the bottom of her purse and fished out the last remaining silver package from the strip she'd used with Rake. She turned it over and over, finally finding those tiny little black numbers. The noise that came from her throat was somewhere between a sob and a laugh. They'd expired three months ago.

"You . . . keep them in your purse like that? All crinkled?"

Lizzie shot the nurse a pathetic, watery-eyed look before completely crumpling into tears. "Yes, Linda, I keep expired, crinkled condoms at the bottom of my purse—right next to the peanut butter crackers, thank you very much—and then use them to have sex with a random Australian man. I'm. A. Mess."

"I'm sorry! I'm so sorry. I didn't mean it like that. Oh, poor dear." Linda gently patted Lizzie's shoulder until she got her sobs under control.

The rest of the appointment was handled with a bit more delicacy, Linda offering Lizzie gentle smiles and painless handling.

"How long until . . ." Lizzie gestured vaguely at the little vials of her blood on the counter, her voice scratchy.

The nurse gave her a soft smile. "Since you're one of the first appointments of the day, I imagine we can get you your results by this evening. Is email okay?"

Lizzie nodded.

Linda stared at her for a moment before reaching out and taking Lizzie's hand. "You have options, dear. Don't forget that. Whatever the results or whatever you decide, we'll be here to help you."

Lizzie choked down a sob and nodded again, pressing her

lips together in an attempt at a smile, before heading out the door.

* * *

LIZZIE SPENT THE rest of the day taking more pregnancy tests that she'd spent an obscene amount of money on and checking her email every two seconds. Right before five, she decided to take one more test, because the ninth time was sure to show a different result, right? She sat cross-legged on her bed, her knuckles white as she clutched the tiny stick in her fist, when her computer dinged with an email. She clicked it open so fast, she almost tore a muscle in her fingers.

She clicked it open, logged into the health portal, and scanned down the labs, all negative for the various venereal diseases, and the tiniest blossom of relief bloomed in her chest. But, at the bottom, sat the one word that changed everything.

POSITIVE

Her eyes scanned back and forth across the line over and over.

hCG 327 mIU/ml   POSITIVE

She somehow managed to unglue her eyes from the screen to look at the stick in her hand. To look at those two pink lines.

Lizzie stared at those two lines. She wished she could shrink her body down and dissolve between those little pink lines, lock herself in a little pink jail so she wouldn't have to face this reality.

She wanted to cry and she wanted to puke. She wanted to run away and curl up in a ball. Her brain was somersaulting in her skull, so many thoughts tumbling over and over one another.

She didn't know what to do.

What was she supposed to do?

Objectively, twenty-seven was a perfectly normal age for a woman to have a baby. Subjectively, Lizzie was now unemployed and barely had enough faith in her abilities to care for herself, let alone an innocent life. Yet suddenly she was faced with the reality of motherhood? But could she give the baby up? Or terminate the pregnancy altogether?

She had options. Options many women weren't fortunate enough to have. But she was overwhelmed by all of them. What did she actually *want*? Questions built in her chest until the pressure threatened to crack her open, fracture her skull, and pop her heart from her chest.

She could practically *see* herself fucking up as a mom. Missed appointments, messy apartment, all those small little functional things that felt like mountains to her hyperactive mind.

But, amid all the flickers of failure dancing through her brain, one image kept coming to the forefront. It started off hazy, but as each doubt surfaced, the image grew stronger. Lighter. It practically glowed on a projector in her mind. A tiny chubby fist with dimpled knuckles wrapped around her finger. Squeezing tight. Holding on to her.

She was suddenly so overwhelmed with the need to have that little hand wrapped around her finger, she wanted to howl.

She collapsed back onto her pillows, staring up at her blank white ceiling as she let the idea tumble around her brain. Could she do it? Could she be a mom? Slowly, the thoughts transformed.

Maybe she could?

Lizzie loved children. She'd always had some far-off dream of being a mom, of finally reaching some point in her life when she had her shit together. It had always seemed like a fantasy. Some alternate-universe version of Lizzie that got to be a mom. The alternate Lizzie had a brain with excellent executive functioning and a steady partner who loved her. She remembered to switch out the laundry and kept a color-coded calendar.

A sharp tang of jealousy filled Lizzie's mouth at the thought of that other version. That couldn't be her. That would *never* be her. But why couldn't Lizzie have at least part of that fantasy?

The longer she stared up at the ceiling, the weaker any other options became, until they didn't take up any more space in her mind.

Lizzie was pregnant.

There was a tiny bundle of cells dividing inside her that would eventually become a full-blown person.

A start of a little life, and she was responsible for it.

And she wanted to do it.

She wanted to see them grow.

Tears fell from the corners of her eyes, and she let them. She wasn't sure what emotion they represented; she felt so many all at once. Each little salty drop that rolled down her cheek was filled with fear and anxiety and doubt, but also love and determination and the tiniest bit of hope.

Chapter 14

LIZZIE spent the next few days crying, applying for jobs, and making endless batches of emo cookies and pity pies.

The kitchen was where her brain vibrated on its best frequency, and as she mixed and stirred and created, she thought.

Lizzie was disastrously prone to impulsivity, but she forced herself to work through every angle of the choice she was making, the undeniable magnitude of the decision. By the time she'd baked her heart out and cried over multiple plates of warm cookies, she knew without a doubt that she wanted to keep the baby.

And she also knew that it was time to really look at what she did for ADHD management.

And there wasn't much.

She had a psychiatrist and a prescription and a mountain of abandoned self-help workbooks piled up in the corner of her room, but when it came down to it, she went at life with a wish and a prayer, flailing about as she barreled full speed ahead and tried to fit into society's definition of normal.

It was like trying to squeeze herself into a life that didn't quite fit. It pinched at her ribs, dug under her arms, painfully straightened her knees and elbows. And when it all was too uncomfortable, sex was her outlet. Her unsanctioned therapy with a quick, feel-good reward that soothed over every aching nerve.

But Lizzie couldn't stay on this trajectory—pushing her brain to fit the wrong mold until the pressure built too high— not with another person to take care of.

So, she decided to start simple.

After having an emergency call with her psychiatrist and confirming it was safe to keep taking her meds while pregnant, Lizzie set a daily alarm to remind her to take them. She set the orange bottle directly in her line of sight on her nightstand, completing a task she'd procrastinated on for years.

It was a small thing, but it felt like a metal band was un- clamped from around her chest, creating a small blossom of hope that the work she needed to do to take care of her brain might not always be quite as backbreaking as she anticipated.

With this tiny boost in self-confidence, she decided to tackle something else she could feel herself putting off.

Lizzie grabbed her phone and scrolled through her texts, searching for the three eggplants and exploding-head emojis she'd marked Rake's name with.

She stared at the last message he'd sent:

> Thanks for a great time. Let me know if you ever
> find yourself in Sydney

Great time. That's all Lizzie ever was. The perfect person in small doses. That bucket list type of person who made for a memorable weekend, a wild story, but was always a little too much to keep around for the long term.

How was she supposed to tell him? She wanted to rip the Band-Aid off; her bones ached with the need to get it over with as soon as possible. But what words do you use to tell a near stranger you're carrying their baby and you want to keep it?

Hey, Rake! Just the girl from Philly that rode your face the first night we met! Wanna hear something hilarious? I'm pregnant lol

Rakeeeeeee. It's ya girl, Lizzie. How've you been? Anyway, have you ever seen the movie Juno?

Remember that time I told you I always come prepared and had a fuck ton of condoms in my purse? Turns out they were expired and guess who's pregnant??? Lol isn't life funny?

She blew out a deep breath and tapped through to his number, pressing the call button before she could overthink it anymore.

It rang.

And rang.

She simultaneously dreaded the sound of him answering as much as the sound of his voicemail.

Just when she thought it would ring forever, Rake's voice came through the line.

"Lizzie?" he answered, his accent purring with a mix of amusement and curiosity.

Lizzie couldn't help the little puff of nervous laughter that escaped her lips. "Hey, yeah. It's me. Lizzie. Not sure if you remember me. The girl from Philly." Her voice was hoarse, tense.

"Like I could forget you, Birdy. How are you?" His words were light, but an undercurrent of sensuality punctuated each one, stirring her pulse. She pushed those feelings away.

"I have something I have to tell you. Something serious."

There was silence on the line, a pause that felt, well, pregnant.

"What's wrong?" he asked at last, all humor gone from his voice.

Tears pricked at Lizzie's eyes again. She couldn't seem to pull herself together. "I—" She took a deep breath, her hands trembling as she clutched the phone to her ear. "I'm pregnant."

There.

The words were out.

They'd left her throat and traveled across miles and wires and oceans and mountains to the other side of the world and into Rake's ears. She'd done it.

But the silence stretched. It grew and pushed, and Lizzie checked that the call wasn't dropped three times before a hoarse noise broke through the line.

"What?" he finally managed, barely an audible whisper.

"I'm pregnant," she said more firmly. "And I . . . I'm planning on keeping it. I just thought you should know."

"Is it . . . are you sure it's mine?"

"Okay, fuck you, I'm hanging up," Lizzie said, indignation flaring across her skin and lighting up in her veins.

"No! No. I'm sorry. Don't hang up." She heard him take a few rattling breaths through the phone, a gulping sound. "That was a terrible way to say that. I'm sorry," he choked out. "I think I'm . . . in shock? I'm not sure. Are you sure, though?"

"Yes, I'm sure it's yours, you giant-cocked dickhead."

"So you aren't—or you *weren't* on birth control?"

"Were *you*?! Oh no, that's right. The pill is the woman's job. Heaven forbid it makes her feel like total shit and she choose not to take it."

"I'm sorry!" Rake's voice was close to a shout.

"Don't yell at me," Lizzie shot back.

There was a pause. "I'm sorry," he repeated, his voice softer, but still holding a jagged edge. Lizzie understood that edge. She was dancing on it herself. "I'm sorry. This is just . . . This is the last thing I expected."

Lizzie snorted. "Yeah, join the club."

"We used condoms."

Lizzie shrugged, even though he couldn't see it. "They were . . . expired," she admitted, swallowing past a dry, tight throat. "I'm sorry. That's on me."

"I—" Rake coughed. "I had just as much ability to check them as you did," he whispered.

Another silence stretched out and threatened to kill her.

"Listen," she said, finding some pretend reservoir of strength in her voice. "I'm calling because I thought you deserved to know. I don't expect *anything* from you, okay? I don't expect you to uproot your life or be forced to play house or do anything just because I want to keep the baby. I just thought you should know." The words were tumbling out of her, a rambling disaster, but she needed him to understand that she didn't need him. She could figure out her mess.

"I want to be involved," he said suddenly. Forcefully. "I want to be involved, please don't try and stop me."

Lizzie's eyebrows shot up to her hairline. "Wait, what? Stop you? I'm saying—"

"I know what you're saying," he cut her off, "but *I'm* saying I want to be involved. If you're keeping the baby, I want to be involved. Completely."

Lizzie couldn't suppress the nervous bubble of laughter that burst from her. She always laughed at the most serious moments. "While I can respect the sentiment, you live across the globe," she pointed out.

"I'm booking a flight," he said, leaving no room for argument, his words punctuated by the rattle of a keyboard.

"*What?*"

"We need to figure this out, and I think we should do it in person. I can be there in thirty-six hours."

"Sorry . . . *what?*"

He didn't respond, more keyboard clicking filling the line.

"Are you telling me you're moving here in thirty-six hours?" Lizzie asked, her heart hammering up into her throat. This was a lot to comprehend, and her brain seemed to be moving in slow motion.

"No, that will take a bit more planning—"

"Yeah, no shit."

"*But*," he pressed, ignoring her comment, "I'm coming to see you. We have a lot to figure out."

"You don't have to figure anything out. I can handle this."

Rake didn't say anything.

"Why are you doing this?" Lizzie asked weakly. For some reason, the idea of him coming, being involved, being a witness to the inevitable mess she would be at this, was agonizing. "I'm giving you an out. You don't have to do this."

There was yet another long pause. This one felt heavy, weighted, something close to pain punctuating the silence.

"Rake?" she prompted at last.

He cleared his throat. "I don't want an out. I'll see you in thirty-six hours."

Chapter 15

AFTER buying a ticket for the next flight Rake could realistically catch to Philadelphia and booking a hotel room, he phoned his boss.

"Hello?" Robert answered in his gruff voice after the third ring. Robert was the president of Onism, a long-standing luxury swimsuit line that was a staple among Australia's richest.

"Robert, hi. It's Rake. Have a minute?"

"This couldn't wait until I see you at the office in an hour?"

Rake looked at his watch. 7:30 a.m. He'd been halfway out the door when Lizzie had called him. "No, sir. I'm sorry, but I'm not feeling great. If we can manage, I think I need a few days off."

"A few?" Robert asked skeptically. Rake never got sick, never took time off, so this request was no doubt odd to his boss.

Rake cleared his throat, fumbling to come up with a lie. "Yes, sir. I visited my mum this weekend, and she had . . . strep," he said, grabbing at the first illness he could come up with. "And I think I caught it. Heading to the doctor in a bit." He drummed his thumb on the counter, hoping that his rustiness at lying could be mistaken for some sort of high fever.

"Pity about your mum," Robert said distractedly, the noise

of a morning household floating in the background behind him. Then, pulling the phone away from his ear he called out, "Betty, have you seen my navy tie?"

"So is a few days okay?" Rake prompted.

"That should be fine," Robert grumbled. "But what about your meeting with Walton's?" he asked, referring to a small, regional department store in the south of the country Rake was scheduled to meet with later in the week, hoping to develop an exclusive marketing campaign with them for Onism's next line of resort pieces.

"Anderson can cover the pitch," Rake said, throwing in a fake cough for dramatics.

Robert grunted in response. "Well, make sure he has the slide deck," Robert added. "Feel better."

"Sir?" Rake said, trying to grab his attention before he hung up.

"Hm?"

"I was wondering if . . ."

"Out with it. I'm running late as it is."

"I was wondering if the U.S. position was still on the table?" Rake pushed out, feeling almost dizzy with how rapidly his world was changing. Things were happening too fast, and he didn't like it. He liked order. Structure. Predictability.

He hadn't always been so buttoned up, so afraid of change. But the past two years had turned him into a man with little motivation to step outside of his routine. A routine that was serving him just fine until he'd met Lizzie.

"I thought you said there was nothing for you in making the transfer," Robert said slowly, his interest piqued. He had offered Rake a position on a new team designated to integrate the brand into the East Coast of the U.S.

Rake had immediately turned it down, saying he was better suited to business development on long-standing projects than starting from scratch.

"I've been thinking on it," Rake lied, "and I'd like the challenge. I have some ideas from my last trip to the States that I believe could really be an asset to the endeavor."

"Oh really? Like what?"

Rake paused, his mind going blank in a desperate scramble for any campaign ideas he could come up with. He was so caught off guard, he started spluttering and choking.

"You really sound like shit," Robert said, then pulled the phone away from his mouth again, "Betty! The tie! Have you seen my tie?"

"Sick as a dog," Rake confirmed, hoping Robert would take the hint and end this.

"Listen, I think Dominic's already completed his team, but I'll talk to him. He's always had a fondness for you."

Rake cringed. He didn't particularly like Dominic. He was an older executive, notorious for his rejection of anything new or experimental in campaigns to reach younger markets, and had an unsavory reputation for his treatment of employees. But what needed to be done needed to be done. Lizzie had dropped a bomb in his lap, but he wasn't about to throw it back at her to deal with alone.

"I've got to run, Rake. Send me a slide deck with some of your ideas, and I'll see what Dominic thinks."

"Thank you, sir."

Robert ended the call, and Rake stood in his small, empty kitchen, slapping his phone against his palm while he stared blankly at the wall.

A baby.

A giant-headed creature that would be in this world in, what, eight and a half months?

He wasn't sure what he felt. Rake had pushed down his emotions so succinctly over the past few years, it was hard to identify when a more complex one bubbled to the surface. Scared shitless was probably the primary feeling.

He looked around his apartment. He didn't spend more time in his home than strictly necessary, and it showed.

It was embarrassingly bare, had been since Shannon moved out. White walls. Gray carpet. His lonely bed sat in one corner of the bedroom, tidily made. A small, uncomfortable couch faced an unimpressive TV in the living space with an empty kitchen he never used attached. A bathroom with only the barest of necessities to keep his hollow self looking the part at his corporate job stood opposite.

It had the effect of a poorly done model apartment, unlived in and sterile. There was no denying the emptiness that made it more sad than anything, haunted by ghosts of could-have-beens. Rake had never been a particularly exuberant or expressive person, but there had been a time that he felt happy and content in this space. Had felt safe to show it.

But that type of vulnerable foolishness was far behind him. Or it was supposed to be, at least. He'd acted like quite the fool in Philadelphia.

Being around Lizzie had opened some trapdoor through his walls, pulling him out of the barren landscape he cultivated for himself and into a bright light. He'd reasoned it was something he'd needed to get out of his system, a few days of indulgent fun, and then he'd cram himself back into his cage upon returning home.

That had turned out well.

Because for the past two weeks, the foolish version of himself had taken the reins in his sleep, and the shower, and second-long daydreams all starring Lizzie and her dazzling smile with just a pinch of something that felt like longing.

Which was *ridiculous*. What, was he *pining*? Having *feelings*?

No. He wasn't.

It had been a lapse in judgment.

A lapse that now meant a child and approximately four

million new responsibilities he had to plan for and execute to perfection.

Rake massaged his temples, making neat mental lists of everything he needed to do immediately, over the next week, and over the next few years. He found comfort in the planning, in the preparation for anything life would throw at him.

This would all be okay, he thought, neatly folding his clothes into his suitcase. He'd make sure everything was okay.

Chapter 16

RAKE was exhausted as he swiped into his hotel room. All he wanted to do was fall face-first onto the mattress and sleep for the next three days. Instead, he chugged down a coffee, hopped into a freezing shower to wake up, then sat on the edge of the bed in a towel, staring at his phone.

He needed to get in contact with Lizzie. Rake was only in the U.S. for twenty-four hours, and he needed to use that time efficiently, like he did with all other aspects of his life. He'd spent the excruciatingly long flight working through multiple plans, and he needed to present her with the options. Like a business meeting.

He'd lay out the pros and cons of different arrangements, stick with the big picture instead of the details, and likely have an agreed-upon decision with designated action items within an hour.

If he could keep his head on straight, that is, which he seemed incapable of around Lizzie.

After one more deep breath, he dialed her number.

"Hello?" Lizzie's voice was like roughened honey, and his heart gave a small kick at the sound of it. Which was bizarre.

"Hi, it's Rake. I made it to Philadelphia. Can we meet somewhere and talk?"

There was silence for a long moment. "Am I being punked?" she asked at last.

"I don't know what that means."

Lizzie sighed. "You're really here?"

"Yes. I'm at the same hotel as last time. Is there a restaurant or coffee shop you like that we can meet at?"

More silence.

More of his heart doing that weird kicking thing.

"I'll meet you at La Colombe on Nineteenth and Walnut. It's a coffee shop. Is an hour enough time?" Lizzie said all of this with another resigned sigh.

"That's perfect. I'll see you soon."

Lizzie hung up the call.

Rake finished getting ready, paying extra attention to his shave, making sure his clothes looked crisp and clean, no matter how rumpled he felt inside.

He was oddly . . . nervous? Which, on one hand, wasn't all that strange. He was about to have one of the most important conversations of his life, of course he was nervous. But the nerves came more from seeing *Lizzie* and less from the topic. Which was a very confusing reaction and one he chalked up to jet lag.

Fifty-five minutes later, he stood outside the coffee shop waiting for Lizzie. He checked his watch every few minutes, the jangle of nerves growing the longer he waited.

Half an hour later, Lizzie rounded the corner in a walk-jog, her red hair blazing about her as she maneuvered through the crowds.

"I'm sorry I'm late," she said, stopping in front of him, her honey-colored eyes with their touch of wildness threatening to swallow Rake whole. "I was busy puking," she added, using the collar of her tank top to dab at the sweat on her red cheeks and forehead.

"Are you, uh . . . are you okay?"

She looked at him, her eyes dancing across his face, and her body seemed to sag under the weight of his question.

After a moment, she smiled. A soft, sad smile that for some odd reason created a tiny, devastating effect along his body.

"Let's go in," she said, pulling open the door and leading the way into the cool café.

After ordering, they grabbed a table in the back corner.

Lizzie's knees started bouncing under the table as she looked around, her eyes darting around the space.

"So," Lizzie said, taking a sip of her iced tea. "You took the world's longest flight to talk? Did you have a topic in mind?" She let out an awkward bubble of laughter that made his heart squeeze a bit.

Rake cleared his throat, ready to get down to business. But all his carefully planned speeches seemed to have evaporated straight from his brain, leaving a tangle in its place. He cleared his throat again. "I'd like to be involved," he said at last. Because this was the one constant he didn't want to compromise on.

Lizzie pursed her lips. "Sending a kid across the world every other weekend for visits isn't particularly ideal," she said, tracing the mosaic pieces of the table with her fingers.

"I—I'd like a bit more than every other weekend. I'd like to be involved on a daily basis or as close to that if we can arrange it."

Lizzie gaped at him, then narrowed her eyes. "I'm not just giving you the baby, you weirdo."

"No. No. That's not what I mean. Obviously, I don't want that. I . . . I mean—"

Lizzie stared at him, her eyebrows arching. Rake blew out a breath.

"I'd like for us to develop an agreed-upon plan of coparenting here in Philadelphia that offers us equal time with the child."

Lizzie gaped at him again. "So, you'll . . . what? Move here? Like it's that easy? What about a job? What about, I don't know, *citizenship*? I don't—" She stopped, her shoulders slumping, and she buried her head in her hands.

"Don't what?" Rake asked.

"I don't even know what you do. What your job is," she said with a humorless laugh, lifting her head to look at him.

"I'm in marketing," he said. "I work on the creative team for a brand called Onism Swimwear. And I'll figure the job thing out. That's for me to worry about."

Lizzie made a scoffing noise. "Well, isn't that just wonderfully cavalier. You don't want to share *how* you'll figure it out. And, again, isn't there that tiny little thing of *you living across the globe*?"

"Are the details that important right now? Don't we have bigger things to worry about?"

Something in Lizzie snapped, a small fire blazing in her eyes, as she propped her elbow on the table, jutting her finger at his chest. "The details matter the most," she said, her brows puckering and eyes turning glossy in her anger. "You come here, tell me you want to be this idyllic father figure, but don't care to share *how* you'll do it? I'm just supposed to have this blind . . . *faith* in you to magically make everything work?"

"Why are you getting mad?"

"I'm mad because you're leaving me in the dark! I'm mad because how can you say that you want to help if I don't know how you plan to even live in the same city?" She punctuated every other word with a jab to his chest.

Rake grabbed her finger, enclosing her hand in his. "I'm sorry. I'm not trying to keep you in the dark." Lizzie let out an indignant snort and tried to pull her hand away, but Rake placed more gentle pressure on his grip. "I'm *not*. Listen, my dad is originally from California, so I have dual citizenship. I just have to look into the details of it. Let me worry about that. And seriously, I'll figure out the job. I already have something in the works. You're carrying a child. You don't need the added burden of tiny details that I can handle."

Her lips twitched. "You don't get it. You're asking for us to be partners in this. I need more than that."

"On the subject of partners," he said, resting their hands on the table and trying to make his touch reassuring as he stared at the spot their skin met, "I think we should get married."

Lizzie jerked her hand from his, her whole body jolting back like his words were a punch, and she hit her head on the wood paneling behind her. She stared at him, open-mouthed, eyes blank, for what felt like ten minutes.

Without warning, her face crumpled like a wadded-up piece of paper, tears bursting from her as she buried her head in her hands.

"Why are you crying?" Rake asked, trying to mask his alarm. He was out of practice dealing with anyone else's emotions, and Lizzie seemed to filter through the entire spectrum of them every few minutes.

"Why am I *crying*?" she sobbed, fixing him with an anguished glare of disbelief. "I don't know, you cyborg. Maybe because I'm pregnant and scared and throwing up nonstop, and my tits hurt so bad I want to rip them off, and my nipples look all weird already, and now some guy I don't know tells me we should get married? Maybe because about ninety-six hours ago I realized I was pregnant, and then you show up here asking me to tie my life to you like I don't have one trillion other thoughts crowding my brain? And to top it all off, you live halfway around the world but still expect me to have this blind confidence in you to secure some job here and all kinds of other shit that makes my brain want to melt straight out of my ears just thinking about it?"

"That certainly is . . . a lot to process."

She let out another choked sob, curling her body around herself like she would lie down in the booth and never stop crying.

Something about it fissured through Rake's sternum. He hadn't known her long, but the Lizzie he did know had seemed like an indomitable force. A woman of fire and steel and energy.

But now, she looked afraid. And soft. And scared.

And it did funny things to the organ in Rake's chest.

Acting on impulse, he moved to her side of the table. She tried to scoot away from him, but he wrapped his arms around her, pulling her to his chest, anchoring her to him.

Her body was stiff and tense, but all at once every muscle seemed to relax, and she went boneless against him. She continued to cry, her sobs slowly turning into soft whimpers until her breathing steadied. She let out the tiniest sigh, one Rake felt right in the hollow at the base of his throat. It made his chest tighten uncomfortably.

"I'm scared," she whispered at last.

Although it seemed impossible, Rake hugged her even tighter. "Me too."

"I don't want to get married," she said. "I don't know you."

Rake nodded, trying to swallow that down. It was true. They didn't know each other. Not much, anyway. But that didn't stop his intense impulse to take care of her. To take care of their child in the way his own parents had. Two parents, one house. As few confusing variables as possible. It was old and antiquated, but he felt so embarrassingly useless, it was the best solution he could come up with.

"I don't want to be shut out," he admitted softly. "I want to be part of my kid's life."

She pulled back, fixing him with an intense stare. "You say that now, but what if you change your mind? What if tomorrow you meet the love of your life and want to start a family with them? Or five years from now? What if you don't like being a dad? What if you don't like the baby?"

"None of those things will happen," he said. He wouldn't let them.

"How do you know?"

He stared into her red-rimmed eyes. "Because some things I just know," he said with finality. Turning away from her gaze—her searching look that felt like she wanted to crack his head open and read all his thoughts, see all his secrets—he sipped his coffee.

"Tell me your plan," she said after a minute. "With details."

Rake took a deep breath. "I'm working on getting a transfer out here. My company is looking to branch into East Coast markets, and I was offered the position shortly before the trip over here, when we met, but I turned it down initially. Now it seems rather fortuitous."

Lizzie chewed on her bottom lip while tapping a spoon on the table, lost in some train of thought.

"What are you thinking?" he asked. He wasn't sure why, but something about her made him want to know every vibrant thought that swirled through her colorful mind. She fascinated him in a way no one else ever had before. He wanted to understand her.

She sighed then chugged down her iced tea. "I'm thinking it's early in this whole . . . pregnancy thing, and I'm scared. I'm scared for you to uproot your whole life and move across the world for a job you don't want, when I'm still in that period where so many things could go wrong. So many. Do you know how many women miscarry in their first trimester?"

Rake shook his head, holding her wide, panicked gaze.

"It's like, ten percent, or something awful," she said. "And what if that happens to me? To us."

That little "us" bounced through his ears and traveled down his throat, locking itself there and making it hard to breathe.

"I feel like I can't have you move here until we're surer this is . . . happening."

"This is happening," he said gruffly, wanting to push away her words. The idea left him cold. Nauseous.

"But—"

Rake cupped his hand around her neck, his fingers curling around her soft skin and tangling in the wispy hairs at her nape. "We can't think about everything that could go wrong. If it does, it does. But I'd rather be here to help you through that part of it too. I can't do much here, Lizzie, and it's kind of killing me. All I can do is physically be here. For whatever comes next."

She fixed him with that look again, like she'd opened a trapdoor in his skull and was seeing his brain. Like she recognized the pain in there. He blinked away, dropping his hand.

He quickly lost Lizzie to her thoughts; he could almost hear her mind whirring like a car engine. Absentmindedly, she reached both hands around his wrist, making a circle with her thumbs and middle fingers, then moving it up his arm until the little cage of her fingers broke, repeating the movement over and over as she thought.

"Okay," she said at last, dropping her hands.

"Okay?"

"Okay, let's do this thing," she said with a goofy grin, equal parts hope and panic. "Let's coparent or whatever-the-fuck. Let's do it. I can't stop you from moving here, and God knows I'll need help."

"Yeah?" A small yellow balloon of optimism slowly inflated in his chest.

"Yeah."

He couldn't resist the need to hug her, and he pulled her close. Never in his life had he had such a strong impulse to touch someone so often. He quickly discarded the notion as some primal instinct for protecting one's mate. Or, coparent, more accurately.

"It's still a no to marriage, though," she said into his neck. Rake nodded. He could live with that. He could figure out a new plan for making their child's life perfect. But an idea did strike him, and he pulled back.

"Would you consider moving in together? At least for the pregnancy and first few months?"

Lizzie's instant look of resistance made him push on. "Just while we figure this out. How to be parents. How to work together. Trial by fire, right?" He wanted to be there. He wanted to be there if there were complications, when the baby cried, when they were hungry, when Lizzie needed something in the middle of the night. He wanted it all.

She still had a wary look, but her resistance was softening. Rake went in for the kill. "It'd be helping me out so much. Give me peace of mind to have you close by if something happens. Help me get used to living in the U.S. Help us both figure out how to do this."

Her wariness transformed into soft contemplation. Even in the short time he'd known her, he'd realized how much she liked to be needed. Liked to be helpful.

"I need to think about it," she said at last, then laughed. "I always make super impulsive decisions and jump without thinking. But this"—she pointed down at her stomach—"I promised myself I'd think through everything with this."

Rake nodded. "What if you stay with me while I'm here? I know being in a hotel isn't real life, but it could give us an idea?"

Lizzie pursed her lips, thinking for a moment, before nodding in agreement. "Okay, baby daddy, you've got yourself a deal."

Chapter 17

RAKE heard Lizzie's phone buzz as they walked into his hotel room. She fished it out from the bottom of her bag and stared down at it before letting out a soft curse.

"Everything okay?" Rake asked, but Lizzie didn't seem to hear him. She started pacing the small room, biting her nails as she lost herself in thought.

He watched her dart back and forth for a minute, but as she paced by him on another circuit, he reached out, pulling her to stand in front of him. "Lizzie?"

She seemed to snap back into her body, blinking up at him. "Sorry, what?"

"Are you okay?" Rake asked slowly.

"Peachy keen, jelly bean," she said with a sharp bubble of laughter, chewing on her cuticles. She tried to slip out of his arms, but he held her still.

"Are you sure?"

She stared at him for a moment, eyes sharp, body tense, before she slumped in his arms, her face wrinkling in some emotion Rake couldn't understand. She had so many emotions that flitted across the surface of her freckled skin, and for some unknown reason, he wanted to be able to identify them all.

"It's just my hair hasn't been washed in a few days, and

I've cried so damn much today, I know my mascara looks like railroad tracks down my cheeks, and I really want a shower since it was so hot today and I'm smelling kinda spicy, but I also don't have any clothes with me, but by the time I grab the trolley to the connection with the Market-Frankford Line and then walked the few blocks to my place, I'd be running *really* late, and I'm not positive I even have any clean clothes, because when I had meant to put in a load of laundry, I'd gotten sidetracked by realizing I'd only unloaded half of the dishwasher the day before, and Indira made it clear she *hated* when I did that because it screwed up the whole system, and then she had to—"

Rake gave Lizzie a tiny shake, trying to snap her out of the runaway thoughts he couldn't follow. "Sorry, but what the hell are you talking about?"

Lizzie blinked at him for a moment before letting out a soft laugh. She stepped away from him, stretching and straining her arms over her head as far as she could before collapsing like a deflated balloon to touch her toes. "I forgot I'm supposed to meet my friends tonight for dinner," she mumbled to her shoes.

"Oh, okay . . ." Rake was still lost. "That will be fun, right? What time?"

Lizzie looked at her phone again. "In thirty-eight minutes," she said, typing something out that Rake couldn't see before jolting back up to standing. "And I think I'm maybe freaking out."

"Maybe?" Rake said, arching an eyebrow.

Lizzie shot him a sardonic glance. "I'm *kind of* freaking out because it's with my *best friends*, and I look like absolute trash and I'm also pregnant."

"What did your friends say about all this?" Rake asked, nodding vaguely toward her torso.

"I haven't exactly told them yet," Lizzie admitted, plopping onto the edge of the bed and slapping her phone against her thigh.

"Why?"

Lizzie sighed. "I don't know. Everything is happening so fast, I'm not even sure when I would've had a chance. I thought about telling them as soon as I found out, but I just felt like I *couldn't*. Probably because my friends are all perfect and responsible and would have a lot of questions for me that I don't have answers for. And when I try to think of answers, I get super overwhelmed, and then it's like my mind is on one of those Tilt-A-Whirl things, and it just gets all"—she made an exploding sound, flashing her fingers for effect—"fritzy."

"Fritzy?"

"Like my motherboard is short-circuiting," she said, tapping her finger to her temple. She gave him a sad smile.

"But what happened? Why—"

"Do you know anyone with ADHD?" she asked suddenly.

His eyes flashed in surprise. "What?"

"Do you know anyone that has attention deficit and hyper-activity disorder?"

Rake scrubbed a hand across the back of his neck, trying to keep up. "I imagine my mates and I had a touch of it in primary school. What does this have to—"

"Anyone that isn't a twelve-year-old boy?"

"What are you on about, Lizzie?" he asked, sitting next to her on the bed.

She took a deep breath and massaged her temples. "I have adult ADHD. It's why I come across a bit . . ." She waved her hand, searching for a word. ". . . all over the place."

Rake nodded, watching her.

She turned so her body was fully facing him, meeting his eyes. "And I'm trying to be more honest about that. Up front. Because for a long time, it was something I was taught to be embarrassed of, but I don't want to live like that anymore." She took another deep breath. "People think ADHD is just code for hyper or distracted, but that's not it. Not for me, at least. It's the inability to focus on or follow through on something that isn't immediately rewarding. And it applies to so many of life's basic things. Feeding myself. Completing a task. Total time blindness. Sometimes it feels like my brain straight-up riots against any normal executive functioning and makes me feel like I can't do anything right. Or I act impulsively, or do something destructive, and I mess life up for people." She stood again, resuming her pacing.

"I forget to take my meds or can't work my way through the steps to set up a doctor's appointment because it's all too much. I let people down. I get in trouble at work. I get myself into situations—this included," she said, pointing toward her stomach. "And it's like at every turn, I'm missing something. I'm forgetting dinners with my best friends. I have to tell them I'm pregnant without a plan. I don't have clean underwear because doing one load of laundry takes me like, eight days."

She stopped, staring blankly at the wall. "And people have such little faith in me to fix things. Or to manage things. But I'm trying. I'm working on it." Lizzie turned, marching to stand in front of where he sat on the bed.

"Will you go with me tonight?" she asked, her eyes pleading. "I know that's probably a lot to ask, but I don't want to face them alone. I love my friends, but they'll have a lot to say and I don't think I can field it all myself."

The raw vulnerability in the way she looked at him would have inspired Rake to agree to just about anything. He reached out, grabbing her hands. "If that's what you want, of course I'll go."

Lizzie nodded rapidly, sucking her cheeks into her mouth until her lips puckered like a fish. "I'll probably say a bunch of stupid stuff, and Thu is a beautiful deviant menace that might flay me alive using only her words. And Indira will probably be mad that I kept it from her. Harper and her boyfriend, Dan, will be there. They might be a bit more chill. They're so in love, I think the world is just a golden bubble of happiness, and every-thing is good news for them at this point but—"

Rake stood up, crushing her to his chest. "Take a breath, Lizzie."

She was tense for a moment before sighing into his chest and wrapping her hands around his waist in a hug.

"I'm sorry I'm such a mess," she mumbled into his T-shirt.

"I'm lost at all this too, Birdy. But we'll take it one hour at a time. Together."

Lizzie was still for a second before nodding into his chest. She sucked in a deep inhale, smooshing her nose against him. "You smell so good, I want to eat you," she said.

". . . thank you?"

They stood like that for a few soft moments, Rake rubbing his hands up and down her back in what he hoped were soothing circles. He had no clue what he was doing, and he was probably doing it wrong, but he felt as directionless as Lizzie seemed. After a few breaths, he realized she was quietly crying.

He pulled back, looking down at her. "Why are you crying again?" he said. He really wasn't sure he could handle more tears.

Lizzie let out a wet laugh, rubbing her eyes. "I'm sorry. I know this is like the eighty-seventh time I've cried today. I'm not even sure why I'm crying. I'd like to blame it on hormones, but I also cry at kittens and bench ads pretty regularly, so who knows." She stepped away from him, using the hem of her shirt to wipe her nose. "I'm sorry," she repeated, "this is so embar-rassing."

"Why are you embarrassed?"

"The crying. Telling you all this. Being a hormone monster. An emotional nightmare. It makes me want to rip my skin off."

"That's . . . graphic."

Lizzie snorted in amusement.

"You don't have to be embarrassed," Rake said. "About any of it. You aren't an emotional nightmare."

She gave him a skeptical look.

"You're . . . alive."

She blinked at him, her eyebrows furrowing. "Alive?"

Rake waved his hand, heat crawling up his skin like he'd just told her something way too honest. "You know. Lively. Energetic. There's a sort of . . . I don't know . . . vibrancy about you."

Good Lord, was he blushing?

Lizzie was oblivious to his discomfort, her eyes lighting up and head tilting as she seemed to chew on the word.

"Vibrancy," she said slowly. "I like that. Sounds very glamorous. Like how you'd describe an old Hollywood starlet."

"Sure."

Her eyes glinted as she stared off. "And perhaps she's a young widow, gallivanting off to Palm Springs or Monaco and throwing lavish parties, taking an endless string of lovers."

"Okay?"

"Rumors start circulating about the sudden death of her late husband, but her elusive beauty is the ultimate distraction. But then, one day at the opera, her lover and her other lover meet and—"

"Lizzie? Don't we have to get ready for dinner?"

"Oh, right, right, sorry," she said, shaking her head. And just like that, she grabbed his hand and pulled him out of the room and off to dinner.

Chapter 18

LIZZIE walked ahead of Rake into the restaurant, her eyes adjusting to the dimly lit space as she scanned the crowd of people waiting to be seated.

Over by the bar, she spotted her four favorite people in the entire world.

Indira was leaning against the bar, while Thu stood in front of her, sipping a cocktail. Harper was perched on a barstool, facing them, with one arm wrapped around Dan's waist. Lizzie watched them for a moment, absorbing the way Thu said something that made Indira throw back her head and laugh. How Dan's body molded against Harper as though he couldn't help but be pulled in closer. Dan stooped to whisper something into Harper's ear, and whatever it was made Harper turn and beam up at him then brush her hand across his cheek.

They were so in love, it was almost tangible, like a delicate force field existed around their happiness. The sight of their pure, open adoration rattled something in Lizzie's chest and tightened her throat. It wasn't jealousy—no one deserved love and happiness more than Harper—but an acute sense of want. And loss. Like she was peeping through a window and seeing something she would never get.

Harper's eyes flicked away from Dan and landed on Lizzie. A goofy grin of excitement filled Harper's delicate features as she started waving, gaining the attention of the rest of the group. All four of them moved toward Lizzie, and it took every ounce of Lizzie's minimal self-control not to break into a dead sprint across the restaurant for a hug.

The four women threw their hands around one another, giggling as they tangled in a tight hug that eased the squeezing feeling in Lizzie's chest. Lizzie eventually freed herself long enough to give Dan his own hug.

"I'm not letting you guys go back to New York," Lizzie said, fixing Harper and Dan with a stern look. "Or you to California," she added, swinging around to point at Thu. "Consider this the beginning of your kidnapping. I've missed you all way too much."

"We've missed you too, Lizzie," Dan said, giving her shoulders a final squeeze.

Thu cleared her throat, making the subtle yet universal face that said, *There's someone weird lurking around us*, causing Harper, Dan, and Indira to shoot glances over Lizzie's shoulder.

Guilt hit her as she realized she'd forgotten Rake's existence in her excitement. She was always doing that. Getting so lost in a feeling, social norms and niceties flew out the window.

She turned, grabbing Rake's arm and pulling him to stand next to her. "So, uh, I'm sorry I didn't mention this sooner," Lizzie said, starting to swing her and Rake's clasped hands, "but this is . . . um . . . this is my . . . uh, Rake, and he's here to join us for dinner."

"Your what?" Thu said, her head snapping back.

"Rake," Lizzie repeated, her leg starting to bounce as she mentally prepared for the onslaught of questions Rake's presence would no doubt cause.

"I'm confused. Are you calling him a rake like a gardening tool?" Indira asked, looking between them.

"Oh, he's a tool, all right," Lizzie said, making herself snort at her own joke. Rake couldn't stand any stiffer at her side.

"My name is Rake," he clarified. "Like the tool," he added, shooting Indira a weak attempt at a smile.

"Yes. Rake. This one is named Rake," Lizzie continued to babble. Her friends sent her a questioning glance. Lizzie waved her hand toward him. "He's my, um . . ." She let the words dangle, shooting a helpless look at Rake, who was similarly at a loss for what they were.

An awkward moment of silence settled around the group as Lizzie's friends continued to stare with open confusion. A light dusting of color spread across Rake's cheeks under the attention. Lizzie had never done anything close to introducing a guy to her friends without at least a prefacing text along the lines of "I'm bringing along the guy I'm screwing tonight," so their confusion wasn't much of a surprise.

Dan broke the tension first, reaching out a hand to Rake. "Rake," he said, nodding at him.

"It's, uh, nice to meet you," Harper said, also reaching out to shake his hand. Thu and Indira followed suit.

"I'm so glad to meet you all," Rake said, his hand hovering in the air after the shake like he didn't know what to do with it. "Lizzie's told me so many wonderful things about you."

This wasn't a line. Lizzie had spent the entire trip to the restaurant gushing about her friends.

Silence stretched after the greetings, and Lizzie had the uncontrollable need to fill it.

"Rake's Australian," she said. Harper and Dan nodded, looking at her with almost pained expressions. Indira and Thu pressed their lips together in an attempt not to laugh. "He's, uh, tall too. What, like, six-two?" She looked to Rake for confirmation, her eyes going a little wonky and wild as she scrambled to force a flow of conversation. "Big muscles."

He gave her an imploring look, an almost imperceptible shake of his head, begging her to stop. She wanted to. She wanted nothing more than to shut her mouth.

But the word-vomit was overwhelming, a projectile coming before she could stop it, completely out of her control.

Silence did this to her.

"Huge dick too."

If Lizzie was uncomfortable in the silence before, it was nothing compared to the silence that struck the group after.

"Oh, Lizzie," Harper whispered, ducking her face to her hand to shield her from the secondhand embarrassment. Indira let out a huge laugh before slamming her mouth shut.

Rake gaped at Lizzie, his face turning white, then pink, then red, then purple. He looked like he wanted to strangle her.

She wished he would.

Her absolute anguish must have been obvious because his anger softened a degree. He screwed up his face tight, eyes squeezing shut, forehead creasing with deep lines, then visibly relaxed like the snap of a released rubber band. His eyes opened, and he gave her a tense but understanding smile.

"And this is Lizzie," he said, keeping his eyes on hers. "She's American. Average height. Great tits. Lovely ass. Likes to embarrass me. We're . . . friends."

"Really great friends," Lizzie added. The type of friends who were so close, they made a baby after knowing each other for forty-eight hours! Yay friendship!

A thick cloud of awkwardness hugged the group, no one knowing what else to say. The tension of it made Lizzie want to scream, but instead, she shuffled her feet, concentrating on keeping them in a single square tile on the floor in an odd little jig of uncomfortableness.

Dan's eyes flicked from her feet to her face, and the kindness and understanding in his look allowed Lizzie to let out a breath. Dan gave her an almost imperceptible nod.

"Table for Dan?" the hostess called from her stand, gathering menus.

"Oh, thank God," Lizzie burst out, her shoulders drooping from released tension. "This was getting a little awkward."

"A little?" Thu said, fixing Lizzie with a look before turning and following the hostess, Harper, Indira, and Rake trailing behind her. Dan laughed, bringing Lizzie into a side hug and walking her toward the waiting hostess.

"I've missed you saying exactly what everyone's thinking," he said, giving her a squeeze. "Don't worry, it can only get better from here," he added, before releasing her as they walked to their table in a single-file line.

Once they were seated around the table with drinks ordered, conversations started to flow. Harper filled everyone in on the gruesome surgeries she'd performed recently, describing them with a grin like the bloodthirsty little angel she was. Thu talked about how much she hated Los Angeles but was glad she'd found a friend in her residency program. Dan said something boring about numbers that made Lizzie's brain groan but had Harper smiling at him like he placed every star in the sky.

And through it all, Lizzie's phone buzzed nonstop on her lap, rotating messages from Indira, Thu, and Harper flooding the group chat so aggressively Lizzie couldn't comprehend how they were also carrying on a verbal conversation.

> Indira
> Lizzie, who is this guy?

> Thu
> what fresh hell is this dearest Elizabeth?

> Harper
> Lizzie!!!!! Do you have a boyfriend???

Thu

Indira, has Lizzie brought him to your apartment
before?

Indira

I've never seen him. She's never even mentioned
him before

Indira

he hot AF tho

Thu

answer us Liz

When it became obvious Lizzie wasn't going to answer their
texts, Thu decided to slap her metaphorical dick on the table
and get straight to it.

"So, how long have you two known each other?" she asked,
taking a sip of wine.

Rake and Lizzie flashed each other a glance before looking
down at their plates. "A few weeks," Lizzie said, dragging her
fork along the tablecloth.

"How'd you meet?" Harper said.

"At a bar," Lizzie responded, craning her neck to look for
their waitress. Having food to cram into her mouth would be
ideal at this moment. She felt the truth scrambling out of her
throat, and she instinctively knew its delivery would be less than
ideal.

"Do you live in the city?" Dan asked Rake.

"I don't, actually. I live in Sydney."

Her friends shot her a curious look at that news.

"And what are your intentions with our lovely Elizabeth?"
Indira said, a hint of a laugh in her voice. "You better not whisk
her across the globe from me."

Rake cleared his throat. "Uh. We . . ."

"What was that?" Thu pressed, sensing his discomfort and pouncing like a tiger on meat. Lizzie's pulse started to punch painfully at her throat, her leg jiggling below the table.

"We're . . . Lizzie and I . . ." Rake trailed off, looking at Lizzie.

"You're . . . ?" Thu repeated.

"I'm pregnant," Lizzie blurted out. And the impact seemed to freeze her friends in place, a piece of bread falling from Indira's fingers, Harper's wineglass halfway to her mouth, Dan's eyes large and dazed as he stared at a spot on the table.

Thu was the first to move, violently shaking her head as if she were removing water from her ears. "You're what?" she said, her voice barely a whisper.

"Knocked up. Bun in the oven. Good ole Rake over here basted my turkey with that massive dong," Lizzie said, nodding toward Rake on her right. She let out a booming laugh of discomfort that made everyone jump.

"What are you going to do?" Thu said, her voice rising. "What's your plan? How long have you known? Why didn't you tell us?"

Lizzie shrugged, dragging her thumbnail across the table.

"What are you going to do, Lizzie?" Thu repeated.

"Thu, come on," Harper said quietly, putting a hand on Thu's forearm. Thu whipped her arm away from her.

"Don't give me that 'come on.' What am I supposed to say? Congratulations on your massive accident?"

"Hey!" Lizzie said, her voice rising. While, yes, le bébé was an accident, it was *her* accident. And she was already quite fond of said accident.

"No," Thu pressed back, never one to beat around the bush or approach a subject with delicacy. "I'm not going to sit here and pretend with you all that this is some great news. You don't even know this guy."

"I know him!" Lizzie said.

"Yeah? What's his middle name?"

Silence.

"How about his birthday? You know that one, Lizzie? Or does he have any siblings?"

Lizzie crossed her arms over her chest and stared down at her lap like a pouty child, shame pricking through her like needles.

"How did this happen?" Thu said.

"Well," Lizzie said, eyes still fixed on her lap, "when a man and a woman get super horny and rub their naughty bits together—"

"Lizzie, stop." Thu's face was serious and stern. "You're an adult. How do you not know the fundamental basics of not getting fucking pregnant?"

"Because I'm a moron, I guess!" Lizzie burst out, hot tears stinging at her eyes. "Because it never occurred to me to check the expiration date on a condom! It's rubber, for fuck's sake, not a carton of milk!"

"You have more sex than anyone I know. How did you even manage to let one expire?"

Lizzie opened her mouth to offer some weak excuse, but the low rumble of Rake's voice cut her off.

"I think it's time you stop talking."

Lizzie's head whipped around to look at him. He was staring straight at Thu, whose eyes widened in shock.

"*Excuse me?*" Thu said, fixing him with a terrifying glare.

"I mean this with as much respect as possible, but you need to stop. Now."

The entire table was frozen in another stunned silence. Harper and Dan shared a similar mask of horror, while Indira's jaw was almost resting on the table. No one *ever* told Thu to do anything, let alone stop talking. Rake had unwittingly stepped into a minefield.

Without warning, Thu threw her head back and laughed, making everyone jump. Ending the cackle as abruptly as she'd started it, she pointed a finger at Rake. "You don't tell me what to do, asshole."

Rake held up his palms in defense. "I'm sorry, but I'm not going to sit here and listen to you berate Lizzie like this. Do you really think she isn't confused enough? That *we* aren't confused enough? And scared shitless and asking ourselves all these same questions? Because we are. Was this planned? No. Do we have a plan? Not really, but we're working on it. You shaming her isn't going to make this process any easier. Lizzie doesn't need someone pointing out all the reasons this situation is less than ideal. She needs a friend." Rake turned suddenly, aggressively, to face Lizzie. She stared at him with wide eyes. "My middle name is Arthur. I was born on January 23. I'm an only child."

Rake continued to stare at her, Lizzie blinking back, trying to process all the different signals vying for her attention. After a moment Rake cocked an impatient eyebrow.

"Well?" he pressed, waving his hand. "Tell me yours."

Lizzie snapped out of it. "My middle name is Marie. It's boring and common, and I've always hated it. I was born on April 1, and I have an older brother named Ryan. And a sister-in-law named Mary. She's perfect."

Rake nodded once. "Great. I look forward to meeting them." Then, without preamble, he turned back to the table, clapping his hands together. "Now that Lizzie and I obviously know each other, I think it's best if we go. You've sufficiently upset her, and I'd like to take her home to rest." He stood, holding out a hand for Lizzie.

In a daze, she took it, looking between her friends. Indira's mouth still dangled open, and Thu sat there with a blank look on her face, the first time Lizzie had ever seen her lost for words.

Harper's eyes flicked back and forth between Lizzie and Rake in a blur, but Dan met Lizzie's gaze with an unabashed grin, one eyebrow giving the subtlest arch of approval before Rake placed his hand on Lizzie's lower back and guided her to the door.

Chapter 19

THE walk home with Lizzie was silent. Sad.

At a bodega near Rake's hotel, Lizzie stopped, telling him to wait there as she popped inside. After a few minutes, she reappeared in front of him, plastic bag swinging, as they continued their silent walk back to the hotel and up to his room.

Inside, Lizzie kicked off her sandals and pulled the earrings from her ears, tossing them on the dresser.

Rake leaned against the wall, watching her. "Do you want to talk about it?" he asked. He had absolutely no clue what the right words would be for this situation.

"No," she snapped, moving farther into the room. Rake blew out a breath. He didn't know how to do this. Any of it. She needed comfort and support, and all he was capable of was standing there like an absolute twat as she continued to hurt.

"I'm gonna have a shower, then," he said, heading toward the bathroom.

He rinsed off quickly, replaying the disastrous dinner on loop. He sensed the true gravity of Lizzie's hurt when he walked back into the room twenty minutes later and found her sitting on the bed, eyes somewhere far away while tears rolled down her cheeks. In a dazed state, she brought the nozzle of a whipped cream canister to her lips and sprayed a mountain of foam into her mouth.

Rake felt rooted to the spot. He didn't know her well enough to know how to help her. She had said she didn't want to talk about it, and he didn't want to push her, but he also didn't know how to comfort her.

Rake cleared his throat, and Lizzie slowly resurfaced from the deep recesses of her thoughts, blinking and looking around the room until her eyes landed on his. They stared at each other for a moment, the heavy weight of vulnerability threatening to push them deep into their awkward shells.

Then, she gave him a sad smile and held out the whipped cream can. Rake moved into action, sliding onto his side of the bed and leaning on the headboard next to her. He took the can and squirted a mouthful of whipped cream into his mouth, passing it back to her. They sat like that for a few minutes, the hiss of the whipped cream nozzle filling the room.

"Still don't want to talk about it?" he asked, then opened his mouth wide for Lizzie to fill it with the sugary sweetness. He'd forgotten how delicious whipped cream was. But everything seemed to taste better around Lizzie.

"No," she responded curtly, nearly drowning him in cream then filling her own throat.

Rake swallowed and nodded. "Okay." He opened his mouth again for another hit.

She looked at him for a second, almost like she expected him to push.

Rake saw the exact moment wariness was replaced with mischievousness in her golden eyes. She brought the can to his face, but instead of putting the nozzle in his mouth, she moved it at the last moment and dropped a dollop on his nose.

"Oh my God, are you serious?" Rake said, fluffy bunches of cream blowing from his nostrils at the laugh he couldn't hold in.

Lizzie let out her signature sonic boom of a giggle, giving him a whipped cream mustache for good measure.

"I just showered!" He jolted away from another incoming attack, turning and rolling so her hand with the can was pinned to the mattress and her laughing smile right below him.

"You look so nice, though!" Lizzie said between giggles. "Good enough to eat."

"Oh yeah? Let's decorate you then," he said. Her eyes went wide with surprise and amusement as he pressed his nose against hers, dragging his face down to her neck and chin as she writhed and laughed beneath him.

"Stop! You'll make a mess!" she gasped out as he moved one hand to tickle her waist.

Rake pulled back to give her a sardonic look. "Oh, we can't have that now. I would *hate* for this to turn into a mess," he said, scooping his finger through the fluff on her chin and bringing it to his mouth. He forgot that she still had the weapon, though, and she used it. She bucked up, throwing him off-balance, and she used the momentum to roll on top of him, grabbing his jaw with one hand and adding a beard to her creation with the other.

Rake let out an exaggerated groan, pretending to fight her off just enough to turn her laughs into screeches of joy. She planted a hand next to his head, leaning forward so her nose almost touched his as she gasped for air between giggles.

It felt like he'd just won the lottery, seeing her laugh. The realization that he'd do anything to make her smile, act any type of fool to see that pain drain from her eyes, hit him hard and fast.

She continued to hover over him, eyes wild and chest heaving as she worked to catch her breath. They shared a smile. An intimate, delicious, decadent smile that sent a sharp bolt of lust down Rake's body to his groin, right where Lizzie straddled him.

Her eyes heated and her body pressed ever so slightly closer to his as she continued to look at him, her sheet of red hair falling over one of her shoulders and trapping them in a soft, glowing cage.

Rake reached up his hand, unable to control it, and brushed his knuckles along her jaw, dragging his thumb over her parted lips.

The touch popped their bubble, reality flooding in at the edges as the echoes of their laughter dimmed, the sounds of traffic floating in through the open window reminding them where they were. What they were.

Lizzie cleared her throat, her smile turning into something stiff and fake as she slid off him in retreat. She put the can of whipped cream on the nightstand and padded to the bathroom. Rake heard her turn on the tap, and he worked to get his spiraling mind and lust-filled body back under control.

The thought of them having sex and getting it out of their system flashed across his mind, but he knew that wouldn't do any good. Not for him at least. There was no reason to complicate things more with intimacy and sex. He needed moments like this to stop happening. Silly moments of play that seemed to spark a fire of want for his untouchable . . . what? Friend? Mother of his child?

She walked back to the bed, damp washcloth in hand. She moved to wipe his cheeks, clean him off, but seemed to think better of doing it herself and handed him the towel. He took it with a silent thanks and scrubbed it over his face, wanting the coarse fibers to wash away the dangerous feelings that seemed to be staining his skin.

These feelings were not real. Rake wasn't supposed to have these feelings at all. Emotionlessness had served him well for the past few years, and there was no reason to reacquaint himself with them. He didn't deserve happiness. Didn't qualify for domestic bliss, the ghosts of his past rattling their chains in his mind and sobering him up from the weird fantasyland he and Lizzie seemed to exist in.

After cleaning off their faces, they worked in silent tandem, stripping off the soiled comforter and pulling back the clean sheet beneath. They plopped into the bed with a safety net of inches between them. Rake stared up at the ceiling, images of his ex, Shannon, floating just above him.

Had he ever felt this way with her? If he had, he couldn't remember. And it seemed impossible to forget joy like this. But what he and Lizzie had wasn't real. Couldn't last. People passed one another in fragments, broken pieces fruitlessly searching for a nonexistent other half, hurting each other more in the process. It was all bullshit, and he'd do well to remember that.

"I wish I wasn't like this." Lizzie's words startled him, and he jumped. He'd thought she'd fallen asleep.

"Like what?" he asked.

"This wrecking ball of a person. I wish I didn't act on impulse and say stupid shit and do stupid things and break any relationship I'm ever lucky enough to build."

The words were raw and honest, and Rake could hear the tears behind them. He didn't know what to say. So instead, he reached out his hand, breaching the valley of sheets between them, and wrapped his fingers in hers. She let out a shuddering breath at his touch and gripped his hand like it was her life preserver in a storm.

"I don't think you break things, Lizzie," he said after a few minutes. She let out a disbelieving snort. "I really don't. I think you make things better. A lot better."

They didn't say anything else after that; the only sound in the room was their mingled breathing mixing with the summer night and city traffic. Rake eventually heard Lizzie's breathing turn into a soft rhythm of sleep, fueling his racing thoughts. He and Lizzie were a mix of blurred lines and one hundred different shades of gray, something undefined, not entirely real.

But her pain was real. It was real and sharp, and he decided then and there that he didn't like it poking at her. And his last thought before falling asleep was that he'd do whatever it took to stop her from hurting. For the sake of their baby, of course.

In the morning, Rake woke to Lizzie staring at him, wide-eyed, and looking more than a little alarming.

"All right, let's do it," she said, before he even had a chance to offer her a good morning.

"Do what?" he asked, still half asleep.

"Live together. Coparent. All that jazz."

Rake blinked as her words soaked into him. A slow smile broke across his mouth. "Really? This is great, I'll—"

"But I have one rule," Lizzie said, placing a finger against his lips, her eyes level and serious. "You can't fall in love with me."

Rake jerked his head back, bashing it against the headboard. He tried to say something—anything—but the words got stuck in his throat and he started spluttering and coughing.

No. No, no, no. Absolutely not, he thought. *I won't fall in love. I doubt I'm even capable of it.* But he couldn't get any of this out as he choked on his own tongue.

Lizzie's stern mouth suddenly broke into a grin, and she started to laugh. "Oh my God, you should see your face." She snorted as she laughed harder. "Calm down, I'm messing with you. I couldn't let an opportunity to drop a classic rom-com line pass me by, though, could I?"

She let out one more laugh before sitting up and getting out of bed, buzzing around the hotel room in a flurry of energy that seemed to have a distinct Lizzie signature to it.

Rake let out a silent sigh of relief. *Good*, he thought. *Good, good, good.*

They were on the same page. No relationship. No love.

Purely platonic coparenting.

Nothing could go wrong.

Chapter 20

Week six, baby is the size of a rainbow sprinkle.

A few hours after Rake left for the airport to catch his flight back to Australia, Lizzie was thanking the goddesses above and below for finally sending her a job interview. After hanging up with a cranky-sounding woman named Bernadette and jotting down the address to the aptly named Bernadette's Bakery for her interview in a few hours, Lizzie squealed then spun in a quick circle around the kitchen floor before ransacking her pantry.

Maybe things will actually work out, she thought as she stood at the stove, whisking her Bad-Ass-Bitch Banana Pudding into luscious smoothness, the soft and delicate scent of vanilla and bananas wrapping around her like a comforting blanket.

Maybe.

As long as she actually got the job, kept the job, figured out how and when to ask for time off for doctor's appointments, magically secured health insurance, and got adequate maternity leave.

The joys (logistical nightmares) of motherhood were filling her already.

The front door opened as she took her mixture off the stove to cool, and Indira, Harper, and Thu's voices filled the apartment. They stopped in their tracks as they rounded the corner to the living room, obviously not expecting Lizzie to be there. She instantly felt so awkward that she did an odd little toe-ball-heel shuffle across the floor to grab a box of vanilla wafers and expel the energy pulsing through her.

"Hi," Lizzie said at last, giving them a flap of a wave with the cookies in hand.

"Hi," Indira said back, crossing the space to wrap her arms around Lizzie in a hug. "We're sorry," she added, placing a kiss on Lizzie's temple.

Lizzie pulled back, tucking her hair behind her ears as she stared down at the floor. "Nothing to be sorry about," she said. "I'm the one that's the idiot."

"You're not," Harper said, giving Lizzie a similar hug. "We were surprised and caught off guard and definitely didn't say the right things . . . Right, Thu?"

Lizzie glanced over at Thu, who still hovered across the room, looking down at the ground. After a beat she looked up, meeting Lizzie's eyes. "I'm sorry," she said. And Lizzie almost fainted from the shock of it. Thu wasn't one to apologize, whether she was wrong or not.

"You really don't have to be," Lizzie said, waving her hands to dispel the tension. She would rather not talk about it. She would rather avoid revisiting the words said between them until the day she died. Then she wouldn't have to feel them.

"No, Lizzie, I do. I was judgmental and bitchy, and I know that . . . Harper and Indira have made sure I know that," she said, flashing the friends a sheepish grin. "But I . . . I worry about you . . . That maybe you won't make the best decisions for yourself, and the last thing I want is to see you hurt. But it isn't my place to judge you. I'm supposed to be your cheerleader, not your mother."

Lizzie swallowed past the lump in her throat, doing a full-body shake to rid herself of the choked-up feeling. She walked across the apartment and gave Thu a giant hug.

"Thank you, Thu-Thu." Lizzie pulled back, looking around at her friends. "I'm really fucking scared," she admitted.

"Do you want to talk about it?" Harper asked, pouring herself a cup of coffee at the counter then moving to the couch. The rest of them followed suit.

Lizzie plopped down on the cushions, all the air leaving her body in a massive sigh. She launched into how she met Rake and their resulting two-night stand. She explained about the condom and taking the pregnancy tests and calling Rake. She told them everything except for the teeny-tiny, minuscule, probably-just-indigestion pangs of feeling in her chest for him. Because Lizzie didn't do relationships. She'd been told her whole life what a burden her feelings were to others, and she'd rather die than subject a partner to that.

"So where did you and Rake leave things?" Indira asked.

"Well, we decided to coparent and stuff. One of his parents is originally from the U.S. so he has dual citizenship, apparently. He also mentioned some job opportunity here that he's going to take."

"And what will coparenting look like?" Thu asked.

Lizzie shrugged. "Uh, well, I think maybe it's going to look like he and I . . . uh . . . living together?" Lizzie shot a quick glance at Indira to see how she was taking the news. The pair had known each other since high school and lived together for the last five years, taking many drunken vows to die together in their apartment.

Indira nodded, unlatching the iron grip of nerves around Lizzie's heart. "I totally get it."

"Are you two, like, *together*?" Harper asked.

Lizzie shook her head. "No. Definitely not. We don't . . . I don't think we . . . We don't feel *that way* for each other. It's more of a totally-platonic-roommates-who-happened-to-have-had-really-great-sex-a-few-times-and-then-made-a-baby situation."

"Pretty run-of-the-mill stuff," Thu added dryly, smiling at Lizzie.

"I know it isn't *normal*," Lizzie said, adding air quotes around the last word. "But I think it kind of makes sense . . . right? We'll both be around to raise le bébé, split finances, et cetera, et cetera. And if it totally sucks, then we get our own places or whatever. I don't know." Lizzie pressed one hand over her thrumming heart and the other over her rolling tummy, feeling overwhelmed.

"And are you going to bone this platonic roommate?" Indira asked, arching a perfect, thick eyebrow.

"We haven't talked about it, but I'm not exactly *opposed* to the idea," Lizzie said, plucking at the couch. The truth was, she'd been dreaming about Rake, naked and sweaty with his head between her thighs, every night since they'd met, and the idea was creeping into her daytime psyche too.

"That sounds a bit messy," Thu said, a soft warning in her voice.

"When am I not?" Lizzie said with a laugh. "And it's just sex. We're both adults. It's fine." The room was quiet for a moment while they all turned that over.

"When are you guys leaving?" Lizzie asked Thu and Harper.

"Thu's flight leaves tonight, and Dan and I are taking the train back to New York at five."

Lizzie nodded, sadness poking at the soft spot between her ribs at the impending goodbye.

"I actually better get going," Lizzie said, glancing at the time on her phone. "I have an interview at a bakery in Fishtown—I'll clean up the kitchen when I get back, Dira," Lizzie said, standing and taking in the mess she'd made. "Thank you guys for . . ." Lizzie flapped her hands at them, feeling overcome with emotions again.

"We'll always be here for you, Lizzie," Harper said, standing to give her a hug. Thu and Indira latched on, and they stayed like that for a few heartbeats, their golden thread of friendship weaving and buzzing through their veins, binding them together.

Eventually, Lizzie disentangled herself, grabbed her purse, and headed for her interview.

* * *

BERNADETTE'S BAKERY WAS in a squat, yellow building off the main strip of Fishtown's thriving, eclectic neighborhood. Pushing through the heavy front door, Lizzie was hit by the familiar smell of sugar and bread and comfort, the constant perfume of her job. She could get high off the sweetness.

But a quick glance around the small shop showed a bakery that looked . . . not great.

Three small tables were crammed in, and a huge but nearly empty pastry case sat by the register. The menu was written in fading chalk on the back wall, smudged in multiple spots. The small glimpse she caught of the back kitchen through the swinging door window looked similarly shoddy.

Whatever.

Lizzie could make due working under a bridge with a trash can fire if it meant she was earning wages.

A tall, older woman stepped out from the kitchen, the mass of her frizzy gray hair nearly touching both sides of the doorway. She pulled off her yellow apron, revealing a billowy top and a long skirt. She had thick glasses and a sharp nose that she looked down as she evaluated Lizzie.

"Hi," Lizzie said at last. Something about the woman was both beautiful and terrifying. "I'm Lizzie. I'm here for the job interview."

Bernadette nodded, eyeing Lizzie closely for a long moment before saying, "Hello. I'd had a feeling our auras would be complementary. Let's take a seat and get to it."

She swept toward the closest table, her multicolored skirt like a fluffy cloud around her ankles.

"My . . . my aura? You can see my aura?" Lizzie asked, taking the seat opposite Bernadette.

Bernadette nodded.

"What color is it?" Lizzie asked, her voice rising and eyes widening with excitement.

"Magenta," Bernadette said, pulling a pencil from behind her ear and a notepad from her skirt pocket. "You have strong blue emissions indicating your creativity, but it's mixed with a vibrant red, which tells me you have a deep connection with the physical world."

"No arguing with that," Lizzie said with a lascivious wink. Bernadette blinked at her.

"The colors combine for your magenta emission, indicating you are high-energy and innovative in taking physical substances and stretching them to new forms."

"No shit?" Lizzie said, leaning back in her chair. "That's so cool. What color is yours?"

Bernadette tilted her head to the side, studying Lizzie for a moment before saying, "Indigo. Shall we proceed with the interview?"

Lizzie nodded, making a mental note to research the hell out of auras when she got home.

Bernadette asked Lizzie a few standard questions about availability and experience, and Lizzie went into her strengths, discussing her skills with innovative frostings and clever takes on traditional pastry shapes and designs.

The interview was going surprisingly well. Lizzie tended to overshare or say something profane or obnoxious when she got excited talking, which she always did when it came to baking, but she and Bernadette found an easy flow. The truth was, it was the one thing in the world Lizzie really believed she was good at. She ditched hobbies at an extraordinary speed, throwing herself into them like a maniac of enjoyment and burning out of interest just as fast if she wasn't instantly an expert at it.

Something about baking—the measuring, mixing, experimenting—allowed her energy to hyper-focus on the task and provided an outlet for her hands to work and shape and play for hours of enjoyment.

Lizzie described her most recent large undertaking—a "cake" for a beach-themed wedding that was more like an art installation. The display covered a large table made to look like the shore, sugary sand and small cakes decorated so realistically like shells and driftwood that some guests were nervous to try them.

Bernadette paused the conversation, letting the silence grow as she eyed Lizzie like she was deciding how much she could trust her. Lizzie blinked back.

"If I hypothetically told you I ran a discreet business on the side, what would you say?" Bernadette finally said, steepling her fingers in front of her.

Lizzie's eyes flicked around the shop, trying to look thoughtful when she was really just confused about whatever the hell the eccentric old woman was talking about. Her eyes landed on a plate of brownies sitting on the counter.

"Oh." Lizzie nodded wisely. "Pot. I'm cool with it, Bernadette. I'm no narc," she said, shooting her a wink.

"What? No," Bernadette said, shaking her head. "I'm not selling weed brownies. It's something else."

"What?" Lizzie asked, leaning closer, a fun thrill of suspense chasing down her spine.

"I . . . hypothetically, might sell"—Bernadette looked over both shoulders despite her and Lizzie being the only ones in the shop—"erotic pastries under the table."

Lizzie was silent for a solid minute, letting that phrase loop around in her mind, before she erupted in laughter. "I— hypothetically—could never think of a job I was better suited for. So you sell . . . what? Penis cakes?"

Bernadette looked offended. "It's not just cock and balls, my dear. These are artistic pieces made with the highest degree of craftsmanship. And the phallic form is so overdone. I specialize in yonic work."

Lizzie gave Bernadette a clueless look.

"Vulvas," she said with a wave of her hand.

Lizzie's eyebrows shot up, her lips pursing in interest. "I'm listening."

"Vulvas, breasts, buttocks . . . all represented in the baked form. Is this work you'd be comfortable doing?"

"Comfortable? Oh, Bernadette, I've been whipping up sexually suggestive croissants and tarts for years. I don't think there's a job I could be more comfortable doing."

"Mind you, these are for our private orders. We have to project a more . . . conventional front for our day-to-day customers."

Lizzie looked around the empty shop, wondering how many of those she would actually be dealing with. "I understand, but maybe if you forced more people to eat pussy-shaped croustades, they'd be less hesitant to eat pussy in other scenarios."

Bernadette's eyes went wide, then she pursed her lips, looking off like she was contemplating the truth in that.

"Who's your main, uh, clientele?"

Bernadette looked a bit sheepish for a second. "Primarily my wife and I's friends and any word of mouth they generate. I'm starting to get more requests than I can track alone, but not enough to base the business off it."

"Would you like to base the business off it?"

Bernadette thought for a moment. "I'd like to sell my products to anyone interested without having my whole shop shut down by angry prudes," she said at last, giving a brisk nod.

Lizzie couldn't help but smile. "Maybe I could help you?"

"How so?" Bernadette asked, tilting her head as she studied Lizzie.

"I don't know, get some hype on Instagram? TikTok? Make

a website? I think if we work on a set menu, things that are clever without being gratuitous, we could maybe generate a pretty solid client base. Especially in this area," Lizzie said, referring to Fishtown's more eccentric tastes. "We could start with online orders, and if they're popular, we can slowly incorporate them into the shop? Not to take away from your, uh, other offerings." Lizzie glanced at the desolate pastry display. Bernadette's eyes lingered there too. "This could be amazing. Celebrate the human body, be creative and fun with it . . . or it could be a disaster. Who knows. But I'm willing to do whatever you need of me."

Bernadette continued to stare at the glass display, lost in her thoughts. After a moment, she let out a gentle humming noise, turning back to Lizzie.

"When can you start?"

Chapter 21

RAKE was learning that convincing his boss to give him a job he previously said he didn't want and then have him send Rake across the globe for said job was a bit more complicated than expected.

He'd been in meeting after meeting, often at odd hours, to accommodate Dominic, who was already in the U.S. setting up shop. Dominic had been hesitant at first, wary that Rake's previous dismissal of the position indicated he wasn't enough of a team player to help Onism's U.S. introduction develop roots. But Rake could be charming and convincing when he needed and had a good track record to prove his skills. He eventually secured a spot as an associate creative director for Onism's U.S. East Coast division.

The rest of his time in Sydney was spent balancing work demands with packing up his sparse possessions and figuring out where he would be living in Philadelphia.

His job had offered him a decent relocation budget that he was trying to stay well within the confines of, searching place after place online, not wanting to bother Lizzie with going to look for him.

When the clock had all but run out, options being snatched up quicker than he could inquire about them on Philly's competitive housing market, he put a deposit down on a furnished unit not far from where Lizzie was currently living, hoping the proximity would make the transition to living with him a bit easier.

What he should have realized was Lizzie probably wanted at least a little bit of say in where they would be living.

"You *what*?" Lizzie asked after Rake told her he signed a lease. He pulled the phone away to protect his ear from her pitch and volume.

"I found us a place."

"And you didn't think to, oh, I don't know, *tell* me about it? Or have me go see it?"

"You're mad," Rake said slowly, his heart sinking. He had thought taking care of this, putting as little stress on Lizzie as possible, would be the right thing. The chivalrous thing.

"Yeah, I'm mad. I would have liked a *say* in the matter. Since I'll be *living* there and all."

"I thought I was being helpful," Rake said weakly. Lizzie huffed.

"Well, tell me about it," she said, annoyance still in her voice.

This was the part Rake was also mildly nervous about. He knew there were a few . . . flaws in the layout of the unit, but it was a steal, and the landlord had agreed to a six-month lease, which meant Rake and Lizzie weren't tied down for too long if it didn't work. He had been so desperate to secure *something*, he might not have thought it all the way through.

"Well," he started, clearing his throat, "it's a newly converted warehouse. 'Industrial luxury' was what the Realtor called it. New appliances. Lots of windows, so good light. I thought you'd probably like lots of windows."

Rake had seen the huge expanse of windows spanning a wall of the unit and had instantly thought of Lizzie, the way she would look with sunlight dancing on the flames of her hair as she stared out over the city. The pang of affection he'd felt at the image was entirely unnerving, but made him click "submit" faster on the application than he'd care to admit.

"How many bedrooms?" Lizzie asked, not jumping at the excitement of natural light as much as Rake had hoped.

"Well, that's kind of the one downside."

"Downside?"

"It's a big space. Huge, really, for Philadelphia at least. Eleven hundred square feet, but the rent was comparable to places half that size."

"*But?*" Lizzie said impatiently, the syllable indicating that she would strangle Rake right now if she could reach him.

"But it's technically zero, um, bedrooms."

Lizzie was silent on the line, and Rake double-checked that the call hadn't dropped. "You still there?"

"What do you mean it's zero bedrooms?" Lizzie hissed.

"It's a studio. A big studio," he added quickly. "Giant. But there's no, um, doors or technical bedrooms."

Lizzie's voice was chillingly quiet. "And how exactly are we going to make that work, Rake?"

"I was thinking . . . Well, I don't have it fully figured out—"

"Title of our memoir," Lizzie grumbled.

"*But* I think it will actually work to our advantage. The space is open-floor and big enough we can both fit our beds, and then we can set up the crib near us, and we won't have to deal with, uh, opening doors and . . . stuff."

"Well, thank God you've relieved me of *that* hassle. Not sure what I would do if I had to open one more *door*."

"There's other good stuff about it too," he pushed on. "It's a furnished unit, for one, so we don't have to buy a bunch of new furniture. And I looked and saw there was a highly rated day-care nearby. The park is only a few blocks away, which will be great to take the baby when the weather's good. Close to grocery stores and the like. I just . . . I don't know. I guess I didn't think it through. Or I did think but not the right way."

Lizzie was silent on the line again, and Rake's heart nearly bruised his sternum with its pounding strikes. Shame washed over him. He was already fucking up. Failing her. Like he seemed to do to every woman in his life.

"Do you want me to try and get us out of it?" Rake said with a sigh, pinching the bridge of his nose.

Lizzie was silent for another moment before saying, "Send me pictures of it. I want to see."

He put her on speakerphone then sent over the link, crossing his fingers and toes that she would like those fucking windows with all their fucking light and maybe save his ass.

He waited a moment, letting her scroll through. "Well?" he said at last.

"It looks really, really nice," Lizzie said, her voice sounding tired. She sounded tired a lot lately, and for some bizarre reason, the idea of her being weary without him there to help her plucked oddly at the base of his throat. Weird.

"Okay," she said after another moment. "What the hell. Let's go for it. That rent can't be beat."

"Really?" Rake asked, relief flooding him.

"Yeah, I do really like those windows," Lizzie said with a tiny laugh, and confirmation that she liked them made him want to punch his fist in the air. Which was also weird.

"I'll try and set up a time to look at the daycare you mentioned," Lizzie added. "Indira, all-knowing-goddess-of-things that she is, mentioned daycare wait lists are long as hell. I already have a few places I've found to put our name down if that's okay with you."

"That's perfect. This'll be great. We'll make it great."

"LOL. It will be pure chaos, and it's best you realize that now," she said, giggling. "I gotta run. I'll talk to you soon."

She hung up, and Rake brought his phone down to his chest, tapping it against the organ in there that seemed to be acting up.

* * *

TIME FLEW BY after that, Rake making his way through an end-less list of work and personal tasks to get done before the move.

For her part, Lizzie seemed to be throwing herself into the deepest corners of the internet with pregnancy research, send-ing Rake weekly texts and keeping him thoroughly updated on every time she puked and just how badly her boobs still hurt. A few days before his move, she sent him a message that stopped him in his tracks and made everything feel that much realer.

Do you want to go to the first ultrasound? Followed immedi-ately by: No pressure or whatever.

Of course he wanted to go. The idea of *not* being there was unthinkable, and he told her such. In a much less dramatic way, of course.

On Rake's final day in Sydney, he drove out of the city to visit his parents. He pulled up in front of the short picket fence surrounding the bungalow he'd grown up in. He stared at the home for a few minutes, suddenly desperate to memorize every crack in the walk-up, every leaf of his mum's rosebushes. He was feeling a bit . . . sentimental? Perhaps? It was hard to know for sure because Rake picked up the emotion by its scruff and tossed it right out of his brain.

Eventually, he pulled himself out of the trance and headed inside.

"Oh, sweetheart," his mum, Leanne, said by way of greeting, wrapping him in a hug as he stepped into the kitchen. Rake stooped down a bit to accommodate her, giving her a gentle pat on the back. "I hope you're hungry," Leanne said, pulling away and trying to subtly wipe the tears from her cheeks. "Your dad has enough food on the barbie to feed an army."

"I simply cook whatever she hands me," Rake's dad, Peter, said, as he walked in through the sliding doors from the back-yard. "Learned long ago not to ask questions," Peter added, shooting Leanne a cheeky wink as she swatted at him with her towel. Rake smiled.

Peter placed a plate of grilled prawns and a platter stacked with enough meat to feed a family of ten at the center of the table.

"How's Lizzie?" Leanne asked as she scooped some salad onto her plate.

Rake had one of those bizarrely healthy relationships with his parents, and he'd told them both everything when he'd returned from seeing Lizzie. While his mum had shed some tears over him moving so far away, she'd been supportive of the situation and had asked Rake about Lizzie every day for weeks.

"She's good," Rake said. "Told me yesterday she feels like she's carrying a big wheel of cheese."

Peter snorted.

"Oh Lord, I remember that feeling, even thirty years later," Leanne said, shooting Rake a smile. "Felt the size of a house."

"She was the cutest thing I've ever seen," Peter said, beaming at his wife. Rake looked on as they glanced at each other with such natural affection.

He wondered why he didn't have that gene, why it felt so unnatural for him to show endearment. Not that he wanted the capability. Fondness led to hurt, and Rake was not interested in *that* experience again, thank you very much.

His parents chattered on in earnest—his mum discussing her book club, his dad talking about their plans to visit friends in Melbourne in a few weeks—and Rake let their words flow around him like a river of contentment. He'd miss them like hell.

When the time finally came for goodbye, both of his parents misty-eyed as they wrapped him in tight hugs, something sharp and strong poked at Rake's ribs and throat, but he pushed it away.

Everything would be okay. It had to be.

Chapter 22

RAKE could barely keep his eyes open as the Lyft made its way from the Philadelphia airport to Lizzie's apartment.

The flight had been long and grueling, the line to get through customs and security even longer. Lizzie had offered to come get him in Indira's car, which they were using to move their stuff to the new apartment, but Rake decided it would be easier for her to focus on getting herself organized and they'd meet at her place.

The car pulled up to the curb, and Rake hopped out, grabbing his two large suitcases from the trunk and giving the driver a quick *thanks*.

Packing had been laughably easy. He'd been able to fit most of his wardrobe into one suitcase, using the other for some work things, a few books, and other odds and ends like sheets and towels. He had sold or donated everything else, wondering if his lack of attachment or sentimental value to anything in his old place meant he was emotionally evolved or just really fucking sad.

Double-checking the address, Rake punched in the door code Lizzie had texted him, then let himself into the building and up the elevator to her floor.

When the flight had taken off and Rake stared down at his

disappearing country, he'd felt something close to . . . well, something kind of close to excitement, at seeing Lizzie again. Which was bizarre, and he shook it off as stress at the time. But now, as he knocked on her door, all he felt was a bone-deep tiredness and an exceptionally strong desire to get all of this done with quickly so he could fall asleep for the next forty-eight hours.

The door swung open, and for a moment, Rake's heart sparked in preparation for Lizzie's brilliant smile, the brick wall of energy that always seemed to crash into him when he laid his eyes on her.

All very normal, emotionally distant physical responses that he was sure he only felt because she was carrying their child.

But instead, Lizzie looked frazzled and pale, a clumped mix of sweat and what looked like flour streaked across her forehead, while alarming splotches of red decorated her giant T-shirt.

"What's wrong?" Rake said instantly, cutting off her start at a greeting.

Her head shot back. "Well, hello to you too, handsome. Nothing's wrong. Why?"

"You look—"

Lizzie laughed and held up a menacing finger. "If you want to live to see our new apartment, I beg you not to finish that statement."

Rake snapped his mouth shut.

"I spent the night puking," Lizzie said, moving aside to let him in. "Midnight sickness or whatever you want to call it. And then I couldn't fall back asleep, so I've been in the kitchen since about four," she added, taking a step into the bathroom off the hall and flicking on the lights.

Lizzie let out a gasp. "Oh shit!"

"What's wrong?" Rake asked again, moving to the door to check on her.

"I *do* look bad," she said with a grin, pointing at her face.

Thick smears of mascara hugged the bottom of her red-rimmed eyes, her hair sat like a rickety bird's nest on top of her head.

"You look . . . good," Rake lied, and Lizzie let out a booming laugh.

"I look ridiculous, you ass." She grabbed a cotton swab and scrubbed at the mascara stains. "How was the flight?"

"Fine," Rake answered, an odd sense of concern kicking at a spot on the left side of his chest. "Have you talked to a doctor about how often you get sick?"

Rake shrugged when she shot him a wry smile in the mirror.

"They say it's all normal. It's actually been getting a lot better. It doesn't even happen every day anymore," Lizzie said. "Last night just happened to be one of the not-so-good days."

Rake nodded as he watched her, inexplicably fascinated as she did seemingly mundane things. She cupped her hands under the faucet and splashed water on her cheeks, soaking the counter, then dried her face with a towel. She ripped her hair out of its knot and tore a brush through it a few times before flipping her head over and bundling the locks back into another crooked bun. All of it was enthralling and Rake couldn't figure out why.

"So that's all you have to say about the flight? *Fine?*" she asked as she pulled her contacts out of her eyes. "Did they feed you? What drink did you get? I always get Sprite. Did you sit next to anyone interesting?"

Rake was about to give the barest of answers when she did something that made all conversation stop in his throat.

As Lizzie flicked off the lights and joined Rake in the hall, she slipped on a pair of glasses.

Huge, round glasses with electric blue frames. She blinked up at him, the thick lenses magnifying her eyes to look twice as big, and Rake worked to hide his smile, pressing his lips firmly together.

She looked so damn adorable, his bones felt like they would break from it.

Or that was probably just the exhaustion talking. He didn't *actually* feel that.

Lizzie's eyes narrowed to zoomed-in slits. "Are you laughing at me?" she said, pushing the giant spectacles farther up her nose, then crossing her eyes.

"No!" Rake said, trying to hide a laugh with a cough.

"Yes, you are! You're laughing at my glasses," she said with mock outrage, punching him on the shoulder.

"I'm not! I just didn't know you needed them."

"Yeah, I'm blind as an infant baby mole rat," she said, tucking her lips against her teeth and giving him a goofy grin.

She was so weird.

"They're . . . nice," Rake teased, eliciting a smile from her.

"Shut up," she said, landing another punch on his shoulder. He grabbed her hand and pulled her into a hug. A super quick one, though. Like, less than a millisecond of contact because he absolutely did *not* do stuff like hugging. Or whatever.

"They're cute," he said, taking a step away from her. "And you could use them as a plate if you were ever in a tight meal situation," he added, following her through the apartment. But instead of heading toward the closed doors on the left, she veered off to the living room and kitchen area on the right.

"Or I can use them as a shovel to bury you alive, maybe get you to shut up?" she said over her shoulder. Rake laughed again.

But the laugh died in his throat as he stopped dead in his tracks and absorbed the indescribable chaos that surrounded them.

Chapter 23

"OKAY, so I'm sensing a bit of an energy shift from you," Lizzie said, maneuvering around stacks of books and piles of pans in the living room to take her spot in front of the stove and stir the compote she was working on. "And I don't want to, like, project feelings onto you or whatever, but I promise there's no need to freak out," she said calmly while she internally continued to freak out.

"I have it all under control . . . Well, Indira does, at least," she added, sneaking a peek at Rake over her shoulder and pointing her wooden spoon toward her bedroom door.

Rake stood like a stunned statue in the center of her living room, surrounded by boxes and bins stacked like a topsy-turvy city.

"I will admit it looks a little . . . disorganized," Lizzie said, stirring her compote even harder, leaning down to huff in the tart sweetness of the berries like the scent could calm the energy buzzing through her brain. She took it off the heat to cool.

Rake's head turned slowly around the room, taking in the tumbleweed of cheap jewelry on the coffee table, the littering of cards and receipts and balls of yarn on the couch, the mountain range of clothes scattered throughout.

His horrified eyes finally turned back to Lizzie.

"Try this. It will help," Lizzie said, grabbing a lemon-bread biscuit from the nearby tray and advancing on him, popping the whole thing in his slack-jawed mouth. She pressed his chin up with her hand, encouraging him to chew.

After a moment's hesitation, his horror-stricken eyes still on her, he abided. Lizzie gobbled down her own biscuit, her muscles relaxing as she tasted the tart zest of the treat, the piped icing that offered just enough sweetness.

Rake blinked a few times then cleared his throat. "Lizzie . . . You knew we were moving today, right? What . . . what happened?" He glanced again around the room.

Lizzie sighed, scrubbing her hands down her face. "It turns out I am physically incapable of packing," she said, moving back to her creation on the counter. "But it also turns out I'm incapable of admitting that fact until the last possible moment," she added, picking up a few fresh berries from the bowl and sticking them into the soft icing.

"And right as I finally resigned myself to slowly suffocating under a pile of my clothes, Indira, sweet gorgeous angel of light and goodness that she is, offered to help," Lizzie added, pointing to Indira, who emerged from Lizzie's room with armfuls of clothes. She gave Rake a big smile before dumping the massive heap of items onto the ground and heading back into the room for more.

Lizzie was doing better with her baby steps of ADHD management—taking her medication every day, drawing to-do lists with bite-sized tasks and actually using them, creating a pattern for when to leave for work—and she felt small whispers of pride at her accomplishments.

But packing was a different story. Lizzie had intended to be on top of her shit and get it done early. But every time she started to load up a box, she'd get distracted, wanting to see if a shirt still fit, wondering what had happened to an old favorite skirt. Which would cause her to then hunt down something else, until the next thing she knew, she'd fallen into a brain trap and was lying on a pile of foam fingers and sweaters, flipping through her favorite scenes of Lisa Kleypas novels.

This cycle repeated on a loop daily, all while she assured Indira she had everything totally under control, too overwhelmed and embarrassed to ask for help.

Then last night, after puking her brains out for a good two hours, she'd finally taken in the absolute shit show that was "packing." She tried moving things out of her room into the living room to see if that offered a clearer picture to the puzzle of where she was supposed to start, but that only made it worse, sending her into a spiral over the sheer impossibility of it all.

So, Lizzie did what she did best. She went to the kitchen to think.

And ended up baking lemon-bread cookies, her summer take on gingerbread, and crafting them into tiny cottages with a thick raspberry icing acting as the cement. Some of the houses were short and squat with intricate piping of green ivy covering the sides, others tall with widow's walks and crystalline sugar dyed to imitate a mosaic of stained glass.

She'd just started piping on shingles and creating manicured lawns from mixed berries when Indira found her that morning. After a minor bit of dramatics on both their parts, and a lot of bribery with personalized lemon-bread cottages and IOUs of pies and cakes, Indira had taken charge and left Lizzie to cope.

"And it's all working out perfectly," Indira said, depositing another load. "I'm making progress, Lizzie's almost built an entire lemon-bread city, and now you're here, Rake, so the three of us will get this done in no time," Indira said, turning kind eyes on Lizzie. "We all hit roadblocks sometimes, but we've got this."

Indira had ceaseless patience and encouragement for Lizzie when it came to issues with her flawed executive functioning, even when Lizzie fell into the trap of anger and frustration at her brain instead of accepting it for how it worked.

"And, um, on the . . . bright side," Lizzie said, "this is pretty much all of it." She waved her hand across the invisible floor of the apartment. "Now it's just a matter of . . ."

"Shoving it in garbage bags and loading up the car," Indira offered, walking over and giving Lizzie's shoulders a squeeze before popping a biscuit in her mouth.

Embarrassment prickled down Lizzie's spine, and she couldn't bring herself to look at Rake. Indira had always been more than accommodating of Lizzie's less-than-ideal habits as a roommate, making her feel safe and valued even when working memory failed or hyper-focus took over and chores were left undone.

But what if Rake couldn't deal? What if she was leaving her safe place to live with someone who fundamentally could not understand her? What if he saw her as lazy or rude or inconsiderate, when it was a disorder of executive functioning out of her control? He certainly wouldn't be the first.

Lizzie sucked in a deep breath and looked at Rake.

The horror had left his features, leaving steady determination in his tired eyes and a soft hint of a smile. "Well," he said, after a moment, "we better get to work."

He moved toward her room, grabbing a garbage bag from Indira's proffered hand, and Lizzie followed.

Rake knelt on the floor, starting to fold her clothes with something like gentleness. Watching his large hands take care of her things created a weird tightness in Lizzie's chest, and she turned away, surveying the room and trying to get her scribble of a brain to pick a task to start with, fighting against the fear and exhaustion that constantly tugged at her since her entire world changed.

Out of nowhere, a hollow *whoosh* filled the room, punctuated by Rake's loud curse. Lizzie's eyes shot to him where he was slowly sinking to the ground.

"Lizzie . . . Do you . . . sleep on an air mattress?" Rake said, staring at her with bewilderment from his awkward little squat as her bed casually swallowed him whole.

Lizzie scrubbed at her tired eyes. "I *really* wish I was in a headspace to come up with something funny or witty to say that makes it less sad, but, yes, I sleep on an air mattress."

She hadn't meant to turn the piece of rubber into her permanent bed, but she also didn't know where to start with buying a new mattress, so she'd avoided it altogether.

She buried her head in her hands for a moment, trying to breathe deeply.

"Are you okay?" Rake asked, the softness of his tone catching her off guard.

"Yeah, I'm okay. I'm just . . ." She gestured vaguely around the room. Indira had moved to the kitchen to start packing away Lizzie's extensive baking equipment. Rake continued to look at her with that quiet fascination of his.

"I'm a little emotional about leaving," Lizzie admitted. "I'm overwhelmed with packing, I feel like a loser for all the shitty stuff I'm bringing, and I'm scared about moving in with someone I barely know. I'm just . . ." She mimicked an explosion with her hands over her head.

"Fritzy?" Rake asked.

Lizzie smiled, a glowing ball of warmth filling her chest that he'd remembered her word for bad brain moments. "Yes. Fritzy. The fritziest fritz."

"You don't have to do this," Rake said quietly, the words coming out a bit thick and odd. "You can stay here, and we can make the coparenting thing work some other way."

Lizzie shook her head. "No, I think it's the best call. I can't dump a baby on Indira right now, and living with you will . . . Well, we'll see what that will do, but I think it's the right choice."

Rake nodded slowly, looking around the room like he was turning her words over in his head. "What are those?" he asked, pointing at a few stacked boxes near her closet door, the only things sealed nicely away.

"Oh. That's just some stuff I never unpacked. Been tucked in the closet forever." She walked over to them, dragging her finger over the shiny tape that held the boxes together.

"How long have you lived here?"

"Five years," she said with a sad laugh. She looked up at him, her eyes glossy. "I can't believe I've lived here for five years and never unpacked these boxes."

"Why didn't you?"

"I don't know," she said absently, fiddling with a worn corner. "It always seemed like a lot of work. They're just knick-knacks and mementos and stuff. Memories. Sorting through it seemed like such a monumental task, and Indira already had the place decorated when I moved in, so my flair wasn't needed."

Rake gave her a small smile, then went back to gingerly folding her clothes. Lizzie stared. There was something about him. Some weird hidden pieces under his calm facade that tugged at her attention. Made her want to know more.

"So how do you feel about all this?" Lizzie asked, grabbing handfuls of random crap and shoving them into trash bags.

"Fine," Rake said, keeping his eyes on his task. "Don't love hearing you've been so sick, but if the doctors say it's normal . . ."

"Yeah, but how do you feel about all of this? Like really, really *feel*?"

Rake shrugged. "Fine. I'm confident we'll find the best way to handle parenting and learn to be decent roommates. Obviously, we have to start talking about childcare and budgeting and things of that nature, but I figured we'd give it a few days as we both settle in."

"Will you miss Sydney?"

"I'll survive."

"Was it hard to say goodbye to all your friends?"

"Not particularly."

Lizzie continued to stare at her gorgeous cyborg, greedy for the truth. He was a puzzle, and she wanted to crack him open, see all the lovely mess he hid in there. She was disastrously curious, and he was her most recent fixation.

"Who do you think you'll miss the most?"

"My parents, I guess? Haven't really thought about it."

"What's your favorite memory? The happiest you've ever been in your entire life?"

Rake glanced at her. "What?"

"Your favorite memory?"

He shrugged. "I've no idea. Never thought about it."

Lizzie chewed on her lip. "Did you leave anyone back home? Someone you have feelings for, or anything?"

"Do you have to ask so many questions?" Rake snapped.

Lizzie flinched at the sharpness of his words, turning to gather more things while she blinked back the sharp and sudden poke of tears. She hated that she was always so quick to cry.

"Sorry," Lizzie said, swallowing past the lump in her throat. She felt like a nosey child.

"I didn't mean to snap at you. I'm sorry," Rake said after a few heavy, silent moments, dragging a hand through his hair. "I . . . all of this is just . . ."

"My fault," Lizzie said, willing her voice to be free of emotion. She pushed to standing, dragging a trash bag toward the door. "I shouldn't have pushed."

They finished gathering up her things in silence, Lizzie dumping handfuls of clothing into garbage bags while Rake nicely folded her bedding and rolled up her air mattress, placing it all in a neat pile by the door. Indira intermittently deposited things in the growing spot from other places within the apartment.

Lizzie dragged her four hundredth overstuffed plastic bag across the room, giving it a kick to keep it wedged in the growing heap.

She turned, reaching for the last two, when Rake grabbed her hand.

"I lost someone," he said, his voice hoarse. "I lost someone a while back, and all of this *is* happening very fast, and I'm trying to be as calm and levelheaded as possible for both our sakes, but I'm not used to, um, sharing so much of myself with someone."

Lizzie stared at where his warm hand touched hers. Her eyes trailed up his arm and over the lines of his face, back to those blue-green eyes.

"Okay," Lizzie said, her voice soft.

"Okay," Rake said, giving her hand a final squeeze before letting her go.

After that, they loaded up Indira's car, making multiple trips over several hours between the two apartments as Philadelphia's humidity sapped their energy.

By the time the final stuff was unloaded into the apartment, Lizzie wanted to collapse with exhaustion, but she took a moment to look around at her new home as she inflated her air mattress.

Exposed brick lined the room. A lofted ceiling with metallic beams hinted at the warehouse it once was, no walls to break up the space. The huge bank of windows looked out on the kaleidoscope of lights punctuating the city, and she pressed her palms and forehead against the glass, absorbing the energy all around her.

"How ya going?" Rake asked, standing a few paces behind her. She looked at his tired reflection in the window before turning and fixing him with a smile.

"Better than a bird with a french fry," she said, which, despite her exhaustion, wasn't a total lie. "Oh, before I forget, would it be okay if I hang these on the wall?" Lizzie asked, darting across the room to grab a folder off her bed. She thrust it at Rake.

"What's this?" he asked, flipping through the pages.

"They're weekly pregnancy sheets," Lizzie said, moving to stand next to him. "I've been panicking about not knowing important things or missing something, and after Pinteresting my heart out, I found this for ADHD moms-to-be. It breaks down things to do or plan week by week." The diagrams were filled with colors and cute doodles instead of excessive text, which harmonized with Lizzie's brain and made everything feel more manageable.

"I know taping a bunch of crap to the wall isn't the most aesthetic, but I think—" Rake's eyes flashed to Lizzie's, and the softness of his look made Lizzie's breath catch in her throat.

"Of course we can," Rake said, marching to a drawer and grabbing tape. "I'll get you a corkboard this week and we can move them to that, but this will work for now," he added, tearing off pieces of tape and sticking the sheets in a grid on the wall.

Lizzie watched him work in silence, her nose and eyes stinging from the flood of emotions that threatened to rip her open.

"And we'll delegate the tasks, obviously," Rake said, as he continued to tape. "We'll have a weekly meeting on Sundays and create workflows and divide up the tasks. This is gre—*oof.*"

Lizzie slammed into him from behind, wrapping her arms around his waist as she buried her face against his back.

"All right there, Birdy?" Rake asked after a moment, turning in her arms, his hands hovering over her back like he didn't know what to do with them.

She pressed closer to him. "Thank you," she said against his sternum.

"For what?"

"For being so enthusiastic about to-do lists."

Rake was silent for a moment then chuckled, his hands slowly lowering to touch Lizzie's back in a soft stroke. "I love to-do lists."

"That makes one of us."

Rake laughed again, the deep, gravelly vibrations a gentle caress against her cheek.

"Think we can actually do this?" Lizzie asked in a quiet voice.

Rake's heartbeat sped up under her cheek, but his voice was smooth and steady. "I know we can."

Chapter 24

LIZZIE spent the first morning in her new apartment happily working—kneading thick and sticky dough that she manipulated into boob-shaped soft pretzels, creating a strawberry-cream filling piped through the imaginary nipples that offset the salty topping. She couldn't stop giggling.

Her new job was going well, and she was thriving in coming up with suggestive baked goods. Bernadette cackled at the macarons with intricately decorated areolas ranging from a soft pink to a delicious brown, and she clapped at the small peach galettes with the fruit slices placed to (not so subtly) hint at a vulva.

It was too damn fun.

Bernadette, glorious angel she was, had been more than accommodating when Lizzie told her she was pregnant, already discussing flexible work schedules after maternity leave or the possibility of Lizzie doing some of the prep from home if her kitchen could accommodate it.

She'd also given Lizzie a few days off to get settled in her new place, but Lizzie was still trying to get a few hours of work done while her creations cooked, navigating the bakery's online presence and posting some of her creations on Instagram, taking #foodporn to new realities.

And it seemed to be working.

Over the past few weeks, Lizzie and Bernadette had seen a steady increase of orders for their vulvalicious offerings, and more than a few people had walked into the shop hoping to see the pastries on display and left disappointed when they explained that was more of an online thing and all they had to offer were normal, non-vagina-esque cupcakes and muffins. Lizzie and Bernadette were discussing the best way to roll out their new menu, and, for the first time in her life, Lizzie felt like she was a valuable member of a team.

Rake also had the rest of the week off to get organized before reporting for work, and he'd spent most of the morning unpacking and organizing the apartment.

Lizzie watched him from where she was sprawled on the couch. He was on his hands and knees, scrubbing at scuff marks on the baseboards from rearranging furniture a few hours before. Lizzie, ogler that she was, couldn't help but admire his perfect ass, lovingly hugged by a pair of jeans that deserved to be framed in the Museum of Modern Art for their stunning effect.

Horny and bored, Lizzie thought over her options.

Yes, this was technically a platonic living situation. But that didn't mean it had to be platonic in the no-one-gives-each-other-orgasms type of way, right? Sex was sex, and they were both adults, so what could be the harm in blowing off a little steam?

Lizzie tossed her laptop on the couch beside her and got up, padding across the room toward him. He looked over his shoulder at her, then sat back on his heels as she got closer, wiping sweat off his forehead.

"So, you're a clean freak," she said, leaning her back against the wall and sliding down to sit cross-legged next to him.

Rake frowned, looking around the immaculate apartment. "I wouldn't say that. I just like to keep things tidy." His eyes rested for a beat longer on what Lizzie had declared her official corner of the place, her garbage bags and boxes shoved haphazardly next to her air mattress, which was already covered in discarded clothes.

"You used a toothbrush to clean between the tiles in the kitchen before I even used it."

Rake shrugged. "We don't know the last time it was cleaned. It just makes sense. Would you prefer I be a slob?" he asked, lifting the neck of his shirt to wipe off more sweat. Although their large windows were thrown open, summer had infiltrated Philadelphia with humidity you could swim in.

"A slob like me?" she said, poking him in the side, letting her hand linger and her eyes go soft as she looked at him, making her intentions obvious. Rake's eyes traveled from her face, down her arm, to where her hand rested against his ribs.

Moving slowly, like she was a skittish animal, he put his own hand over it, giving her a gentle squeeze before removing her fingers and depositing them safely back to her lap. She blinked at him. That was . . . not the reaction she was expecting.

"You're not a slob," he said, picking up his rag and wiping more at the sparkling baseboards. "You just don't have anywhere to put your stuff yet. We'll get you a dresser."

Lizzie snorted. "Dresser or not, I assure you, I'm a slob. It always drove my mom nuts." She got on her own hands and knees, mimicking his posture. Rake glanced at her (cleavage) then quickly away, color rising in his cheeks.

He cleared his throat. "Other people's messes don't bother me. I just like to clean up my own. I enjoy cleaning, I guess."

"Do you?" Lizzie purred, plucking the rag from his hands. "Maybe I should give cleaning a fairer shot then, if you enjoy it so much." She dragged the cloth up and down the baseboards, slowly, seductively, making sure her breasts pushed together and ample cleavage showed as she did it.

She heard Rake swallow, and she glanced up at him through her lashes. He was staring at her face with such obvious focus, it was clear he would much rather be looking at her chest.

She slid forward an inch, moving closer, still looking up at him, trying to give him ideas of what she could do from this position. Lizzie slowly reached out her hand, dragging her palm up his thigh.

"Or, we could take a break from cleaning and do something else enjoyable," she said, smiling to herself at the obvious bulge growing at the front of his jeans. She inched closer still, dragging the tip of her finger over the shiny metal of his button, enjoying his hiss of breath as she did it. Lizzie watched as Rake stared down at her hand, his chest moving with his shallow breaths. Slowly, she pushed the button through the hole then pinched the tongue of his zipper.

Rake jerked back like she'd shocked him.

"Nope. No. No. We can't. Sorry. No," he said, crab-walking away from her across his shiny floors.

Lizzie's head shot back in confusion. "What?"

"We . . . we can't have sex," he said, redoing his button.

"I assure you, we can," Lizzie responded with a laugh, shucking off her T-shirt and crawling toward him.

"I mean, we shouldn't," he said, slamming his eyes shut and swallowing. "We shouldn't have sex."

Lizzie stopped her pursuit, her heart sinking and mortification pricking at her skin. "What? Why not?"

"Well, uh . . . sex got us into this . . . situation, didn't it? I was thinking it'd probably be better if we didn't continue to . . . do . . . it. Since we aren't getting married or pursuing that aspect, it will make our, uh, cohabitation less messy."

Lizzie flinched, the words feeling like a punch to the chest. Her brain whirred into overdrive, rejection flooding her veins.

"Cool, cool, cool, cool," she said, shooting to her feet and moving toward her stuff. "Sexless parents living together. Sounds more like a marriage than not, huh? Should have let you put a ring on it if it meant I could have an orgasm." She let out a horrified little laugh, her mind diving into a tailspin. Rejection and shame and embarrassment dug their claws into her back and wouldn't let go.

"Calm down, Birdy," Rake said, scrambling to stand. "This isn't because I don't *want* to. It just would complicate things even more."

Lizzie could hear the words, could even picture their order in her head, but all she could feel was the weight of *I don't want to* and *complicate* and *messy* pound at all her pulse points. She tore through her garbage bags and pulled out workout clothes, throwing them on in a flash. Hot, embarrassed tears welled at her eyes, and she wanted to strangle herself for letting him see. The tears were making it so much worse.

"Where are you going?" Rake asked, coming up behind her.

"For a jog. Maybe jog right into the river. Who knows, ha ha, see you later." She knew how unhinged she must seem to Rake, but she couldn't control it. Even the smallest whisper of rejection shattered her into a million sharp pieces of embarrassment. She'd always been this way.

"Lizzie, come on. I just meant—"

She shut the door behind her before she would have to hear more words that could hurt her.

Chapter 25

LIZZIE'S mind was lulled by the rhythm of her feet hitting the pavement. She tried to match her breaths to her steps—in, in, out, out—her chest squeezing as she moved faster. Ran farther.

It'd been a while since she last laced up her tennis shoes, but her body fell right back into the tempo, her thick thighs and muscular calves rejoicing at the delicious burn of their use. She had picked up running on a whim a few years back, signing up for a marathon training club after seeing a group of cute guys walk into the running store.

She'd hooked up with one of the guys and ended up completing the marathon, throwing herself into the sport like she did everything else: with unadulterated hyper-focus.

That is, until she got bored with it. Just like she did with everything else too.

That was Lizzie's pattern—a new shiny high to chase, a bucket list item to check off, all pursued with fanatical zeal. And then the inevitable lull of monotony creeping in at the edges made her sprint toward the next thing to snag her attention.

She turned, heading back for Rake's place. Their place? Probably just Rake's place after the total meltdown she'd had.

Lizzie knew she'd overreacted. What he said made sense; they definitely shouldn't be having sex.

But that was her pattern too: overreact, feel rejected, flip out, flee.

Her brain felt like a giant scribble of complex patterns, and she wished more than anything she could raze it over, flattening out the nooks and crannies and complexities and react rationally for once.

She stopped at the corner, walking the rest of the way to the building to catch her breath, Rake's words still stinging her skin. She knew that, in a more direct sense, *she* had rejected *Rake*, by turning down his offer of marriage, but she had known he offered out of pity. A natural, albeit outdated, offer to take responsibility for their situation. But even that had the feeling of rejection snaking its way through her veins. She didn't want to be anyone's obligation.

But now the rejection felt more acute. She'd never had her body rejected before. Sex was something satisfying she could offer people, and his rational reasoning for them not doing it still upset her balance. Hurt her feelings.

She took the stairs up to their place, and, with a deep breath, opened the door.

And darted for the bathroom like the embarrassed little chickenshit she was. She decided to wash her sweat off first before talking to Rake.

Lizzie rinsed off quickly, her muscles still restless and itching for stimulation, even after her run. She was glad some of the worst parts of the first trimester were behind her, her projectile vomiting seemed to only happen once a week or so, and the overwhelming tiredness had slowly subsided, but it also meant her body and mind needed more of the usual constant stimulation—like she would literally die if she had to be still and alone with her thoughts for too long.

She finished up her shower then stepped out, wrapping a towel around herself. The washer and dryer were housed in the bathroom closet, and she slid open the door. She'd moved a metric ton of dirty laundry to their new home, and she'd thrown it in for a wash first thing on moving day like a productive little hummingbird. But now she cursed herself and her minute-long spell of productivity as she remembered she never transferred it to the dryer.

Feeling frustrated at all the day's shortcomings, she opened the washer's lid, bracing herself for the all-too-familiar smell of moldy, forgotten clothes.

She was surprised to find it empty.

Maybe she hadn't forgotten? She checked the dryer, but that was empty too. Her eyes fell on a tiny shelved cart, pushed into the shadowed corner. She flicked on the closet lights, and there were her clothes, crisp and folded like they belonged in a department store. She looked at the neat stacks, noticing the similar ones of Rake's clothes on the shelf below.

She'd never seen her things so organized, shirts and pants in separate piles, arranged in a color gradient from light to dark. Looking closer, she saw that Rake even folded his *underwear*. Tidy stacks of boxer briefs, lined up and wrinkle-free.

Something about seeing their things together, the image of Rake's large hands folding her cheap, flimsy clothes, handling them with such care, plucked at her heart and tightened her throat. Staring at the fabric until her eyes blurred at the edges, she realized how little she knew about the man she was living with. They couldn't be more different: She was an explosion, while he was an intricate code, sometimes free and flirty, more often guarded and confined.

It bothered Lizzie that she couldn't pin down who he was, the essence of his personality, but she sensed a hurt buried deep down below that gorgeous golden skin.

Why did he not have someone to do things like this for already? Why did he agree to take on her tornado of chaos?

Lizzie straightened, grabbing some clothes off the cart and making sure not to disrupt the piles. She was being too emotional again. Probably pregnancy hormones on top of her already excessive default of dramatics. It was the only explanation for all these pesky *feelings* she'd been having.

She threw on the clothes and wiped the raccoon smears of makeup from under her eyes, taking one last deep breath before opening the door. Rake was lying on the bed, his arm thrown over his eyes. As Lizzie moved closer, she heard the steady rumble of his sleeping breath, and it unsettled her that she already knew how he sounded when he slept. Two days ago, she didn't know that about anyone.

She got on the other side of the bed, sitting cross-legged as she looked down on his sleeping form. Damn, he was beautiful. Objectively gorgeous.

His dirty-blond hair stuck up at odd angles against the pillow, the muscles and veins of his lean arms were finely made, and his lips were slightly parted as he slept. Lizzie placed her palm over his chest, feeling his heart knock against it, before she gently shook him awake.

He started like a bat out of hell, making Lizzie jerk back.

"What's wrong?" he nearly yelled, jolting up.

"Sorry!" she said, throwing up her hands. "I was trying to wake you gently. Clearly, I didn't."

Rake blinked at her a few times, then scrubbed his fists against his eyes to rid them of sleep. He rubbed his large palm over his chest, right where she'd touched him. "You scared the shit out of me, Birdy."

"I'm sorry," she said again.

"No, it's fine. I'm jet-lagged as hell and must've dozed off. I didn't hear you come in."

She looked into his eyes for a moment before staring at a spot on his shoulder, trying to formulate her words.

"How was your run?"

"Rejection Sensitive Dysphoria," she said, at the same time he spoke, and he quirked his head to the side.

"Sorry, what?"

"A doctor once told me it's called Rejection Sensitive Dysphoria. RSD. It's a part of having ADHD. For some people, at least."

"I'm sorry, I'm not sure I follow," he said.

Lizzie took a deep breath, squeezing her eyes shut. She didn't like talking about it. She didn't like the way people made her a diagnosis. The way people always seemed to "understand" her behavior once they had a label for it. But she was also determined to be her own advocate, seeing endless online advice that articulating her experience was a form of radical self-care.

She opened her eyes and met the lovely blue-green of Rake's. "You know how I kind of *minorly* flipped out earlier?"

Rake's lips quirked at the edges. "Very minor."

Lizzie smiled back. "I know what you're saying makes sense. It's the right choice, us not having sex. I get it. I agree."

Rake looked at her wearily. "But?"

"But, I flipped out like that because I . . . I automatically took that smart, adult decision as a personal rejection. It's part of RSD. It's like this *visceral* reaction when I sense rejection or that I've disappointed someone or done something wrong. It feels like a punch square in the chest. Or like my stomach dropped out of my body, folded itself inside out, and then wrapped around me and tried to suffocate me. It's an overwhelming, primitive type of pain."

Rake continued to stare at her, the corners of his mouth turned down in a small frown.

Lizzie breathed out. "I'm doing a terrible job explaining it. I'm sorry, I'll stop." She moved to slide off the bed, but Rake grabbed her hand, squeezing it gently. Lizzie wanted to cry out at the relief of the reassuring touch.

"No," Rake said, "keep going. I'm listening."

Lizzie looked at their hands, and she twined her fingers between his. "I tried to explain it to my mom once," Lizzie said, the words quiet. "She had taken me to a child psychiatrist, convinced I had some disastrous imbalance because I was so sensitive and emotional. 'You're too much, Elizabeth. Too much for one person to be,'" Lizzie said, mimicking her mom's prim voice.

"My mom wanted to put me on more meds—I was already on stuff for ADHD, but she didn't think it was enough. She wanted something to calm me down, I guess. Sedate me more likely," she said with a wry smile that Rake didn't return. He continued to look at her with a steady focus, like she was the center of all his attention.

"The psychiatrist told me it was part of having ADHD," Lizzie continued. "We'd known I had that for a while . . . not hard to miss." She let out a genuine laugh, plucking at the comforter with her free hand. "I felt so . . . *understood* after the psychiatrist told me RSD was a thing. Like I could finally understand why I always felt things in a way that was too . . . too *big*. Too sharp. But on the flip side, happiness felt like I could burst with it, overflow with it.

"I tried to tell my mom about it—how every punishment for not keeping my room clean or forgetting to do something or messing something up felt like a catastrophe. Like I was the world's greatest failure."

Lizzie traced the index finger of her free hand over the grooves of their knuckles, enjoying the slight dusting of blond hairs across Rake's.

"What did she say?" Rake prompted, giving her hand another squeeze.

Lizzie looked at him then down at the bedspread, dropping his hand and smoothing both of hers over the sheet. "She told me it was nonsense and I was too defiant and headstrong for my own good. That she was only trying to help me and do what's best for me. Helping me be 'normal.' She took me to a different doctor. One that put me on meds like she wanted. I didn't feel quite as much after that."

The room was silent, heavy. Lizzie needed to break the tension. Dissolve it. She didn't like all the feelings that were diffusing through the walls like ghosts. She blew out a raspberry and grinned at Rake, trying to blink past the tears that felt like little pinpricks in her eyes.

"Anyway, that's why I flipped. And I'm sorry. You're right, it would be ridiculous for us to continue having sex if we're going to do this as platonic coparents. And I hope you don't think I'm too crazy to do that with now." She gave him a goofy look, hoping to make him laugh.

His face was sharp lines and deep furrows as he continued to look at her. Lizzie's body began to vibrate under his gaze, wanting to move. Get out of the room. She didn't want to hear him break it off. She didn't want to see the end of one more failed attempt to fix a disaster of her making.

Slowly, he reached up a hand, cupping her cheek. He brought his head forward, resting his forehead against hers. "I've never thought you were crazy, Lizzie. Weird? Yes. Crazy? No. And you shouldn't think of yourself that way either."

Lizzie let out a shaky breath, the tension in her shoulders easing a bit. It was so easy to fall into that trap and let the mean voice in her head dig its claws in. Tell her that her brain wasn't okay. That it didn't fit in this neurotypical world and that it was wrong.

She tried to be conscious of that internalized ableism and shut that shit down, but it was nice to hear someone else say it too.

She wrapped her arms around his neck and hugged him. She wanted to melt into the feeling of him hugging her back. Hugs were miracles. Drastically underrated daily miracles.

They stayed like that for a few minutes, just holding each other, little buoys in the absurdity of this curveball life threw at them.

Chapter 26

Week ten, baby is the size of a hermit crab.

Two days later, Rake's alarm blared, and he jolted up from the bed, panting and disoriented. He'd been having a dream moments before. A vivid one.

A *recurring* one that involved a great deal of nudity and moaning from his totally platonic roommate/coparent.

"Morning, you great barrier queef," the object of his fantasy said from her side of the room. Lizzie sat cross-legged in the center of her air mattress, the blue light of her laptop reflecting in the saucer lenses of her glasses.

Rake almost had to bite his knuckles to suppress a groan.

The problem with seeing Lizzie like this every morning— while he was uncomfortably hard and still heard the echoes of her moans in his dreams—was that she was too damn precious and peculiar for her own good.

Rake's own good, more accurately.

Something about her was crawling under his skin, working its way into his system, making him feel . . . *things*. And feeling was something he'd given up the second Shannon had walked out the door two years ago.

"Why are you so pouty this morning?" Lizzie asked, her voice snapping him out of the uncomfortable memories.

"I'm not pouty," he answered. He was sexually frustrated, confused, and needed her to turn away so he could get to the bathroom without her spotting his erection and giving him hell about it. But definitely not pouty.

"What are your thoughts on cream pies?" she asked suddenly, staring at her computer screen.

A thousand lewd images flashed through Rake's mind. "I beg your pardon?" he said, his voice cracking. "It's a bit early for porn, isn't it?" he added, nodding toward her laptop.

"It's never too early for porn," she answered evenly. "But I mean for Bernadette's. Some sort of cream pie or a cream-filled donut shaped like a butt. Is that too obvious?"

Rake let out a breath. "Well, you are known for your subtlety. I'd hate for you to ruin that."

Lizzie looked up at him, flashing a wide grin. "Excellent point. Are you ready for today?"

The first ultrasound was scheduled for that afternoon, and Rake had been a jumble of nerves and anticipation all week.

"Can't wait," he answered honestly. "We should leave around eleven thirty, yeah?"

"Sounds good," Lizzie said, her attention back on her laptop.

Rake decided to take his chances and got out of bed, making his way to the shower to get ready for the appointment.

* * *

"I DON'T MEAN to rush you, but we are about to be very late," Rake said to the closed bathroom door a few hours later.

Lizzie had decided to make last-minute fruit tarts that morning, losing herself in a mountain of sugar and fruit while Rake became utterly engrossed by the focused pucker between her eyebrows. Her small smile as she laid the fruit slices in concentric patterns. The sinfully delicious scent of her and the dusting of flour on her forehead as she popped one straight into his mouth and made him chew.

"Thank you for the warning, Father Time," Lizzie said with a laugh before opening the door.

She breezed out, her bare feet padding along the wood floors. She wiggled into a pair of wedged heels then ran her hands down her stomach, smoothing the tight red fabric of her dress that clung to her body, accentuating every curve.

"Why are you so . . ." Rake tried to swallow past his dry throat, his eyes scouring over the jut of her hips, the swells of her breasts. He couldn't drag his gaze away. The dress was just so damn . . . *red*.

"So what?" she asked absentmindedly, grabbing her giant purse and riffling through it.

"Why are you so dressed up?" he finally managed, his voice cracking.

Lizzie looked down at herself like she hadn't realized she was wearing a dress that was threatening to kill him. She shot Rake a goofy grin. "Oh, this? I wanted to make a good first impression."

"For who?" he choked out.

"The baby, obviously."

"Obviously."

She let out her sonic boom of a laugh. "I'm kidding. I know I won't be able to wear stuff like this for much longer, so might as well work it while I can." She emphasized this point with a shake of her hips that almost made Rake's knees buckle.

"It's very . . . red," he said, cringing at the words. What was the matter with him?

"Whoa, nothing gets past you, kid." She patted him on the cheek as she moved past to grab her phone. "I know they say redheads shouldn't wear red, but I've never been a fan of social constructs of feminine beauty and rules of fashion. Plus, wearing red makes me feel like Jessica Rabbit."

Rake wasn't sure what the hell she was on about, but as she bent over to pick up a tube of lipstick that had fallen to the floor, her tight skirt riding up in a way that showed nothing but had him picturing everything, he didn't really care. He had the urge to move to her, bunch the fabric in his fists and shove it up to her waist, see the full roundness of her ass, touch every sweet hidden freckle that covered her skin.

But he couldn't do that.

For reasons he couldn't quite remember but he knew existed, and there was some important reason to abide by them.

He was being ridiculous. The only reason he wanted her like this was because he'd made it forbidden, and therefore wanted her all the more. It was the only logical explanation for his near-constant state of arousal around her.

"What's wrong with you?" she said, pulling him out of his fantasy as she stood back up. "You're staring at me all weird."

"Am I? Sorry. I was just thinking that you look very nice."

Lizzie blinked in surprise, like she wasn't used to compliments, but she recovered quickly, beaming at him.

"Thank you. I was going for a sort of cool-future-mom look that says I'm serious about parenting but also still pull a ton of dick, ya know?"

Rake nodded. "A bit cliché and traditional for an ultrasound, but I think you nailed it."

Their eyes met and neither could control their giggles, breaking up some of the tension in Rake's chest.

"Okay, let's go. Our ride is downstairs," Lizzie said, looking at her phone.

The drive to the doctor's office was quiet, Lizzie's jiggling legs making the whole car shake.

Rake was feeling fine.

Totally fine, save for this odd sensation that he was taking off on a flight and leaving his stomach on the ground. He wasn't sure what that was all about.

At the clinic, Lizzie filled out a few forms, and by the time she was done, they were escorted to an exam room, the nurse handing Lizzie a paper gown and a plastic cup for a urine test, letting them know the doctor would be in shortly.

Lizzie nodded with uncharacteristic quietness then headed into the bathroom.

"Everything all right?" Rake asked after a few minutes. For some reason the shut door and her silence were making him uneasy.

"Yeah," Lizzie said with a tiny laugh, "I'm having stage fright and can't get any pee to come out."

She emerged a few minutes later, her tight red dress replaced with the boxy paper gown. Lizzie hopped up onto the exam table, her knees instantly bouncing again and making the whole thing shake while she bit her nails and looked around the room. Rake wanted to comfort her, gather up all her anxious energy and throw it out the door, but he was too frozen by his own nerves and knotted stomach to do much of anything.

With a knock that made them both jump, the door opened and the obstetrician walked in, giving Lizzie and Rake a warm smile.

"Hello, I'm Dr. Herrara. It's a pleasure to meet you," she said, first shaking Lizzie's hand then Rake's. "How are you feeling today?"

"Good," Lizzie said, blowing out a breath. "Nervous, actually. Is it normal to be nervous? Why do you think I'm so nervous? Is it like an intuition thing and something is about to go really wrong?"

Dr. Herrara sat and rolled her chair closer to the exam table. "Nerves are perfectly normal. It's a big day, but we'll check everything out and get a clear picture on how the pregnancy is going. Do you mind if I ask you some questions on your medical history and the pregnancy thus far?"

Lizzie nodded, and Dr. Herrara launched into an endless list of questions.

After what felt like hours, Dr. Herrara finally asked Lizzie to lie back and put her feet in the stirrups. Rake moved toward the head of the exam table, hovering over Lizzie.

"All right, I'll be inserting the probe now," Dr. Herrara said gently, positioning herself between Lizzie's spread legs.

Lizzie sucked in a breath as Dr. Herrara inserted the wand, and Rake looked down to see her eyes squeezed shut and brows pinched together.

"Okay?" he asked, watching as his hand, seemingly detached from his body, reached down and smoothed back Lizzie's hair. Seeing her discomfort created a weird plucky feeling in his chest.

She squinted one eye open at his touch. "I'm fine, just kind of cold and weird down there," she said, squirming on the table. "I'm sure you hear that a lot," she added, shooting him a grin that morphed the uncomfortable feeling in his chest to something softer and sweeter. But equally confusing.

"I'm sorry. Try and relax your pelvic floor, the pressure should ease soon," Dr. Herrara said from below the tent of Lizzie's paper gown.

"All right, here we are," Dr. Herrara said, using one hand to move the mouse on the portable computer next to her, clicking a few buttons on the ultrasound machine. She turned the monitor so Lizzie and Rake had a clearer view. "There's your baby."

Rake stared at the screen, seeing a black ellipse in a sea of static gray, a tiny blob floating in the blackness.

It was the most beautiful thing he'd ever seen.

He glanced down at Lizzie, wondering if she was similarly awestruck by what they were witnessing. Their bewildered eyes locked, the moment splitting open between them, time spreading out and emotions refracting around them like a kaleidoscope, fear and love and excitement and worry and a sharp sense of joy. They turned back to the screen.

"And here's the heartbeat," Dr. Herrara said, clicking another button. A steady, methodic whooshing sound filled the room, a tiny blinking pulse on the screen matching the rhythm and becoming the center of their world.

Lizzie's hand squeezed around Rake's in a viper grip that traveled up his arm and fisted around his heart. Everything felt real and magnified and terrifying, like all this time he'd been living in a box, and the sound of the baby's heartbeat crumbled the walls to dust and left him overwhelmed by sunlight.

Dr. Herrara turned off the machine shortly after, offering a few last-minute notes that neither Lizzie or Rake really heard in their dazed state. Lizzie got changed, and they checked out, receiving a small printout of their beautiful little bean baby.

Outside on the sidewalk, they stared down at the grainy picture, each pinching a corner of it between their forefinger and thumb. Rake's heart felt like a giant flapping bird that threatened to burst from the cage of his chest and take off in flight. He didn't know what to do with all these feelings.

At the same moment, Lizzie and Rake tore their eyes away from their perfect blob and met each other's gaze. Rake watched as Lizzie's features transformed from blank and slack-jawed to a delicious grin. It was a grin that could rival a star in the way it dazzled—the way it lit up the constellations of her freckles and creased the edges of her eyes where one small tear rolled out of the corner. It was impossible to look at that smile, to look at their blob, and not feel the same enormous grin break across his own face and fissure through his body.

They stood there for a moment, as a sea of people parted around them, moving along with their day as if Lizzie and Rake didn't hold the single most precious photo of the most gorgeous smudge in the history of the world in their hands.

Rake couldn't say what came over him, whether it was the way Lizzie's tongue darted out to lick her lips, or how his blood heated and his pulse quickened with the enormity of the moment. But he had to touch her.

He crushed his mouth to hers, wanting to imprint her happy smile onto his heart. And, Lizzie being Lizzie, she didn't act surprised at all. She molded into him as if it was the most natural thing in the world for Rake to kiss her like his life depended on it. And that's what it felt like.

Happiness and one hundred other unnamable emotions flooded him so sharply, so painfully, he needed to anchor himself to the moment, to her, or else he quite simply might die from the feelings. He hitched her body closer, one hand cradling the back of her skull while the other snaked around her waist. She twined her arms around his neck, deepening the kiss, her tongue sliding over his in a way that drew all his attention to the silk of her mouth.

She pulled him toward her, causing them both to stumble until her back met the building behind her. Lizzie let out a soft groan that echoed in his bones, static electricity humming just beneath his skin, against her lips. He wanted her. Badly.

And that thought was enough to make him realize he needed to stop.

He tore away from the kiss, turning his back and rubbing his knuckles across his lips in a vain attempt to lose the feeling of her on them.

"Fuck," he said, dragging his hands down his face then turning back to her. "I shouldn't have done that. I'm sorry."

Lizzie was panting, her cheeks and nose burning with color. Rake didn't miss the flash of vulnerability in her eyes after his words, but she straightened her spine, brushing a hand over her hair and down to her stomach.

"It's fine," she said, plastering on a teasing smile. "I know even on my worst days I'm nearly irresistible, and what with you having the emotional range of a caveman, it only makes sense that you would get all primal after seeing proof of your giant spawn in me."

Rake let out a hollow laugh, still trying to get a grip on his pounding heart.

They made their way back home, opting to walk while Lizzie kept up her usual stream of observations. Rake listened to every word, seeing hundreds of beautiful things he never would have noticed without her clever eye.

When they finally made it back to the apartment, the air conditioning was a relief from the raging humidity.

"So," Lizzie said, patting her hands awkwardly against her hips and looking around. "We're going to be parents . . . It seems more real now."

Rake ran his hands through his hair. "It does."

They stared at each other, small bricks of shyness and intimacy and lust stacking up between them. In typical Lizzie fashion, she bulldozed through them.

"Wanna order some pizza?" she asked, kicking off her heels and fumbling for the zipper on the back of her dress. After a moment of contortion, she dropped her arms and backed toward him. "Will you unzip me?"

Rake swallowed, his whole body heating and throbbing as if she'd just asked him to bury his face between her thighs. Doing as she asked, he pulled down the zipper, the scratch of its teeth from her neck to her hips reverberating around his skull. The dress dropped in a red wave, pooling at her feet. She stepped out of it and moved toward the bed area, completely unaware of the impending physical crisis she just thrust upon Rake.

He stared, all her luscious curves hugged by black nylon shorts that covered her skin from mid-thigh up to the edge of her strapless bra.

It shouldn't look sexy. But it did.

"What are you wearing?" he asked, his voice coming a little hoarse.

She glanced down at herself, then snorted. "Ridiculous, isn't it? It feels like a sausage casing. I always tell myself I should stop wearing them, but I'm a tragically vain creature and like the smooth lines." She plucked at the nylon on her stomach, and it made a slapping noise when she let it go.

It shouldn't have sounded erotic. But it did.

"Plus, they help prevent chub rub," she said.

And now he was picturing rubbing.

Lots of it.

Her thighs pressing together with his hand between them.

His chest moving against hers.

Her hands scratching down his back.

His cock—

"What's chub rub?" he asked, his voice three octaves too high. For the four hundredth time that day, he told himself to get a grip.

"Thigh chafe. I get a heat rash from my inner thighs rubbing together with enough friction to start a bonfire," she said with a laugh, getting on her knees to dig through her garbage bags of clothes, the material stretching so hints of her skin showed through the dark nylon. "But the thigh fabric on these helps, and it doesn't ride up much. Indira and I call them full-body condoms." She laughed again, and Rake swallowed down a groan at the way it made her overspilling breasts bounce in her bra.

"So, pizza?" she repeated. Lizzie pulled out a T-shirt and workout shorts, then pivoted a bit, still on her knees with her back now to him. She reached her arms behind her and undid the clasp of her bra, and Rake made a strangled, choking noise.

"What was that?" Lizzie asked, throwing the large T-shirt over herself and turning her head to look at him over her shoulder.

Her oversized T-shirt and extra-tight bicycle short–looking things should not have made him even harder than he was. But they did.

He scoured her face, trying to find any hint that she knew what she was doing—that she was the single most tempting creature he had ever seen and he wanted to devour her. There wasn't any indication she knew. She was sexy and beautiful in her ridiculous outfit without even trying. And she wasn't his to touch.

"Pizza sounds great," he said, whipping around and heading for the bathroom. "Get whatever you want. I'll leave my wallet on the table."

"Where are you going?" she asked, and Rake could hear more plucking at the spandex.

"Shower," he croaked out, moving as fast as he could toward the bathroom, for the coldest, longest shower of his life.

Chapter 27

LIZZIE was learning all sorts of interesting things about her baby daddy. For starters, he took exceptionally long showers.

The pizza had been delivered over twenty minutes ago, and she waited impatiently for him to emerge. Lizzie sniffed at the closed box, salivating like a dog. She glanced at the firmly shut bathroom door then lifted the lid. It wasn't like he'd know if she ate some of the toppings. Maybe she could even convince him the pizza was delivered with a missing slice. She didn't want to be rude and eat without him, but the water had stopped some time ago, and at this point she assumed he was either jerking off or had diarrhea.

Either way, she didn't want to knock and interrupt him, but she was also close to perishing from starvation.

She walked over to the door, about to press her ear to it so she could gauge how much more time he'd need to take care of business, when it was pulled open.

She jumped back, looking as busted as she felt. But her guilt of being caught was quickly replaced by one single thought.

Body. Body. Body.

Rake stood in nothing but a towel, his skin still damp from the shower. Little droplets of water kissed and hugged the muscles of his torso and traveled down to his navel and below the towel's edge. Ah, to be a drop of water resting between that V at his hip bones to then slip down below and caress that lovely dong.

"What are you doing?" Rake asked, retreating a step into the bathroom like she was going to pounce on him.

Lizzie cleared her throat, trying to drag her eyes from the planes of muscles up to his face, but her vision got tangled in the wet mess of his hair, looking boyish and beautifully mussed from the towel he must have run through it.

"Are you sick?" she asked, her voice sounding too sultry, even to her own ears.

His eyebrows pinched together. "No? Why?"

"You just took a while. I thought maybe you had . . ." She trailed off, trying to lift her horny eyes from the slight bulge they'd noticed in the front of the towel.

"Had what?"

"Diarrhea," she whispered, making eye contact with his nipples.

"What? No!" Rake said, horrified. A blush touched his cheeks.

"Oh, don't look so scandalized. Everyone poops." She gave him a teasing poke in the abs. He flinched, the spot ticklish, but Lizzie was the one to giggle. She catalogued the reaction, her brain wanting to soak up every detail.

"Oh my God, please stop," he said, lightly smacking her hand away and gripping the towel tighter around his waist. "I realized five minutes in that I didn't have any clothes, and we're out of clean towels, and it took me a second to find one that wasn't damp and make sure it was mine and . . ." He trailed off, running his hands through his hair. "Did you order the pizza?" he said, maneuvering past her toward his dresser. Lizzie watched the muscles of his back tighten and release with every step.

Get a grip, you horny monster.

"Yep," she said, trying to sound casual as she flopped onto the couch. She bit into one of the throw pillows and kicked her feet for a second while he wasn't looking, needing to get out some of the naughty energy building inside her. She could hear him searching through his drawers, the whisper of fabric as he pulled a T-shirt down his body. She threw open the pizza box and shoved a slice into her mouth. Fuck it, she needed stimulation from something.

"What toppings did you get?" he asked, moving around the TV stand toward the couch. He sat down, his thighs slightly spread and inviting, the loose fabric of his workout shorts riding up to show the definition of muscle and dusting of leg hair. She wanted to perch like a horny little bird on his lap. Even his kneecaps were sexy. It was ridiculous.

"Pineapple," she said through a mouthful.

"Bold choice."

"Oh shit, do you not like pineapple? I forgot how controversial of a topping it is. It's what Indira and I always get."

"No, I love it. Great pick."

"Ugh, coparenting will be such a breeze at this rate," she said, holding up her hand for a high five. He slapped her palm, and they shared an indulgent smile. Buddies. Partners in crime.

Clueless idiots.

He leaned forward and grabbed a piece. A long strand of cheese dangled from the end, and he lifted the slice high, catching the string between his teeth.

Lizzie watched, completely enraptured by the swipe of his tongue to grab the inch of cheese that stuck to his chin. She shoved the remaining half of her slice into her mouth so she wouldn't say anything stupid or obscene or embarrassing or make this already bizarre situation of a sexually charged platonic living arrangement any worse.

Rake gave a grunt of approval as he bit into it, and Lizzie almost spit hers out.

Pizza was supposed to be safe, not sexy.

But Rake made it look very, very, *very* sexy.

She was about four seconds away from a heaving bosom.

"Wanna watch TV?" she asked, reaching with grabby hands for another slice. She needed to keep her mouth full and eyes distracted if she was to avoid mauling him.

"Sure."

She turned on the TV and flipped to the Travel Channel, her favorite. It was one of the fifty identical shows where a host roamed around an exotic city, and Lizzie was hooked instantly. She nestled more firmly into the couch, tucking her feet up under her.

"God, could you imagine seeing a place like that in real life?" Rake asked, nodding his head at the gorgeous landscape on the screen. A waterfall tumbled from the edge of thick jungle brush, white foam cascading into tiered pools of soft turquoise water—a delicious color that reminded Lizzie of Rake's eyes. She could almost feel herself floating in the warm water, little triangles of sunlight falling through the canopy above and creating a kaleidoscope of aquamarine.

"I've been there," she said, shooting him a sly smile from across the couch.

He snorted. "Bullshit."

"I have! It's called Kuang Si Falls. It's in Laos." The show's host relayed similar facts on a few-second delay, and Lizzie pointed at the screen. Rake still looked skeptical as he leaned over and squeezed the fleshy spot above her knee, making her yelp at the tickle.

"I have pictures! I went the spring I turned twenty."

"*That* was your spring break? *Laos?*"

"What can I say, I'm very cultured and worldly." Lizzie sniffed, tossing her hair back over one shoulder and pushing her glasses up her nose. Rake arched an eyebrow. "Okay, maybe not cultured. But well traveled."

"How'd you afford it?"

"Growing up, I hoarded away every dollar I was ever given.

My family isn't big into sentimental things, so nearly every holiday and birthday, I received money from one family member or another. And then the second I was old enough to get a job, I did. I spent any time I wasn't in school working. I always said I was saving up for college, but I feel like part of me always knew I wouldn't end up going. And then I'd find any other way to make some side cash. Did you know you can make, like, $180 a month selling your blood plasma?"

"I did not," Rake said, looking at her like she was a bizarre creature.

"Yup, easy money. So, I saved up every penny, and then once I graduated high school, I took off. Too much world out there for me to see, and I couldn't wait another minute." The truth was, she would have lived in a cave in the woods to avoid staying in her mother's home for one more day, if it had come down to that.

"Where all did you go?"

"All over. I'd usually pick a country to start, get a one-way ticket, and go as far as I could."

"You didn't run out of money?"

"I *always* ran out of money," she said, laughing at the memories. "But I'd make do. I'd find a gig here and there, friendly strangers willing to feed me. This one time, I was staying in a hostel in Beijing, and I ran out of money to pay for the night. I met these German girls in a similar bind, and we started busking outside the hostel. One of them sang, and the other girl and I tap-danced. We earned enough money to get our bunks back and split a hot pot."

"You tap-dance?"

"No, not at all—I'm a terrible dancer. But I'm great at faking my way through things. Give 'em the old razzle-dazzle," she said, throwing in jazz hands for emphasis.

"That's amazing. What happened to the German girls?"

"I'm not sure," Lizzie said with a shrug, her brows pinching together as she tried to remember. They'd parted ways soon after, just another two faces in a constant ebb and flow. Lizzie was always great at meeting people, but never as good at keeping them. "I think they headed home after or something. Hard to remember."

"Who would you travel with?"

"Oh, no one. I always went alone."

"Alone?" Rake asked, sounding like a mother hen. "Wasn't that lonely?"

"Lonely?" Lizzie repeated, the word tasting funny. "No, never. Being alone is half the fun. I did exactly what I wanted exactly when I wanted to. Never had to ask someone else what they wanted to see or eat or if they were okay staying in shitty hostels. Total freedom." Her favorite feeling in the world. Lizzie valued freedom more than oxygen.

"But having no one to share the memories with? Isn't that . . ." Rake trailed off, studying her closely.

Sad. The word he was searching for was *sad*.

But it wasn't sad. Lizzie had been able to find people whenever she'd needed to. If sadness crept in at the edges, she'd approach a friendly smile, fall into bed with a beautiful stranger. It had been exactly what she wanted. What she needed. Faces and names passing by in a gentle stream around her.

Lizzie shrugged. "I didn't need anyone to share them with. The experience was for me. Not anyone else."

Rake nodded, but she could tell he didn't really understand. "Where else have you been?" he asked, still watching her carefully.

Lizzie chewed on her pizza, thinking. "All over, really. I set up somewhat of a home base in Prague, and then would travel from there. On that trip," she said, nodding back at the TV, "I went on to South Korea and Japan. I really wanted to see Vietnam, but I ended up spending too much time in Japan and had to get back to Prague for a monthlong nannying job I'd snagged."

"Too much time doing what?"

Lizzie wiped her hands on one of the flimsy napkins that came with the pizza. "I met a guy," she said with a laugh. "I try not to live with regrets, but one I'll always have to bear is that I was so preoccupied hooking up with a Turkish guy staying at the same hostel that I missed out on an entire country."

Lizzie thought she saw Rake's jaw tick, but he smoothed his features, smiling. "Sounds like quite the life," he said. "Ever make it to my hemisphere?"

"South America, yes. But never Australia."

Rake made a disapproving noise.

"I'd love to go, though," she added. "I have to see the reef before humans destroy it."

"Ahh, you definitely have to go. I'll take you someday."

Lizzie's eyes went wide, and she blinked at him. Rake snapped his mouth shut, the words dropping heavily onto the couch between them, snuggling up like little monsters for an awkward cuddle.

"Want some water?" she asked, bolting up and clambering over the back of the couch toward the kitchen.

"Yeah, that'd be great," Rake said, clearing his throat.

Lizzie pulled out the water pitcher from the fridge, filling two cups. She chugged down a cold glass, then another. She also made sure to draw a penis in the condensation of Rake's glass for good measure.

She went back to the couch, handing him one of the drinks and settling herself on the far end of the love seat. She needed a bit of space from Rake and his kind words and lovely eyes. He was making domestic bliss all too comfortable.

"That's cool," Rake said, pointing at the TV. The show's host was touring an open-air market and had stopped at one of the stands, watching a woman weave a rainbow of threads into a textile. Her fingers worked quickly, and she gave a broad smile at the camera, pride radiating out of her. "Every inch of that place is covered in fabric."

"You like stuff like that?" Lizzie asked, perking up.

"How could you not? The time and focus that goes into it, the colors, it's incredible."

"Wait here." Lizzie tossed down her plate and bolted toward the bedroom, hurdling over her air mattress like a track star. She pushed aside some of her garbage bags and pulled out her securely taped boxes—boxes she hadn't opened in years. She ran her hands over the cardboard, the memories buzzing and humming, ready to be remembered.

She tore into them, riffling through one, then another, until she found what she was looking for.

She looked at the textile, then hugged it to her chest, rubbing her cheek against the rough wool and tangling her fingers in the fringe at its edge. She pressed her nose to it and inhaled like she could breathe in the happy moments the fabric held, allow them to soak into her soul. Smiling, she moved back toward the couch.

Lizzie stood in front of Rake, allowing the fabric to unfold with a flourish. It was a magnificent explosion of colors—geometric shapes in fuchsia and bright blue, blocky birds lined up in green and purple, linear zigzags of orange and red, all of it glowing against the dark green background.

"Isn't it amazing?" Lizzie cooed, looking down at the weaving. "I got it in Guatemala. The woman even taught me how to embroider one of the flowers." She ran her finger over the raised yellow threads of a wonky flower, the single imperfection in the glorious masterpiece.

"It's amazing," Rake said, pushing off the couch to get a closer look. He pinched the edge between his thumb and forefinger, touching it gently as though it might dissolve in his grasp. "The colors are unreal."

"I know. That's what drew me to it. I saw the woman working on it, and I couldn't stop staring. I sat there and watched her weave for hours." Lizzie remembered the feeling, like each strum on the loom was harmonizing with something in her brain, plucking at her neurons until they were all focused on the creation of the vibrant piece.

"You should hang it up," Rake said, carefully studying the stiches.

Her eyes flew to his face. "Really? That'd be okay?" The idea of gazing at the textile every day, seeing it hanging proudly on a wall, hummed through her bones and set a large grin on her face.

"Sure. It's too cool not to show off. What else have you been hiding in those boxes?"

And so it began. Lizzie plundered into her stored-away memories, reliving all the joy she had put to rest so long ago in that drab, brown cardboard. She'd always meant to show off her travel mementos, but Indira had liked a more minimalistic decor. And something had always held Lizzie back from even asking.

Once she'd sealed up those boxes, she'd been afraid to re-open them, like all the happiness the objects held would rush out. Leave her. Or worse, they'd act as a taunting reminder of the freedom she'd felt in those different places, and what a cruel trick it was to actually grow up.

But as she unpacked them, surrounding herself with treasures— smooth pebbles from a volcanic beach in Iceland, carved cedar trinkets from Lebanon, an evil eye from Turkey—she wasn't homesick for those places. Instead, the memories zipped through her veins in pleasure.

She made a mess of Rake's recently cleaned floors—*their* floors—but he didn't seem to care. He watched the unveiling of every item from the boxes, his eyes lighting up as though they held special meaning for him too, asking questions and laughing at her stories.

"You look so happy," Rake said. And she was. Little starbursts of happiness sparkled through her as she looked at her memories. Nothing had ever fulfilled her quite like traveling, not even sex. She felt most whole and present and complete somewhere, anywhere, that wasn't her parents' house.

And that's how they spent their night, Lizzie rediscovering small pieces of herself she'd long stored away, and Rake welcoming every single one to their new home, the picture of their little blob baby the center of it all.

LIZZIE and Rake were starting to find a flow in their cohabitation. They would both wake up early, Lizzie spending the day at the bakery making and shipping out orders for what she called "vulvalicious sweet treats," while Rake would head to the office, playing catch-up on the team's first few weeks of work without him.

Dominic was dismissive of most suggestions from Rake and any other team member, saying only traditional campaigns geared at the rich and WASP-y would serve the luxury swimsuit line in their East Coast launch, and trying to persuade Dominic otherwise was the verbal equivalent of stepping on a Lego.

Rake was often forced to stay late at work as they finalized details on their upcoming website rebrand, an important photoshoot, and a big launch party happening in a week. He'd also picked up a handful of freelancing gigs that took up any spare moments, wanting to hoard away every dollar he could before the baby was born.

After sitting at a desk staring at his computer screen for hours on end and suffering through endless meetings that could have been summed up in an email, it still caught Rake off guard to come home to an apartment so bursting with life.

Lizzie was noise and smiles and brightness. She always had

the music blasting as she worked in the kitchen, making him sample hot cross buns shaped like plump butts or something she joyfully referred to as "cinna-boobs" the second he walked in the door.

He'd sit at the kitchen counter for hours, listening to her talk and think out loud, sampling her delicious products as often as necessary until he felt sick from all the sugar, and she'd finally collapse on the counter and say her brain bank was empty.

At night, they'd retreat to their separate beds, Lizzie's air mattress pushed against the wall near his normal bed frame. He felt like shit having her sleep on an air mattress, but no amount of pressing would make her budge on it.

And through all of it, Rake had the indecent urge to touch her. Hold her. Brush off the constant smears of flour on her nose. Breathe in the scent of her delicate sweetness edged with something tart and delicious until he was delirious from it.

Lizzie's energy tugged at him like the moon pulls the tide, and there were countless moments when he wanted to give in to the current.

And he couldn't, for the life of him, figure out what the bloody hell was wrong with him.

He wasn't this poetic, *feelings*-type person.

And he certainly wasn't about to give in to such a foolish impulse and screw up their agreed-upon plan.

No. He'd ball his fists at his sides every time she walked past. He'd keep his head down and eyes slammed shut when she pranced out of the bathroom in nothing but a towel. And, he'd (eventually) figure out how to shut off the lobe of his brain that generated constant daydreams of Lizzie Marie Blake.

Besides his dizzyingly intrusive thoughts, everything was fine. Incredibly fine.

One night a couple weeks into their cohabitation, Rake woke up needing to pee. He blinked at the ceiling for a moment

Chapter 28

before letting out a gruff yawn, then rolled out of bed, stumbling through the dark toward the bathroom.

But, in a moment that caused his life to pass before his eyes, his toe caught on something at the corner of his mattress.

And he went down.

Hard.

Whatever he'd tripped over was tall and rubbery and collapsed beneath him.

His sleep-logged limbs didn't balance him, and his mind moved in slow motion as he fell, registering that it was Lizzie's air mattress by the time he was halfway down on it.

"Oh, fuck," he groaned, his knees smacking the floor beneath.

Lizzie screamed as she woke, her body jerking up from the collapse of the air mattress, and her knees hitting him squarely in the chest.

"What the hell?" Lizzie said with a hoarse yell, continuing to kick and twist. Rake groaned again, the wind knocked from his lungs.

He rolled to his back, groping around for one of her legs so she'd stop kicking the life out of him. "Lizzie," he wheezed, "it's me."

Lizzie stilled for a moment, the hiss of her rapidly deflating mattress the only sound in the room. "What are you doing on my air mattress?"

"I had to pee," he said, sucking in a breath.

"You what?"

"Pee! I had to pee!"

"Why were you trying to pee on my air mattress?"

"I wasn't! I tripped over this ridiculous thing," he said, slapping the thick rubber.

"I think you popped it," Lizzie said after a moment.

"You think?" Rake said, the whistle of escaping air emphasizing his sarcasm.

Both their bodies rested on the floor at this point, tangled in the sheets and plastic, and their breaths came in heavy pants from the commotion.

And then Lizzie started giggling.

It was quiet at first, almost imperceptible. But the sound grew to wheezes and snorts, her whole body shaking with laughter.

And Rake was utterly defenseless against the tidal wave of laughter that broke in his own chest. He didn't know how long they lay there, laughing and shaking on the wreckage of her bed. Eventually, the need to pee outweighed the fun, and Rake sat up.

"Get in the bed," he said to Lizzie as he stood, reaching out a hand to help her up.

"I can sleep on the couch," she protested.

"No" was all Rake said, turning her shoulders and giving her a gentle push toward the bed.

After handling his bathroom needs, he returned to the site of his near demise, folding up the useless plastic so Lizzie wouldn't similarly trip over it. He snuck covert glances at her form on the bed while he finished his task, his heart pounding with hard strikes against his chest.

With a deep breath, he walked over to his side of the mattress, sliding under the sheets and leaving half his body hanging off the edge so he wouldn't accidentally touch Lizzie. Which was the totally normal way to handle the situation.

"This is very one-bed-at-the-inn," Lizzie said after a minute, giggling as she squirmed next to him.

Rake was trying to keep his breathing steady—which had become jagged and short for no apparent reason whatsoever the second he slid next to her—and he offered a grunt in response. He stared up at the ceiling, hyperaware of Lizzie's untouchable body just a few inches from him.

"Go to sleep," she said, poking him in the ribs. "You're lying all stiff and weird."

Stiff indeed, Rake thought, her breath pushing soft clouds of air onto his cheeks. Living with Lizzie was making him randier than a teenage boy.

"I'm all wired now," he said, clearing his throat.

"Too much excitement," Lizzie said with a yawn.

"Which part was most exciting for you, Birdy? Me shattering my kneecaps or you double kicking me in the chest?"

Lizzie let out one of her booming signature laughs, making the bed shake. Rake loved her laughs—loved how easily he could pull them out of her and how little sparks of happiness seemed to travel on the sound—but he decidedly did *not* love her laughs when they were two inches from his ear.

"Jesus Christ, Lizzie. Now you've gone and blown out my eardrums too. Any other bodily injuries you want to inflict before the night's up?"

Another laugh bubbled to the surface, but she clamped a hand over her mouth, sending the vibrations through the mattress.

"Glad you think it's so funny. If I didn't know any better, I'd think you're trying to kill me."

Her laughter continued, making him smile. A foreign sense of pride swelled in his chest, knowing he was the source of her joy. He wanted to make her laugh forever.

"I'm serious," he continued. "At this rate, you're going to be carting me around to endless doctor appointments in my old age with the damage you're inflicting."

Her laughter started to fade, but he picked up momentum with the joke.

"And, in retribution, I'm going to make sure they're all at the most inconvenient times of day. You'll hate it." He laughed to himself, picturing an elderly version of Lizzie trying to drive him to appointments around the city. They'd probably fight over directions. And laugh.

After a moment, he realized how quiet and still Lizzie had

become. He squinted at her, making out subtle traces of her face in the dark. The deep pucker between her eyebrows. The way she chewed on her lip.

"What's wrong?" he asked, reaching over and giving her arm a soft squeeze.

"Nothing," she said, shaking her head and pulling her arm away.

"No, tell me. You look upset. Did I offend you? I was only joking."

"No, it's just . . ." She stared at him, the dark room turning her usually vibrant and bright eyes into dark searching pools.

"Just . . . ?"

"You said, 'old age,' which means we'd—" She paused, swallowing. "Which means we'd have to still be together for that to . . . happen."

Rake blinked. "Right. Right . . ." he said, his mind somersaulting. "Total joke. Once the little one comes of age I'm sure we'll . . ." He waved his hands around in a vague motion.

"Right," Lizzie said, nodding. "Right. Yeah. We'll . . . yeah."

An awkward silence snuggled in between them. Lizzie cleared her throat.

"Well, good night, then," she said, turning away from him and tucking her knees up toward her chest.

"G'night," Rake whispered back, trying to ignore the odd poking sensation in his gut.

Chapter 29

Week thirteen, baby is the size of a half-eaten corn dog. And has butt cheeks.

About a week later, Rake woke up with a raging boner.

That was torturously cradled by Lizzie's ass as they spooned.

Which, unfortunately for Rake, was his new disaster of a morning routine.

He always woke before Lizzie for work, saving himself at least a little bit of embarrassment. But the softness of these summer mornings and the sweetness of her skin caused all his common sense to drown in a warm pool of pent-up horniness and tempting bad decisions.

Grappling for self-control, he rolled away from her, sitting up and swinging his legs off the side of the bed in a rush, the sunlight from the cracked window blinds making him squint. He scrubbed his hands through his hair and down his face, begging his erection to leave him alone. He tried to think about work and the big launch party happening that day.

Dominic had been particularly foul and abusive to the team over the past week, everything down to the color of napkins for the event making him bark and snap, commonly stating that they were all tasteless morons dead set on ruining the Onism brand before it even gained legs. While Rake was making decent progress on securing exclusive campaigns with key distributors, he was rapidly burning out from being a rat on a wheel in the process.

Lizzie stirred on the other side of the mattress, and he glanced at her over his shoulder. What he saw caused an odd shaky feeling in his chest, his breath catching for a moment in his throat.

She had rolled to face his side of the bed, one arm reaching out into the space he had just left, her hair spilling in red waves across the pillow. A triangle of morning sun sliced across the room and glowed against her skin, a soft pink obvious below her outrageous freckles.

She looked so soft. So lovely. Like an exquisite painting too precious to ever touch.

Which was ridiculous.

Because it was Lizzie. Loud, vibrant, exuberant Lizzie who thrived on human contact, and he needed to stop being so weird about her. Stop being so . . . damn emotional.

In a flash—because Lizzie seemed incapable of doing anything subtly or slowly—her eyes blazed open, sparking as they roamed around the room before landing on Rake.

"What are you staring at, weirdo?" she said with a yawn, stretching her arms over her head.

"You have a big booger hanging out of your nose," Rake said, aiming for an aloofness he didn't feel.

"What!" Lizzie rubbed the palm of her hand against her nose, crinkling it in a way that Rake found disastrously adorable. And arousing. What was *wrong* with him?

"Did I get it?" she asked, pushing up to sitting and tucking her top lip against her teeth.

Rake tried to bite back a smile as he pretended to study her nose carefully. "No, still there."

Lizzie scrubbed again, even using the collar of her shirt to pinch her nose. It should have been gross. It wasn't.

"Now?"

Rake sighed. "No, it's . . . Oh wait. What's that?"

"What?"

Rake pulled a concerned face. "Lizzie, I'm not sure if you're aware of this, but . . ." His eyes flicked away from her.

"Aware of what?" she said, touching her face all over.

"I hate to be the one to break the news—and please don't burst into hysterics—but it seems as though you have a little spot on your skin right"—he circled his finger around—"there," he said, touching the tip of her nose.

Lizzie stared cross-eyed at his finger before jerking back, grabbing a pillow, and flinging it at him. "You mean my *freckles*?" She let out a booming laugh. "You had me scrubbing my face over a freckle?"

"I told you not to get hysterical."

"You're right, this does come as a shock," she said, rolling her eyes and getting out of bed. "I only have 4.2 million freckles on my body, but I didn't know there was a booger-shaped one *right there*."

She moved toward the kitchen, and Rake's legs twitched with the bizarre impulse to trail after her.

She had on tiny cotton shorts that barely covered her generous hips, and a thin tank top that would likely kill him. Any progress he'd made on controlling his erection was shot to hell, and he tried to adjust himself without her noticing. God, he desperately needed a wank.

But there was no damn privacy in their place. It was moments like these that he *hated* himself for getting an open floor plan apartment. What a fucking *idiot*. It wasn't like he jerked off with a great deal of regularity before all of this. He'd lived in such a gray hole of self-pity that masturbation often felt like more work than it was worth, but he'd had no way to anticipate just how potent Lizzie's presence would be.

He imagined little blood ever reached his brain with how

frequently and furiously she turned him on. And she didn't seem to have a bloody clue. He'd seen her in her seductive mode, and he'd thought that was irresistible. But Lizzie in the morning? In her tiny scraps of pajamas, moaning over a cup of coffee?

Or Lizzie in the evening, home from the bakery smelling like sweetness and sin as she pulled off her work clothes in the middle of the goddamn apartment to change into her "comfy clothes" and ridiculously thick glasses?

Or Lizzie at *night*? Her body so close on the bed, he could feel the heat of her? Hear her soft breathing? Smell the traces of sugar on her skin?

Those things were the definition of irresistible.

And yet, he resisted.

"Why are you just standing in here?" Lizzie asked, padding toward him with a proffered cup of coffee. He took it, and she used her free arm to wrap him in a little hug. Rake reflexively shifted his hips away.

While Rake didn't cross the touch barrier, Lizzie sure as hell did with stunning frequency. She touched and hugged and reached out her hand like human contact was essential to her existence—like she had so much energy, her body couldn't contain it all and she needed to pass on the warmth of it to whoever was near.

It did odd things to Rake's composure.

"Shower," Rake said gruffly, disentangling himself from her warmth and her smell and her damn hair and making a beeline for the bathroom.

Slamming the door, he pressed his back to it, squeezing his eyes closed and trying to think of anything, *anything*, that would remove the imprint of her touch from his skin. He brought his coffee mug to his lips and took a scalding sip. Burning off the roof of his mouth seemed to help take his mind off Lizzie's body, so he gulped down a bit more.

After feeling as though he'd properly collected himself, he opened his eyes and flicked on the lights.

And what he saw almost caused him to faint.

Panties.

Panties *everywhere*.

And *bras* for Christ's sake.

He was surrounded by a sea of red and pink and blue and black lace. Straps and strings. Bows and the random rhinestone. A bra here, a thong there.

It wasn't often that Lizzie did laundry, but when she did, the results were almost more of a mess than what needed to be cleaned. And apparently her delicates were no exception.

She had bras draped over the shower rod. Frilly underwear hanging on the edges of the mirror and on the towel hooks. Two pairs were draped over the back of the toilet, another hung from the vanity knob. It was like walking through a maze in her underwear drawer.

It was hell. Absolute torture.

Rake did what he could to ignore them. He descended deep, *deep* down into one corner of his brain that was still able to find cool indifference to the world around him. But that tiny corner wasn't a great match for the burning flame of his heated blood, the pounding of his pulse in every inch of his body as he maneuvered around Lizzie's most intimately acquainted articles of clothing.

With shaky hands, he pulled the bras from the shower rod, trying his best to gently stack them together before placing them on the washing machine in the closet. He pinched only a millimeter of lace as he lifted a pair of underwear and retrieved his towel from the hook below, replacing them as though they'd burned him. He gingerly transferred the panties sitting on the toilet to wait with the bras so he could put down his towel.

After being certain he'd cleared a decent path, he turned on the shower, pushed the curtain aside, and stepped under the spray. He closed his eyes and tried to let the water relieve the tension in his shoulders, the pounding of his pulse.

He couldn't keep doing this, keep thinking like this. Neither of them wanted a relationship, and marriage had been swiftly rejected, but they both needed to be in their child's life. And Rake recklessly hoped that they would do such in camaraderie. As a team.

But a team wasn't performing at its best if one of the players desperately wanted to fuck the other.

Rake scrubbed the water from his face and opened his eyes, looking for his shampoo. But a tiny scrap of red lace on the edge of the tub caught his attention instead, just an inch peeking out below the wrinkled edge of the curtain liner. Slowly, so slowly one would think he was about to reveal a severed head, he pulled the curtain back.

And looked at those torturous fucking panties. Stared at them for one . . .

two . . .

three . . .

Fuck it.

Rake snatched up the fabric like it was food and he was a starving man, then fisted his cock, no resistance left.

He could picture Lizzie, wet and soft in the shower with him, her curves slick and yielding as his hands traveled all over her. She'd throw her head back as he dragged his teeth along the column of her throat. He could hear the sweet moan she'd let out as his lips traveled down to her breasts, taking the nipple of one between his teeth, pinching the other with his fingers. He could taste every freckle he'd lick along her body.

He continued to stroke his cock, pressing his other hand that still gripped the panties to the cool tiled wall. He was so far gone, he could practically feel her hips rubbing against him, her body bent over and shaking for relief. He'd drag his hand over that perfect ass, spanking and squeezing the tender flesh until she writhed against him, *begging* for him to push inside her. His hand would trace around to her front, gliding over her soft lips, finding the spot that would make her moan and pant and scream for him. And then, only when he was sure she was close, *so close*, would he surge into her.

A strangled growl broke from his throat as he imagined pounding into her warm, wet heat. The way she'd call his name right before she came. *Rake. Come. Now. Come with me. Rake.*

And he'd—

"Rake?"

The reality of Lizzie's voice—her *close* voice—scared the soul from Rake's body. He jerked up so fast, he went light-headed, seeing stars.

"Sorry to barge in, but I need to grab my makeup. I'm going to be late for work."

Rake was disoriented, no blood reaching his head, as she moved farther into the bathroom. He couldn't keep his balance with his head spinning, the shower tiles twisting and turning as he tried to get a grip.

His feet slid across the tub floor, his hands clawing at the walls and the curtain, neither of which offered any support.

"Are you—"

Before Lizzie could get the question out, Rake's legs slid out from under him, and he fell with a loud smack onto the bathtub floor, ripping the shower curtain down with him.

The only noise he heard for the first second was the ringing in his ears, the distant sound of the water falling around him.

Then, with perfect, sonic boom clarity, Lizzie's voice broke through his haze.

"Oh my God, is that my *thong*?"

Chapter 30

LIZZIE stared with an open-mouthed grin at Rake's spread-eagle form in the tub. She knew this was a very serious matter and he could have hurt himself, but she was notorious for laughing at the absolute worst possible times.

"You okay?" she managed to choke out, trying to swallow down the nervous giggles.

"Fine," Rake said, his eyes wide with horror, one hand (unsuccessfully) covering his erect penis and the other fisting her underwear.

"You sure?" she asked, pretending to cough over a laugh.

Rake was quiet for a moment, still staring up at her, before he closed his eyes and turned his head. "I think I'd like you to leave so I can die in peace, please," he said.

"Oh, calm down, drama queen," Lizzie said, no longer hiding her amusement now that she was pretty sure he was unharmed. Besides his pride. Obviously.

"Let me help you up." She moved forward, bending over the tub to offer him a hand. He ignored it, pushing his way to standing. Lizzie handed him a towel, pressing her lips together to hide a grin.

"I'm sure this happens to every guy," she said, smiling at the glare Rake shot her. "I'm just worried you sprained your wrist too, because that fist was *flying*."

Rake stomped out of the room, and Lizzie followed.

"And I'm honestly surprised it took this long for an incident to happen," she continued.

Rake shot her a confused look as he gathered his clothes in his hands, still refusing to speak.

"You have an 'I masturbate a lot' type of vibe, and I can't believe I haven't walked in on you sooner."

Rake blew out an angry breath, slamming his underwear drawer and heading back toward the bathroom, clothes fisted in one hand.

"I feel like I could toss a tomato at you and you'd hump it," Lizzie continued, practically running after him in her pursuit to apparently be the most annoying person on the planet. "You look like—"

The words died in her throat as Rake spun on his heel, splotchy patches of red staining his cheeks, annoyance flashing in his beautiful eyes.

"Do you ever stop talking?" he growled, before taking her face between his hands and placing a rough kiss on her lips.

It was the kind of kiss that stole the air from her lungs. Like dropping down the largest hill on a roller coaster, losing yourself to a free fall, and hoping you never touch the ground. It was a kiss that made her skin prickle and her heart stutter.

On instinct, she molded herself against him, pleasure points sparking in her breasts, her belly, her hands—every millimeter of her body that touched his coming to life. He tasted like citrus and sin, and she couldn't get enough of it as he deepened the kiss. She felt like a raw nerve, something coming unhinged in her chest as he sipped at her lips, pressed her for more as his tongue explored her. It felt like every moment of want and lust and hunger over the past few weeks clicked into place, weaved into a beautiful tapestry of this kiss.

And just when she thought she might fracture apart from the magnitude of it, he pulled away.

And took two steps back.

His chest heaved as he stared at her with something like bewilderment and fear, while she, on the other hand, swayed forward as though he were a magnet she couldn't fight.

"We won't talk about this again," he said, his voice low and rough.

Lizzie didn't know if he meant the kiss or the masturbation or the fall, but she was too dazed to ask, her skin still humming. She nodded numbly.

"I'll see you at the launch party," he said, fixing her with a final, level stare before turning around, walking into the bathroom, and shutting the door behind him.

Chapter 31

LIZZIE pounded her fist on Indira's door. She pounded and pounded and pounded like maybe she could take an ounce of her built-up horniness and confusion and expel it through her fist. She was more likely to punch a hole through the wood than solve her ailment.

"Jesus Christ, Lizzie," Indira said, swinging the door open and gracefully sidestepping Lizzie's rogue fist. "Who died?"

"*Indiraaaaa*," Lizzie whined, propelling herself into the familiar apartment and flopping onto the couch face-first. "I have a very real problem."

"It's nice to see you're being so stoic about it," Indira said, pressing her lips into a firm line in a failed attempt at hiding her smile.

Lizzie turned her head to glare at her. "I'm serious!"

"What's your problem, sweet Elizabeth?" Indira asked, sitting on the coffee table and stroking a motherly hand over Lizzie's hair.

"It's Rake."

"What about Rake? Do I need to kill him?"

"No. He's killing *me*," Lizzie said, rolling over and draping a dramatic arm across her eyes.

"Could you try actually telling me what's going on, or do

you want to keep going like this? I just need to know if I should start drinking."

Lizzie pushed up onto her elbows, fixing Indira with the most serious expression she could muster. "I'm so horny, I think I might die."

Indira stared at Lizzie for five long seconds, her face inscrutable, before she burst out in explosive laughter.

"I'm serious!" Lizzie said, collapsing down. "It's like this cold war of sexual tension. I mean, you've seen his face. But then that body? Holy. Fuck. I accidentally walked in on him spread-eagle in the shower this morning and nearly swooned."

Despite Lizzie's serious tone, Indira kept whooping with laughter.

"It's not funny! I want to run my teeth down his thighs like a cheese grater. I want him to spank me so hard, my soul leaves my body. I want to gnaw on him like a piece of Laffy Taffy then shrink my body down so I can build a permanent residence in between the muscles of that hot V thing he has. And I've never, *ever* wanted to suck dick so bad in my entire life. He's making me feral."

"You've always been feral," Indira said, wiping at her eyes. "You've just never not had an outlet for it. Why don't you guys have sex and get it out of your system?"

"We made a pact," Lizzie said, pulling a pillow over her face and biting the fabric. "He said if we're doing this coparenting thing platonically, we shouldn't also be having sex."

"*Damn* him and his rationality," Indira said dryly.

"What am I going to do? I feel like I'm one more peek of his damn kneecaps away from combusting or jumping him."

"Oh sweet child, just masturbate. It's not that hard."

Lizzie bolted up to sitting. "You think I haven't been? You think I'm not sneaking off to the bathroom every chance I get? He probably thinks I have IBS at this point. It's not helping. *Nothing* is helping. I'm just a dehydrated, horny mess."

Indira must have seen a semblance of the torment in Lizzie's eyes, because her face softened. "I'm sorry. I imagine it's actually very hard to be pregnant and horny and unable to do anything. I wish I had better advice for you. You could go on a date, though, you know. You never had a problem finding sex before all of this happened."

Lizzie turned this over in her mind, but for some reason, the thought of a stranger's hands on her, once such a delicious image, made her queasy. She didn't want a random person touching her. She wanted Rake. Only Rake. And that was terrifying.

"I don't know. It just feels weird to do that. Like it's . . . wrong or something."

"It shouldn't," Indira said, studying Lizzie. "You'll need to get back out there eventually, right? Or what, you're just going to live the next eighteen years of your life like this? Horny and living with some guy, not together but also not seeing other people? You'll want to find someone to be with eventually, won't you?"

Lizzie was quiet, trying to picture herself happy with this "someone," but Rake's stupid face kept popping up instead.

"I'm just being ridiculous," she said at last. "I'll get over this. It's probably hormones."

"Do you want to stay here?" Indira asked. "Move back in? There's no shame if living with Rake isn't working."

"Living with Rake is actually kind of fun," Lizzie admitted, plucking at the couch cushions. "I'm the one making things more complicated than they need to be." She wouldn't tell Indira about the kiss. That would provoke dozens of questions that Lizzie had no answers for. She knew the kiss meant nothing in the grand scheme of things.

They sat in silence, Lizzie staring down at her hands, feeling the weight of Indira's stare.

"I should go," Lizzie said at last. "Rake invited me to some swimsuit launch party whatever thing, and I need to finalize a few orders at Bernadette's before I get ready."

"That sounds glamorous."

"Only the classiest for yours truly and le bébé," Lizzie said, grinning and rubbing her hand over her barely-there bump. She stood and moved toward the door.

"Love you!" Indira said as Lizzie stepped out into the hallway.

"Love ya back," Lizzie said, then shut the door.

Out on the street, Lizzie's phone rang and she groaned when she saw GOLDEN CHILD flash across the screen. Ryan had been reaching out to her with greater frequency over the past few weeks, regularly sending her condescending texts like Hi. How are you? Or How've you been?

Ha! As if Lizzie couldn't see right through that little passive-aggressive stunt.

Still in a pissy mood, she answered the call. "God, Ryan, could you be more obvious?"

There was a long silence. "Lizzie?"

Lizzie blew out a breath. "Yes, Lizzie's Sausage Shop, we'll pork it, you fork it."

"Obvious about what?" Ryan asked.

"With your obsessive texting and calling." Lizzie sighed. "I know what you're doing."

"I hardly think texting you twice a week to see how you're doing is obsessive," Ryan said, sounding genuinely confused.

"I know why you're doing it."

"Why I'm doing what?"

Annoyance and indignation flooded Lizzie. She wasn't stupid enough to think her brother would reach out to her without an ulterior motive. "You're texting me because you think I'm going to mess up this dumb-ass cake, and you're scared, so you think that by texting me regularly, it will remind me I have to make it. News flash, Ryan, I know what I'm doing."

. . . for the most part.

Lizzie knew what she was doing *for the most part.*

Silence flooded the line for three heavy seconds. "That's

really why you think I text you?" Ryan asked, his voice soft and bewildered. "To harass you about a cake?"

"Well . . . yeah. What else would it be?" Lizzie said, scraping the toe of her shoe against the concrete.

Ryan let out an incredulous laugh. "To. See. How. You. Are."

Lizzie pulled the phone away from her ear and gave it a wide-eyed look before responding. "Yeah? Why would you want to do that?"

"Because you're my sister? Why the hell else would I want to?"

This tripped Lizzie up. While Ryan had never shown Lizzie open disdain, he was such a perfect shining golden star of a child, Lizzie had always assumed he found her as . . . unpalatable . . . as their parents did.

Ryan sighed. "Look, I don't exactly understand how I screwed this up, but I apologize. I've just been texting you to check on you. That's all. I-I'm . . ."

"You're what?" Lizzie said, her throat feeling a little tight.

"Looking forward to seeing you in a month," Ryan said, his voice without inflection.

He might as well have told Lizzie he thought she was the greatest sister in the world for the small kick start of happiness it gave her heart. A slow grin broke across her cheeks, and she couldn't help letting out a tiny laugh. After a few moments, she remembered she was on an actual phone call and it was expected of her to respond.

"Oi, bruv, I be damn'd. Lookin' forward ta seeing you too, good sir. Only two fortnights' time, I reck'n," Lizzie said, putting on a thick and awful Cockney accent because Ryan saying he was excited to see her felt a tiny bit serious, and Lizzie did not do well with serious conversations.

Ryan was silent again on the line, then a rusty chuckle came through. "No one would say two fortnights. They would just say a month," Ryan said.

"Wha' you on about, then?" Lizzie said, making him laugh even harder. She couldn't help laughing too.

"You're ridiculous," Ryan finally choked out through his giggles. "I have to run, but I'll talk to you soon."

"Bye, Ry," Lizzie said, then hung up the call.

Chapter 32

LIZZIE met Rake outside of a swanky high-rise in Center City a few hours later, having spent the day telling herself over and over that the kiss meant nothing and she was making it a way bigger deal than it was.

Rake looked nothing short of devastating in his black suit and black dress shirt. If Lizzie were a cartoon character, her eyes would have popped out of her head while *AHOOGA* blared at full volume as she watched him lean against the building and scroll through his phone.

God really spent his time on that one, Lizzie thought as she stepped toward him and tapped him on the shoulder.

"Hi," she said. "You look ridiculously good and it's borderline obscene."

Rake blinked at her for a moment before giving her an embarrassed smile. "You clean up well yourself, Birdy," he said, eyeing her up and down. "I'm starting to doubt you own anything other than red dresses."

She waved off the comment then dragged a hand down the lapels of his suit coat, unable to resist touching him. "No, for real," she continued, still ogling. "This suit makes me wish I was a snake, so I could unlatch my jaw and swallow you whole."

Rake blinked again, opened his mouth to say something, seemed to think better of it, and shook his head.

"Let's go," he said, placing his hand on her lower back to guide her into the building.

They rode the elevator up to the rooftop in silence, Lizzie fidgeting and smoothing down the skirt of her bloodred dress, tangling her fingers in the overlay of lace, while Rake typed away on his phone.

When the golden doors of the elevator slid open, Lizzie was slapped with the news that swimsuit launch parties were her waking nightmare of ADHD overstimulation.

Bumping music and chatter crashed at her from both sides, sending a sharp zap of energy from her brain down her spine. A glittering sea of nicely dressed people fanned out across the rooftop, all circled around a sparkling pool where models in swimsuits lounged and laughed, every color and texture tugging at her attention. They were swallowed into the crowd, Rake leading Lizzie to a table of name tags while she gawked, all the shininess of the scene devouring her brain like warp-speed ivy.

"Here you go," Rake said, handing her a marker after scribbling his own name on one of the tags. "Do you want a drink?" he asked.

"Tonic and lime," Lizzie said, giving him a smile. "Oh, and have them put it in a fun glass," she added as he headed toward the bar.

Turning back to the table, Lizzie uncapped her pen. With a stroke of genius, she scribbled *Sek C. Baudy* across the white square, making herself snort. She slid it over a bit, hoping it might give someone else a laugh, then wrote out *Lizzie* on a fresh sheet.

"Here you are," Rake said, handing her the glass. "Shall I introduce you to some people?"

"Let's do it," Lizzie said, taking a sip of the tonic then grabbing a name tag off the table and slapping it on her chest.

They made a circuit around the rooftop, Rake stopping to introduce her and chat with coworkers she'd heard him speaking to many late nights. Even when he left the office, his work never seemed to really end, always someone else to call, some other fire to put out, some side job to complete for extra income. Lizzie admired his work ethic but often found herself wondering if anything else in his life would ever matter as much as his job.

Lizzie received more than one funny look as they made their way around the party, but she brushed it off as people being curious about who she was in relation to Rake. She made sure to introduce herself before Rake had a chance to stumble over an identifier for her. Lizzie was doing the best she could to stay focused on the small talk, but she missed more than half of what people said or asked, the noises and action of the party sinking its claws into her attention, turning her brain this way and that.

"Lizzie," Rake said, steering her toward an imposing older gentleman who sipped a glass of scotch as he surveyed the party, "I'd like to introduce you to my boss, Dominic. He's responsible for getting the line to be such a success already."

Lizzie flicked a look at Rake for his oh-so-subtle ass-kissing before fixing Dominic with a smile and reaching out her hand. "Great to meet you."

Dominic lifted his hand to shake, his gaze snaking an appreciative path down her body, but it snagged halfway through, his eyes locking on Lizzie's right tit.

"What the bloody hell is written on your chest?" Dominic said, his eyes flashing with a bizarre mix of horror and lewdness. Gripped by fear at the look, Lizzie clutched her boob, then looked down.

And her heart sank.

She'd been walking around this fancy party, talking to Rake's clients and coworkers, trying to be classy and charming, with the name *Sek C. Baudy* written in block letters across her chest.

And Lizzie, by no uncertain terms, wanted to die of embarrassment on the spot.

"I'm so sorry," Lizzie said, her eyes flashing between Dominic and Rake, every inch of her skin stinging with mortification as she replayed the funny looks she'd received.

"Lizzie, it's—"

"So, so sorry," she repeated, ripping off the tag and taking a step back.

And right as she did, she collided into the people behind her.

The crash of champagne glasses and a silver platter echoed around the party.

Lizzie was suddenly drenched in booze while hors d'oeuvres slid down her back before plopping to the ground, following the platter to its demise.

She turned, seeing two horrified servers looking down at the mess, broken glass and sea scallops covered in a green sauce littered around their feet.

"Jesus Christ," Dominic said gruffly, making Lizzie's body jolt in shame.

"Fuck, I'm so sorry," Lizzie said, for what felt like the thousandth time in five minutes. She dropped down, grabbing handfuls of scallops and flinging them on the platter while trying to avoid the shards of glass. "I can't believe—I'm sorry. What a mess. Here, I'll—"

"It's okay. You go get cleaned up," Rake whispered, squatting next to her and placing a hand on her back. "I'll get someone to take care of this."

Lizzie nodded, squeezing her eyes shut tight against the pressure of tears and embarrassment threatening to consume her as Dominic continued to mutter about the giant fucking mess.

She stood, unable to meet Rake's eyes, and hurried toward the bathroom.

Chapter 33

AFTER calming down the profusely apologetic servers and getting the mess taken care of, Rake turned to Dominic, preparing for his worst.

The lines of Dominic's face were deeper than usual, his nostrils flared as he glanced around, trying to gauge the disruption's effect as curious eyes lingered on them. Dominic existed on precision and style, and Lizzie's mishap pressed every one of his nerves.

"I'm sorry, Dominic. She's a touch clumsy."

Dominic held up his hand, his voice low so no one else would hear. "Rake, you can't bring women like that to events like this."

Rake blinked, not understanding.

Dominic looked at Rake then sighed, his anger easing like he was about to import a life lesson to a small child. "I get it. Being young can cloud your judgment when it comes to mixing business with . . . pleasure," Dominic said, shooting Rake a conspiratorial glance. "But you have to be wiser than this. You're representing the company. The brand. Girls like her aren't a good look for events like this."

Rake opened his mouth, but no words came out.

Dominic clapped his hand on Rake's shoulder in a friendly gesture, but his grip squeezed harder than necessary. "Don't get me wrong, girls like that are always a good time," he said in a lascivious whisper, "but leave that for your private time. And I tell you this from making similar mistakes myself when I was your age. You have a great career ahead of you, and I'd hate to see something like that . . . tarnished."

Rake stared at him, his mind reeling as he tried to figure out what to say.

"Glad we had this talk," Dominic said with one more pat on Rake's shoulder. He plastered on a grin and walked away, mingling with his clients.

Rake scrubbed a hand down his face, feeling like an absolute wanker as he played back the conversation. He hated hearing Dominic talk about Lizzie that way, but he also couldn't challenge his boss and get fired on the spot. He doubted Dominic even meant it. He was probably as stressed and tired as the rest of the team and lashed out at the nearest target.

"Rake?"

Rake spun around to see his coworker Andrew typing away on his phone as he started to speak. "The photographers are ready to get the 'candid,'"—Andrew paused his typing long enough to add air quotes—"shots of the models with the golden hour, but we need your approval before we start."

"Right," Rake said, following Andrew toward the shallow end of the pool where the models were clustered in their black-and-white swimsuits, long-limbed and smiling radiantly as they gently splashed in the water.

Rake shared a few words with the photographer, confirming the aesthetic goals of the shots, then clapped his hands, telling everyone to get to it.

Rake watched with disinterest, trying to avoid the suggestive smiles some of the women sent him. After a few minutes he rearranged the order, pulling a few girls out for a smaller focused shot. They were all naturals, smiling and posing with professionalism that made Rake confident they'd have plenty of images to use.

He was about to call it a wrap and let the models and photographer go back to actually *candid* candids, when a husky voice spoke near his ear.

"These suits are divine," the woman purred, placing a hand on his shoulder. She gave him a honeyed smile, lips full and dark red, her catlike features framed by waves of silky black hair. "I'm Sasha, by the way," she added.

"Rake," he said, giving Sasha a brief smile before turning his attention back to the pool.

"And what do you do, Rake?" she asked, pressing closer to him under the pretense of moving out of the photographer's way. She didn't step back.

"I'm on Onism's creative team."

She let out a tinkling laugh like that had been a hilarious joke, and he shot her a funny look. She was undeniably gorgeous and friendly, and the Rake from five years ago would have jumped at her obvious flirtation. But, at this point in his life, he wasn't interested. And after dealing with Dominic, the last thing he had patience for was small talk. Strangely enough, even the *idea* of engaging in flirty banter with this woman made his skin crawl, and an image of Lizzie flashed full force through his brain.

"I'm a model," Sasha said, dragging a hand down her lovely figure. "Obviously."

"You're doing great work," Rake said, hoping his tone sounded professional as he gestured toward the pool. She giggled again.

"It's easy when these suits are so glamorous," she said, finally stepping away to do a full spin as she ran her hands over the crisscrossing fabric that went from the top piece to the bottom. "Oh, am I all tangled back here?" she asked, stopping with her back toward him, her fingers resting on the fabric near the curve at the base of her spine. The weaving pattern was tucked and bunched, forming a small ball of knotted material.

"Yeah, looks a bit twisted," Rake said, clearing his throat as he glanced up from her perky butt and put all his focus on the photographer.

"Would you fix it for me?" she asked, glancing over her shoulder at him, eyes sultry and heated. Rake's jaw ticked as he looked down her body. He nodded, quickly plucking the strings of fabric into place.

"All set," he said, gesturing toward the photographer and pool in the hopes she'd walk away and break up the intimate dynamic that seemed to be choking him.

"You're the best," Sasha said, placing a hand on his chest, then popping up on her tiptoes to place a kiss on his cheek. "I better get back to work, but find me later if you get a spare second," she added, sauntering back toward the pool and shooting him one last sultry smile as she caught him watching her walk away.

Rake felt himself blush.

Like an *asshole*.

What was *wrong* with him?

Why did he have so many . . . *feelings* all of a sudden?

Why did seeing Lizzie in her red dress make his heart feel like it would beat out of his chest? Why did her laugh feel like a punch to his gut with an iron fist? Why did Sasha catching him checking her out make him feel like a guilty piece of shit?

He'd been doing astonishingly well the last few years with composed neutrality on all things, but now it was like his motherboard was short-circuiting and his brain was a mess of emotions.

He scrubbed his hands down his face in frustration.

And when he opened his eyes and looked across the party, his gaze landed on the redheaded source of so many of these ridiculous fucking feelings.

And she looked pissed.

Their eyes locked for one tense moment, before she turned on her heel.

And took off in a dead sprint.

Chapter 34

LIZZIE knew, objectively, that running away was not the subtlest of party exits. But, subjectively, she was feeling too overwhelmed and insecure to care.

She'd never struggled too much with loving her body. She liked her thick thighs and round hips. Found satisfaction in her big boobs and soft curves.

But, standing by that pool—bloated, sweaty, stained, and smelling like scallops—while a literal *model* flirted with Rake, every ounce of Lizzie's confidence seemed to evaporate from her body. She was only human, after all.

A human woman feeling a lethal combination of jealousy and possessiveness as she watched the gorgeous woman lean into Rake as he smiled down at her.

Lizzie's heart felt like it collapsed in on itself, folding over and over like a piece of paper until it was a sad little square.

In a totally platonic roommates/coparents way.

A teeny-tiny corner of her brain—the feminist lobe that she'd worked hard to develop but seemed to be shriveled up at the moment—told her she was being ridiculous. That the woman was her sister-in-arms and shouldn't be disliked for her beauty. That internalized misogyny would *not* get the better of her, and she would be cool, calm, and collected for once in her life.

But it was watching Rake gently touch the woman's back, seeing the smiling woman place a kiss on his cheek, that made a sharp little monster in the pit of Lizzie's stomach rear its head and snap its jaws.

And when Rake had looked at her, she couldn't do anything but bolt.

She tore off her heels and legged it out to the street, barreling the few blocks to their apartment. She could hear Rake yelling her name behind her, but she didn't stop.

Lizzie burst into their apartment, walking an erratic circuit around the space as Rake crashed in a few seconds behind her.

"Damn, Birdy, you're fast," Rake said, his chest heaving. He rested his palm on the wall, bending over slightly as he tried to catch his breath. Lizzie wanted to put her hands around his stupid throat and squeeze.

"Fuck you," she said, reaching at her side and unzipping her dress, letting it fall to the floor in a sweaty heap. She moved toward the kitchen for some water.

"Excuse me?" Rake no longer sounded out of breath. Instead, a sharp, thick tone punctuated his words.

"Fuck. You," Lizzie said again, mocking his accent as she enunciated the words.

"You are wildly misinterpreting what you saw, and I don't appreciate the tone."

"You don't appreciate my *tone*?" Lizzie boomed, turning on him. "Well, I don't appreciate you . . . you . . ."

"Me what? Doing my job?" he said, taking a step toward her. "Trying to provide for you? For us? Need I remind you that we aren't together? That *you* decided on that? Or is that only for you to point out when the situation suits you? I don't belong to you. And you don't get to make assumptions about what you think you saw."

All of this was true, but it only fueled her anger. "Hate to break it to you, pal," she said, jabbing her finger in his chest, "but I'm playing the pregnancy card here and now. You want to be involved? Then do that without eye-fucking the women at your work. Be the good little baby daddy you said you wanted to be."

"Don't shove your fingers in my face."

"Don't make a fool out of me!" she said, pushing past him toward the bed. "You need to get your rocks off, pal? Well, sorry, but the no-sex rule was yours, not mine."

"You won't let me finish a sentence and explain it to you," he said, fisting his hands in his hair as he followed her. "She—"

"I mean for fuck's sake, just masturbate like a gentleman. You don't have to involve another woman in this shit show," Lizzie said, getting down on her knees to rummage through her things. Her body was buzzing, frantic for some sort of release from the overwhelming surge of emotions—a disastrous combination of anger, pent-up horniness, and the whisper of genuine feelings she may be having for Rake.

Rake let out a bark of a laugh. "Oh, is that all I have to do? That'd be nice, but I can't get two minutes alone to do so without you barging in!"

"Listen, buddy, you're the one who was so jazzed about us not having *doors* in our apartment. The lack of privacy is on *you*," Lizzie said, turning on him. "But go ahead! Ejaculate everywhere! See if I care! Just don't flirt with random women in front of me and expect me to be cool with it."

Rake stared at her, and something about the close way he studied her, like he was searching desperately for an answer, plucked at her heartstrings. His face morphed from sharp confusion to soft understanding.

"You're jealous." He said the words slowly, bordering on a question.

Lizzie's whole body stiffened, rage spilling off her in waves. "What? As if, you cocky asshole," she spat, riffling through her next bag of things.

"You're jealous," he said again, this time with more conviction. "This is a jealousy thing."

She scoffed then turned on him, brandishing the vibrator she'd been looking for like a weapon. "This isn't a jealousy thing," Lizzie shouted, "it's a respect thing. A frustration thing. I'm frustrated and horny and angry. But instead of finding some random dude to bang, I'm going to have a good old-fashioned angry masturbation session. Like a *lady*," she added, flopping on the bed.

"So be gone, you great Australian brute. I have things to attend to that don't involve your ridiculous notions of jealousy. You can use the shower to take care of yourself." She gave him a dismissive wave then flicked on the toy, revving it to life in her palm.

She gracelessly lifted her hips and pulled her underwear down. Rake still stood in the corner, looking at her with a mixture of heat and humor and curiosity.

"You don't get to stand there and watch," Lizzie said, balling up her panties and chucking them at him. They didn't come close to hitting him, hovering in the space between them for a split second, before fluttering to the ground in a pile of red.

Their gazes locked for an angry, heated moment before Lizzie let out a huff and looked away, moving the toy down her body. He wasn't worth her attention.

But he also wasn't a presence that was easily ignored, try as she might to focus on the task at hand. Sex, even solo, usually absorbed her full attention, centered her racing thoughts. But Rake's lurking body tugged at her mind, pulling her focus from the orgasm she needed.

Out of the corner of her eye, she saw him move forward slowly, bending down to retrieve the panties. He lifted them, rubbing the silky material between his fingers, the movement branding her as though he'd caressed her the same way.

Rake folded the flimsy fabric into a small, neat square, then tucked them into his back pocket.

"Those won't fit you," Lizzie said to the ceiling, letting her head loll back into the pillows as she turned up the intensity on her toy, enjoying the vibrations softly pulsing against her. She tried to focus on the feeling of silicone between her legs, instead of remembering Rake's touch. She squeezed her eyes closed, trying to drown him out of all her senses.

"And I said leave," she added.

She hated how much she secretly liked that he was watching. Knowing he was looking at her sent a jolt of lust through her body, the tension building along her spine. She hated that it was thoughts of him that were getting her closer, instead of the mechanical toy that usually absorbed her mind during these moments.

Sex wasn't supposed to have thoughts, only sensations.

"I don't plan on just watching." His voice was closer now, a gravelly whisper mixing with the vibrations humming through her body, pooling low in her belly and high in her chest.

Lizzie let out a gasp as tension built, taking her closer and closer to that mindless peak where she'd get rid of these mixed-up feelings for Rake. Her hips started grinding in a delicious rhythm. So close.

Almost

There

She sucked in a breath when she felt pleasure cresting over her, ready to ride the wave, but Rake's hand wrapped over hers, lifting it and the toy. Lizzie jolted.

"Are you fucking kidding me right now?" she snapped, glaring at him. He hovered over the mattress, his hand pressing hers against the sheets while his broad expanse of chest filled her view.

"What the actual fuck—"

Rake cut her off, pressing his lips against hers. Lizzie felt herself melt into the sensation of his hot mouth, before she remembered herself and pulled back, ready to snap again at him.

"I like when you get jealous, Lizzie," he whispered against the corner of her mouth before biting into the pillowy flesh of her bottom lip. She hated the groan that escaped her.

The room felt humid and stifling, his large form blocking out the light and creating a hazy golden glow around his body.

Rake started kissing her again, slower now, almost tender, and the hint of emotions made her squirm and push for more.

Tenderness was dangerous, and she needed to avoid it at all costs.

One hand still pinning hers to the bed, he used the free one to skim down her neck, his fingertips tickling her oversensitized skin, making her arch.

He continued his journey, allowing his palm to graze along her body, barely touching the swell of her breast, splaying across her ribs, then farther down over the curves of her stomach and hips, traveling down her thigh to her bent knee.

"What are you doing?" she said, breaking away from his kiss, pushing her spinning head into the pillow as every nerve ending zeroed in on the pressure of his hand on her knee.

"Can I touch you?"

The question caught Lizzie off guard. She'd never been asked so overtly, with such blatant need encased in restraint. It unnerved her.

"Because what you've been doing was . . . ?" she said, trying to lighten the tension.

"Lizzie." Something about the edge in his voice forced her eyes to his. He looked wild, desperate. She couldn't hold his gaze longer than to give a tiny nod.

"Say it," he growled, squeezing at the flesh of her thigh.

"*Yes*," Lizzie gritted out through clenched teeth.

He shifted, kneeling between her parted thighs. He let go of her wrist, bringing both hands to rest on her knees, pushing her open, looking at her with wolfish hunger.

Rake stared at her until she couldn't stand it, and Lizzie tried to squirm away. He soothed her by finally dragging his hands down the insides of her thighs, his fingers exerting different pressure points across her wet heat that sent sparks across her eyes. Her body started to relax again, waiting and desperate for him to touch her exactly where she needed.

He didn't make her wait. Spreading her even more with one hand, he used the other to push into her while his thumb moved in a circular rhythm that had Lizzie's neck tensing and back arching. Their eyes locked over her body, and it was too much. Too close. Lizzie needed to escape what she saw in his look. She'd never been shy about sex. Never abashed about being naked or touched.

But something about the way Rake studied her body, responded to her sounds, made her feel overexposed. Shy. Like he saw too much.

"I've missed hearing you moan," he whispered, his voice like a caress down the center of her body, pleasure igniting along every nerve.

"I thought you said no sex," she ground out between pants, trying to shoot him a coy smile.

"Do you ever stop talking?" he asked, plunging in deeper and curving his fingers in a way that stole the breath from her lungs and had her vision blurring at the edges. Rake hummed in satisfaction. "I guess that does the trick," he said, moving to press his smile against the inside of her knee as she shot him the dirtiest look she could muster.

But she wanted more.

Lizzie wanted pressure and sweat and teeth.

She sat up, tearing at his suit jacket and ripping off his belt buckle. She had him stripped to his boxer briefs in no time. Lizzie pushed him down on the bed, straddling his hips as she ground herself against him.

Rake groaned and pressed his head into the pillows, tendons

and muscles sticking out of his neck as she rubbed back and forth against his length.

And damn did it feel good—powerful—to see him undone beneath her. To watch him unravel as every muscle in his body tensed and hardened. His groans shot currents of lust from her breasts to her clit, all of it building higher and higher.

With a sudden grunt, he lifted her, flipping her on her back and positioning himself over her again. He ground into her with speed and pressure, his boxers damp between them as his hips pumped, the tip of his swollen cock hitting her in the perfect spot over and over until Lizzie cried out, her fingernails digging into his back, the orgasm jolting through every corner of her body.

"Fuck," Rake grunted out, following her into the mindless bliss.

He collapsed to the side of her, rolling onto his back, and they stared up at the ceiling, panting and sweaty.

A weighted silence filled the room.

"I feel like a teenager," Rake said after a few moments, shooting a gross look to his sticky abs and destroyed boxers.

"Who doesn't love a good dry hump to completion?" Lizzie said, awkwardness settling around them as they continued to lie there. They were quiet for a few minutes.

"We probably shouldn't have done that," she said when the continued silence became unbearable.

"Probably not," Rake agreed, still staring up at the ceiling.

"It was a one-off thing," Lizzie added.

"Totally. Won't happen again."

Lizzie nodded, ignoring the way her heart felt like it might punch through her chest. Getting up, she swung her legs off the side of the bed and headed toward the bathroom, walking off any weird feelings that were trying to cling to her.

"Yup, never again," she said, shooting him a smile before

closing the bathroom door behind her, unable to shut out the emotions swirling through her stomach.

It would all be okay. It was nothing.

One little slipup didn't mean anything.

. . . Right?

Chapter 35

Week seventeen. Le bébé is the size of a crème brûlée.

Lizzie and Rake were doing really well at their "never again" agreement. Over the following month, they only broke it five times.

Which was truly remarkable since Rake was so damn hot and Lizzie was so damn horny. But could either really be blamed for screwing each other senseless one morning when the coffee took an extra-long time to brew? And, really, it was only economical and environmentally friendly for them to shower together from time to time. If *perhaps* a dick slipped into a mouth or fingers into a pussy now and then while Rake *maybe* growled about how sexy he found her tiny baby bump or the swelling of her breasts, it was a small trade-off for trying to preserve water.

But the crucial point was that, after the most recent time, they'd *firmly* agreed to no more totally platonic hookups.

And they'd already gone five days without one.

Growth was a beautiful thing.

A huge reason for their recent success was the disgusting heat wave melting the city. The building's air conditioner was tuckering out, and the coolest they could get their unit was a staggering eighty degrees, causing Rake and Lizzie to say fuck it and open the windows and invest in some fans.

It was a particularly unbearable night, soft city noises and curls of humidity pushing in the open window, adding to Lizzie's discomfort. She flopped and flailed beneath the suffocating sheets, unable to find any relief. After another minute, she let out a loud, suffering sigh, peeking over at Rake's sleeping form as she did so. When he didn't even twitch, she gave it a more aggressive attempt.

Still nothing.

"Hey," she whisper-yelled, poking his bicep. "Rake. Hey."

Rake squinted one eye open and looked at her, his cheek smooshed into the mattress. "What, Birdy?" he mumbled, his voice heavy with sleep.

"Can you turn on your tiny-ass fan?" she whispered, sitting up and nodding at the small thing on his nightstand. He blinked at her a few times before rolling and flipping it on.

"I was sleeping," he said, turning back to stare up at the ceiling, his voice less groggy.

"That's so weird," Lizzie said, kicking the sheets off them both. "Because I wasn't."

Rake was silent for a few seconds, before he let out a sigh and sat up, swinging his legs off the bed.

"Come on, let's go," he said, grabbing their crumpled quilt and tucking it over one arm.

"Go where?" Lizzie asked.

Rake didn't answer, just reached out an impatient hand and gently tugged her from the bed. He marched them toward the door, dropping her hand to grab two pillows off the couch as they went. Lizzie smiled, a gooey, delicious smile as she followed his sleep-rumpled form out the door and down the hall. His hair stood on end, his T-shirt and sleep shorts lightly wrinkled and clinging to him. These simple things shouldn't have caused a punch of tenderness to strike her in the chest, but they did.

He pushed the button for the elevator, then scrubbed at his face, shaking his head as he tried to wake up.

"Are you abducting me?" Lizzie asked with a grin.

Rake yawned in response.

Lizzie hadn't noticed at first, but he had hit the up button for the elevator, the little green arrow illuminating and pointing toward the ceiling as the doors slid open. Lizzie moved in after him and watched as he hit the button for the top floor. Lizzie looked at him with raised eyebrows.

"I've been meaning to show you this for a few days now," he said, as the floors dinged past. When they reached their destination, he held his arm against the door, ushering her out. "Now seems as good a time as any."

He stepped in front of her, moving down the hall to a small door at the end. Rake turned the knob and pushed against it, the noise echoing into the stairwell as it unstuck from its frame.

Rake seemed fully awake now, bounding up the stairs and turning to give Lizzie a wide, boyish smile over his shoulder as he reached another door at the top. He pushed it open, holding it for her as she stepped out onto the roof.

Lizzie's eyes went wide, and she let out a coo of excitement as she took in the scene. Their building wasn't the tallest by any means, but also not the shortest, allowing city lights to twinkle above and beside her, giving her the feeling of being surrounded by glowing stars. Real stars strained to compete in the inky summer sky. The energy of the city hummed into her veins, her body starting to relax for the first time all night.

"I had no idea we could get up here!" Lizzie said, turning on Rake, who was leaning lazily against the door, watching her reaction with a smile.

"I'd hoped it would be a surprise," he said, pushing away and walking toward her. He fluffed out the quilt, allowing it to softly fall to the rooftop. He dropped the pillows onto it and held out a hand to Lizzie to join him.

And then she burst into tears.

Rake's eyes went wide with fear, and he reached her in two long strides, pulling her into a hug.

"What's wrong?" he said, placing a palm on the back of her head as she cried into his chest. "Do you want to go back downstairs?"

"No!" she wailed, tightening her arms around his neck.

"Then why are you crying?"

"You're so damn lovely."

"What?" he asked, pulling back to give her a confused frown. "You're sad because I'm lovely?"

Lizzie shook her head, hoping he wouldn't notice the snot she'd gotten on his shirt. "I don't actually know why I'm crying," she choked out between sobs. "I think I might be feeling a tiny bit hormonal."

Rake was silent for a moment before letting out a soft laugh. "Maybe the tiniest bit," he confirmed. He placed his hands on her shoulders, steering her to the little nest he'd made. He laid her down on it, making sure she was comfortable before taking up his own pillow next to her.

"This okay?" he asked, turning his head to look at her.

Lizzie sniffed then let out a contented sigh. The night was still hot, but something about the freedom of an open sky cooled her. "This is perfect," she said.

Lizzie wasn't sure how long they lay there, staring silently up at the stars, but every second felt divine, a soft peacefulness threading around them in a golden connection. Her brain gave up its somersaults of things she needed to do, things she needed to learn, in preparation for the baby. She didn't dwell on how she'd fuck things up or all the things out of her control. Instead, she reached out and held Rake's hand as they watched the night float on around them.

"You know how people always say they feel smaller when

they stare up at the stars?" Lizzie said after some time. She heard Rake shift his head to look at her.

"Yeah. I feel that way," he said, his voice soft.

"I've never understood it," she said, continuing to look up. "I've always tried to make sense of it. But, when I stare up at the stars, I feel the exact opposite."

"What do you mean?" His words were a whisper, curling around her heart.

"I always feel bigger looking up at the stars," she said, raising her hands, pulling one of his with her, to gesture at the sky as she sought out the words. "It's like I'm looking up at all the energy that lives inside of me. Like whatever divine being or miracle of science that made all these beautiful stars, also made me. Whatever allows for stars to exist also allows for me to exist. It feels empowering—elevating—to know that I can exist among something so beautiful."

Rake was silent, and Lizzie could feel the press of his stare. She regretted the words. They had made sense in her head, but she'd never been great at articulating the grand feelings that swamped her. She probably sounded ridiculous. She squirmed on the quilt, letting go of his hand and pushing her hair out from under her neck.

"You never fail to surprise me" was all Rake said.

Lizzie snorted. "Yeah? How's that?"

"That was quite poetic of you," he said, a smile in his voice. But, as if sensing Lizzie's need to break the seriousness, he added, "and not even one dick joke for a full ten minutes. You'll be a boring, serious mum by the time the little one is ready to come out."

Lizzie giggled, rubbing her hands over her belly. "Don't be ridiculous. I was just about to point out how that group of stars over there looks just like an uncircumcised penis blowing a load."

Rake let out a deep, rumbling laugh that made her smile as their eyes met.

And that's when she felt it.

Little tiny bubbles low in her belly. Small happy pops that made her body freeze, her eyes go wide.

Rake jolted up at the look on her face.

"What's wrong?" he said, his hands hovering over her like he was afraid to touch her, but desperately needed to. "Are you okay?"

Lizzie nodded, but her face must have still looked serious based on the panicked way Rake continued to stare. She cleared her throat. "I think . . . I can't be sure, but maybe the baby is kicking?"

The tension in Rake's face dissolved into heart-melting tenderness, his mouth going soft and slack as his eyes traveled down her body to rest on her stomach.

"Really?" he asked, his voice hoarse. "What . . . what does it feel like?"

"Like a tiny little flutter," Lizzie said. "I can't be sure. It stopped, it was only a moment. It could be gas for all I know, but—" She paused, the tiny popping feeling returning. A smile spread across her cheeks, threatening to crack her open. "It's happening again. Touch me. Touch me!" She grabbed his hand, placing it right above her pelvis. Rake was still, save for a tiny tremble Lizzie felt in his fingers.

After a moment, he spoke. "I don't . . . I'm so sorry, but I don't really feel anything." He looked pained, as if it was the most important thing in the world for him to feel the baby kicking and he was a failure for the barely perceptible vibration not reaching his hand.

"Don't be sorry," Lizzie said, reaching out to cup his jaw. She dragged her thumb over the stubble along his chin. "You'll feel it. We still have a while. I promise you'll feel it before the little one gets here."

His face cracked, so many emotions flitting across its beautiful surface, before two small tears welled up in the corners of his eyes. He blinked, trying to pull away. Lizzie sat up, gripping his face in both her hands.

"Hey," she said, tilting his head so she could meet his eyes, "what's wrong?"

He shook his head between her palms, a sad smile tugging at the corners of his lips. "Nothing's wrong."

"Liar," Lizzie said, giving him a tiny rattle. "Talk to me."

He blew out a deep breath that traveled over Lizzie's skin like a cool breeze. "There really isn't anything wrong," he said at last, meeting her eyes. "It's the exact opposite. I'm just so damn happy to be a part of this. So happy you're letting me."

Lizzie's brow furrowed. "Letting you? I'm not . . . It's not about *letting* you do anything. I'm . . . I'm glad you're here with me."

"But you don't—I mean, you didn't . . ." He let out another deep breath. "You didn't have to do this, or tell me, or any of that. But you are. We are. Together. And it . . ."

Two more tears rolled down his cheeks, and he extracted himself from her grip, dragging his own hands across his face.

There was that thing again. That feeling. That tiny inkling that poked at Lizzie's heart, whispering that he'd been hurt. Was hurting. Pretending he wasn't. She decided, if there was ever a moment to push, this was it.

"Rake?" He looked at her. "Why *did* you want to be a part of this? Why . . . What made you uproot your life for this? Jump into it like you have?"

He swallowed, staring at her like a wary animal torn between bolting and submitting.

"You don't have to tell me," Lizzie rushed out. "You really don't. But I . . . if we're going to do this parenting thing together, I want to know as much of you as I can."

Something about that seemed to push his decision.

"Do you remember when I told you, while we were moving, that I'd lost someone?"

"Yes," Lizzie said. The sadness in his tone when he'd said it sometimes played on a loop in her mind like a tragic melody. "Did someone you love die?"

Rake shook his head. "I didn't lose them in that way—poor choice of words—but it was one of those things where everything changed and crashed and burned so quickly, it almost felt like it."

Lizzie cocked her head to the side, giving him a confused look.

After a deep breath, he started again. "I had a girlfriend. Shannon. We dated for a little over two years, and I was going to propose."

Lizzie nodded, her breath seeming to get locked in her throat.

"She was everything I'd always assumed I'd need in a partner. Beautiful, smart, good job, nice family . . ."

"She sounds great," Lizzie said, her voice scratchy.

Rake shrugged. "She was—*is*—in many ways. But she was never particularly affectionate, but I'm not either, so I tended to ignore it."

"I think you're affectionate," Lizzie piped up. He was.

It was in the small things he did. The way he always asked her about her day, how she was feeling. Let her force-feed him endless baking experiments. How he endured her teasing and poking, letting her under that serious facade and rewarding her with his smile.

Rake gave her hand a quick squeeze. "I did love her, though. I had bought a ring. But the last month or so of our relationship, she'd been acting more distant than usual. It was odd. We never fought. Not once. It was always as cordial as talking to a work acquaintance. And that never bothered me until that last month, when we drifted further apart. It was like I could touch her, but she wasn't there. I was searching for some sign that she even cared I was around."

Rake was quiet for a moment, staring out at the city.

"Then, one day, I get home from work and I flip through the mail on the table, and I see a clinic bill sitting there for a termination of pregnancy. It was this bizarre flood of confusion. I was instantly worried, but also didn't fully understand. She hadn't said a thing to me. We'd never even talked about kids . . . Isn't that weird? I was with her all that time, and I never even asked how she felt . . ."

Rake dragged his knuckles along the edge of his jaw. "So, I asked Shannon about it. And the same moment I was told she'd been pregnant was the same moment I was told she wasn't. I didn't know I could feel so many things at once. It was this weird mix of relief and confusion and sadness and one hundred other things that muddled my brain."

He was silent for a moment, eyes somewhere far away.

"I would have gone along with whatever Shannon wanted. It was always her choice to make—and I respect her decision—but I wanted to be there for her. I wanted the chance to be the partner I was supposed to be in her life. I always thought that us not fighting meant we had this perfect relationship of communication and openness. But, in reality, I guess we were just going through the motions of it. Together, but alone."

"I'm sorry," Lizzie whispered. And she was. Having recently been in the position, she knew how hard the decisions that come with an unexpected pregnancy can be for some, but she also could understand the pain of having no idea about a partner's situation at all.

"But when I pushed her, when I asked *why* she didn't tell me she'd been pregnant. Why she didn't want us to go through the termination together, she admitted she'd been cheating."

Something sharp and acidic dropped into the pit of Lizzie's

stomach and pulsed through her veins. An odd sense of protectiveness, of indignation that anyone would cheat on Rake—put him through that type of hurt—made her blood sting and skin itch.

"She told me she didn't know who the father was," Rake continued in a soft whisper. "And it's strange. It might not . . . I don't know . . . it might not even have been mine, but I still felt this sense of loss. Maybe it was more for the relationship or the future I'd thought we'd have. Maybe the loss of Shannon . . . Even now I can't really parse it out."

He was quiet for a moment, and Lizzie watched as the ghosts crept in from the corners of his memory. "All I do know is that it physically hurt to find out we weren't this partnership I thought we were. We weren't a unit. I wasn't . . . worthy of that, I guess. I don't know. It's probably stupid to feel like I lost something I never really had."

Lizzie's heart ached and squeezed as she watched the pain play out across his features. "I never would have expected it to hurt that much," he said at last. The words were almost inaudible, not meant for Lizzie. Not even meant for Rake. But for the universe. For whatever grand entity coordinated pain and loss and mourning like puppets on strings.

"We broke up after that. Obviously," he said, giving Lizzie a sad smile that she couldn't muster up the ability to return. "Shannon told me I was too obsessed with work. Never did enough to notice her at home. I'm sure she was right," Rake said with a sigh, dragging a hand through his hair. "I was a shit boyfriend. I never realized . . . It sounds so *stupid*, but I never realized she even wanted me home as much as she did. She was rather serious and dedicated to work herself, and I didn't think. I . . ."

He looked up at the sky, waves of blame and self-loathing radiating off his skin.

"She's actually married now," Rake said. "Happy." He said that last word with whispered reverence. Like it was some elusive, magical concept he would never fully understand. "And I'm happy for her. I really am. It took me a while to arrive there, but I mean it.

"I kind of . . . I don't know, shut down after it all happened. I never wanted to be in that situation again. I didn't want to fail someone in a relationship or go through the pain of being cheated on like that, and I . . ." He swallowed, his eyes tracing over Lizzie's features in a gaze that felt like a caress.

"So when you told me you were having the baby," he continued, "I decided I wanted to do whatever I could. Be here however you would let me. Because I didn't want to miss my second chance to be someone's partner."

Lizzie wanted to hold him. Soothe his aches. Take away that pain. But she also knew she couldn't. It was his to bear. His to work through.

She lay back down on the quilt, gently tugging at his shoulder until he followed her. She turned on her side, looking at him, and he mirrored the motion.

"We aren't—" Lizzie paused, trying to find the right words, sifting through them. "We aren't a partnership in the traditional sense. Or the romantic sense. We probably don't make any sense," Lizzie said, dragging the pads of her fingers along the bridge of his nose. "But we're in this together. And I'm glad you're doing this with me."

Rake reached out, grabbing her hand and bringing it to his chest. He stared at her for a moment before saying, "I'm glad too."

Chapter 36

LIZZIE and Rake had done the unthinkable: They'd fucked each other out of their systems.

Which was awesome.

SO. GREAT.

Because, no, Lizzie didn't walk around constantly hoping Rake would touch her. And no, she didn't stay up all hours of the night wondering what he would do if she made a move.

None of that on her end! Nope! They couldn't be more platonic.

And *if* Lizzie was maybe feeling a little bit of pining/horniness, she channeled all that energy into her baking. Bernadette's online sales of erotic pastries were booming, and they'd recently introduced some of the tamer pieces to the pastry display case. What neither Bernadette nor Lizzie expected was for a local reporter to catch wind of their shop filled with tuile tacos filled suggestively with fruit and butt-shaped cookies with intricate frosting lingerie and run a story on them that spread like wildfire on Twitter. The resulting daily lines to get into the shop sucked up most of Lizzie's focus, and she thrived on the success of their creations.

She was also gaining momentum in her work to manage her ADHD. Lizzie was learning that making to-do lists into cartoons and pictures made her brain hum with excitement to get started, and she was successfully keeping a notebook and crossing things off her list. She'd also found a surprising type of fun in timing herself on tasks and learning her patterns, creating a routine that accommodated her habits instead of forcing her to do things the "right" way.

And Bernadette, quirky angel of graciousness that she was, encouraged Lizzie through it all, working with her to find a flow for the shop that allowed them both to thrive.

The progress wasn't linear and the process was far from easy, but it felt undeniably *good* to learn herself. Nurture her brain instead of rewire it.

Lizzie's phone rang as she walked to her apartment from the subway stop, Mary's name lighting up the screen.

"Hi, Mary," Lizzie said as she picked up the call.

"Lizzie! How are you?" Mary had a voice like Snow White, and Lizzie had, more than once, hinted that she should narrate children's audiobooks.

"Hanging in there. How about you?"

"Good, good. Just finalizing some stuff for the big bash," Mary said, referring to the anniversary party for Lizzie's parents that was two days away. "Wanted to check in on the cake and make sure you didn't need anything from me."

"Nope, all good," Lizzie said, stopping in front of her building and leaning against the rough stone to finish the call. "I finished building it today and I'll put the final decorations on it tomorrow before I drive up."

Mary had requested a minimalistic three-layer cake, and Lizzie was going with the popular semi-naked frosting look with sprigs of flowers and clusters of fresh fruit. She was also desperately nervous that her mom would absolutely fucking hate it.

"Are you bringing anyone to the party?" Mary asked, catching Lizzie completely off guard.

"I, uh, I hadn't thought about it. Am I allowed?"

Mary giggled. "Of course you're *allowed*, Lizzie. I'll put you down with a plus-one."

"I—well—I—"

"Sorry, Lizzie, I have to run. Call me or Ry if you have any issues. We'll see you tomorrow at your parents' for dinner, right?"

"Uhh."

"Great! See you then." Mary hung up the call.

Lizzie pressed the back of her head against the building, staring up at the sky. *Fuckkkkkkk.*

Should she bring Rake? On one hand, he was so put together and competent and beautiful that he might distract from the inevitable evaluation of Lizzie's shortcomings from her mother. But on the other hand, did she really want to subject him to the passive-aggressive contempt that Claire Blake had spent a lifetime gorgeously perfecting?

She decided she'd paint Rake a very realistic portrait of what the weekend had in store and let him decide.

Rake's laugh greeted Lizzie as she walked through the door. Padding into the apartment, she found him on the couch with his laptop, smiling at the screen. He turned that smile on her, and her body ached with how adorable he was.

In a totally platonic way, of course.

"Hold on just a second, Mum," Rake said, looking back at the screen. He clicked a few times then turned again to Lizzie. "I'm video chatting with my parents if you'd like to meet them. No pressure," he said.

Lizzie broke out in a cold sweat. She'd never met a guy's parents before. She knew as an inherent fact that she was *not* the kind of girl a mom would be happy to see her son with.

"Won't they hear me say no?" Lizzie whispered, shooting a nervous glance at the laptop.

"I muted it," Rake said, giving her a bemused look. "But I think you'll really like them."

Lizzie didn't doubt that for a second. It was a rarity for her to meet someone she didn't instantly find something to like, and anyone who'd had a hand in making Rake was undoubtedly a perfect sunbeam of a person.

Rake was studying Lizzie closely, as if he were seeing her inner turmoil like words written across her skin. "And I have no doubt they'll adore you," he said, scooting over on the couch and patting the seat.

Lizzie looked at him for a moment then gathered some courage, moving to sit next to him. "Do they know about le bébé?" Lizzie asked, halting his hand from unmuting them.

"Of course," Rake said. "Mum texts me almost daily to ask how you're doing. She's been dying to meet you, I think."

"Cool cool cool cool cool," Lizzie said, her leg starting to bounce. Rake gave it a gentle squeeze then turned the video back on.

"Mum, Dad, I'd like to finally introduce you to Lizzie."

There was a racket of noise as a jolly middle-aged couple on the screen leaned in and started speaking over each other, the commotion sounding like sunshine and softness.

"Shut it, Peter. Let me go first," the woman said, shooting a scolding look at the man before turning back to the screen. "Oh, you darling girl, it's so nice to finally put a face to a name. I'm Leanne, Rake's mum. He's been telling us so many things about you."

Lizzie shot Rake a horrified glance, and Leanne and Peter let out a hearty chuckle.

"Wonderful things, I assure you," Leanne said, still grinning at the camera.

"And I'm Peter," Rake's dad said, waving at the camera.

Lizzie waved back, a genuine smile breaking across her face. "It's so great to meet you."

Peter and Leanne launched into conversation, asking Lizzie about the pregnancy and how she was feeling before shifting to questions about her baking. They cackled with laughter when

Lizzie hesitantly explained the erotic pastry side business Bernadette had originally hired her for.

"What I wouldn't give to take a bite out of one of your delicious arses," Leanne said, clapping with glee. "What a riot."

"You should come visit!" Lizzie said without thinking. Rake
shot her a surprised glance, the corners of his mouth kicking up
in a soft smile.

Leanne and Peter were quiet for a moment, looking at her.
"You wouldn't mind?" Leanne asked at last. "Because we'd absolutely love to make the trip. Obviously, we'll wait until you
feel settled, and we'd hate to be a bother with a baby on the
way, but—"

"I'd love to meet you in person," Lizzie said, meaning it.

"Well," Leanne said, she and Peter glancing at each other
softly before beaming into the camera. "We won't take up any
more of your time," Leanne added, flapping her hand toward
the camera. "Rake, you take good care of her."

"Of course," Rake said, waving. "I'll talk to you soon." After
a few more seconds of prolonged goodbyes, Rake shut his laptop.

"I know they're a lot," he said, turning to Lizzie, "but—"

"They're *wonderful*," Lizzie said, nestling deeper into the
couch. "Which makes what I'm about to ask you suck even
more."

Rake's smile dropped. "I don't like the sound of that."

Lizzie huffed out a laugh. "I have to drive up to my parents'
this weekend. It's their anniversary, and my brother and his wife
have organized this big bash. I'm making the cake."

"And?" Rake prompted after a moment.

"*Andddd*," Lizzie said, plucking at the couch. "My sister-in-
law said I could bring someone if I want, and I should probably
check in with my mom and she'll probably say no, but if you
want—I mean, if you'd be interested in getting out of the city
and maybe—"

"Of course I'll go with you, Birdy," Rake said, getting up and moving to the kitchen. "Just let me know what time we need to leave and what I should pack. I'm excited to meet your family."

"Oooh, I'm gonna stop you right there, buddy," Lizzie said, sitting up on her knees and turning to watch him over the back of the couch. "This will not be a joyous *Family Stone* lovefest. This will be a stuffy and passive-aggressive weekend, to say the least. And if they find out I'm pregnant . . . God save us."

"You haven't told them?"

"No. I don't tell my family anything if I can help it."

Rake looked at her, crossing his arms and leaning back against the counter. "If you're dreading it so much, why go?"

"Because some things you have to do. Suffer in the name of character development or whatever." Rake opened his mouth to say something, but she cut him off. "I really better check with Queen Claire Blake that it's even okay I bring you."

Lizzie scrolled through her phone then made the call, putting it on speaker so she could simultaneously flip through Instagram on her phone. It felt impossible for her to focus solely on a conversation. It also helped to lessen the blow of her mom's harshness if she was slightly distracted by pretty pictures.

"Blake residence," Claire's refined voice answered, and Lizzie's spine stiffened.

"Hey, Mom." The line filled with silence, and Lizzie hoped for a second that the call had magically disconnected.

"Elizabeth. How are you?"

Pregnant. Confused. A tiny bit scared.

"I'm fine!" *Silence.* "I got a new job."

Her mom made a small humming sound, innocuous to an untrained ear, but Lizzie knew it as the soundtrack for disapproval.

"Another new job. Congratulations."

Rake frowned down at the phone, but Lizzie waved a hand

to get his attention and smiled. *It's okay. This is our talks going well.*

"Did Mary tell you I'm making the cake for your party?" Lizzie asked, hating how the pitch of her voice reached a new octave.

"She did."

"I, er, I think it's going to be really nice! Mary picked a very tasteful design. I think you'll like it."

"Oh, wonderful. I'm sure it will be lovely," Claire said, not sounding sure at all. "Even though your father doesn't indulge in sweets . . ."

"Oh. Yeah. I forgot. Well . . . I don't know. Hopefully you like it. Or Mary at least." Lizzie rested her palms flat on the back of the couch, lowering her head to bang it softly against her hands a few times. Claire remained silent.

"I've . . . There's a new person in my life," Lizzie blurted out. She still hadn't decided on what label to use for Rake. Baby daddy was the most accurate, but she might send her mom into a tailspin with that phrasing.

Her mom hummed again, the noise sounding like grating steel and disapproval.

"I'd like to bring him. To the anniversary party, I mean." Lizzie glanced over at Rake, and he nodded, a soft smile on his lips.

"Is that so? It's only supposed to be for family and our close friends."

"Well . . . uh . . . he's like family to me," Lizzie said honestly. "I'd like for you to get to know him." *Maybe when you see the gorgeous, wonderfully starchy father of my future child who keeps his hair well trimmed and carefully folds his underwear, you won't judge me as harshly.*

The silence lingered, making Lizzie squirm.

"Well, we'd be happy to host him," her mother said at last, sounding resigned.

"Yeah?" A wary voice in Lizzie's head told her not to get

excited, not to even go to the damn thing. But she couldn't extinguish the small starburst of happiness in her chest. Just like that, she was a girl again, desperate for a bond with her mom.

"We'll see you tomorrow. Please dress appropriately."

"So is that a yes or a no to titty tassels?" Lizzie asked, snickering.

Claire let out a sigh. "Goodbye, Elizabeth." She hung up.

Chapter 37

Week nineteen, baby is the size of a flying squirrel. Lizzie is convinced that's what she's actually carrying based on how much the little one moves around in there.

The next afternoon, Rake and Lizzie drove away from Philadelphia, traveling north toward the Pocono Mountains in an SUV they'd borrowed from Indira. Rake was typing away on his phone; Dominic had immediately rejected his request for a half day but had made the ever-so-generous concession that he could work remotely for the afternoon. Rubbing the heels of his hands against his tired eyes, he sighed, setting his phone down and giving himself a short break.

He looked over at Lizzie, who'd been disorientingly silent for most of the trip. Rake was learning that she had two modes: endless talking or complete silence. She was either exquisitely present or completely gone. He could see her chewing on the inside of her cheek, somewhere far away in her thoughts. He wanted to know every single one, understand the gears and wires that made up such a unique person. He could tell by the furrow of her brow and the tension in her jaw that something was bothering her.

"What are you thinking about?" he asked, tugging gently on

a lock of her hair. She snapped back into her body, blinking like she wasn't sure how she got there.

"Mirrors," she said, glancing over her shoulder as she changed lanes.

Rake blinked. "What?"

"I guess reflections more," she continued, keeping her eyes on the road. "Like how the hell can I look in a window, see a partial reflection, and then make eye contact with someone next to me in that weird half reflection? It's a see-through material, and yet I can make eye contact on its surface? Isn't that weird?"

"Weird indeed," Rake said with a soft laugh. "What else is on your mind?" Rake could tell window reflections weren't the only thing consuming her thoughts.

"I'm worried about the cake," Lizzie answered, her eyes flicking to the rearview mirror for the thousandth time. "I'll be so fucked if something happens to it." Lizzie had spent over an hour packing and securing the cake in the trunk.

"I've no doubt you could fix it even if something did happen, but I'm sure it'll be fine."

Lizzie chewed on her lip, shooting him a quick glance out of the corner of her eye, and he gave her a reassuring smile.

"Why did you become a baker?" he asked.

Lizzie shrugged. "Just your run-of-the-mill get-rich-quick scheme every girl plans out."

Rake laughed. "No, seriously."

She shrugged again. "There's nothing else I was really good at. I don't have a degree, and I blew through all my money traveling. When I came home and tricked Indira into letting me crash at her place, I made enough batches of pity cookies I decided to make it a job." She laughed, but Rake remained silent. She glanced at him.

"Why do you do that?" he asked.

"Do what?" She tried to smile, but it didn't reach her eyes.

"Pretend like you don't do great things. Wave off your accomplishments. Why?"

A loud burst of uncomfortable laughter ripped from her throat, making him flinch.

"I'm not . . . I don't . . . If I can do it, literally anyone can."

"That's not true," Rake argued. "You're clever and creative and clearly have excellent business sense, seeing how much you've grown the bakery. So why are you so mean to yourself?"

"Mean?" Lizzie's mouth twisted. "I'm not *mean* to myself. I love myself. I love my body and my looks, and I've never doubted any of that stuff. I have tons of confidence."

"Appreciating your own physical beauty isn't the only component of being nice to yourself, Birdy. You should appreciate your mind too." He said it gently, in a way that didn't mean to poke but just gently lift a veil.

Irritation blazed through her.

"Why don't you rein it in, Dr. Phil. It's not like you actually know me."

A painful stab of hurt rocketed through Rake's stomach. "Sorry," he said quietly, turning to look out the window. "I didn't mean to upset you."

They sat in a loaded silence for a few miles, before Lizzie finally spoke. "A therapist suggested I try it."

Rake turned his attention back to her, arching an eyebrow.

"Baking, I mean," she continued. "When I was younger, my mom had me in and out of psychiatrists' offices. She was always taking me to a new one. I think a big reason is that they would tell her I wasn't actually that bad. They'd tell her that, more than anything, I was just a spirited person who happened to have ADHD." Lizzie frowned for a second. "But to my mom, it was abnormal for a child to be so loud and hyper and obnoxious. Especially a girl. I honestly think for a long time she didn't even believe it was possible for a girl to have ADHD. By the time I was sixteen, I'd started really leaning into the wild child role she'd cast me in," she continued, a small smile tugging at her lips.

"I was drinking and smoking and wearing tiny-ass skirts. I was on Adderall and it helped in school, but there are some facets of a personality that medicine just can't change. And my mom didn't like that.

"So she took me to this psychiatrist and all but demanded I be put on something stronger. The doctor told her I was taking the most suitable dosage she was comfortable prescribing to a minor, but she suggested I find a productive and creative hobby. She suggested baking," Lizzie said, glancing at him to reward him with that gorgeous smile.

"In perfect Claire Blake form, my mom thought the woman was an idiot, but for some reason, the idea stuck with me. So I looked into it and signed myself up for some baking classes at the community center and fell in love with it. I fell out of it for a while, but once I came back from my globe-trotting years, I threw myself into it. Took classes and courses and turned it into my job." Lizzie adjusted her rearview mirror as she spoke. "I like making things that make people happy, and using my hands. It's like getting to play all day. Freeing and fun and one of the few things in this world I can lose myself in in a good way."

"I'm glad you found your calling," Rake said, reaching across the console to give her knee a friendly squeeze. "And I'm very proud of how hard you work. How well you're doing at Bernadette's. It can't be easy to come up with all of those ideas."

Lizzie's head whipped over to look at him, a bizarre mask of fear covering her face.

"What's wrong?" Rake asked, alarm rising in his chest.

Lizzie continued to stare at him, and Rake glanced quickly at the road. That seemed to break her out of her trance.

"No one's ever said that to me before," she said quietly, focusing her eyes out the windshield.

"Said what?"

"That I work hard. That they're . . . proud of me," she said, her voice a rough whisper.

Rake opened his mouth to say something, but words failed him. That seemed so wrong to him.

Lizzie deserved all the praise in the world. She did so much that warranted pride every single day. The woman was a force of nature, a vibrant living flame that lit up everything she touched.

Rake couldn't process that the people who raised her could look at their incredible creation and not burst with pride. Not say the words every day.

"Well, I am," Rake said at last, looking out the windshield. "Proud of you. Incredibly proud."

Lizzie nodded but didn't say anything for the rest of the drive.

Chapter 38

RAKE couldn't name anything that was glaringly off about the Blake residence as he looked around the family room—pristine furniture and spotless china surrounding him—but there was something undeniably *cold* about it. Sterile. Like walking through a well-preserved museum of an idyllic upper-middle-class residence, but certainly not a home.

Claire had opened the door upon their arrival, giving Lizzie a rather stiff hug and Rake a brief handshake before retreating into the kitchen to check on dinner. Rake had been introduced to Lizzie's father, Douglas, who was a portly man who oozed self-importance, before he strode off to his study to take an important business call.

Rake looked over at Lizzie as she stood in the corner, waves of uncomfortable energy radiating off her. It seemed impossible that a firebolt of a person like her could ever have grown up in such a dull, contained space.

Perfectly placed frames lined the walls, almost all of them holding an image of the man Rake assumed was Lizzie's brother, Ryan. Rake could only find two pictures of Lizzie: One was of her in her graduation gown and cap, her red hair spilling out from beneath, thick black liner rimming her eyes, a certain mischievousness to her smile. The second was a family photo, everyone dressed in black pants and a white top. Douglas, her father, was seated in a leather chair, Claire resting her hands on his shoulder as she stood behind him, both with perfect smiles. Ryan looked young, maybe eight, his hair gelled and combed, a reserved smile on his own lips as he stood next to his dad.

And then there was Lizzie, her eyes wild and grin huge, her two front teeth missing. Her arms were stiff at her sides, the tension visible in the tiny little body, like she'd been told to hold still and the effort to do so was physically challenging. Rake loved the picture so much, he wanted to steal it.

The doorbell rang, and moments later it opened, a friendly female voice calling out hello. A couple, just a few years older than Rake and Lizzie, entered the living room. The woman was impeccably dressed, and layers of honey-colored hair framed her delicate and lovely features. The man was a younger version of Douglas, offering a genuine smile as he took in Lizzie and Rake.

"Lizzie!" the woman said, stretching out her arms and walking toward the corner. "I'm so glad to see you. It's been so long."

"Hi, Mary," Lizzie said, wrapping her arms around the petite woman, an uncharacteristic level of delicacy in the way she did it. Lizzie usually hugged with the joyful force of a bulldozer.

Ryan cut in, giving Lizzie a hug that seemed to catch her by surprise. "It's good to see you," Ryan said, pulling back.

Ryan and Mary turned to Rake, crossing the room with smiles as they shook his hand.

"And so good to meet you!" Mary said, her voice bubbly and kind. "Glad you could make it this weekend."

Claire walked in, Douglas right behind her, and she beamed as she looked at her son.

"Ryan, Mary, so glad you're here," Claire said, moving to them with outstretched hands, her greeting one hundred degrees kinder than anything she'd given to Rake and Lizzie. "Dinner is all ready," she said, looping one arm through Mary's as they walked toward the dining room.

A pristine white tablecloth covered the table, fresh flowers in a crystal vase sitting in the center of the grand display of china. Each setting had already been served, steaming roast and vegetables placed in perfect portions on each plate.

They sat, Rake and Lizzie on one side, Ryan and Mary on the other, with Claire and Douglas at either end.

An awkward silence fell over the table as they settled in. Rake glanced at Lizzie, her body humming with energy as her eyes flicked around the room—plates, ceiling, flowers, silverware, corner—no spot safe for her to land on.

Mary delicately cleared her throat. "Tell us about yourself, Rake," she said, fixing him with a kind smile. "What do you do for work?"

Rake gave his basic spiel about marketing for Onism and mentioned some of the freelance projects he'd picked up, wondering, for the first time, why adults spent so much time working and the rest of their time talking about work. Rake noticed the subtle pursing of Claire's lips as he explained Onism was a swimwear line, but Mary and Ryan both asked interested, if not predictable, questions about it.

"And what do you two do?" Rake asked.

"I'm an electrical engineer," Mary said, her smile bright. "And Ryan practices law like Douglas," she added.

"They're both exceptionally accomplished young professionals," Claire said, nodding toward Mary.

"Mar is an absolute genius," Lizzie said, smiling at Rake. That's what was so remarkable about Lizzie: Her pride and adoration for the people around her felt like the most genuine force in the world. She gushed about the accomplishments of others with unfettered joy.

"*Mary* is quite smart, yes," Claire said, cutting a small bite of roast. "She and Ryan both attended the University of Pennsylvania," she added. As though Rake gave a fuck.

"What was Lizzie like as a kid?" Rake asked abruptly, the

tone and direction of Claire's comments raising his hackles. He directed the question toward Ryan, hoping he could inject good humor into this rapid spiral of awkward tension.

Ryan chuckled. "Lizzie has always been a firecracker," he said, shooting her a big smile. Lizzie returned it with a hesitant quirk of her lips.

"From the moment she learned how to walk, she was always into trouble," Douglas said, taking a bite of food and chewing loudly. Rake watched Lizzie's smile slip, her shoulders curving into a protective shell as she looked down at her lap.

"But she was the funniest kid," Ryan interjected, smiling again. "Lizzie, remember your Superman cape?"

Lizzie's head shot up, a genuine smile curving her mouth. "I totally forgot about that. How old was I? I feel like I was really little for that."

Ryan nodded. "I was in my superhero phase around eight, so you were probably, what, five?" Ryan turned to look at Rake, humor lighting up his features. "Lizzie was obsessed with Superman," he explained. "She used to beg me to lift her over my head so she could pretend like she was flying."

Lizzie snorted beside Rake, but there was no missing the harsh glance Claire shot her at the noise.

"She found this red towel in the linen closet and made me pin it onto her every day. Every. Single. Day." Ryan rolled his eyes with good humor, looking at Lizzie.

She let out one of her signature laughs. "Oh my God, the towel." She slapped a hand to her forehead, her shoulders bouncing with giggles. "I was obsessed with having my cape," she said, turning to Rake. "Refused to leave home without it. I'd run around with a fist in the air while using the other to hold back the cape."

Lizzie continued to laugh, but Claire caught her eye, giving the subtlest shake of her head while she made a soft shushing sound, delicately pumping her hand toward the ground to tell Lizzie to lower the volume.

Lizzie's laughter dimmed to a throat clearing, her cheeks flushing a violent red.

"The thing was twice your size," Ryan added. Mary laughed next to him, smiling at the siblings. "I wonder what ever ended up happening to it?" Ryan asked, turning toward Claire with a smile.

"I threw it away," Claire said, daintily cutting her vegetables. "She wouldn't stop wearing it. Always demanding we pin it on . . . The fits she would throw if we told her no." The woman let out a tinkling laugh, shaking her head. "Had to get rid of it to find some peace."

Lizzie pushed her hair behind her ears, her cheeks heating to a deeper crimson as she blinked down at her plate again.

"It was the Hulk phase after that," Ryan carried on, lost in the happiness of the memories and completely oblivious to the tension threatening to crack the room in half. Lizzie shot him a pleading glance across the table, and Mary gave his hand a squeeze, but he didn't notice.

He turned his attention to Rake, all smiles. "She got ahold of a pair of scissors somehow and cut all her pants into knee shorts, like the Hulk wore." Ryan laughed, and Rake couldn't help but smile at the image of his Lizzie, a round-faced, freckled little girl, running around with frayed shorts pretending to be a big green monster.

He reached under the table and grabbed Lizzie's hand from where she had them shoved under her thighs. He laced his fingers with hers.

"She even figured out that if she made tiny little cuts at the top of her shirts, she could rip them off when she'd 'Hulk out.'" Ryan laughed even harder and grabbed his wineglass, taking a sip. "When she'd get upset, she'd tear her shirt straight down the middle and let out a yell like she saw in the cartoon. She'd crack herself up so much by doing it, I don't think she remembered why she was even upset afterwards."

"I hope our kids are as creative as you were, Lizzie," Mary cut in, leaning forward a bit to catch Lizzie's eyes. "Sounds like you were such a fun child."

"That's one way to phrase it," Claire said, carefully cutting another bite of food.

"She certainly was an adventure," Douglas added through a mouthful.

"Well, I think she sounds like a wonderful kid," Rake said, not a trace of subtlety in his words. Lizzie squeezed their still-clasped hands, sending him a cautious glance.

"Must have been," Rake continued, holding her eyes, "to become such a wonderful adult."

"Yes, well . . . her father and I certainly did our best," Claire said with a sigh and almost sorrowful smile.

Rake opened his mouth to say something—he wasn't sure what, but he wanted it to be as subtly cutting as Claire's words—but Lizzie cut him off, lobbing a question at her dad.

"How's the firm, Dad? Business still good?"

Douglas launched into an incredibly boring and detailed account of his job as a lawyer, directing a great deal of the conversation to Rake as if he gave a damn. Rake couldn't care less about Donna the paralegal or the influence of small-town politics on the practice. He didn't care about some big catch Mr. Blake made in a contract. He didn't even pay attention to what kind of law the man practiced.

All Rake cared about was Lizzie. Hurt seeped from her body like perfume. It wasn't obvious; she kept a controlled smile plastered on her lips as she nodded at her father, but Rake could feel it. He wanted to pick her up, throw her in the car, and speed all the way back to the safety of their home. He wanted to erase her memory of the past few hours and build her up, layer by layer, until she knew how much she glowed as a person.

But instead, he sat there, holding her hand and trying to

channel all those thoughts into the spot where their palms touched, wanting to heal the thousands of small cuts she was being subjected to at the table.

"And how's work going for you, Lizzie?" Ryan asked, taking a bite of food. "Are you still at that place near Callowhill's med school?"

"Your sister has found a new location to prepare coffee," Claire said with a sip of wine.

"I'm a baker," Lizzie corrected in a quiet tone Rake wouldn't have guessed possible for her. "But it's going well. I work for this older woman, and she's given me a lot of creative freedom."

"That's great, Lizzie! You've always made the best treats," Mary said. "I actually read the funniest article, and I meant to send it to you," Mary continued, setting down her fork and knife. "It's about this bakery in Philadelphia that sells these, shall we say, not-safe-for-work pastries. My jaw was on the floor looking at these things!"

Rake felt Lizzie stiffen next to him, and he scrambled for a conversation change.

"What do you mean, unsafe for work?" Claire asked before Rake could divert the topic.

"Well, they're . . ." Mary blushed, ". . . erotic, I guess would be the best word for them. They're subtly—well, some are subtle, some are just plain obvious—decorated baked goods to look like private parts. Mainly women's."

Claire's silverware clattered to the table, and Rake felt waves of anxiety cascading off Lizzie's skin.

"The depravity of people these days," Claire said, shaking her head. "The overt need to oversexualize everything. Nudity is a private affair, not something for public"—she waved her hand, searching for a word—"consumption," she landed on.

"I think it's rather clever," Mary said, exuding a calming energy around the room. "But have you heard anything about it?"

Mary asked Lizzie. "I was stunned that someone could come up with so many different ways to do . . . *that*."

Lizzie shot Rake a horrified look as she opened her mouth, like she was begging him to stop what she was about to say.

"That's the shop I work at," Lizzie blurted out, whipping her head to stare at the space in front of her like she could see the words hovering over the table, and she wanted to grab them back. "It's called Bernadette's Bakery, and we specialize in sexually suggestive pastries."

"Oh, for God's sake," Douglas said, dropping his silverware with a clang and rolling his eyes.

The rest of the table was silent.

Mary blinked at Lizzie, her pretty mouth dropping open in surprise. Ryan looked more confused than anything. But Claire's displeasure radiated off her in palpable waves as she stared at Lizzie.

"This is your idea of work? This is your *job*?" Claire said, her voice a whisper. "Something so . . . so tasteless and tawdry?" Color rose on her cheeks. She pinched the bridge of her nose and closed her eyes like someone had struck her. "You've always had so much potential, Elizabeth. Every door open to you. And this is the one you chose? An *erotic bakery*? Why would you do this? Do you enjoy embarrassing us?"

"Mom—" Ryan said weakly.

"Lizzie is extremely hardworking and clever and deserves respect," Rake said, his temper flaring. "Her work may be . . . *unconventional* to you, but it's hers and she's happy and that should be enough."

"Excuse me?" Claire said, looking at him as though she'd forgotten he was there. "That's quite a declaration from someone she'll likely grow bored of by next week. Who even *are* you to her?"

Lizzie stood, nearly knocking her chair over with the abruptness. She bolted from the room, the sound of her feet pounding up the stairs echoing around them. In a move that stunned them all, Ryan shot up, following behind her.

"I'm her goddamn partner," Rake said, pushing back from the table and throwing his napkin on his plate. "And I'm really fucking proud of her."

Rake walked out of the dining room, ready to mount the stairs when he felt a hand on his arm. Turning, he found Mary staring at him in earnest.

"Would you . . ." Mary drew in a deep breath, her eyes flicking up the stairs and back to Rake. "Would you let Ryan try? To talk to her, I mean. I know it's probably not who she wants to talk to right now, but Ryan wants to at least try."

Rake stared at her for a moment, his heart tugging him up the stairs, but the sincerity in Mary's eyes convinced him to at least give Ryan a shot to be a good brother to Lizzie. He nodded.

Mary's shoulders sagged at the gesture. "Thank you."

They stood in awkward silence at the base of the steps, the gentle clink of silverware against dishes and phrases like *she'll never change* and *I hope no one at the club hears about this* drifting from the other room as her parents continued their dinner.

"He feels a lot of guilt, you know," Mary said at last, her eyes roaming over the wall of photos dedicated to Ryan. School pictures and sports shots, graduations and marriage all frozen in perfect snapshots of what an outsider would think was a family of three. Ryan, Douglas, and Claire, smiling at the camera.

"Guilt for what?" Rake asked, not really caring. As far as he could tell, they'd all tried their damnedest to crush Lizzie down, and he couldn't wait to get her back to the sanctuary of their apartment.

Mary shot him a knowing look. "He's starting to realize how unfair it's been. How differently they grew up. I don't think he really understood it as a kid, but he sees it now and he's trying to figure out how to change it."

Rake let out a rude snort and Mary's lips pursed. "He is. The guilt eats him up. He's been trying to reach out to her more, but he's dense and bad at expressing himself. He's trying to make amends, I think."

"Amends for what, though? *Why* were they treated so differently?"

Mary sighed, moving closer to the wall of picture frames. She stood in front of a large wedding photo, her flowing white dress contrasted with the perfect blackness of Ryan's tux, a waterfall of flowers cascading from her hands. Douglas and Claire were on either side, beaming as though they'd been the ones to tie the knot.

"I wish I knew," Mary said, her voice cracking and surprising Rake with the genuine emotion in it. "It always seemed weird, to be completely honest. But if it's not your family, how much can you push for details? Who are you to come in and turn over the stones of a family dynamic?" She reached out, tracing a manicured pink fingernail over their smiles. "Ryan and I were high school sweethearts, but I've known the family longer than that."

Mary turned and looked at Rake. "What you have to understand is that a small, wealthy bubble of a town like this comes with a sort of ingrained natural order of things. I'm not sure what it was like where you grew up, but here, it was always that you loved your town, you lived and breathed for Friday night football and homecoming dances. Your family belonged to the country club, and you'd play tennis in the summer while your dad golfed and talked business. You ventured as far as the closest university, then came back and settled here, bringing up the next wave of devotees.

"But Lizzie was always a little different. A little wild for what this small town was used to. My sister was in her grade, and Ry and I aren't much older, and she always had this . . . *something* about her. This—I don't know—zest for life that many people didn't know what to do with. Her parents included."

"It's a parent's job to know what to do with their children. To love them, *zest* and all," Rake said, not amused with the excuse for how Lizzie was treated.

Mary shook her head. "I agree. I'm not excusing their behavior. I'm trying to explain the reality of it. A place like this—small, idyllic town built on white picket fences and perfect families with two point five kids and church on Sundays—someone like Lizzie throws off that image."

Mary was silent for another moment, looking at the photo. She ran her finger over an invisible smudge on the glass.

"Lizzie didn't come to our wedding, she was traveling, but it almost seemed like Claire was relieved she wasn't there. Like she'd thought of every possible mistake Lizzie could make and decided it ruined what she expected for her son's wedding.

"I tried to keep my mouth shut. I didn't think it was my business to get involved, but I eventually had to confront Ryan on it all. Why Claire talked about her daughter with such weariness. Why Ryan didn't really try with Lizzie."

"And?"

"And . . . he didn't know. He said it's how it's always been."

"I'm sorry, but that's bullshit," Rake said, glancing up the stairs.

"I agree," Mary said, nodding. "And after digging into it more with Ryan, he knows it too. It was like Lizzie was more than Claire or Douglas bargained for, and they didn't want to try. Ryan's working on it, in his own way, and I hope they can build a stronger relationship than they have now."

Rake opened his mouth to respond, but at that moment Ryan came clomping down the steps, his head hanging in defeat.

"Any luck?" Mary asked, her tone implying she already knew the answer.

"No," Ryan said, scrubbing his hands over his face. "She wouldn't come out. I said a few things through the door, but who knows if she even heard me."

"I'll talk to her," Rake said, taking the stairs two at a time.

Chapter 39

LIZZIE heard the padding of feet down the hallway outside her room, the *snick* of the doorknob turning, and the creaking wood floors as someone moved toward her hiding place. Out of the corner of her eye, Rake's shoes appeared.

"Lizzie?" he said after a moment, turning in a circle to look around the room.

"Down here," she said softly, twining her fingers into the box springs above her.

After a moment, Rake's hands and knees appeared in the crack from under Lizzie's bed as he lowered himself to the ground, moving fluidly until his whole body came into view. He lay on his stomach, pressing his cheek into the wood to look at where she lay underneath her old bed.

Lizzie's gaze shot up to the underside of her mattress. She didn't want to look into his eyes and see the events of the last twenty minutes reflected in them. She didn't want to see knowing pity, a sad understanding that she'd always been this *thing* no one knew how to deal with. After a few breaths, he finally spoke.

"What are you doing down here, Birdy?"

Lizzie continued to study the floral pattern of her mattress, frantically trying to plug up the dam of sadness that threatened to burst in her chest.

Slowly, Rake slid his hand across the floor, twining his fingers in her limp hand at her side. The warmth of his skin nearly tore her apart, emotions thick in her throat and pulsing just under her skin, seeming to pool at the spot where he touched her.

She swallowed a few times, squeezing her eyes shut against the sting of tears, until she felt confident that she could get words out.

"Do you remember your first time? Having sex, I mean," she asked, pressing her palm more tightly against his.

There was a short beat before Rake answered. "Yes."

Lizzie's lips quirked. He was getting better at not questioning her zigzags of conversation. She rolled her head to look at him, and it felt like opening a vein. Everything was about to pour out of her, the least she could do was look at him while she did it.

"I do too. It was Chris Petrakis. It happened right here," she said, pointing up at her mattress. Rake's eyes flicked up then back to her, a muscle ticking in his jaw as he waited to hear her point.

"But what was kind of funny was how much later it happened than everyone guessed. Rumors started circulating that I was a slut by the time I was thirteen. I got boobs super young, so of course everyone assumed I was sleeping my way through the school, and the boys were all too happy to say I'd given them a hand job or whatever."

She traced the curling pattern of her bedspring, the cruel words of teenage boys and girls circulating through her mind. "I flirted and stuff, but I never really did anything until I was eighteen. Chris was the town's bad boy, and I'd been stupidly obsessed with him. He always had that undeniable cool factor, you know? Smoking, skipping class, big fuck-yous to teachers, whatever. Looking back, he was less of a bad boy and more of a privileged asshole, but any guy that wears a leather jacket and rides a motorcycle has instant appeal."

Lizzie had always fantasized that Chris was misunderstood, just like her. She daydreamed they'd find each other and talk and connect over being the pariahs of their small, dumb town. That he'd see her and he'd like her and he'd accept her exactly as she was.

Stupid.

"I'd known for a while that I wanted to lose my virginity to Chris. We'd been flirting and tiptoeing around it for months, and I was ready," Lizzie said, a tear reopening in her naïve little heart.

"One weekend, a few weeks before high school graduation, my parents went out of town, and Ryan and I threw a party. He was already home from college for the summer, and he was able to buy us booze and stuff."

She could still feel the energy of the night. The gentle warmth of an early summer darkness, clouds of cigarettes and marijuana and freedom mixing into a heady cocktail of pretend maturity. Lizzie had felt wise and womanly that night, on a mission to enter some new secret club with her body. She wanted to feel wanted.

And the way Chris's eyes followed her, she knew she was. She'd pulled out every trick teen magazines had taught her— flirty glances, tinkling laughs, arm touches, and eyebrow arches.

"I'd been drinking, getting up that liquid courage. And he had asked me to dance—turns out he was a terrible dancer. That should have been red flag number one, huh?" she said, trying to cut through the growing tension in the way Rake looked at her.

It didn't work. His eyes sharp and brows pinched together, and Lizzie pulled her hand away, locking her fingers around the metal links of her box spring.

"After a few songs, he asked me if I wanted to go up to my room to talk." She sent a sardonic glance at her mattress. "Talking was pretty much him squeezing my tits and asking me if I wanted to fuck—very romantic and subtle. I gave an adamant yes, picturing orgasms and sensual touches and laughter and cuddles after. In reality, he laid me down on the mattress, rolled a condom on, pushed my skirt around my hips, then jackhammered me for about three and a half pumps until he was done. It was like I didn't even need to be there. It hurt like a bitch too."

Lizzie could still feel the heavy press of his sweaty body against her, hear the grunt he'd made as he finished. She remembered thinking it was odd that she could feel so empty with another person that close to her.

"He pulled out, took the condom off and tied it up, then looked around my messy room for a minute—like he was trying to figure out what to do with it—then just tossed it on the bed next to me and walked out. I stayed in my room the rest of the party, staring up at the ceiling." Lizzie's breath rattled around her aching chest. "I don't really know what I had expected. I guess just something more. To feel wanted or—or I don't know, appreciated."

Loved. You had wanted to feel loved.

The words were like a sharp jab to her psyche, and she pushed the thought away. Lizzie had wanted her body and her brain to be desired. For someone to see her as she was and think she was enough.

"But for some reason, that hurt me so badly. Like I wasn't a person, just this mess."

Lizzie was quiet for a few moments, praying she would eventually build a callus over the way the memory still cut her.

"My parents came home the next day, the place was still trashed, and of course they put most of the blame on me. And Ryan let them. He was always such a little shit." She turned, giving Rake a sad smile. He looked like she'd punched him in the gut. She went back to staring at her mattress.

"I still went to school on Monday expecting things to be different. For Chris to *care*. For *feelings* to be there." She let out a deprecating laugh. "But he ignored me. I went up to him at lunch, and he looked right through me. I'd never felt so invisible. My mom had looked through me before, when I'd been 'too much' as she likes to call it. But this hurt worse. I think because I thought he had really *seen* me . . . Obviously I was wrong."

Lizzie wanted to reach into the void of time. She wanted to grab that sweet young girl with her heart on her sleeve and hug her. Comfort her. Hold her like she needed to be held. Tell her things would hurt, but she'd survive the pain.

Lizzie felt Rake's finger brush her cheek, and she realized she was crying. Soft tears for that young girl who had thought her body a gift and had seen it transformed into something disposable. She nuzzled closer into Rake's touch. After a few quiet moments, she continued. She wanted to get it all out. She wanted the poison to leave her.

"The worst part of it all, though, was how my mom reacted."

Rake's touch turned firmer, protective—his fingers weaving into her hair and holding her head, his palm a rest for her cheek.

"I was a wreck after that. I had my mom come pick me up from school. Good ole Rejection Sensitive Dysphoria keeping me on brand." She shot Rake a knowing smile, his lips a tense line as he watched her. "She came and got me, and I told her everything. Told her about the sex and how he'd treated me . . ."

Lizzie's throat burned as she spoke, pain slicing through her as she remembered sitting in the passenger seat, tears streaming down her face as she'd confessed to her mom—as she'd reached out for any source of comfort she could find. Any validation that would make her feel okay. For a woman she loved to tell her she was worthy of all the affection she so desperately craved.

Her life had been a series of these moments. Lizzie making a mistake and turning to her mom, hoping for a safety net, starving for the affirmation that she could mess up and still be loved.

And every time, Lizzie was disappointed. Her mom's lips

would purse and her tone would turn pained, like Lizzie's failures were a personal reflection of Claire as a mother. Like Lizzie was attacking her with every shortcoming.

"When we finally got home, she shut the car off and turned to me. The way she looked at me . . . She started talking like she was imparting some great *wisdom*. Asking what I expected, acting the way I did. Telling me I'd never find someone to love me if I continued to be this overwhelming of a person. This careless and easy. This *messy*."

Even now, the words delivered with a tone of kindness and care, slapped and stung at her skin, shame vibrating in her bones. "And maybe I'm overreacting, but it's always felt like she knew exactly what to say to hurt me the most."

Rake let out a deep breath. His hand moved from her head to her waist, sliding her out from beneath her mattress. Lizzie let him. She let his hands guide her body, his touch keep her on the floor so she wouldn't sink too far into the memories. He hovered over her, hands planted on either side of her head as he stared down. She looked back up, feeling the heat of his body, absorbing the tenderness in his look.

"I pretty much left after that," Lizzie continued, watching Rake's pulse beat at the base of his throat. "I had to. I was surrounded by people but so fucking alone. I couldn't take it much longer. I powered through to graduation, booked myself a plane ticket, and bounced."

She'd spent the summer fucking and drinking her way through Europe, working odd jobs when she could. She unlearned every restriction she'd created for herself, feeling everything she'd always tried to suppress. She leaned into pain and lust and freedom and happiness, oftentimes all at once. And if it all ever became too much, there was always a body or a drink on hand to smooth down the sharp edges for the night.

Lizzie had managed to stitch herself back together, slowly, in each new city she'd discovered. She found pieces of herself in art museums and coffee shops, in cobbled streets and pulsing clubs. She learned to love her sensuality, embrace sex and lust without shame. But she was never able to convince herself that anyone else would ever want her both body *and* mind. Even though she came to accept her distracted, impulsive brain, she knew no one would want to deal with her outside of tangled bedsheets.

By the time fall had rolled around, she'd abandoned any intention to go back home. But through it all, a tiny piece of her always hoped—with a desperate, human type of strength—that she could one day win her mom's approval. One day, their past would be erased and they would have the closeness and love and affection for each other that Lizzie had always been hungry for.

"Tell me what you're thinking," Lizzie said, reaching up her hand to trace over Rake's stern features.

He let out a breath. "I'm thinking," he said slowly, closing his eyes for a moment before meeting hers with unparalleled focus, "that I adore you."

Lizzie swallowed. She hadn't been expecting that.

"I'm thinking," he continued, his voice low and rough, "that I want to murder every person that's ever hurt you. Get my knuckles bloody on anyone that ever dared to try to dim your shine."

Lizzie's mouth opened, but she couldn't find any words, could barely hear him over the wild and reckless clanging of her heart against her chest. Small tears bloomed at the corners of her eyes.

"And I'm thinking," Rake said, using his thumb to brush the tears away, "that I value you. On a deep and terrifying level. And it makes me scared to lose you, because my life would never be the same without you."

Lizzie searched his face, absorbing the tenderness of his words and the way he looked at her. Part of her wanted to run from it, afraid that she'd ruin it. Destroy this small fragile thing between them. But another part of her, the bold and brazen part, wanted to absorb it, dance in the storm of what the emotions might hold.

She sat up suddenly, Rake moving back to give her room, and she wiggled her dress up her body. Rake's hands stopped hers right before she pulled it over her head.

"Lizzie, we don't—"

She touched her finger to his lips, quieting him. "Just hold me," she pleaded softly. "I just . . . I just need to feel your skin on my skin."

She watched Rake swallow, tracing the movement down the column of his throat, before he nodded. She pulled off her dress and tossed it to the side.

"You too," she whispered, pointing at his clothes. Rake nodded again, his eyes traveling over her body, landing on her face. He sat up, his hands shaking as he worked the buttons of his shirt, a sweet vulnerability wrinkling the corners of his eyes. Lizzie reached out her hand, tracing the planes of his face, feeling his skin. He nuzzled closer into her touch.

He threw his shirt into a pile with her dress, then stripped off his pants. Lizzie's eyes landed on his tented boxer briefs, and an autopilot reflex made her reach for him, but he put a finger on her chin, nudging her eyes back up to him.

"Let me just hold you," he whispered, repeating her words back to him.

Lizzie nodded, the moment feeling heavy and poised for pain or pleasure. She felt fragile, her heart a delicate globe of blown glass teetering on the edge of a shelf, primed to break.

She stood up, reaching out her hand to help him to his feet, and laid herself on the bed, pressing against the wall to accommodate him on the narrow mattress.

Rake pulled her tight against his chest, tucking her head under his chin and running his large hands over her skin, like he was stitching together all the invisible cuts and nicks that still hurt her. Under his touch, she surrendered to the feelings that had been piercing her gut and tightening her throat. Rake let out a soft hum of pleasure as he cherished her body, giving every inch of her skin loving affection.

Lizzie splayed her palm across his chest, feeling the gentle rhythm of his breaths, the ticking of his pulse. She wanted to sink her fingers into it and grab his heart. Own it. Or take her own out and shove it next to his.

Rake pulled back after a moment, brushing her hair off her face so he could look into her eyes. Lizzie felt exposed under that look, and she fought every instinct to pull away, to squirm into action. She saw the moment Rake registered her urge to retreat into herself, like he could see through her skull into her wild brain, and it made him smile.

"I love your freckles," he said, ducking his head to kiss a dense cluster above her breast, giving her words and touch and sensations to focus on.

She let out a breathy laugh, twisting her fingers into his hair. He let out a grunt of approval at her soft tug.

"They're like a work of art," he said roughly into her skin. "*You're* a work of art. You're unlike anything I've ever seen."

Lizzie pulled him closer, emotion making her throat thick and painful. He took a deep breath, inhaling against her skin, his exhale filling her with a soft, golden shimmer of adoration.

"And your eyes? They kill me. My heart hasn't beat in a steady rhythm since you started looking at me with those honey-colored eyes. I swear they change color with your mood. Browner when you're mad. Glints of yellow when you're excited. Small hints of green when you're laughing."

Lizzie's lips parted. She wanted to say something. Anything. She wanted to pour words into him and fill him like they were filling her. But she couldn't remember how to speak.

"Don't get me started on your hair," he continued, dragging his fingers through the strands. He caught a handful of the ends, and brought them up to his nose, inhaling deeply. "I should have known you'd wreck me with hair like this. It's become my favorite color. If I were a poet, I'd fill volumes about your hair. I'd find a smarter way to describe it than long and thick and orangey-red."

Lizzie laughed, moving to rub her nose against his. He planted soft kisses across her cheeks.

She let out a shaky breath, squeezing her eyes shut for just a moment. Lizzie was flooded by endless feelings. They were sharp and soft and delicate and fierce, and they all threatened to kill her or give her life. But she didn't resist. She decided she would drown in all those feelings if it meant she could feel them with Rake. They looked at each other for a long time, eyes skimming and tracing features, memorizing them. There were certain words that were still unsaid—syllables still too scary to utter.

A soft knock on the door disrupted their private oasis. Lizzie's eyes flicked to it across the room as Ryan's voice traveled through the door.

"Lizzie? We are about to take off. I'd really like to talk to you."

Lizzie sighed, turning her eyes back to Rake.

"You should talk to him," he whispered, placing a kiss on her forehead. "We'll come back to this. But you should hear him out."

Lizzie swallowed and nodded. She wasn't sure she'd ever actually be able to use words again.

"Give her one minute," Rake called, breathing in Lizzie's skin one last time before sitting up and pulling her with him.

He reached down, grabbing her dress, then turned to her, dressing her gently. He grabbed his own clothes, standing to shove his legs into his pants and quickly buttoning up his shirt, before striding across the room and opening the door, Lizzie following a few paces behind.

Ryan and Mary stood in the doorway, both with drawn and serious expressions on their faces.

"Ryan has something he wants to ask you," Mary said at last, giving Ryan a little nudge.

Ryan cleared his throat. "Lizzie, I know . . . I . . . Do you two want to stay with us tonight? I'm guessing you wouldn't want to stay here, but it's late and we'd hate for you to have to drive back to Philly. We don't live far, and we have a guest bedroom in our basement."

Mary nodded, giving Lizzie a warm smile.

Lizzie glanced at Rake, and his look told her he'd go along with whatever she wanted.

"Okay," Lizzie said, staring into Ryan's eager and anxious eyes. She really did love him, and she still had a reckless shard of hope that they could come to know each other better.

Ryan nodded, looking like he was going to leave it at that. Mary nudged him again. Ryan cleared his throat.

"And, I just want to say. I'm sorry Mom and Dad are so shitty. And I'm sorry I've been . . . complicit in it."

It was Lizzie's turn to nod, emotions building in a steady pressure between her eyes and nose. She couldn't think of what to say.

So, instead, she threw her arms around him, hugging her big brother with all the strength she could muster. And he hugged her back.

After a moment, Lizzie pulled away, fixing Ryan and Mary with a grin.

"Let's get the fuck out of here," she said.

Chapter 40

MARY and Ryan's home was cozy and warm. They all made themselves comfortable in the living room, Lizzie and Rake snuggling into the plush love seat while Mary and Ryan sat on the light gray couch covered in pillows and blankets. The whole house held a softness that Lizzie wouldn't have pictured for Ryan, a domesticity that she never associated with her brother. She realized that, as misunderstood as she'd felt by him growing up, she didn't really know him either. And she wanted to change that.

The four of them talked for hours. While there was a tang of awkwardness at first, it quickly dissolved as they started laughing and joking with one another, carefully navigating the new territory of closeness they stood at the perimeter of.

Mary eventually yawned and stretched. "I'm dead tired," she said, standing up. "I better head to bed. Lizzie, do you still plan on going to the party tomorrow?"

"No," Lizzie said, shaking her head. "The cake is already at Mom and Dad's, and I don't think it'd be worth more fighting to show."

Mary nodded. "I understand," she said, reaching out a hand for Ryan. "Your parents weren't so happy with us either after

Ryan went off on them," Mary added, folding up her blanket. "I'd be surprised if they even want us there tomorrow."

"You went off on them?" Lizzie said, her gaze whipping to Ryan.

He blushed. "I . . ."

"It was probably the closest I've ever seen Ryan get to telling someone to go fuck themselves," Mary said with a delicate laugh, catching Lizzie off guard. Lizzie didn't even know Mary *knew* cuss words, let alone said them.

"It was a necessary conversation," Ryan said, looking down at his feet.

Lizzie stood up and moved to him, giving him another hug. "I love you," she whispered into his chest. She heard him swallow.

"Love you too, Lizzie."

They said their good-nights, and Rake and Lizzie headed downstairs to the guest bedroom. An unspoken thread of need tethered them together as they walked into the room. The night had been raw, heavy, and more words needed to be said, but first, they needed to communicate in the way they'd first learned with each other.

When the door was shut and locked, they turned to each other, eyes searching. Without saying anything, Rake started unbuttoning his shirt and Lizzie lifted her dress up and over her head. She moved to stand in front of him, their breaths mingling in a delicate cloud in the few inches that separated them.

In the space between a breath and a heartbeat, her lips found his, the touch soft and tender as their bodies met.

Rake ran his fingertips along her skin like he was touching the surface of a bubble, delicate and focused and careful.

Lizzie broke the kiss long enough to reach back and unhook her bra and slide off her underwear, Rake removing his remaining clothing as well.

Lizzie reached out her hand and Rake took it, pressing his

body against hers, skin and heat and hunger. Walking backward, her lips and limbs tangling with his, Lizzie made her way to the bed and Rake prowled over her.

They kissed and touched and held each other, a garden of pleasure blooming across Lizzie's body. She arched her hips against him, wanting and ready, desire pulsing beneath her skin. But Rake pulled back.

He caged her between his forearms, covering her with his broad expanse of chest. He stared down at her, forcing her to look back.

"I need to say one thing," he panted over her, stilling her movements, "before we continue."

Lizzie bit back a frustrated groan. "Listen," she said, arching up to touch him again. "I love talking to you, I do. But right now, I really, really, *really* want to be done with the talking part."

"This is important," he said, and the serious look on his face made her still her greedy hands that wanted to touch and grab and caress every inch of him.

"When we were talking at your parents' house, I mentioned how much I love your freckles. Your hair. All those things."

Lizzie nodded, basking in the memory of his praise like a kitten in the sun. "You did. I thoroughly enjoyed it. You can tell me other body parts you like during what we were about to do, though," she said with a soft laugh, straining her head up to kiss his shoulder.

"No, that's the point."

Lizzie gave him a confused look, so he pressed on.

"Your brain," he said.

"What about it?"

"I adore your brain the most." He threaded his fingers through her hair, sparking up every nerve ending with the gentle tug. "More than your freckles or your eyes or this deliciously round arse of yours." He reached down, giving her butt a playful pinch that made her giggle and squirm.

"I think about your brain constantly," he continued, his eyes piercing into hers. "It fascinates me to no end. I want to know every corner of it, learn the secret colors of your thoughts. I'd do anything for a map of it."

She let out a rough chuckle, about to say something self-deprecating, but he cut her off like he could read her thoughts. He pressed his mouth to hers in a deep kiss. He kissed her and claimed her until she opened for him on a gasp. He moved away, placing soft brushes along her cheek. Her jaw.

"You don't understand what a privilege it is to know you," he said, whispering the words into the shell of her ear. "You don't understand how it changes a person to hear you laugh. And, God, the way you make me laugh. You're the funniest person I've ever met. Even when you aren't trying."

His words traveled, hot and humid through her skin, an expanding cloud of bubblegum pink in her chest, until she felt like she would burst from the affection, like the kindness would rip her open at the seams.

She reached up, pressing her lips to the spot just above his pounding heart. Rake smiled down at her as her head fell back to the pillows.

Lizzie had been naked in front of countless people, but she'd never felt so bare as when he looked at her like that, like she was the answer to every question he'd ever thought to ask.

She pressed her palm to his cheek, and he kissed it, moving down her arm. Kissing her collarbone, her breasts. Licking the space between each rib. Nibbling the skin at her hips. He traced a broad hand between her thighs, and she fell open for him. He let out a smug hum of approval, pushing himself farther down her body. But instead of going straight where she wanted him, he took his time, resting his cheek on the curve of her belly, breathing her in again.

She threaded her fingers in his hair, and they stayed like that for a lingering moment. He moved with the rise and fall of her shallow breaths, his warm exhales against her skin the most delicious thing she'd ever felt.

Rake turned his head to look up at her over the planes of her body. "You'll probably never fully grasp how wonderful it is to know a person like you exists."

A firecracker of emotions erupted in her chest, sharp and sparkling, taking her breath away.

It was the closest she'd ever felt to a person, and the intimacy of it started to press in against her, unsettling her. She wanted to hide behind wildness, fall into the protection of the physical act.

But Rake wouldn't let her. No, he was going to force her to experience every feeling she'd been denying. She was going to stare into the face of those scary beasts.

As he kissed and licked and nibbled his way back over her, she felt cherished. Sheltered. Like the covering of his body would keep her safe from the pain of the past. Every cruel word and misunderstanding, every moment of being an endless liability pinged off him like he was her armor.

He continued his slow mapping of her body, whispering sweet, hot words against her skin. Branding her with his touch. Only when she was quivering and whimpering, aching with need, did he line himself up at the entrance of her body, and Lizzie tilted her hips, angling to take him in.

Rake stared into her eyes as he slowly pushed into her, sparks flashing in her vision at the raw pleasure of it.

When their hips were flush, Rake stilled, taking the time to sip at her lips, caress her breasts, roll her nipples between his fingers.

Instinct and years of other bodies told her to move, but Rake held her still, gripping her hips, making her feel.

"I'm taking my time with you tonight," he whispered against her throat. "Making you wait and wait until you're blind with the need to come."

"I think I might be there already," she ground out, her body clenching around him, begging for more. Rake laughed softly, but didn't give in.

In those immeasurable moments of exquisite stillness, Lizzie felt everything. Each pulse and jump of their joined bodies felt like an electric shock to her system, a shower of stars obscuring her vision. Sweat pricked her skin, her body trembling with need. She memorized the feel of his teeth bared against her shoulder and her nails digging into his back.

And when she thought she'd break from the primal need, the near-painful tension in the center of her being, she began to beg. With three subtle nudges of his hips, Rake sent her over the edge, the climax devastating her in endless shudders and spasms, her head pushing back into the pillows as she groaned and sobbed, Rake's teeth clamping lightly on her neck as he growled against her.

As the sensations died away, some heavy emotion she couldn't name tore at her chest and caused tears to well in her eyes. Before she could brush them away, Rake was there, kissing them, tasting her emotion.

He started moving in earnest, hips pumping as he hoisted her leg to wrap high on his waist. A foreign flair of possessiveness shot through Lizzie as she watched him move. She wanted to mark him, be every notch on his bedpost, be his good night and good morning.

Rake grunted loving, dirty words against her skin, building her up to that peak again, until they both tumbled over.

The pleasure was decadent, rolling through her in exquisite waves as she held him close.

When the earth stopped spinning, she pressed her face into the crook of his neck, breathing him in.

They lay there for a while, Rake on his back and Lizzie on her side, one arm and leg draped tightly over him.

"Do I remind you of a koala?" she asked, nuzzling into his chest.

A soft chuckle vibrated across her skin, and he smiled against her hair. He was quiet for a moment, lightly dragging his fingertips up and down her arm.

"You certainly remind me of home, Birdy." He pressed his nose against her temple, breathing in deeply.

She glowed at his words. "Why do you call me Birdy?" she asked after a moment, tangling her fingers in the light hairs of his chest.

"I must have known you'd leave me henpecked," he said, nuzzling his cheek against her temple and making her giggle at the drag of stubble.

She smacked him on the shoulder. "Tell me the real reason, you ass."

Rake was still, breathing her in and out, before he sighed. Pulling back to look at her, he searched her face.

"My nan's name is Robyn," he said at last, dragging the backs of his fingers down Lizzie's cheek. "She's a lovely woman. Beautiful, warm, vivacious . . . a wonderful person to be around. Same with my grandpa. They were one of those couples that always seemed young and alive, regardless of how old they actually were." The corners of Rake's mouth curved in a smile at some private memory.

"And my grandpa adored Nan. He was always kissing her cheeks or holding her hands, and she was always making him laugh, giving him these bold, bright smiles. They were just . . ." He trailed off, wrapping a lock of Lizzie's hair around his finger as he thought.

"He always called her his Little Bird. 'Dance with me, Bird.' 'What's for dinner, sweet Bird?' 'Come have a perch, Birdy,' and he'd pat his knee and she'd walk over and sit on his lap, draping her arms around him, and they'd laugh and giggle like teenagers. Even being a kid, it was impossible to witness two people so enamored and not realize how special it was."

He stared at Lizzie for a long moment, his brows furrowed,

as if he was trying to understand something, solve a puzzle by mapping the freckles on her face. "My grandpa died a while back."

"I'm sorry," Lizzie said automatically. And she was. She wanted to know every person who shaped Rake. Collect every memory people had of him from any stage of his life.

"Don't be," Rake said, watching as he trailed his hands up and down Lizzie's arms like he couldn't stop touching her. "He lived a long, happy life. It was hard to even be sad at the funeral because it was filled with so much love and happy memories. But what I'm trying to say is 'Birdy' wasn't something I'd heard in years. It's not something I ever said."

He stopped his curious fingers, looking fully at Lizzie, his eyes piercing in their intensity. "But when I saw you at that bar, when you smiled at me like that, the nickname slipped out. I didn't even realize I'd said it until you laughed. Something about you . . ." A gentle blush covered his cheeks as he looked away and cleared his throat. "That and your nose looks like a beak at some angles."

Lizzie was silent for a moment, absorbing his words, before she burst into laughter at his cheeky ending. She felt so much all at once, it was impossible to contain everything inside her, and it didn't take long for her giggles to make the whole bed shake. Rake joined her, both laughing wildly as they lay tangled in the sheets.

When their cackling subsided and sleep beckoned, Lizzie decided to be brave.

She decided to tear off a corner of her heart, carefully fold it into a tiny paper airplane, and gently toss it at him, letting it glide to a stop at his feet. He could either pick it up or step on it, and she was scared of either option.

"Rake," she whispered, running her fingers along his arm, his palm splayed across her belly, cradling the gentle swell of her little bump.

"Hmmm?"

"Do you think . . ." She cleared her throat, her voice barely audible, as she pressed her hand over his. "When we go home, things will be . . . different?"

Rake was quiet for a moment before answering. "I hope they are."

Chapter 41

LIZZIE and Rake woke up early the next morning with every intention of getting on the road as soon as possible. But Mary knocked gently on their door shortly after, telling them that Ryan had run out to get bagels. And Lizzie had a really hard time saying no to any circle-shaped carbs.

Even though they'd been at Ryan and Mary's for less than twelve hours, Lizzie had still managed to empty her suitcase like a small tornado had whipped through the guest room, and by the time they were packed and upstairs, Ryan was back, a delicious spread of bagels and cream cheese was sitting next to steaming mugs of coffee.

They sat around the table, talking and laughing as morning sun filtered in through the white curtains, casting a soft haze over the conversation.

Ryan was in the middle of suggesting the four of them go to a Flyers hockey game sometime in the winter when the doorbell rang. Mary went to answer it, and a choked noise of surprise left her throat.

"Claire. Hi. What are you doing here?"

A cold dread flooded through Lizzie's system.

"Good morning, Mary. Is Elizabeth here? I need to speak with her."

"Uh, um . . ."

Without giving herself enough time to think better of it and run and hide, Lizzie stood, moving toward the door. Rake grabbed her hand, and she looked at him.

"It's okay," she said, giving his hand a squeeze before letting it go. "She and I are long overdue for a conversation." He looked wary, but let her go.

"Hi, Mom," Lizzie said, rounding the corner to the front door.

Claire nodded, giving her a tense smile. "Mary," she said, turning to her, "may we use your sitting room?"

Mary looked uncomfortable, but she nodded, swooping her arm toward the room off the entrance hallway.

"I'll . . . Let me know if you need anything," Mary said, before turning and leaving.

Tension radiated throughout the room, slapping against Lizzie's senses. She waited, head bent as she stared down at her lap, peeking at her mom and preparing for things to turn ugly any moment.

Finally, Claire daintily cleared her throat. "I wanted to say that I regret how things ended last night."

Lizzie's eyes went wide as she wondered if hell just froze over and the end of times was upon them. Was Claire Blake about to apologize?

Claire continued, "I'm sorry if you felt our reaction to your career news wasn't as . . . *enthusiastic* as you wanted. But I would hope you could understand my perspective. Hopefully we can move past this . . . For my part, I'm prepared to forgive *you*, Elizabeth," she said softly. Almost kindly.

Lizzie jerked back like her mom slapped her. "Forgive *me*?" Lizzie said, looking around the room. "For what?"

Clair blew out a breath through her nose as she looked at Lizzie, searching for patience. With a smile that didn't quite reach her eyes, she leaned over and held Lizzie's hand. Lizzie knew that her mom was trying to make the touch comforting, but Claire's skin was cool and foreign.

"You pulled quite the dramatic exit last night," Claire said, as though this all should be obvious. "And you dragged Ryan and Mary into the theatrics. On a weekend that is supposed to be celebrating me and your father, no less. And this isn't the first time you've centered the attention on yourself over the years."

Lizzie blinked. "You expect me to apologize for . . . getting upset? After what you said to me?" Lizzie was trying to understand . . . she was *always* trying to understand the disconnect between her mother's expectations and who Lizzie was.

Claire pulled her hand back, sighing again. "I do, yes. I expect you to apologize for making a scene. I expect you to apologize for your belligerent reaction to my genuine concern for your career choices. If I don't take your future and career seriously, who will?"

"I'm pregnant, Mom." The words were out before Lizzie even realized they were in her head.

Claire sat there, expressionless and unblinking.

"Rake's the father," Lizzie added. Anything to break up the silence.

Something in Claire's face snapped, a wave of anger rippling across her composed features. "Jesus, Elizabeth. This is unacceptable."

"Do you not like Rake?"

"My feelings on him are irrelevant," Claire said, her lips twitching as she spoke. "The issue is you and your careless decisions. Your reckless behavior. Do you have any idea how this will look? For you? For us?" Claire rubbed her temples. "A child out of wedlock? What were you thinking?"

Lizzie felt herself cowing to her mother's sharp voice, shame prickling across her skin, that mean voice in her head gaining volume as it told her what a mess she was.

But that wasn't true, was it? She wasn't ideal or conventional by any standards, but she also wasn't this mortifying wreck her mom painted her as. Claire hadn't even asked how Lizzie was doing. How she was feeling. All she'd thought about was herself.

"I don't really care," Lizzie said, looking straight at her mom.

Claire blinked. "Excuse me?"

"I don't fucking care."

"Don't use that language," Claire said.

Lizzie ignored her. "I don't care what you tell people at the stupid country club. I don't care how it feels for you to hear the news so suddenly, because you've never given me any indication that you actually give a fuck about what I do unless it messes up your idea of perfection."

"How could you say that to me?" Claire asked, astounded. "I won't sit here and be spoken to this way."

"Go ahead, Mom. Leave. And then what? Say something else passive-aggressive and cutting on your way out? Ignore me for a few more years? You've already done that so thoroughly, I doubt my worth with every person I interact with. So go ahead, say something bitchy." Lizzie could feel her anger welling up inside of her like a red-hot burst that threatened to burn her alive.

Claire sniffed, looking at her nails, sharp judgment and disapproval pushing out of her and cutting Lizzie's skin like shards of glass.

"All my life I just wanted you to see me, Mom," Lizzie said, her voice cracking on the words as she spoke through a knot in her throat, tears threatening to spill over onto her cheeks.

"I do see you, Elizabeth," Claire said through tight lips. "You're sitting right in front of me."

"Not literally, Mom. I wanted you to *understand* me."

Claire tilted her head. "Why do you insist on this narrative that you were so neglected? You were clothed and fed. You had a great education, every opportunity before you. Parents who only wanted the best for you. I've tried with you. Indulging your ridiculous hobbies. Putting up with your theatrics. How can you sit there and complain? How can you be so ungrateful?"

"Because that isn't love, Mom!" Lizzie shouted, throwing her arms out to her sides. "Love isn't trying to force me into some mold you've decided I needed to fit. Love is making a child feel safe. Encouraging them to find themselves. I've spent so much of my life doubting myself, hearing your words over and over every day that I've second-guessed who I am for years. And I'm not perfect—God, do I know how far from perfect I am. I make a lot of mistakes. But I'm *trying*. Does that matter to you at all? The effort I make to be better?"

"Elizabeth, your mistakes are all avoidable. You don't think. You don't listen. That's your problem."

"No!" Lizzie jabbed her finger at her mom, the words coming hot and sharp from her chest. "That's *your* problem. All I ever wanted was for you to love me."

Her mom sighed. "I've said this before and I'll say it again, I love you as every mother loves her child. I'm not sure why you can't see that."

"Because you don't show that. It's all conditional."

"And what would you have me do? How would you have me prove it to you?"

Lizzie took in the almost bored look in her mother's eyes, the subtle dismissal in the way she tapped her perfectly manicured nail on the arm of her chair, the almost imperceptible arch to her eyebrow that made it all seem like a ruse. How *would* Lizzie want her to prove it?

It wouldn't be some grand gesture of tears and declarations. It wouldn't be a long list of things her mom liked about her.

More than anything, it would just be a sign that the woman gave a damn. Even the slightest sign of distress that her daughter ever questioned if she was loved.

But, looking at this woman, with her perfectly tailored blouse and ramrod-straight posture, she knew she'd never get that. And it hurt. It was a pressure that built in her chest and pressed on her heart. But it was a good hurt. It was a hurt that could maybe one day be healed.

"Nothing," Lizzie said at last, looking her mother in the eye. "There's nothing you could do."

"Nothing?"

"Yup, nothing."

"Then what, pray tell, was the point of all of this?"

"The point was realizing that I can love you and also need you out of my life."

Her mom's head jerked back, the first hint of emotion thawing her features. "Excuse me?"

"You heard me. I love you. I'll always love my mom. But you're toxic as fuck."

"Don't you dare speak to me like—"

"I'll speak to you however I want. I'm an adult woman having a discussion with a fellow adult. I don't need you in my life. I don't need you hurting me, making me doubt myself, judging me. You may be my mom, but you aren't my family."

"What is that supposed to mean?" Claire stood up, using her height to look down at Lizzie.

"I have a baby on the way that I already love so much, it feels like my bones could crack with it. I have people that love me. I've found friends that accept me more than you or Dad ever will. I have Ryan, who doesn't really get me, but he wants to learn. I have Rake—"

Claire let out a cold laugh. "As if anything you have with that boy is built to last. You don't have a stunning track record."

Lizzie chucked those cruel words straight out of her brain. "Believe whatever you want, but he and I care about each other. And regardless of him, I have myself. I love myself. I can take care of myself."

"Because you've done such a good job so far," Claire spat out.

Lizzie straightened, looking at her mother, as if seeing her for the first time. It was like looking at a stranger. Lizzie wanted to reach into the woman's skull and force her to understand. Force her to want the relationship Lizzie wanted. But she couldn't. All Lizzie could do was protect her heart, step away from the thing that had always hurt her.

"Mom, I think you should go."

"This isn't your house."

"Okay, then I'll go. Either way, I think this conversation is done."

"Is that so?"

"Yeah, it is. My life is too full to try and make room for someone that doesn't want to be there."

After one last glance at her mom, Lizzie left the room, heading straight to Rake, who stood tensely near the table. She registered his worried look the second before she crashed against him, wrapping her arms around his waist, burrowing her face into his chest. He rubbed his hands up and down her back, and placed kisses on the top of her head.

"You okay?" he asked as she pulled back.

"I am," she said, wiping her running nose on the back of her hand. Then she looked at him fully and smiled. "Let's go home."

Chapter 42

Week twenty-two, little one is the size of a brioche à tête.
Harper called and told Lizzie that le bébé's adult tooth buds are
now formed. Which is weird as hell.

Over the next few weeks, a foreign domesticity perfumed Lizzie
and Rake's apartment. It was sweet.

Warm.

Them.

They'd started acquiring odds and ends for the baby's arrival, Rake swearing and sweating as he tried to put the crib
together, Lizzie getting a new pack of outrageous onesies from
Etsy delivered at least once a week. Both arguing over what type
of nipples they should get for the bottles, like either had a clue,
and stockpiling diapers at an alarming rate.

Rake was slowly, carefully relinquishing control of his feelings, letting them out into the world, finding the courage to
trust that Lizzie would welcome them. And she did.

She was ever the lightning bolt of a person, saying and doing
ridiculous and wonderful things that made Rake smile like a
fool for hours on end. He'd get home from a grueling day at
work, his battery empty from the vain attempts to please Dominic, and there'd be Lizzie, in the kitchen with flour on her nose,

or sprawled out on the couch with a book. Some days, he would beat her home, and she'd waddle in, her baby bump growing, and she'd plop right at his feet in front of the couch.

"You know that thing people do where they manipulate the muscles in another person's shoulders and neck?" she'd say, turning to look at him over her shoulder.

"A massage?" Rake would ask.

And her face would light up in mock surprise. "Oh, that's so sweet of you to offer. Yes, thank you," she'd say, pulling her hair to the side and sighing in pleasure as he worked the muscles. She'd eventually clamber up to the couch, pushing her feet into his sides until he started rubbing those too, smiling the entire time as she talked about her day.

At night, he'd love her, devoting himself to pleasuring every inch of her body. She was radiant, lighting up the dark room like the moon glowed through her, her freckles constellations across her skin.

Rake couldn't name the exact moment, but at some point, Lizzie had become painfully real to him. She wasn't some fun indulgence, some wild mystical being that lived beyond the scope of real life. She was flesh and blood and pain and determination, and the dimensions of her were so vast and deep, Rake didn't know what to do with himself. All he knew was that he cherished her in a way that scared him to pieces.

One Saturday afternoon, Rake stood in the kitchen, grating an endless stack of carrots for a carrot cake Lizzie was baking. She'd run to the market on the corner, saying she absolutely could not go another second without tater tots and would be back soon to pick up where she left off on the recipe.

Rake was exhausted but glad to be doing something that wasn't work-related. An ad campaign had fallen through with Nordstrom that week, and Dominic was on a new level of berating the team, having everyone working close to twelve-hour days to find an alternative that would have a similar market impact.

A call rang on Rake's phone, trilling through the Bluetooth speaker he'd been playing music on. He glanced at the screen, Dominic's name flashing across. With a sigh, he quickly wiped off his fingers with a towel then answered the call.

"Hi, Dominic," he said, returning to his grating and letting the call go through his speakers.

"Rake. Got a minute? I've got some news."

"Of course. What's up?"

"I've been working on Nicholás from Nordstrom's, trying to get him to reconsider, and I've made some headway. But he wants a meeting over dinner. My wife and I are meeting him and his wife at Barclay Prime at seven thirty on Monday, and I need you there."

Rake blinked, taking that in. He set down the carrot and grater, placing both palms on the counter as he stared at the speaker. This had the potential to be huge for him. He'd been poised to make a generous commission on the project, and seeing it successfully executed could potentially put him in Dominic's good graces.

"That sounds great," Rake said, his mind already creating a to-do list to get ready, things he'd need to prepare. "I'll talk to Lizzie, but there shouldn't be a problem in us being there. Do you want to meet at seven to go over a few things before dinner starts?"

Dominic was quiet for a moment, then rumbling laughter crackled through the speaker.

"You can't be serious," he said at last.

Rake frowned. "I'm sorry?"

"That redhead from the launch with her tits hanging out?" Dominic said, still chuckling.

Rake's mouth opened, the words humming around his skull but not making sense.

"Listen, Rake," Dominic continued, all humor gone from his voice. "I know I'm hard on you, but it's because I think you have potential. But that's *if* you play your cards right. And that includes exuding a certain sense of refinement. Parading around someone like *that* . . . well, let's just say it's not the best look."

Rake continued to stare at the speaker, speechless.

Dominic sighed. "I pulled a lot of strings to get this dinner, so make sure you're focused, yeah? I need you clearheaded and ready to lead. If this goes the way we want it, I imagine there will be a title change and bonus in your future."

"I . . . uh."

"It's nothing against her," Dominic continued, the tone of his voice indicating his attention was elsewhere. "Just use your head."

"I'll . . . I'll take care of it." Rake cringed.

"Good. We'll talk more on Monday," Dominic said, then hung up.

Rake continued to stare at the speaker, feeling like an absolute prick.

The whole conversation had derailed, and he'd felt incapable of processing it in real time. And what was he supposed to say? He needed to keep his job. He needed to make and save as much money as possible in preparation for the baby. He couldn't jeopardize that by challenging Dominic, no matter how out of line he was.

When things calmed down with the company and Rake felt more secure in his position, he'd have a talk with Dominic about how he spoke about Lizzie. He'd make it right when the timing was better.

Rake hung his head, still feeling like an asshole.

And that's when he heard a sniff and the soft padding of feet toward the kitchen.

Panic flooded Rake. Lizzie was home? He hadn't heard her come in. His head jerked up, his gaze fixing on her watery eyes.

"Lizzie," he whispered.

Lizzie cleared her throat, fixing her face into the saddest

smile Rake had ever seen. "Have a great dinner," she said, tossing her bag of frozen tater tots on the counter.

"Birdy." He stepped toward her, but she put her hands up, moving away from him.

"No, this is great. So great. I hope you get that title change." The last words were almost an imperceptible whisper, but they punched Rake in the chest.

"I'm sorry I didn't tell him off. I just—"

"Why would you?" Lizzie said, closing her eyes and pressing the heels of her hands into the sockets. "You don't owe me anything. None of this is real."

If her previous words were a punch, these were a knife to the gut.

"None of it?"

Lizzie shrugged in defeat. "Nah. I guess I just got carried away, didn't I? How typical of me. We're nothing but strangers, after all. Two strangers and a soon-to-be baby. This is a relief, if anything. Consider it taken care of," she said, throwing his words to Dominic back at him.

"A relief?"

"Of course. Now we know exactly where we stand," Lizzie said, moving toward the bed. She picked up her clothes off the floor, shoving them into bags. "I'm this embarrassing piece of shit that got knocked up, and you're some hero doing the world a favor by offering to help out. But hey, we had some good times, huh?"

"Lizzie, stop."

"No," she snapped, turning her sharp eyes on him. "You stop. Stop looking at me like I'm pathetic. I'm not pathetic. And I'm not some problem to be swept under the rug so you can impress your boss."

"That's not what I'm thinking!" Rake yelled, fisting his hands in his hair. "If you would let me get a word in, I could explain this to you. But you won't. You'll do what you always do, steamroll through a conversation. Have something decided in your thick skull and never let any words get through to you."

Lizzie stared at him, hurt cracking through her beautiful face. "Wow."

"What am I supposed to say, Lizzie?" Rake continued, his voice straining. "I'm doing my best. Do you want me to lose my job? Do you want me to tell Dominic to fuck off?"

"Yes! That's exactly what you're supposed to say. You want to pretend to be the hero? You want to try and make this something it isn't? Then that's exactly what you were supposed to say, you idiot."

"So I can sit around here doing nothing? Not provide for you? Live off you? Be some deadbeat right in time for our child to be born?"

"How do you not get it?" Lizzie said, stomping her foot. "I don't need you to provide for me in some archaic domestic facade. I'm a big girl, and I can figure out how to survive with or without your financial support. The only thing I've ever needed was someone to stand up for me."

"I do stand up for you! I do. Remember when Thu was out of line? How about that whole shit show weekend with your parents? I'm always on your side."

"Being on my side and snapping at people you don't know or give a damn about is one thing, but defending me—going out on a limb for me—when the other person's opinion actually matters in your life? That's the fucking hard part. That's the part that matters."

"Lizzie, I'm sorry. But don't throw away all we've built over this one thing. I'll make it up to you."

"Yeah?" she said, not bothering to look at him while she shoved more things in a bag. "How's that?"

Rake was at a loss for words. His entire life seemed to be spinning out of control in a tornado around him, and he couldn't grab on to any of the pieces and make them still.

"I uprooted my entire life for you. Isn't that enough?"

Lizzie stopped, dropping her bag and fixing him with a look that made his heart twist painfully.

"Don't," she whispered. "Don't you fucking dare. I gave you an out. You moved here for your own conscience. To heal your damaged little ego over a woman who cheated on you. Don't put that on me. I'll make this perfectly clear: I don't need you. I don't need your money, or your job, or your apartment, or your support, or anything else. All I needed was for you to care."

Rake was silent, frozen to the spot.

Say something, his brain screamed at him. *Fix this.*

But he shut down, all ability to form words completely lost. The familiar feelings of shame and inadequacy and heartbreak— all the things he'd felt when Shannon left—came flooding back to him. Immobilizing him.

Without another word, Lizzie picked up her bag, slung it over her shoulder, and walked out of their apartment.

Chapter 43

LIZZIE spent most of Saturday night and all of Sunday sobbing and FaceTiming with Harper and Thu while Indira spooned her and rubbed comforting circles on her back.

"Fuck him," Thu said on repeat, throwing in threats of bodily harm every few hours to keep things spicy. Harper, for her part, created a broken heart playlist for Lizzie at record speed, and Lizzie listened to it on loop while she wailed.

"I feel like such an idiot," she said through choked sobs.

"You're not," Indira said gently.

"I *am*," Lizzie said. "I let myself develop feelings for him when I knew from the start it would be a disaster, that I would ruin it. I break every relationship I touch."

Indira was quiet for a moment, her lips pursed. "Lizzie, what relationships have you *actually* ruined? And don't say your parents because you and I both know that is on them, not you."

Lizzie sniffed, having trouble thinking of one.

Indira pounced on the silence. "You see, I can't think of one you've ruined all on your own. Look at the friendships you have. Harper, Thu, and I love you an unhealthy amount. Seriously, it's almost obsessive."

Lizzie let out a wet laugh.

"And I know things aren't perfect with Ryan, but from what you've told me, you're both trying. And you get on great with Mary. And Bernadette? That old lady thinks you're a star." Indira visited Bernadette's regularly, always taking a few minutes to talk with Bernadette about how everything was going.

"Do you want my opinion?" Indira asked, playing with Lizzie's tangled hair.

"Always," Lizzie said, wiping her nose on her T-shirt. "You're a literal psychiatrist."

Indira smiled at that. "I think you've heard a story about yourself for a very long time. I think the people that were supposed to love you the most actually hurt you the most. I think you were told so many times that you were destructive that you came to believe it. And I think it's always stopped you from pursuing relationships. The loving, romantic kind that you deserve."

Lizzie opened her mouth, but no words came out.

"Am I saying you're perfect? Of course not," Indira continued. "And I'm not invalidating the struggles and obstacles your ADHD presents, that would do you a disservice. But what I am saying is, just because your brain works differently from neurotypicals, it doesn't mean you deserve to be valued any less. It doesn't mean your love is a burden or a liability."

Lizzie turned this over. Indira's point felt dangerous. Scary. Like maybe if she started accepting that she deserved to be loved, she'd consciously start wanting it . . .

Who the hell was she kidding? Of course she wanted to be loved. There was nothing in the world she wanted more than to love and be loved in return.

"But if what you're saying is true, then why would Rake let Dominic talk about me like that?"

"Because Rake is what we call emotionally constipated," Indira said with a small smile. "Just like sometimes you say or do the wrong thing, Rake definitely said and did the wrong thing.

It doesn't excuse it, but his shitty response doesn't reflect on your worth."

"This is . . . a lot to think about," Lizzie said, rubbing her fists against her eyes. "I think I need to go to bed," she added, glancing at the clock. She couldn't keep talking about it. Her brain felt crowded, and any other profound statements from Indira would be like pouring water over glass and expecting it to absorb.

"Of course," Indira said, reaching over to turn out the light, the pair snuggled in Indira's bed. Lizzie knew she had to find a place of her own, but she'd give herself a few days before starting the search.

"And you don't mind going to get my stuff tomorrow?" Lizzie asked, punching her pillow into a comfortable position. Lizzie didn't want to go back into the apartment. She didn't want to feel the happy memories poke and pinch at her skin as she gathered the rest of her stuff.

"Of course not," Indira said. "I'll go during lunch."

"Thank you," Lizzie said with a yawn, allowing a dreamless sleep to take her.

Chapter 44

LIZZIE was not at peak performance for work on Monday. She'd burned two batches of cupcakes for the store's new Yonic Boom flavor—peach cake with a lemon curd filling, topped with pink buttercream suggestive of labia—and was close to a mess of angry tears when Bernadette approached her.

"Why are you dimmed, dear?" the woman asked, patting at her mass of gray curls.

"Dimmed?"

"Your energy. It's faded today."

That was all it took for Lizzie to start sobbing. Bernadette wrapped Lizzie in a tight hug, rocking her gently from side to side as she cried, humming as Lizzie's tears eventually subsided.

"Tears are so healthy," Bernadette said, pulling back to retrieve a tissue from the pocket of her chunky knit cardigan. "They're the body working. All of those feelings and emotions flow through every corner of your body like oxygen, and when they're finally released as tears, it's your body saying it's prepared to let those emotions go."

Lizzie blinked at Bernadette. "Really?"

Bernadette shrugged. "While I did make that up, I think it's a rather nice notion."

"I do too," Lizzie said, breaking into a smile.

"What's bothering you?" Bernadette asked. She pulled Lizzie toward the front of the shop, flicking the OPEN sign to CLOSED while they had a lull in customers.

Lizzie told Bernadette. She poured her heart out to the old woman, explaining Rake and their inability to stay platonic and the way his failure to defend her cut like a knife. She explained what a fuckup she so often felt like, how many fears and hopes she had about the future. She cried and talked, and Bernadette sat there calmly, nodding along.

"Do you know why I hired you?" Bernadette asked after Lizzie finished.

"Because our auras were complementary and I was willing to bake titties all day."

Bernadette opened her mouth to say something, thought about it, then nodded. "That's the long and short of it, yes," she said, a small laugh in her voice. "But it was more than that."

Lizzie looked at her, blowing her nose on a thin napkin.

"All my life, I've had these strong cosmic . . . feelings," Bernadette continued, fiddling with the many rings on her fingers as she spoke. "These nudges of energy that point me in the direction I'm supposed to go. And I trust them. Fiercely. And by trusting them, I try to plan for them, accommodate them. Sometimes I get it wrong, but many times I get it right. And I was planning for you."

Lizzie's eyes shot wide. "Shut up. You predicted me? That's so badass, Bernie."

Bernadette smiled. "Not you specifically, dear, no. And I'm not psychic. But I had a feeling about this bakery, like I was holding things down until the right energy could fill the space and allow it to shine. I started making the erotic treats on a whim, and it made my wife and our friends giggle. But something about it felt like that energy nudge. So, I kept doing it, trying not to question this odd little hobby."

Lizzie smiled.

"Over the past few years, I've sensed my time running this shop myself was coming to an end, and I began to plan for what the next phase in my journey will look like."

Lizzie held up a hand. "Bernadette, I'm begging you, if you're about to tell me you're closing the store and I'm out of a job, this is objectively *not* the best moment."

"Hush, child, let me finish." Bernadette picked up one of Lizzie's hands. "What I'm telling you is you're the energy this store always needed, exactly what it's been waiting for. What I've been waiting for."

"Bernie, you're going to make me cry again," Lizzie said, dabbing at her eyes.

"Which is why, at the end of the year, I'm making you a co-owner of Bernadette's Bakery."

Lizzie's mouth dropped to the floor. "You're *what*?"

"I'm handing over the reins, dear. I'm old, and my wife and I are feeling called to travel. Explore and play. I want to learn to share some of the responsibilities that keep me here. And I know you are the perfect person to do that with. The finances are in good shape, our customer base strong, and I've watched your talent blossom. I'm ready to entrust more of the bakery into your incredibly capable, creative hands."

Lizzie stared at Bernadette, trying to process this. "But . . . but what if I fail? What if I lose you money?" Lizzie said, fear snaking across her gut. "I don't know how to run a business. I don't know what I'm doing."

"Don't you?" Bernadette said, looking at her closely. "Because in the time you've worked here, you've gotten our website and ordering off the ground, created enough buzz to generate lines out the door, learned the bookkeeping, and are thriving with the increased responsibilities I've handed you."

Lizzie opened her mouth, but Bernadette quieted her. "And I'm not *dying*, Lizzie," she said with a laugh. "I'm not leaving you high and dry. We'll be partners until maybe one day you won't need me at all. I'll be around to troubleshoot. To help however you need."

"I don't know what to say," Lizzie whispered. She loved this shop like it was a piece of her own heart, and the idea of co-owning it felt too delicious and terrifying to believe.

"Say 'thank you,' and then get back to work," Bernadette said, cupping Lizzie's cheek. "We have plenty of time and we'll work out the details as we go."

Lizzie launched herself at Bernadette, wrapping her in a giant hug. "Thank you," Lizzie said, a small tremble of excitement vibrating through her body. "I can do this."

Chapter 45

RAKE was absolutely miserable at work on Monday. He hadn't slept in two days, and Lizzie had ignored all his texts and calls. He was a fool, and he wanted her back. He'd do anything to get her back.

He tried to focus on work, but his brain was stuck on Lizzie, wondering if she was okay. Wondering what he could do to fix this.

His office phone rang, the loud noise making him jump.

"Hello?" he answered, not bothering to check the number.

"Come to my office," Dominic said by way of greeting. "We need to strategize." Then hung up.

Rake sighed, slamming his phone down with more force than was necessary. He buried his face in his hands, wishing he had any excuse in the world not to go talk to Dominic. After a moment, he stood and headed to his office.

"Shut the door," Dominic said without looking up from the file in front of him.

Rake did as he was told, taking a seat at the open chair in front of his desk.

"We need to hit Nicholás hard with the pitch tonight," Dominic said, finally putting the file down and glancing at Rake. "I want you to figure out a way to make that market research shine and fluff up those return projections. I think that's what's given him cold feet."

Rake nodded. There was only so much he could do to change the outlook of the numbers he'd already run without outright lying to the man.

"And we need to play up the refined sexiness of it. We need something young and fresh to really capture his attention and attract the millennial buyers."

"I thought young and fresh violated the tried-and-true luxury of the brand," Rake said dryly, repeating the sentiment Dominic had pounded into the team.

Dominic's eyes narrowed. "Onism will always be about refinement and class," he said. "And I'll make sure every campaign reflects that, but the point is to also grow brand awareness in our new market. Or have you forgotten?"

"Was just clarifying the approach," Rake said, staring at him with a level of disinterest that seemed to pique Dominic's annoyance.

Dominic leaned back in his chair, giving Rake a look of cool appraisal. "Is there something you'd like to say, Rake? Or would you prefer to keep staring daggers at me?"

Rake paused, torn between two extremes. Part of him wanted to grab Dominic by the throat and make him take back every foul word he'd said about Lizzie. The other part of him wanted to retreat to the safety of placating his boss, bending over backward and putting the company first, maintaining his job and the security it offered.

He tried to go for a happy medium.

"Actually, there is," Rake said, mimicking Dominic's reclined posture. "I have an issue with the way you spoke about Lizzie during our call this weekend."

Dominic's brows rose in surprise, then he rolled his eyes. "You must be joking. I can't waste any more time on this. What you do in your personal life is your business, just don't bring that messy thing around to client events and we'll be fine."

Rake jolted up, slamming his palms on Dominic's desk and leaning forward. "Shut up," he said through gritted teeth.

"Excuse me?" Dominic said, slowly standing, the lines of his face taut and trembling at Rake's insubordination.

"You heard me," Rake said, a hot type of fury singeing every muscle, his voice rising. "You can't speak about her with that kind of disrespect. I won't tolerate it for another fucking moment."

"I should fire you on the spot for speaking to me like that," Dominic said, sizing Rake up. "I don't know what the bloody hell's gotten into you, but you better get to your office and pull yourself together before you say something else you'll regret."

"The only thing I regret is not saying this sooner. I'm not going to bend over backwards day after day at this company for you to speak about someone I love with such contempt. I'm done putting this place first. I quit."

Dominic's eyes widened, and Rake felt similarly surprised that those words had left his mouth.

"You can't quit," Dominic spit back. "Our meeting is tonight."

"You can take your meeting and your luxury and your derogatory opinions about my partner and shove them up your arse."

Rake found a deep satisfaction in the way Dominic silently gaped at him like a dying fish.

Rake pushed off the desk and, after grabbing a few personal items from his own office, tore out of the building with a triumphant stride.

But, after walking a block, post-outburst clarity sent Rake into a total fucking panic that almost had him crawling back and asking for his job.

Holy hell, what was he *thinking*?

He just *quit*? With a *baby* on the way?

Was he an absolute *idiot*?

He squeezed his eyes shut, fisting his hands in his hair. As reckless as the move had been, he couldn't regret what he'd done.

He'd lost himself in that job for years, using it as the perfect excuse to avoid actually living.

It was like he'd been looking at life through a peephole, and then Lizzie came into his world and bashed the door down, dragging him out into the sun. He'd been a fool to try to rebuild that wall.

Rake rang Lizzie as he kept walking, but the call went to voicemail. He had to find her. He had to apologize. Beg for forgiveness.

Rake was so lost in his thoughts as he opened the door to their apartment, it took him a second to register that someone was already inside, and the shock made him jump out of his skin.

"What the hell are you doing here?" Indira yelled, clutching her chest, presumably just as surprised to see Rake.

"I live here! What are you doing here?" Rake said, trying to get his heartbeat under control.

Indira gave him a sheepish look. "Lizzie gave me her key and asked me to get her stuff."

Rake blinked, the words circling around his gut in cold, sharp jabs.

"No," he said at last, shrugging out of his suit jacket and dropping his keys on the counter.

"*No?*" Indira said, sending him a piercing glance.

"No. Lizzie isn't moving out. She's coming home."

"Is that right?" Indira said, folding her arms across her chest.

Rake held her gaze for

One,

 Two,

  Three.

"If she wants to," Rake said at last, hanging his head in defeat.

"Good boy," Indira said, relaxing her arms. "But to me, it doesn't seem like she wants to."

"Listen," Rake said, desperation in his voice. "I messed up. Horribly. But I want to make it up to her. I'll do anything."

"Why don't you start by telling your boss to suck a fat one?"

"I already did," Rake said, pointing toward the door.

Indira's eyes shot wide.

"In different terms, obviously," Rake clarified, shaking his head. "I quit."

Indira's jaw fell to the floor. "You quit your *job*? Are you stupid?"

"I'll get another one," Rake said, dragging his hands down his face.

"Right, because the economy is so stellar."

"Indira, I get it. But I'll figure it out. I have savings. I have connections. I've already been doing freelance work on the side, and I'll take every job that comes my way to keep Lizzie and the baby comfortable and afloat, but I couldn't keep working there."

Indira looked at him closely, studying him like he was a specimen under a microscope.

"Lizzie is special," she said at last, the words filled with love.

"Believe me, I know," Rake said, his voice cracking. "She's the best person I know. I love her so much, sometimes it feels like my heart might crack with it. And I need to tell her that. And if she wants nothing to do with me after, fine. I get it. But I can't live with myself if she's out there thinking she isn't the most important thing in the world to me. So please, don't take her stuff, not yet. Let me try."

Indira continued to study him, her full lips set in a stern line, her copper eyes seeming to bore into Rake's skull. And then, she smiled.

"All right," she said. "Tell me the plan."

Chapter 46

LIZZIE headed into work later than usual. Bernadette had called, saying some random stuff about energy alignments and morning meditations she needed to do in the shop before anyone could come in. The gist Lizzie took from it was that she could get a few extra hours of sleep.

Indira had been too busy at work the day before to get Lizzie's things from Rake's apartment, and Lizzie had spent longer than she'd planned searching for a dress that fit over her bump in the hodgepodge of crap she'd thrown together.

Objectively, things could be worse for Lizzie. She had a place to live, a job that was morphing into the most exciting career opportunity she could ever hope for, and friends that were coddling her to the highest degree, but a sadness still penetrated deep into her bones.

She felt hollow. Fragile. Like if someone were to touch her, she would crack into a spiderweb of broken glass before shattering to the floor.

She missed Rake with an intensity that scared her. That made her feel like she would never be able to let him go. It had taken all her strength not to answer his calls or texts over the past few days, but when he hadn't reached out last night, his silence had wounded her in a fresh way.

If she were being honest with herself, she'd admit that she maybe, sorta, kinda loved him in the most devastating way humanly possible and wanted him back.

But she wasn't being honest with herself.

And she also wasn't going to submit to being someone's shameful secret. She had too much to offer the world than to be hidden away in some apartment, not deemed suitable for public spaces.

When Lizzie got to Bernadette's, the blinds were closed and the door locked. Lizzie rattled around her giant purse until she found her key and let herself in, trying to focus on work and not Rake.

When she stepped into the dark space, it took her a moment to process what she was seeing. She blinked, turning in a full circle, her jaw dragging on the floor.

Hundreds of candles lit up the space like a galaxy created just for her. Bunches of flowers sat on all the tables, filling the room with their sweet fragrance.

And in front of the counter stood Rake. His tall, broad form was covered in a ruffly yellow apron, splatters and stains decorating the front. His face was serious, eyes watchful, following Lizzie's movements like she was a skittish animal about to bolt. His usually neat and tidy hair was a mess, and flour was smeared on his cheeks and neck. Lizzie was unable to do anything but gape.

"Hi," he said at last.

"Hi," Lizzie managed to choke out, staring at him in wide-eyed shock.

"Can we talk?" he asked, wringing his hands together in an awkward little knot in front of him.

Lizzie tamped down the impulse to throw herself into his arms. Searching for composure, she gave a haughty sniff. "Not sure why I would subject myself to that. It's a well-known fact that the Australian accent is the vilest sound to penetrate the ear," Lizzie lied. She was obsessed with his accent.

Rake's serious expression slowly morphed into a smile. "God, I've missed you," he said, letting out a small laugh. "I made this for you," he added, turning to grab something on the counter behind him.

When he faced her, he was holding a large, wonky-looking cake.

"It's supposed to be a heart," he said, staring down at the lumpy mess. "I asked Bernadette and Indira for help, but they both told me if I wasn't prepared to take on this labor of love solo, I didn't deserve you."

Lizzie glanced over Rake's shoulder and saw the telltale curls of both Bernadette and Indira duck below the kitchen window.

Lizzie stepped closer, looking at the splotchy pink icing, trying to make out the words written in terrible cursive on the top.

She realized it said *Rake ♥s Lizzie*, and she sucked in a breath.

"It's really ugly," she said, tears pricking her eyes as she dragged her gaze up to him. "I love it."

Rake's eyes glistened. "I, uh, I have something else for you," he said, setting the cake down. He reached into his back pocket, pulling out an envelope. He handed it to Lizzie.

With shaking fingers, she took it, tearing open the seal. It took her a moment to comprehend what she was seeing.

"Plane tickets?" she asked, looking up at him.

"Flight vouchers," he said. "Three of them."

"For . . . ?"

"It's . . . well, it's a promise of sorts. Obviously, I'm a clueless idiot and have no idea when babies can fly and the practicality of it, but I want to take you to Australia someday. You and the little one."

Lizzie continued to blink at him. "Why?" she asked, unable to form more than one word at a time.

Rake dragged his hand across the back of his neck as he looked up at the ceiling and smiled.

"Because I want to show you where I grew up," he said, his voice hoarse. "Take you to a new corner of the world to explore. I want you to meet my nan and I want my mum to babysit our child. I want to introduce my friends from uni to the girl of my dreams, so they can see what a lovesick idiot you've made me. I want to show you off and hold your hand. I want to take you to the beach and ogle you in a bikini. I want to take you camping and make love to you under the stars. I want to hand over all my old memories because I only want new ones with you."

She blinked, trying to breathe past the lump in her throat. She chewed on the inside of her cheek and looked around like she wasn't sure he was talking to her.

"I have . . . I'll probably have to work," she said at last.

Rake nodded, his face looking solemn. "For what it's worth, Bernadette said she's fine running the shop any time we decided to go. If you want to go, of course."

"And you expect Dominic to give you time off your job?"

"I told Dominic to go to hell."

Lizzie's eyes snapped to his face, confused and wary. "You did?"

Rake nodded. "I told him that no one gets to disrespect you like that. I told him he could shove the stupid job up his arse because I don't want it."

"I . . ." She trailed off, not sure what to say. Lizzie looked at him. Really looked, taking in the beauty of his face, the sincerity of his eyes. Her heart felt stretched by the flood of emotions, like he had captured every star in the night sky into his cupped palms, enhanced them with whispered words of love, then let them float into her chest. Fill every inch of her.

He reached out, softly tracing his fingers across her cheek. Lizzie's eyes fluttered closed at the touch.

"Why?" she finally asked, looking at him.

"Why?" The question made Rake laugh. "Because I love you. Because life was a shadow before, but you're the sun. And I want the world to know that I'm an absolute fool for you and nothing makes me happier."

"You love me?" A small burst of fear shot across her nerves.

"Yeah, Birdy, I do. I love you like a heart beats or a fish swims. It's automatic and unavoidable, and I wouldn't change a thing about it. You've busted into my heart and carved your name into every chamber."

Lizzie laughed, hot tears trickling out from the corners of her eyes.

"I don't expect you to love me back. Not yet, at least," Rake continued, taking a step forward, putting one hand around her waist. "Not until I can make it up to you. But all I want is to make it up to you. To show you every single day how much I love you. So let me take you to Australia. Or let me just take you home. Our home. Everything is so empty without you, Lizzie."

"I've missed you," Lizzie whispered, the happy tears rolling down her cheeks. Rake wiped them away. "And I'm a little scared," she added honestly. "I'm scared I'll mess this up."

"I'm scared I will too," Rake said, giving her a brilliant smile. "I've made a million mistakes, and I'll make a million more. And I love you enough to know you will too. But we'll do it together."

"I love you too," Lizzie said, an uncontrollable smile breaking across her face.

Then Rake kissed her. It was soft and perfect and made a sunrise of happiness bloom in Lizzie's chest. She broke away, starting to laugh.

"What's so funny?" he asked, resting his forehead on hers.

She grinned, taking his hand from her cheek and dragging

it to the soft swell of her belly. Rake's eyes shot wide as he felt it.

"Told you you'd get to feel the baby kick," she said, more happy giggles bubbling up from her throat. "I think she's trying to tell us she loves us too."

Epilogue

Baby is 7 lbs. 2 oz. of perfection.

Evie Blake-Thompson was born at 3:06 a.m. on a Thursday. She came into the world, red-faced and screaming almost as loud as her mother.

Almost.

Within two seconds of existence, Evie had Rake and Lizzie wrapped around her dimpled little finger.

The couple tumbled, tripped, and fell into the terrors of parenthood, constantly looking at each other with fear that they were messing up, only to dissolve into giggles at their matching expressions of horror. They were clueless and scared, but none of that mattered compared to the overwhelming happiness that tethered them together.

Evie had a single tuft of bright orange hair that sat at the front of her head, refusing to ever lie flat and making her parents giggle every time they looked at her, their precious baby learning early how to giggle along too. Every time little Evie gave them a gummy smile, it was like a supernova went off in their chests.

Ryan and Mary were endless help in those first few months, making the drive into the city on weekends and random days to help with cooking or diaper duty, Ryan going out of his way to check in with Lizzie, not just on what she may need from the store but also how she was feeling.

When Evie turned twelve weeks old, Lizzie decided that a party was in order.

Entrusting most party planning details to Mary and the cake to Bernadette, the new back patio of the bakery was transformed into a soft little oasis of pastels and baby animals. Rake's parents flew in from Australia, immediately enamored with their grand-daughter, bewitched by every coo and gurgle.

Harper, Thu, Indira, and Mary threw themselves into aunt roles with fierce determination, all trying to outdo the other in spoiling sweet Evie.

"She's too cute to be real," Harper said, bouncing Evie lightly in her arms and eliciting a smile. "How do you not sit there and stare at her all day every day?"

"It's hard not to," Lizzie said, glancing at Rake, who stood across the patio sharing a beer with Dan, Ryan, and his father.

Some nights after putting Evie down, she and Rake would spend hours sitting in front of the crib, holding hands and watching her sleep, grinning like lovesick fools.

"Why do I have the urge to gnaw on her cheeks?" Thu asked with an alarmed look as she stroked a finger over Evie's downy skin.

"It's cute aggression," Indira chimed in, making funny faces at Evie. "It's the brain's defense against the overwhelming on-slaught of positive feelings."

"I'm *begging* you to go on a monthlong vacation so I can babysit," Mary said, making Lizzie giggle as she took a bite of lemon bar.

"Have the totally platonic coparent roommates discussed entering totally platonic holy matrimony?" Thu asked, taking Evie from Harper and rubbing circles around the baby's back.

Lizzie glanced at Rake again, happiness spearing through

her as he felt her gaze and met her eyes, giving her a tender smile that warmed the center of her chest.

It felt borderline subversive to allow herself to be loved as fiercely as Rake loved her, like she was breaking every rule life had set for her, only to discover the most delicious reward for her defiance. It was diving headfirst into something that terrified her.

But loving Rake was nothing but pleasure. Soft and sweet. Strong and mighty. Their love was whispered sighs and booming laughs. It was the astonishing pink of a perfect sunset and the inky black of a night sky. It was everything.

"We've talked about it, but no," Lizzie said, still holding Rake's eyes as she spoke. "It's not something we need to do, and we have our hands full enough with sweet little Evie here and her constant pooping and peeing."

Rake and Lizzie knew they belonged to each other in every way that mattered, and for them, that was enough.

* * *

As THE DAY wore on, the warm spring afternoon morphed into a cool evening, and Rake held Evie closer to his chest, tucking blankets around her. His daughter yawned, her mouth forming a perfect little O before she nuzzled closer to him, and Rake thought his heart might crack in two with all the love he felt.

He thanked Mary, Bernadette, and Bernadette's wife, Annie, for their help in the party, then saw his parents into a Lyft to their hotel, with promises of breakfast bright and early the next morning. Peter and Leanne wanted to suck up every second they could with Evie.

Rake held Lizzie's hand as they walked home, paying close attention as she pointed out her love of a piece of bright graffiti or the way the gnarled roots of a small tree made her think of fairy homes.

"That latticework reminds me of the design you did on the pies for the holiday party," Rake said, pointing at a cast-iron fence.

Lizzie beamed at him. "I can't believe you noticed. That's how I came up with the idea," she said.

The booming bakery and Rake's savings and freelance work had kept them afloat, and after a few months of searching, Rake had secured a job he loved at a midscale marketing firm that worked with local businesses to enhance their brand and customer reach. It felt good to work with small-business owners, helping them succeed in the city he now felt was home.

When they got back to the apartment, Rake put his perfect daughter in her crib and pulled Lizzie to their bed.

Lizzie giggled, an effervescent, sparkly type of laugh as they touched and kissed, making love slowly and quietly, soft flames of pleasure igniting between them.

"Let's have five more," Rake said in the aftermath, gently tracing his fingertips across Lizzie's soft and lovely body.

"You want more kids?" she said, playing with his hair.

"I want a swarm of them," he replied.

"That's good," she said, a mischievous grin breaking across her lips. She leaned closer to whisper, "Because I have a surprise for you."

Rake froze, his eyes moving at a glacial pace to stare in horror at her stomach. Yes, he wanted more children. But in like, ten years. When maybe he'd gotten at least three full nights of sleep. He gulped.

"That's . . ."

But Lizzie's choked laugh stopped whatever lie he was going to spew. He looked up at her. She was shaking with giggles.

"You should see your face," she said, snorting so hard, she had to bury her head in the pillow to control the noise. "I'm kidding, you idiot! Holy God, could you imagine? We'd *die*."

"You're pure evil, you know that?" he said, gripping Lizzie's thigh and making her squeal quietly into the pillow. He truly had found himself a little rogue.

"Me being knocked up again would serve you right," Lizzie said, finding the strength through her laughter to look at him. "Walking around topless like you do all the time? Holding a *baby* for crying out loud? It does things to a woman."

"I'll try to dress more conservatively," he teased. "I can't keep tempting fate." They shook with silly giggles until they collapsed into a deep sleep.

A few hours later, their daughter cried.

They woke up in a disoriented tangle of limbs and bedsheets, their wild eyes meeting in the early morning hours.

And then they smiled at all the noise.

ACKNOWLEDGMENTS

Writing is a fickle pursuit. Some stories pour out of you, while others feel like pulling teeth (and I'm somewhat of an expert on that). Lizzie and Rake's story was an unequivocal joy to write. A product of the COVID-19 pandemic, this book was a bright light in a dark time, a safe place to frolic and play with ideas about love and growth and laughter and to see someone with ADHD, like me, be loved and cherished. Quite simply: writing this story made me happy. And that happiness was made possible by the love and support of so many people, and I am overflowing with gratitude for every single one of them.

Ben. I love you. I could fill a book with how much you mean to me, but those three words are at the heart of it. Thank you for encouraging me, cheering me on, and letting me disappear into these fictional worlds. And thank you for always letting me talk through my writer's block. Your suggestions are almost never helpful because they always quickly derail into a murder mystery, but I still appreciate the effort.

My editor, Eileen Rothschild. OH MY GOD I LOVE WORKING WITH YOU. Thank you for embracing my voice and making me a better writer. You are a brilliant editor, and I still pinch myself that we get to work on all these books together.

My agent, Courtney Miller-Callihan. You are quite possibly

the coolest person I know. Thank you for caring about me and my work. You make publishing a better place, and I admire you so much.

Mom, thank you for loving me as I am, doing your best to support the many *many* (expensive) special interest/hyper-focus hobbies I picked up over the years. I hope you never read this book so we can still make eye contact.

Dad, thank you for your endless supply of humor and laughter.

Chloe Liese, I'm not sure I'd ever finish writing a book if I didn't have you to turn to for everything from craft to crassness. I'm so lucky to know you, and your work is a gift to the world.

Megan Stillwell, you are a national treasure and one of the most incredible women I know. I'm constantly awed by you. Thank you for being my friend and a fearless sounding board for ideas.

Hamda Shakil, you deserve all the happiness in the world. I can't believe I'm lucky enough to know you.

Sarah Hogle, thank you for being a fearless author and fierce friend. Helen Hoang, I treasure our talks more than you could know, and I'm so grateful for you. Rosie Danan, Rachel Lynn Solomon, Elizabeth Everett, and Evie Dunmore, thank you for being so supportive of my work. I admire you all endlessly.

Jacque, thank you for your invaluable advice as a beta reader; your insight was everything. Elisabeth Wise, thank you for copy-editing my first draft of this novel; your impeccable work made all the difference.

A huge, never-ending thank-you to my team at St. Martin's Griffin. Lisa Bonvissuto, every interaction with you leaves a smile on my face! Thank you for being so fabulous. Alexis Neuville and Maria Vitale, you two are absolute stars and I'll never be able to express how much I appreciate the work you've done. Brant Janeway and Marissa Sangiacomo, thank you for championing my books and helping them reach readers. You two are amazing.

Thank you to Chrisinda Lynch, Joy Gannon, and Hannah Jones for making my extremely rough Mad Libs–esque draft end up a polished and gorgeous book.

Kerri Resnick, you *SVU*-loving creative genius. I don't know how you create the endlessly stunning work that you do, but you've made the world a better place with it.

As I write these acknowledgments for my sophomore novel, my first book, *A Brush with Love,* still hasn't even released, but I've already been indescribably touched and humbled by the support so many of you have shown for my work. Stacia, Esther, Mae, Amelia, Sarah Estep, Lindsay Grossman, Joana, Chloe, Marianne, Andrea Daniels, Ginger, Katie, Kris, Ashley, Hannah, Tara, Amanda, Hailey, Amanda, Katie Holt, you all have moved me deeply with your love and support. I can never thank you enough for your kind words and your encouragement. You've helped make this journey the best part of my life. Thank you to every reader that took a chance on my writing and for spending your time with my goofball characters.

And, finally, thank you to everyone who's engaged with me in conversations about neurodiversity and mental health. Every message means the world to me, and I am incredibly privileged and lucky to be able to talk so openly about the beauties and struggles that come with being ADHD and autistic. Every brain is beautiful, and they all deserve love exactly as they are.

ABOUT THE AUTHOR

Ben Eisdorfer

MAZEY EDDINGS is a neurodiverse author, dentist, and (most important) stage mom to her cats, Yaya and Zadie. She can most often be found reading romance novels under her weighted blanket and asking her boyfriend to bring her snacks. She's made it her personal mission in life to destigmatize mental health issues and write love stories for every brain. With roots in Ohio and North Carolina, she now calls Philadelphia home. She is the author of *A Brush with Love*.